THE NECKLACE OF KALI

ROBERT TOWERS THE

NECKLACE OF KALI

HARCOURT, BRACE & COMPANY NEW YORK

FOR MY PARENTS

PREFACE

For the sake of any Indian reader that *The Necklace of Kali* may be fortunate enough to have, I would like to make it clear that this novel is not primarily about India but about a little group of Westerners, chiefly American, who were living in Calcutta fourteen years ago. As such, it presents a necessarily limited view of the country. I have tried, as carefully as possible, to ignore the advantages of hindsight and to see these Westerners, their acquaintances, and their corner of the Subcontinent as a very limited observer in 1946 might have seen them. My narrator suffers both from his background and the peculiarity of his vantage point; his opinions of India, though generally sympathetic, must not be taken as either comprehensive or prophetic or even typical.

Although I have set *The Necklace of Kali* in a specific time and place and have occasionally referred to public figures, the characters of the novel are entirely fictional. The personnel of the American Consulate General, as I have invented them, are not intended to reflect the actual consular staff of 1946, and any resemblance to my former colleagues or to other persons, living or dead, is entirely coincidental.

PART I

CHAPTER I 🙿 IN those days I was working in the American Consulate General in Calcutta. This was my first post—later I was stationed in Shanghai and, finally, at the time of the great State Department purge of 1953, in Melbourne. On my appointment as vice-consul, I had been offered a choice of either Calcutta or Chungking and had chosen Calcutta—largely for reasons that now strike me as rather disreputable. Thanks to a boyhood absorption in Kipling, I thought of India as being picturesque in a way that a remote province of China (most of that country was, in the spring of 1945, still occupied by the Japanese) could not possibly be. Furthermore, Chungking would have all the inconveniences of a garrison town overrun by American troops—and by that time I had already had more than enough of army life. Finally, I expect that my choice was influenced much more than I realized by the genteel Anglophilia which pervaded my parents' home in Baltimore.

In any case, by the time this story opens, I had been working for nearly a year in the Visa and Passport Section of the Consulate General. My job was largely routine, often exasperating, never engrossing; outside the office, however, there were plenty of things to catch and hold my interest. After two hundred years, the weird old body of the British Raj was at last thrashing like some foundering dinosaur toward its extinction—though no one could have guessed, early in 1946, that its final shudder was so near at hand. I looked and listened and meanwhile lived very comfortably in a six-room flat in Harrington Mansions. I was unmarried in those days and shared the flat with a fellow vice-consul named Ralph McClure. We had a staff of four servants —by no means an extravagant number.

And I went to a lot of parties. My job—minor but official— brought in a steady patter of invitations from the members of the American colony and the other consulates. Furthermore, my circle of acquaintances—American, British, and Indian—had now grown to include perhaps four hundred people, most of them addicted to the social drug. During the "season," comprising the months of cool weather from November to April, I could have gone out for cocktails or dinner (and usually both) every night of the week. Although as a boy and as a student at Swarthmore I had always read a great deal, there were now long stretches during which I never opened a book.

Still, as many parties as there were, there were never too many for the person with whom I was most deeply involved at the time. This was a Southerner named Dorothy Eustace, a divorcee who had originally come out to India with the American Red Cross and had stayed on to work for a British firm. Her social gluttony still astonishes me whenever I think of it.

It is, of course, important to be accurate about (and fair to) that self I am now describing—a self that has since been defaced, reworked, and overlaid almost beyond recognition. I was too intelligent to have been merely a contented lightweight. I kept myself informed, read the newspapers, argued politics, held opinions, and glanced, at times rather wistfully, through the portholes of my social life. Some warmth or liveliness must have broken through the social glaze; otherwise I cannot account for the genuine affection my friends had for me—and I now have in mind such friends as the Chaudurys, to whom I had never lifted a cocktail glass and said "cheers." Judging from a photograph which shows me sitting at my desk at the Consulate, I must have made a pleasant, not too chilling, impression upon my visa applicants; in that photograph I see myself as a polite, carefully dressed, stocky, dark-eyed, dark-haired young man with an agreeable, rather controlled smile. Once Dorothy Eustace, when she was very angry at me, said that I reminded her of a smug young bank officer who, years before, had refused her a loan in Atlanta. I am certain that my visa applicants did not find me as formidable as that.

My story properly begins toward the end of that season, on a Saturday night early in March, when Dorothy and I went to a large cocktail party at Government House. This was not as grand as it sounds, for the party was given not by the last British Governor of Bengal but by one of his four aides-de-camp, a captain in the Grenadier Guards named Ronny Powell. It was held in the A.D.C.'s Wing and was, for a few minutes, honored by the presence of the Governor himself; otherwise, Ronny's "do" had little to distinguish it from any other Calcutta party (I am using "Calcutta," of course, in a highly restrictive sense). Dorothy and I saw the same people we ran into at least once a week, for Ronny's special friends were the Jungly Wallah Set, a shifting population of rich Indians, Persians, Armenians, poor but ingenious White Russians and Central Europeans, and assorted Americans and Britons, all of whom I remember now through a haze of late hours and cigarette smoke; this group, constituting Calcutta's own brand of café society, took its name from a night club, the Jungly Wallah, which had been its headquarters for several years. I enjoyed myself at Ronny's party, but by eight thirty I had had enough. Dorothy, of course, protested. "John, I can't begin to understand you," she said in her hoarse Southern voice, pronouncing "can't" as though it had been spelled "caint." "Just one second ago you swore you were having the time of your life." But after ten minutes of parting banter with Colonel Drummond, the Governor's Military Secretary, and then five minutes of mixed greetings and good-bys, she came away without further complaint.

As we drove across the paved courtyard, I heard a sudden roar of singing from the A.D.C.'s Wing. A group of voices, chiefly male, had begun "Roll me o-ver, in the clo-ver," and I was glad we had left in time: it was always harder to tear Dorothy away from a party once the singing started. The March air was incredibly tender and fresh after the hot cigarette fog, and I filled my lungs triumphantly. I had had a good time, I was not too drunk, and I had had my way. We pulled up before a pair of immense iron gates—surmounted by the gilded lion, unicorn, and crown of Britain—and waited for the two turbaned durwans to swing them open. Behind us lay the columned expanse of Government House, gleaming and vast like the backdrop for some extravagant ballet. Looking over my shoulder, I caught for an instant the glow of yellow satin curtains and the sparkle of chandeliers in the Yellow Drawing Room, where H.E. the Governor and his lady were entertaining the High Commissioner of Malaya. And for the first time that evening I caught the reverberations of the old palace, the palace of

Wellesley, Bentinck, Dalhousie, Lord Curzon, and the other viceroys whose names still beat like a drum through the ugly city, evoking the imperialist glamour, summoning up the gold-and-scarlet of the British Raj. This, to be sure, was an excitement most easily induced at night, when ungainly proportions and peeling walls didn't matter.

The two durwans saluted and we passed through the gates into Hastings Street. In the distance I could hear the ragged strains of another song—"Bless 'em all, bless 'em all—the long and the short and the tall." Dorothy began to hum the tune and leaned her head on my shoulder, rubbing against it gently, much as she often rubbed her face against the shaven but still harsh stubble of my chin. Breathing in the warmth of her hair, I said, "Dot, let's not go to Firpo's for dinner. Let's go back to the flat and see what we can pick up there."

"What's wrong with Firpo's?" She pulled away slightly. "Are you feeling sick or something?"

"I've had enough crowds for the evening. I'm just not in the mood for a big restaurant, that's all."

"Suit yourself," she said in a disappointed voice. But she made no further objection, and in a moment or so snuggled back against my shoulder.

By the time we reached Harrington Street, Dorothy was in high spirits. We touched fingers and smiled at one another as we got into the lift. Removing her hand from mine to apply lipstick, she grinned wryly into the mirror of her compact. How well she looked! Her white teeth and vermilion lips and turquoise-blue eyes shone with almost the brilliance of costume jewelry against the ruddy tan of her skin and the darker bronze of her hair. Big-boned, long-waisted, with large, rather low-slung breasts, Dorothy held herself with athletic grace, despite the fact that her outdoor life consisted of nothing more strenuous than sunbathing. She did not look younger than her thirty-two years, but she wore them with perfect relish and ease, as though basking in the high noon of her physical life. I always felt slightly pale beside her.

Meanwhile the ragged little lift wallah, who was piloting us slowly to the sixth and top floor of Harrington Mansions, stared at Dorothy with the pitiless curiosity of a child—in this case a child with a wrinkled brown face, drooping mustaches, and a mouth bloody with betel-nut juice. Unabashed, she returned his gaze and proceeded to powder her nose and cheeks with such defiance that I began to laugh.

"I'd give ten rupees for his thoughts," said Dorothy, snapping shut her compact.

"You're like all Southerners," I said. "You can't imagine a dark-skinned man looking at a white woman without wanting to undress her."

"You're like all Westerners who've lived in India a year," she returned. "You can't imagine that any Indian servant understands a word of English."

The lift came to a creaking halt. "Salaam, sahib," said the lift wallah as he pulled back the door. He touched the rag that was wound about his head in a makeshift turban.

"Salaam, lift wallah," I said, stepping out of the lift after Dorothy. I unlocked the door of the flat and switched on the light in the entrance hall. It was now nearly ten; Ghulam, my bearer, had no doubt retired for the night, and I decided not to ring for him. While Dorothy disappeared into the bathroom, I went to the pantry to get ice for our drinks and to explore the contents of the refrigerator. A dim light, I noticed, was shining under the door of the little room that lay beyond the kitchen and scullery. This was the room occupied by the two Muslim servants —Ghulam and the apprentice bearer who was known as the chokra; the cook and the "Untouchable" sweeper had separate quarters of their own in the compound of Harrington Mansions. I could hear low voices and, at one point, the sound of coughing or gagging—I couldn't tell which. A few minutes later, as Dorothy and I were sipping our whisky-sodas, Ghulam appeared at the door of the living room and salaamed.

I returned the salaam and said, in a mixture of English and Hindustani, that we would get our dinner, that Ghulam could go to bed.

The bearer gave the quick sideways nod which, in India,

signifies assent, but he did not go away. Barefooted, dressed in his livery of white jacket and loose white pajama trousers, and wearing the red tarbush of a Muslim bearer, Ghulam stood irresolutely in the doorway, his eyes cast down, his usually bland face now gloomy and set. Then he said, "Chokra sick, sahib. Chokra very sick."

"Wait here," I said to Dorothy. "I'd better have a look."

In the little whitewashed cell behind the scullery, I found the chokra lying on a charpoy, covered with a thin spread of garishly printed cotton. Without his tarbush and jacket, the boy, who was about fourteen, seemed almost unrecognizably young and childish as he raised his enormous, glistening, lemur eyes to the light; weak and fretful, he was several times racked by long spasms of coughing. The place smelled of damp brick and stale rags.

"How long has he been sick?" I asked. Though I had seen the chokra only intermittently during the last busy month (the boy regularly helped Ghulam serve dinner when there were guests), I did recall noticing a bad cold that seemed to hang on for a long time.

"Three, four, maybe five weeks," said Ghulam, counting on his fingers.

"Why didn't you tell me?"

Ghulam looked blank, as though he had not understood, and I decided there was no point in recriminations. I returned to the hall to telephone Dr. Harlestoun. He turned out to be dining with his wife at the Saturday Club, and when I telephoned there, I had to wait nearly twenty minutes before I heard the physician's curt Scottish voice on the other end of the line. After a few noncommittal grunts while I apologized and then told my story, Dr. Harlestoun promised to come in about an hour's time unless there seemed to be a special emergency; I agreed that there wasn't. Then I rejoined Dorothy, who was sitting rather forlornly in the living room, having finished her highball, and suggested that we get something to eat while waiting for the doctor.

"You don't reckon it's cholera or the plague or something, do you?" said Dorothy as we sat down to our supper of cold ham, warmed-over rice, and stewed fruit.

"Nothing that melodramatic." I untied my black bow tie and loosened the collar of my dress shirt. "It looks like a bad case of flu to me," I continued. "The boy's had a cold for the last month."

"Poor kid." But Dorothy was not really interested in the chokra. She wanted to gossip about Ronny's party. For her the sensation of the evening had been the appearance of my close friend and fellow vice-consul Philip Sachs, in the company of Diane Cummings. Diane was a startlingly beautiful Anglo-Indian girl with pale-olive skin, dark eyes, and gloriously improbable blond hair; she ran a beauty shop on Park Street and was well known as the mistress of a handsomely pensioned Indian princeling called the Nawab of Chittagong. "This must mean a real break," said Dorothy. "She's never appeared in public with anyone but Shaheed before." Then she added that Philip had better watch his step. "Everybody," she said, "knows how jealous and Oriental Shaheed is about Diane. Suzy Mitchell says all the servants in the flat he keeps for her are eunuchs."

I laughed, then choked, spraying out bits of ham and rice.

"What's so funny?" she asked. "I wouldn't put it past him." She paused while I caught my breath and then remarked that Diane didn't strike her as Philip's type. "You know what I mean. Philip's such a snob you wouldn't expect him to go for someone who's so obvious. I'll admit Diane's very beautiful, but she's also obvious as hell. She's a first-class piece and that's obvious the minute you see her."

I laughed again. "How do you know Philip goes for her?" I demanded. "After all, this is the first time you've seen them together."

And so we talked and laughed and ate, and then, promptly at the end of the promised hour, we heard the noise of the lift outside and the ringing of the bell. I opened the door for the heavy, slow-moving Scot and introduced him to Dorothy, who beamed at him with the same hectic smile that she had earlier employed for Colonel Drummond. "I think it's just wonderful the way you doctors put aside pleasure for duty," she said. "Especially on a Saturday night." Dr. Harlestoun grunted amicabily, muttered "nottatall," and followed me into the kitchen. A moment later he was bending over the chokra, his stiff dress-shirt front buckling as he did so. There was another grunt as he shone a flashlight into the boy's throat. Breathing heavily, he tapped and thumped at the bird-ribbed chest, which glistened as though it had been polished with brown wax; then he took out his stethoscope and muttered directions to the chokra in Hindustani. "He'll be all right where he is tonight," said the doctor, straightening himself after finishing the auscultation, "but tomorrow I'd best try to get him into the Medical College Hospital. I take it you'll help with the expenses? Otherwise, the lad will simply be lost in one of the charity wards—assuming that there'd be room for him."

I nodded and looked down into the terrified eyes of the boy, who had just swallowed a big capsule.

"I shall telephone you in the morning—shall we say about ten? I think arrangements can be made by then, though of course Sunday's rather a bad day."

When we returned to the dining room, Dorothy rushed forward, exclaiming, "John, you simply must persuade Dr. Harlestoun to stay for a drink! That's the *least* we can offer him after putting him to such trouble." Dorothy could never resist trying her charms on an older man.

"That's terribly kind of you, I'm sure," said the doctor with a heavy rumbling of *r*'s, "but my poor wife still has her heart set on a bit of dancing. She made me promise to hurry back. I daren't disappoint her."

"What do you think is wrong with the boy?" I asked as we were waiting in the hall for the lift. "It looks like flu to me."

Dr. Harlestoun wrinkled his freckled forehead. "I can't be sure what it is until some tests have been made, and I see no point in speculating just now, if you don't mind."

Coming back into the living room, I took Dorothy by the hands and lifted her from her chair. "Let's go to your place now," I whispered. "I'm afraid Ralph and Marcia will come barging in here any minute and bring half of Ronny's party with them." I kissed her playfully and then more searchingly, and I forgot about the chokra. "Now that I've got you all to myself," I said, "I want to keep you that way."

Dorothy nodded, her eyes closed, her face suddenly still and subdued. No matter how brightly her colors had flashed all evening, Dorothy often faded a little at the immediate prospect of love-making, even when she was the one who had begun the overtures. I was used to this brief wilting, but I didn't understand it, especially in view of the wild urgency that was sure to come later.

I drove back to Harrington Street just at dawn. The city at this hour seemed oddly pure, enclosed in a glass dome of motionless gray light. The trees and dense shrubbery in the gardens of Ballygunge glistened with a wet blackness and the streets, too, were wet from the heavy mist. In the doorways, which were their only homes, coolies were still sleeping, curled up on mats, with cotton shawls pulled over their heads against the chill air; others slept under their carts or rickshas. Only the dogs were active, nosing about in mounds of uncollected refuse, and even the dogs were more like gray shadows than starved animals in the quiet pallor of dawn. Not for half an hour or more would the gathering light expose the spots of mange on their yellow flanks or wake up the scavenger crows to their noisy, swirling, all-day battle for scraps.

Still wearing my black dinner jacket but without a tie, I crouched forward over the steering wheel. Dorothy's alarm clock had flung me into the automatic process of dressing and leaving; now sleepiness, fatigue, and a rising thirst hurried me along with a kind of numb determination. Dorothy always banished me at this time, insisting that I go away long before her bearer, Kassim, set about his day's work. I had often made fun of her scruples, pointing out that Kassim could hardly, after four months, be ignorant of what was going on; I had even accused her of being unwilling for me to see her in the harsh light of morning. But these taunts gained nothing: not once had I passed a full night at her side or stretched out my hand, as the sun pressed against my eyelids, to touch the warm shoulder or cheek or the tickling hair close to my face.

At Harrington Street, I woke up the grumbling lift wallah, who had been asleep on the floor of his cage; then I let myself into the flat, drank a glass of water, and began to undress. Remembering that Dr. Harlestoun would call at ten, I set my own alarm for eight thirty. Thank God I'm alone, I thought, five minutes later, as I subsided toward a sleep that would last only three hours. Our love-making had been the best in many weeks—the least fuddled by alcohol—and I had again felt the old excitement and tenderness of our first few nights together. Yet, as had happened so often before, Dorothy would not let me sleep but kept nudging and pressing against me, unappeased, whispering endearments that lay upon me like an excess of blankets, silently beseeching me to provide her with all that she had ever missed in life. "Thank God . . ." I repeated sleepily. For, in spite of my protests at being chased away at dawn, I found an unspeakable relief in the contact of my own bed; cool and dry, it freed me from the exigencies of touch, allowed me to thrash and roll as I pleased.

"Chokra gone, sahib," said Ghulam when I walked into the dining room a little after nine.

Drowsy and confused, I gazed stupidly at the bearer. Ghulam's white jacket was wrinkled and soiled as though he had slept in it and his round face was unshaven, his eyes bloodshot; only the red, tasseled tarbush looked spruce. "What . . ." I began, my hand moving up to the lapel of my bathrobe as Ghulam's words began to work their way in. "He's dead?"

"No, Sahib. Gone away."

"Gone away! Where?"

Ghulam did not know. The boy had stolen away during the night while the bearer was asleep. Maybe he had gone to his own village—Ghulam didn't know. Maybe the chokra had heard the doctor sahib talk about the hospital and was afraid.

I dashed through the kitchen and scullery, past the astonished

Cookie, and entered the little room. The empty charpoy looked as desolately flimsy as its late occupant; there was a tangle of cotton spreads at the foot. The chokra's jacket and tarbush, which I remembered hanging on a nail in the whitewashed wall, had disappeared. Ghulam must have known, must have connived. The bearer's charpoy was less than three feet from the chokra's; the boy could hardly have got up, gathered his few possessions, and gone out without waking the older man. But, as I knew very well, there was nothing to be gained by accusing Ghulam.

I telephoned Dr. Harlestoun immediately. After a silence and then a cough, the Scot's voice rumbled slowly. "The lad'll be dead in a month. I'm convinced he has advanced consumption —galloping consumption. Both lungs sounded very bad." And he added, "This terror of hospitals is common enough, you know. I should have thought of that last night. I didn't realize the boy could understand me."

Putting down the receiver, I stood irresolutely by the telephone. The boy has to be stopped, I thought; and at the same moment I realized that I didn't even know the chokra's name, though he had worked in our flat for over half a year. Chokra, Cookie, Sweeper—they were all known by their functions; only the bearer had a name. I returned to the dining room to question Ghulam, who, looking very glum and sulky, was setting the table for breakfast. I told the bearer what Dr. Harlestoun had said, and the Indian lowered his eyes but did not change his expression. There was little to be learned. The boy's name was Hassein Khan, and he had been recommended to Ghulam by another bearer, who had worked for the Mowbrays on the second floor of Harrington Mansions; this bearer, Ghulam believed, was an uncle of the chokra's; Ghulam did not know where the bearer worked now, the Mowbrays having returned to England just after the new year. "What is the name of the chokra's village?" I asked. My mind was already racing ahead to the possibility of sending money or of writing to the district medical officer.

"Near Dacca, sahib."

"Yes, but what's the name of the village?"

Ghulam's face became even more resentful. "Near Dacca, sahib. Not know name of village."

There was nothing to be done. Among the five million Muslims who lived in the Dacca district of Bengal, how was an illiterate boy named Hassein Khan to be found? The chances were, of course, that he would never reach his home, that he would die unnoticed along the road or in the suffocating crush of a third-class railway carriage. Shaken by this last thought, I went sadly into the bedroom. I did not get dressed but lay on my bed, my eyes fixed upon the immense, four-bladed electric punkah that hung spider-like from the ceiling. A fourteen-year-old Muslim boy had waited at the table, polished shoes, and dusted furniture for half a year at thirty rupees a month (Ralph and I, as Americans, paid slightly more than the standard British rate for a chokra) and had then dropped, almost soundlessly, quite casually, out of sight. I could see him twisting and spinning as he fell toward the dark sea.

A noise of running water came from the bathroom. Ralph was up. Soon Ghulam would serve us our Sunday breakfast. Suddenly I found myself breathing hard, reluctant to get up—as if the prospect of this day and of the whole future had become a dead weight against my chest.

CHAPTER II ❀ DOROTHY telephoned about eleven. "Hi, swee-tie, did I wake you up?" Her Southern voice was hoarse, drawling, and playful.

"No, I had to get up about nine to see about the chokra." And I told her what had happened.

"That's aw-ful," said Dorothy. "Poor boy. What an *aw*ful thing to happen." Then, after a decent pause, she came to the point of her call. Suzy Mitchell, one of the Jungly Wallah regulars, had just telephoned to say that she was getting together an impromptu party for that evening. It was to be a farewell party for Dick Zimmer, who was with Caltex Oil, and his wife, Mary Lou; they were leaving for Manila at the end of the week. Dorothy had accepted for both of us.

"But, Dot," I said, "I told you I was going to the Chaudurys' tonight."

"It must have slipped my mind. Can't you get out of it?"

"I don't want to get out of it."

"But this will be your last chance to see the Zimmers," she wailed. "Besides, it's bound to be a good party."

"Dot, I hardly know the Zimmers."

"But you're *always* going to the Chaudurys'."

"That's not true. They're my closest Indian friends and I haven't laid eyes on them in nearly a month." Then I said, "Look, why don't you come to the Chaudurys' with me. They'd be delighted."

"Like hell they would. Besides, I'm not in the mood to nibble Indian candy and talk about politics or communism or whatever you talk about there."

I laughed at this and then said, "Why don't you get Phippsie to take you to the Mitchells'? I'm sure he'd like a chance to say good-by to the Zimmers." Phippsie was the nickname of Major Phipps, the most persistent of Dorothy's middle-aged British admirers.

"You aren't very funny."

"I'm sorry, Dot."

"Then you absolutely refuse to go to the Mitchells'?"

"My God, you don't give up easily, do you?" I was now

15

angry. "You didn't really forget I was going to the Chaudurys'. You resent the fact I have friends you don't like. That's the real point. Whether or not I go to the Mitchells' is strictly secondary."

"I wish you'd stop putting motives in my mouth. The truth is the Chaudurys don't like *me*. They make me nervous as the devil. I don't trust people who won't take a drink."

Again I laughed, though I was still angry.

"What's so funny?" she demanded. "It *happens* to be true. Well," she continued after a pause, "call me if you change your mind."

"I'm not going to change my mind. Good-by, Dot."

I had hardly returned to the living room when the telephone again rang. God damn her, I thought, certain it was Dorothy. But it turned out to be an English friend of mine, Martin Fenwick, who wanted me to join him for lunch at the United Services Club. I agreed at once, but thinking about it a little later, I was puzzled. Martin, I knew, was also going to be at the Chaudurys' that evening. I wondered if he wanted to see me on business. Martin was a member of the Indian Civil Service, and it was just possible that something had come up involving his department—the Labour Department of the Government of Bengal—with the Consulate General. In any case, I was glad enough to have lunch with him.

When I told Martin about the chokra, he shook his head and then continued to eat his soup. I waited for a comment. None came. Finally I said, "Am I making too much fuss over all this?"

"Not at all. Not from your standpoint. But what you've told me isn't very interesting. A Muslim boy has tuberculosis and is going to die. Perhaps he's already dead. What else did you expect? You've been in Calcutta for nearly a year and you've just seen India bare her teeth. That's all. She bares her teeth a hundred thousand times a day."

I fell silent, rather hurt by Martin's tone. Then the bearer brought our cold lamb, and we began to talk easily once more as we ate. Later, during a pause, Martin suddenly put down his knife and fork and stared at two Englishmen who were hunched over their curry several tables away from us.

"Look about you," he said. "Have you ever seen a seedier, more pathetic lot of aging men?"

I followed his glance around the great still white dining room with its dozens of hushed bearers and its widely separated tables, at which sat a dozen or more Englishmen—an occasional spotting in the vast white room. These were members of the I.C.S., of the Indian Forestry Service, the Indian Police, the Calcutta Port Commission, the Geological Survey of India, captains and majors of the Indian Army; these were the lowly administrators of India, men very different from the Clive Street tycoons and the generals and the chief secretaries who were at this moment stuffing themselves at the Bengal Club, three blocks up Chowringhee. "I find them admirable," I said. "They won't retire to England with a half-million pounds and they won't get the highest decorations of the Empire. But meanwhile they work hard and learn all there is to know about criminal gangs in Calcutta, or bird life in the Sundarbans, or rock formations in the Tista gorge—whatever it is. I consider that an enviable existence."

"And they'll nurse their ill health and spend their few post-retirement years at some desperately seedy hill station, reading the memoirs of their nineteenth-century predecessors. Or so they would do, if the British Raj should last another twenty years—which of course it won't."

The Englishman smiled at me, a bad-toothed smile that cut deeply into his lank, yellowish cheeks. At thirty-four, Martin looked seedier and unhealthier than any of the older men surrounding us; he was a veteran of dysentery and malaria, and was still taking drugs for the malaria. His gauntly handsome face was almost the color of khaki; he had dark-gray eyes, with muddied whites, and a ginger-colored stubble of mustache that matched his hair, giving him the over-all appearance of having been steeped, head first, in a bath of pale varnish. He had a dry, clear enunciation, with the merest trace of a Midland accent.

"Of course it won't last," I said. "That's part of the appeal. It's a melancholy, stoical sort of life. Very interesting in its way but doomed to final disappointment. Doesn't a sense of impermanence add a kick to your work in the Labour Department?"

"Do you mean my own impermanence or the Department's? No, there's very little kick, as you call it, in my work. It's much too swampy." Martin's manner again became remote.

It was not until we had nearly finished our coffee that Martin revealed the main purpose of the lunch. "What I've been wondering," he said, "is whether you might be interested in joining me on a trip to Benares in about a fortnight's time? I have some records to search there, but mainly I want to explore the place more thoroughly than I have done before. Steep myself in it for ten days or so. Then, if we want, we can go on to Lucknow or Delhi for a few days before flying back to Calcutta." He lifted his napkin and rubbed at one of his teeth. "Mainly, quite apart from the business, which merely gives me an excuse, I feel an urgent need to get away from Calcutta for a while—I rather need to sort things out a bit for myself—and I should very much like your company if you'd care to come. Does this sort of thing interest you at all? Could you wangle some leave at this time?"

"Of course I'd be interested." But, with my blood racing at the mere prospect of such a trip, I had to draw back from the brink to review the reasons why I shouldn't jump at Martin's offer. "I'll have to see," I stalled. "I'll have to speak to the Consul General and let you know." I had leave coming to me; Mr. Hubbard would worry and fret about transferring Mary Buxton or Ralph McClure to the visa office, but there was no likelihood that he would turn down my request. Only one reason, in fact, loomed ominously in the way of the trip: Dorothy could be counted on to react violently and bitterly and implacably against the whole project. And with justice—for although nothing definite had ever been said, I knew she assumed we would take our leaves simultaneously, spending the time together at Puri or Darjeeling or some other resort; and I knew, guiltily, that I had done nothing to discourage this plan whenever she hinted at it. On the contrary, I had taken it for granted myself. And now I *had* to go to Benares. Until Martin had spoken, the old city had been only a dark whisper at the edge of my awareness, but now I knew that I would be crushed beneath my disappointment if I couldn't go there. The oppression I had felt earlier in the morning suddenly became intolerable. Calcutta was hateful, my life dreary and jangling, Dorothy nothing more than a willful and querulous voice on the telephone. I had to throw off the weight, run free for a while. And then come back.

But the image of Dorothy's rage flared like a wall of fire across my path. I would have to risk the shattering of everything we had established together, and the mere thought of this made me wince with panic. I can't do it, I decided; I can't do this to her. And I looked up with shame and misery toward Martin.

"I can make all the arrangements," he was saying. "We could take along my bearer. He's damn good at traveling. Unless, of course, you have other ideas." He paused to stroke the little patch of reddish-yellow bristles over his lip.

"Martin, I can't—" I had trouble catching my breath. I knew what was about to happen. "Martin, I think I can manage it. Martin, I'd like very much to go—I really would! I'll try to work it out." This was the first real decision I had made in a long time, and it seemed as if I hadn't made it at all. I can still take it all back, I thought—but I also knew that I wouldn't.

Martin signed his chit for the lunch and we left the dining room and walked slowly through the high, white-painted marble-floored hall. We stopped to look at several of the late-eighteenth-century engravings that lined the walls; it was an oddly uncluttered India that they depicted: palely tinted, spacious, neoclassical in feeling. Descending the wide stairs, I noticed—as I did whenever I visited the club—the sign that read: LADIES WILL NOT USE THIS STAIRWAY.

"Will Anila be at the Chaudurys' tonight?" I asked, referring to the Indian girl with whom Martin had been carrying on a more or less public courtship or affair—I wasn't sure which.

"Yes, of course."

"Good. I haven't seen her in weeks."

We paused in the dim coolness of the hall. The club had a sort of white-marble purity about it, a stillness like that of a great public monument, and we were a little reluctant to leave it. Outside lay Chowringhee with its tearing crowds and its pavements spattered red with betel-nut juice.

"G-g-go ahead and ask him, Ramesh," said Harold Porter, a black-bearded Englishman who taught mathematics at the Dhurrumtolla Street Trade School. "Ask him wh-wh-why the Americans chose to drop the bomb on an Asiatic c-c-country instead of Germany."

"Oh, dolling, why must you be so rude to poor John?" said his stout Indian wife, Mira. "One mustn't hold him responsible for everything his country does, must one?" She looked about with a nervous smile. Having broken with her Brahman family to marry Harold, who was both a half-invalid and a communist, Mira Porter did not have an easy time of it.

"Don't worry," I said. "I've been asked that before. You've heard my answer, haven't you, Ramesh?"

"Yes, but you'll never convince any Indian that racism didn't have something to do with it," said Ramesh Chaudury. "They'll never take your word that the bomb wasn't ready in time to use it on Germany."

"That's quite true," said Philip Sachs. "Indians are racially incapable of accepting such a fact."

Ramesh gave a loud laugh and clapped his hands exuberantly. "What a lie! What a lie!" he cried out good-naturedly. "Ah, my dear Philip, my dear John, you should not waste your breath defending Uncle Sham. After England, you are the most hypocritical nation on earth. You needn't deny it!" Ramesh gestured widely, spreading his long fingers like spokes and then clasping his hands against his chest. He had the true Bengali love of verbal extravagance, and during one minute of rhetoric his long stallion's face could register passionate grief, humor, scorn, outrage, and warm affection to match the onrush of his words. "For once I shall not pick on Martin here. For once I shall spare England. Instead I shall expose Uncle Sham. I shall tell you how he preaches democracy and lynches his poor Negroes. Now don't interrupt me!" he shouted. "I shall show how he preaches liberty and equality and yet takes England's side whenever the question of Indian freedom comes up. Oh, I know he pretends not to, but he always does so in secret. And he preaches a welcome to all the oppressed of the world and yet he will not let me or Sujata or any other Indian or Chinese or Japanese emigrate to the States. He preaches individualism, yet to him we are not individuals but Asiatic hordes, swarming hordes like insects!"

"Ramesh has the true newspaperman's love of accuracy and distrust of exaggeration," said Martin Fenwick.

"Oh, please, please, no more politics for just now," cried Sujata Chaudury. She signaled to the bearer to pass around a basin of rose water and a towel for her guests, who had eaten their curry and rice with the fingers of their right hands.

"I should never have allowed my wife to leave purdah had I known she would interrupt her husband and his male friends in their conversation." Ramesh grinned at his wife as he dried his fingers.

"Better still to be in purdah if the men are going to talk such nonsense," said Sujata, staring back boldly. Sujata, of course, had never been in purdah.

The bearer next brought in a plate of mixed Indian sweetmeats. These he handed to Sujata, who in turn passed them among her guests.

I loved to watch her. Small, bespectacled, wrapped in a sari of flowered cotton, she moved always with a kind of plump gracefulness, whether in greeting her guests or touching the braided hair of her little girl. Her four-months pregnancy was beginning to show in the added straightness of her stance, enhancing, if anything, the delicacy of her movements and gestures. Yet mixed with this poise there remained a touch of the traditional shyness of the Indian woman before the friends of her husband; occasionally, when she had said something witty or laughed loudly or disputed a point, her round face would suddenly be crossed by the startled look of a child frightened by its own boldness. Then she would laugh again and glance with renewed and happy confidence toward Ramesh.

After a few minutes we all went into the tiny, whitewashed living room, where the women sat on the comfortless teakwood chairs and couch, while the men squatted on the flowered Kashmiri mats on the floor.

"Since we are forbidden to talk by Sujata," said Ramesh, "I shall have to play records for you instead." He took a battered album from the bookshelf and squatted with it beside the hand-cranked phonograph in the corner. With his white dhoti tucked around his brown shanks and his collarless shirt hanging out— for Ramesh always wore Indian clothes except at work—he looked like a follower of Gandhi about to begin a demonstration of cottage spinning; there was nothing in his appearance to suggest the staff writer for the *Amrita Bazar Patrika*. In addition to being a journalist, Ramesh was a food crank (and a tremendous authority on native tonics and laxatives), a teetotaler, a minor politician on the farthest left of the Congress party, and a writer of Bengali verse which had won him a narrow fame in his own city and province; he was also an erratic but warm-hearted host and a very good man, deeply fond of his English and American friends, whom he constantly harangued and baited.

"You shall listen first to the singing of Abdul Karim Khan and then to Rajaswari Datta," he announced, as he lowered the record onto the spindle. There was a prolonged scratching and then the first weirdly quavering note plucked from the sitar; then another; then the first tapping of the drums; and finally, after sitar, drums, and sarod had come together, the high, wailing falsetto of the singer.

I settled back on one elbow and watched as Ramesh sank almost instantly into a state of happy absorption. The Indian's expression shifted from trancelike mobility to sudden grimaces of joy, as though the rasps and quaverings of the music had shot along his bones. He seemed to be summoning, even extorting, the sounds from the performers. I glanced at Sujata. Her absorption was less mobile than her husband's but she was also "following through" the involutions and twistings of sound. Her round, placid, dark-olive face, her glasses, the plain sari, the squatness of her rounded body—every detail about Sujata was commonplace, yet there was an emanation from her, a sense that she was powerfully rooted in life and that, being so rooted, she could afford to follow the music anywhere it led her. They're an enviable couple, I thought, and instantly I was depressed, for I imagined that they had achieved some harmony in their life together that it would never be my luck to reach. I was again the small boy forced to listen upstairs to the sound of my parents dining below. This harmony of theirs spread outward through the bare little room, warming its white walls.

Then I saw that Sujata had detached herself from the music and was watching me. She smiled. How glad I was that she liked me! She knew that I was something more than an agreeable consular hack—she knew it far better than I did! And she and Ramesh had both known it from the start; I'd never have to prove my worth to *them*. Reassured, I gradually let myself down into the subtle net of music. After months of listening to what had seemed only baffling and outrageous noise, I was now beginning to catch the patterns of the drums, the high and intricate line of the melody against the steady drone of the bass. I felt mainly happy now, though there was a sharp grain of unease buried just below my consciousness that gave me a twinge from time to time; I would remember the chokra or think of Dorothy and the scene I still had to face.

Ramesh got up to change a record, and as he did so Anila Chatterjee, who had been listening with closed eyes, looked up and exclaimed, "What heavenly music! It has lifted me up and carried me away on its flood—carried me into the world of the artist. What agony to be brought back!" Then she glanced down at Martin, who was sprawled on the floor, and said, "You're laughing at me, Martin!"

"No, he's not," said Philip Sachs. "He's only pleased like the rest of us at how well you've stood up under the strain of travel."

I glanced at my colleague with affection. Philip had been enjoying himself all evening. He was now leaning forward on his elbows, lordly and grinning, his heavy Roman face alive with pleasure.

"Am I being so terribly silly?"Anila turned ruefully toward Philip. "But how can I help it if that's the way I really *feel?*"

"My dear, that's exactly the way *I* felt," said Philip. "We can't *both* be wrong."

Everyone laughed. Anila, too, began first to smile and then to giggle in a way that completely demolished her efforts to pout. She knew better than to stick to a role, once its effectiveness had clearly passed.

"At least you must admit that I do make an effort," she said. "Even at the risk of seeming affected. You know, I'd much rather be thought affected than natural. I *loathe* natural people —I always think they just aren't trying."

Anila got her laugh. I wished I could like Anila as much as I enjoyed looking at her; it was curious how little her appearance reflected the clever, disjointed, slightly bitchy quality of her mind. For Anila, the daughter of a rich Calcutta landowner named Mohan Chatterjee, had all the soft ripeness of the legendary Eastern beauty. Just now she was leaning back in such a way that her breasts strained against the confines of her crimson silk blouse; they were real melon breasts, large and perfect globes, the breasts of the yakshis carved in Hindu temples. And they went with her other features—the faintly aquiline nose; the full lips; the heavy, carefully plucked brows that nearly met beneath the spot of red paint on her forehead; the immense, kohl-darkened eyes; the delicately rounded hips. Anila's beauty was almost too sumptuous to be real, and this disquieting note was played up by the elaborateness of her black-and-gold sari. Altogether, she made a most improbable companion for the yellowed Englishman sprawled on the floor at her feet.

Ramesh played another Indian record and then the party dissolved into general talk. Sujata brought in another plate of crumbly sweetmeats made from milk and curds; they were achingly sweet and as perfumed as if they had been soaked in attar of roses. Ramesh offered drinks—lemon squash and tea, and for those who insisted on alcohol (for Ramesh did not enforce his principles on his guests) there was some harsh local gin.

All evening I had been expecting Martin to bring up the trip to Benares, but the Englishman, once the political bantering was over, had kept very much to himself (and never very far from Anila), watching and listening and smiling, very seldom speaking. At last I said to Ramesh, "Did you know that Martin and I are planning to visit Benares? What advice can you give me about the place?"

"Are you now? I say, how splendid!" And Ramesh at once began to stamp about with as much enthusiasm as if he were going with us. He got out an old book, which had belonged to his father, of faded, sepia-colored photographs of the city, laid it in the center of the floor, and summoned everyone to look on while he pointed out things we simply had to see; he had spent ten days in Benares several years before, giving a series of lectures on journalism at the Hindu University. "It's quite probably the oldest city in the world," said Ramesh, "and from the river, at least, it's the most beautiful." Then his equine face became shadowed and he drew back a little from the book. "But I have very mixed feelings about Benares. It is the heart of the old India. A very superstitious place. Very dirty."

"It's the most G-g-g-god-infested city in the world," said Harold Porter. "Everything that is most r-r-rotten in India breeds in the slime of B-b-b-benares. I d-d-d-d-detest the place!"

Anila Chatterjee squatted at my side. "Did I understand you to say that *you* and Martin are going to Benares?" she asked in a low voice.

I stared. Was it possible that Martin hadn't told Anila about his plans?

Anila, meanwhile, was saying, "Of course I knew Martin was planning such a journey, but I hadn't realized you were going along. What a sly dog he is! He told me he wanted to get away, to be by himself." Then, as if she revealed too much, Anila added enthusiastically, "You will both have the most delicious time, I'm sure. What fun it will be!" She stood up, smiling, clutching the rustling black-and-gold brocade of her sari, and moved away.

Then Philip's voice sounded abruptly in my ear. "I've got to go now. I suppose you want a ride?" His face was flushed and savage as he stood towering above me, his hands clasped behind his back; Philip had made no comment at all about the trip, nor had he looked at Ramesh's book.

"Well . . ." I glanced up in surprise, wondering what had come over Philip. For a moment I thought of staying longer and getting a lift with Martin, but decided against it because of Anila. So, getting to my feet, I said, "Well, it is pretty late. I suppose we really ought to head back into town."

The Chaudurys protested, but Philip walked firmly toward the door.

When I said good night to Anila, she held out her soft, tawny hand with its whitened nails and murmured, "Do take care of my Martin."

"I expect he's the one who'll be looking after me."

"Oh, how lucky you boys are. I'm terribly glad you're going to have such a lovely trip."

Sujata bade us good night in the darkened hallway, where Philip had halted his headlong departure just long enough to be civil. "Please ask me again," he said.

"Of course, Philip. We've loved having you." Sujata then peered rather solemnly at me from behind her silver-rimmed glasses. "Ah, John, we do love you and we see you so seldom. At least I do—Ramesh is more fortunate. What an impossible life you do lead," she went on. "One foot in Mayfair and one foot in Bohemia. I positively wonder you're not split up the middle."

"My God, is it as bad as that?" I felt a little rebuked and at the same time touched by her affection.

Ramesh accompanied us along the dark pathway that led through the looming tenements of Kalighat to the square where Philip had parked his Bentley. The lights in the tenements were all out, and we could see nothing as we stepped carefully along, with Ramesh in front. Then, as we turned a corner, the air lightened and we came into an opening in the midst of which was a large tank, the bathing and laundering place of the local Hindu population. Here the thick clumps of bamboo and other vegetation gave the square the appearance of an unexpected clearing in a dense tropical forest. In the tank itself the huge Bengal stars were reflected in those few clear patches of water where the thick green mantle of scum had been broken by recent bathers.

"It looks as though all my worthy neighbors are in bed," said Ramesh as we reached the car. "These good nationalistic clerks and shopkeepers are very suspicious of us, you know. They even spread rumors that Sujata sleeps with our European visitors." We shook hands and he went away.

The Bentley still had the special smell of a new car—the smell of the most elegant car I had ever driven in. Resting my head against the slick leather of the seat, I closed my eyes. Philip was cursing softly under his breath as he jerked angrily at the wheel. Suddenly the car shot forward with a tremendous burst of speed, tearing through the narrow roadway, which was hardly wider than the car itself. "For God's sake," I shouted. Then there was a strident screeching as the car jolted to a stop, its headlights not eight inches from a stucco wall just ahead: the road had taken a right-angle turn. I could hear windows being raised and shutters flung open from the buildings on three sides; a baby cried, and there was a babble of Indian voices. As Philip backed the car away from the wall and shone the headlights down the road in front, three or four coolies, their faces weirdly bleached, and grimacing in the sudden light, leaned forward, propped on their hands, from the doorways in which they had been sleeping. A male voice called out in Bengali from somewhere above; since there was no answer, the voice called again, thin and shrill with anger.

"I'm frightfully sorry," Philip shouted at last in the most insolent pseudo-British tone he could muster.

"Oh, this is veddy bad," came the high-pitched voice in babu-English. "Such a noise in the night to disturb people that try to sleep. This is really too bad of you."

"I *said* I was frightfully sorry." Philip was again yanking at the steering wheel.

Another Bengali voice, also shrill and angry, came from another quarter. In the fusillade of words that exploded from all sides, I thought I could make out "Chaudury" repeated several times. For a second I was seized with a kind of panic; I felt surrounded, cut off, and the looming tenements, their blotched and leprous walls suddenly flashing toward me out of the dense night, had closed in with a strident menace that had little to do with the voices screeching from the upper windows. Then, as my panic ebbed away, anger toward Philip surged in a flood.

"You're acting like a baby. What the hell's the matter with you? Have you completely lost your mind?" These were the sharpest words I had ever spoken to Philip, and I flung them out, hating Philip, not caring at all if this friendship, which I had carried along with gentle hands and soft words, should fly to pieces in my face.

Philip, who had at last turned the car and was driving forward again, slowly now, said in a subdued tone, "Don't rebuke me, John. I can't stand it if you rebuke me."

Astonished by Philip's meekness, I said nothing. We made our way at last to Russa Road, entering it near the turnoff to the temple of the ferocious goddess Kali, from whom the district of Kalighat (and possibly Calcutta itself) took its name. Now we were on a wide avenue, a continuation of the Bhowanipore Road which led ultimately into Chowringhee.

When Philip spoke again, the old belligerence had re-entered his voice. "So you are going to Benares with Fenwick," he said, and I for the first time realized what had caused the outburst:

the mere fact that Philip was not going along—had not even been invited—had been enough to send him into a tantrum! "I like Martin well enough," Philip continued, "but I can't imagine he'd be a very exciting traveling companion. He's too dried up and enervated and down at the mouth. It would bore me silly to have to spend even a full day in his company, let alone ten days."

"I'll take along a good book," I said.

But Philip's next words uncovered another level. Again his voice changed; now it was aggrieved, querulous. "I hadn't said anything about it, but I'd rather hoped you might wait until I had some leave due me. Then we could have gone together on a really splendid trip. Maybe as far as Ceylon or even Afghanistan. Maybe visit the Buddhist caves at Bamian. Something on that order."

"Well," I began, " 'preciate—I'm glad you wanted to include me in your plans. But I need to get some vacation now. I want to see Benares very much and I get along very well with Martin. Besides," I added, hesitating a second, "I couldn't afford to go all the way to Ceylon or—"

"Of course I would have expected to contribute something to your extra expenses on such a trip. It would have been well worth it to me for the sake of really congenial company."

I laughed this off a little uncomfortably. "That's a reckless thing to offer."

"I wasn't joking. But obviously you don't intend to change your mind."

"No, I'm afraid not."

I was angry again. Why the hell, I thought, can't people keep their hands off me? Philip was as demanding as Dorothy, who at least had certain rights. Although I sometimes worried over my reluctance to let people into the enclosure of my life, I still resented it when someone tried to force an entry. Why should I do battle over my perfectly private desire to spend a couple of weeks in Benares? I didn't want to skirmish with Philip when the real issue, with Dorothy, still had to be faced.

Although I did not speak again, Philip must have sensed

my anger, for in a few minutes he said, "I want to apologize again for that outburst back in Kalighat. I'm afraid I was behaving rather childishly. I've been upset all day, as a matter of fact."

"I'm sorry to hear it."

"Over nothing very important. I won't go into it now, if you don't mind."

I was happy enough to let it go at that.

CHAPTER III ❦ MONDAY and Tuesday passed, and I still had said nothing to Dorothy about the trip. Mr. Hubbard, the Consul General, raised more objections than I had expected and, characteristically, postponed giving me a final answer. I saw no point in upsetting Dorothy prematurely.

On Wednesday morning, as Ralph and I were finishing breakfast, Ghulam led an awkward-looking Muslim boy into the dining room and said, "New chokra, sahib. Very good references." The boy was about fourteen, long-nosed and shy, with a faint line of hair over his upper lip. He salaamed to both of us, touching the lower rim of his fez; then, at Ghulam's murmured command, he rummaged into his open shirt and pulled out a bundle of papers from his waistband. I looked at the grimy, dog-eared letters, obviously penned by different scribes, and signed illegibly by former employers. "Looks all right," I said and passed the references to Ralph. He, too, looked and nodded. There seemed nothing else to do.

"Chokra can wear old chokra's uniform," said Ghulam, who was eager to clinch the deal. He glanced sympathetically at the boy's soiled shirt and ragged trousers.

Ralph caught my eye and shrugged his shoulders, as if shivering a little under a bleak wind. I nodded. "All right," said Ralph. "Same wages."

"What's the chokra's name?" I asked.

"Abdul, sahib. See, written here," he said eagerly, pointing to the references, which the boy still clutched.

"That's all right," I said.

Half an hour later, as I was driving to work, I was held up, at the corner of Old Courthouse Street and the Esplanade, by a large herd of water buffalo. The enormous animals lurched forward unevenly, jostling into one another, plunging and raising their great heads, plopping dung into the street. In the already concentrated sunlight of March, the backs and upper flanks of the buffaloes shone with a polished blue-black gloss, supple and rippling; but their legs and sagging bellies and drooping horns were still caked with the yellow mud of their last wallowing place. I had often seen such herds before, in the busiest sections of the city, but now I stared with unbelief at this jungle eruption surging and thundering in front of my car. The three buffalo-drivers looked wild, too—almost naked and nearly as black and shiny as their animals.

Watching them, I was suddenly overwhelmed with the conviction that I knew nothing about India. My year in Calcutta had barely opened a crack to peep through. What did I really know about Ghulam, whom I saw and spoke to many times a day? Did he miss his wife and children, who lived in a village near Mymensingh? Did he resent having only two weeks a year —his vacation—to spend with them? Did he mourn the dead chokra, who for six months had slept only three feet from his own charpoy in the musty little room behind the scullery?

The herd rumbled past, and I was able to drive up Old Court-house Street to the entrance to Esplanade Mansions—the building that housed the Consulate General. From a distance, Esplanade Mansions—with its shuttered windows, its balustrades and balconies, its pale-yellow walls—had a kind of Mediterranean glamour, the look of a Riviera hotel. But at close range the effect crumbled like the made-up face of an old actress on the point of tears. Even on this fine, clear, sun-washed day, the building seemed unwholesome, as though its gutters had failed to drain off the fluids that yellowed and blotched its damp walls. Nothing in this city holds up, I thought, parking my car between Philip's gleaming Bentley and the olive-drab Army Cadillac which was reserved for the Consul General's use. This is the junk heap of the world, I thought, again aware of the same unease, the same strangeness of vision that had come over me a few minutes before.

Ralph drove into the compound just behind me, and we entered the building together.

During the midmorning, as I was going over the visa dossier of an Anglo-Indian girl named Nellie Lawrence, I got a call from the Consul General. Once again he moaned about the difficulties of granting me leave at such a busy time. Stalling and mumbling, his Milwaukee voice rasping through the receiver, Mr. Hubbard wondered if there'd be time to break in Mary Buxton at the visa desk before I left. I told him I could easily teach her enough to hold things together for two weeks.

"You're sure about this?" he asked.

"Yes, sir. There won't be any problem at all." I spoke confidently, knowing now that he had decided to approve my request.

I hung up and, with a tremendous effort, wrenched my thoughts away from Dorothy. For an instant I stared at Miss Lawrence as if I had never seen her before. "Now, let's see," I said, turning again to the papers spread on the desk between us.

As an Anglo-Indian, a Eurasian, engaged to an American soldier back in the States, Miss Lawrence had to prove that at least fifty-one per cent of her blood was European. If she could do that, and if her other documents were in order, she could then apply for a number from the British immigration quota; if she failed, I had no choice but to reject the application, for the United States allowed no quota for Asiatics. Concentrating now, I scanned each of the papers in front of me: the declaration of intent to marry signed by ex-Sergeant Leroy Latchford of Tulsa, Oklahoma; the letter from American sponsors; the medical certificate; the guarantees of support from Leroy Latchford's parents; the statement from their bank; and, finally, the incomplete proof of Nellie Lawrence's bloodline. Then I turned to the document she had handed me just before the C.G.'s call. It was a brief note, in green ink, stating that the undersigned (Mrs. Doris O'Malley) knew Mrs. Florence Da Susa, of Ranchi, grandmother of Nellie Lawrence, to be of purely English descent. That was all; no affidavit, no notarization, no proof. As I read it, I could hear the quiet breathing of the brown girl across the desk; she was leaning forward, and I could smell her hair and the staleness of her clothes.

"It's just what we've been waiting for, isn't it, Mr. Wickham?" Her voice had the high, chirping singsong of the Anglo-Indian.

"I'm afraid it isn't. Didn't I tell you last time that it had to be an affidavit—a *sworn* affidavit?" I tried to control my exasperation.

"Oh, dear, perhaps you did. It's all so confusing, isn't it?" She gave me a tremulous smile, as if to admit she hadn't expected the green ink to accomplish very much. She was a rather plain girl, with high cheekbones, a wide mouth almost purple with lipstick, and a mass of black hair that tumbled to the shoulders of her ruffled blouse; like so many of the girls who came to my office, her style of looks and dress was hopefully derived from Rita Hayworth. "I've given you such a lot of papers," she went on. "I should think by now there must be enough."

"Almost but not quite." Once again I went through the documents with her. One of the grandmothers was admittedly a pure Indian; her husband, however, was clearly in the open—a railway worker, born in Leeds, who had spent twenty years as an assistant stationmaster in Asansol. Another grandfather, named Da Susa, came from one of those Goanese families that had been mingling Indian and Portuguese blood for four hundred years. It was Mrs. Da Susa we were working on now, a "completely English woman," who would have clinched the case if only her marriage certificate hadn't been lost along with the rest of her papers. "We need an affidavit sworn before a magistrate," I repeated. "A note like this doesn't mean a thing." Ordinarily I would have settled for less—anything remotely plausible would have done—but in Miss Lawrence's case I had to be especially careful: her skin was so dark that the United States Immigration Service would be certain to examine her papers rigorously—and I knew they would not hesitate to deny her the right of entry if the dossier seemed incomplete.

"I think I understand now," said Miss Lawrence. "I'll try again." Then she added, "He still wants me, Mr. Wickham. Leroy still loves me. You should see the letters he writes. He says it's driving him crazy, all this waiting."

"Just get me that sworn affidavit and I'll send you along."

After she left, I sat for a moment, listening to the click of her heels down the corridor. I could hear my American secretary, Mary Haakinson, talking to a passport applicant in the next room. Then I picked up my telephone and asked the switchboard operator to call Mrs. Eustace at Saunders-McNab —the firm of managing agents where Dorothy had worked ever since she quit the American Red Cross. There was a chance she might be free for lunch. We had a date for the following evening, but I decided it might be better not to wait.

Dorothy's coffee cup rattled as she placed it on the saucer. With her vivid bronze hair and glowing skin and clear blue eyes, she looked as though she had spent the morning on a tennis court instead of in the Clive Street office of Saunders-McNab, Ltd. Just behind her head the fronds of a potted palm rose like an extravagant fan.

"So that's what's been on your mind," she said. "From the way you've been stalling and beating around the bush, I thought at least you were going to propose to me. Or something like that."

"As you know, I'd planned to take a trip with you, and I still do." My mouth was dry and I had to make an effort to go on. "I can get another ten days or so later this year and we can go to Puri or Darjeeling or something. It's just that I feel the need to get away for a bit right now," I continued, lapsing into Martin's diction, "and this seemed like a good chance to see Benares. I've always wanted to see it. And I'd be with someone who really knows the place and could show me around." I paused for a moment, painfully aware of how remote and rehearsed my voice sounded. From across the green-tiled dining room of the Great Eastern Hotel, beyond the potted palms and the white tables and the army of hushed bearers, came the thin strains of Bela Szabo's Continental Ensemble; he was playing "Sentimental Journey," as if to mock my enterprise. "Besides," I resumed, "you said you couldn't get leave before May at the earliest, and I feel it would do me a lot of good to get away for a little while right now."

"To get away from *what?* From *me?*"

"For God's sake, Dorothy—"

She had looked away, and I believed I could see the flash of tears. Suddenly hating my selfishness, I longed to cancel the whole trip.

"You're all alike," she whispered, still looking away. "You and Harry Eustace and all the rest. You're all alike."

It's coming now, I thought, bracing myself. But Dorothy did not storm and she did not cry. Whatever tears I had seen or imagined had vanished when she turned her face toward me, and the whites of her strong blue eyes were clear.

"Look, John, you don't have to account to *me* for everything you want to do." Like her eyes, her voice was clear and strong and faintly scornful. "*I* don't own you. And you don't own me. I reckon we're about even on that score. That's the way we both want it, and that's the way we'll have it. There's nothing I hate worse than being possessive."

"You're not possessive, Dot."

She eyed me sharply. "Neither are *you,* John." She lifted her cup, took a long, reflective sip, and then said, "When's this trip going to take place?"

"Exactly eleven days from now." I was drunk with relief. The crisis was over; that fantastic resilience of hers was coming into play. "Meanwhile," I said, "I have to break in Mary Buxton at the visa desk. I hope she won't be too ruthless and efficient with my Anglo-Indian girls."

As we were leaving the dining room, Dorothy stopped at a table where Sir Ronald McAllister, the chairman of Saunders-McNab, was lunching with several business friends; among them was Dorothy's admirer, Major Phipps. I watched from a distance while she laughed and joked, rearing back, both hands on her hips. The gentlemen were delighted and kept waving and calling to her when she walked away.

We parted at the entrance of the hotel. "I'll see you tomorrow night," I said. "A little after seven."

Dorothy grinned at me. "That's right," she said. "I've never broken a date with you yet, and there's no point in beginning tomorrow. So long, Johnnie."

Nothing's happened, I thought, as I walked up Old Courthouse Street toward the Consulate. I had gone to encounter Dorothy with the great sword of my resolution gripped in both hands, and now I was leaving, tremendously relieved and a little crestfallen. I still winced under the lashing of her controlled bitterness and my own guilt. I had hurt her and I was ashamed, but much more than that I was relieved. The sky hadn't fallen. Nothing was irreparable. I was going to Benares—and Dorothy would be waiting for me when I got back. At least, I thought, I've risked a blowup, and I can do it again when I have to. There was a flickering of masculine pride. But meanwhile I was very glad that the *status quo* was still intact—though I couldn't have said why I so much dreaded the possible shattering of it.

CHAPTER IV ❧ ON the afternoon of our third day in Benares, Martin took me to call on an Englishwoman, a rich old maid named Miss Roper, whom he had known years before in Calcutta. Having spent much of her life traveling around the world, Miss Roper had now settled permanently in Benares, where she ran a clinic for pregnant Hindu women. Wiry and determined and resourceful, she lived by herself in a small apartment in one of the crumbling old palaces overlooking the Ganges. Just now, we were sitting on the thickly cushioned floor of a marble-canopied alcove or balcony, from which one could look down, through a pierced screen of peach-colored marble, to a bathing ghat some sixty feet below. Miss Roper had been talking steadily for nearly an hour.

"Dear me, no," she was saying in her dry, rather belligerent voice. "I certainly do *not* think of myself as a Hindu. I'm merely Church of England gone native." She gave a tug at the fold of the cheap cotton sari which hung over one bony shoulder, and the movement caused the bracelet of tiny silver bells on her wrist to emit an elfin tinkle. "In the first place, I couldn't even if I wanted to. You have to be born a Hindu, you can't become one. I have no caste. I'm an outcaste. In fact, I'm *quite* untouchable." Restlessly, she took a cigarette from a sandal-wood box near her bare feet and held it up for Martin to light. "Now," she continued after a few puffs, "Henri Nigot and Claude Bazin—they're coming here for tea on Friday—you'll like them immensely—perfectly charming—anyway, they *pretend* to be Hindu. They observe the dietary laws—complete vegetarians—practice yoga—wear dhotis—all that sort of thing. Of course it's all perfect rubbish. They really aren't any more Hindu than I. Can't be. One has to be born a Hindu."

I was listening, entertained and respectful, to Miss Roper, but more and more my attention was drawn to the fantastic panorama of the ghats below. Sweeping southward in a great crescent, glowing in the torrential light of afternoon, the city poured itself down to the yellow river in cascades of steps and mounds of tumbled masonry. On these steps—the ghats—thousands of pilgrims clustered like black bees swarming toward the water; above them rose golden temples, layer on layer, and white palaces whose walls reflected the wavering lights of the Ganges. Even above the dry continuum of Miss Roper's voice I could hear the sound of bells and temple gongs carried across the water. "They've lived together for years," Miss Roper was saying, "and have never quarreled—not once. Quite extraordinary. Henri has written a perfectly marvelous book on the Hindu temple. Every other word is Sanskrit. Perhaps you've seen it." And a little later, having exhausted the subject of her French neighbors, Miss Roper began to discuss the problem of the stray bulls. "I've been making the most unconscionable nuisance of myself, trying to persuade the town authorities to pen up the vagrant scrub bulls. They wander about, you know, mating quite at will and quite spoiling the stock of cattle. The cows are mostly dried-up runts now, and every year the breed gets worse, thanks to those dreadful scrub bulls. Some of them are hardly bigger than a pony. Undoubtedly you've seen them. Miserable, unwholesome little beasts. They should be penned up, every one of them—ideally of course, they should be castrated, but that's quite out of the question in a place like Benares. Each year the cows give less milk and the prices rise and these wretched people can scarcely afford a drop, the price is so outrageous. But the authorities simply won't listen to me. 'Continue to hand out pills to expectant ladies,' they tell me, 'but leave our poor bulls alone.' Poor bulls indeed!"

Miss Roper broke off to light another cigarette, and during the pause a drum began to beat outside. Leaning forward, I peered through a wide quatrefoil in the marble screen. Then Martin and Miss Roper also moved forward on their cushions to have a look.

On the ghat immediately below, a fat old sadhu—a holy man in orange rags—was being lifted by two young Indians into a small boat; another young man, standing by, was beating on a drum suspended to his waist by a strap. Each of the three disciples was naked to the waist, their shoulders and chests shining like polished amber in the afternoon sun. Their dhotis hung in folds down to their ankles, and as the men went about

39

their task, the lower folds of the snow-white cloth got wet and clung transparently to their brown shins. The fat old man maintained an awkward and rigid sitting position; his hands were folded in his lap and his bald, shining head was thrust forward at a curious angle, as though he had fixed himself in some kind of cataleptic trance. Very gently and cautiously the young men descended the stairs until they were nearly waist-deep in the swirling yellow water, and then they gently lowered the sadhu into the front of the skiff, maintaining him always in his inconvenient sitting posture. One of them placed a loose garland of white and scarlet blossoms around the sadhu's bare, honey-colored shoulders. Then, suddenly, the old man's head lolled forward on his chest, and I realized for the first time that I was watching a corpse on its way to consignment to the sacred waters. The three disciples settled themselves into the skiff and pushed off, two of them paddling, the third still beating his drum. On the ghat, perhaps fifty bathers continued to rinse out their ears and nostrils, spout water from their mouths, climb the steps again, and change into a fresh white dhoti, letting the old one drop in a wet, yellowed heap about their ankles. None of them took the slightest notice of the skiff and its freight. And at the head of the stairs, squatting in a circle, were five Brahman students, all with heads shaved bare and shiny except for a long topnot, all wearing the sacred thread slung round the neck and hanging down one naked side, all chanting, in a half-drone, half-whine, the lines of Sanskrit which their guru had, presumably, set for them to memorize; their chant reached my ear mingled with the sound of bells and gongs and the now distant thumping of the drum. Looking down, with my forehead pressed against the smooth marble of the screen, I was aware of motion and noise, but I was also aware, very strangely, of a profound stillness in which all sound and motion seemed to drown, a stillness in which my own heartbeat seemed to echo louder than the funeral drum. This overwhelming sense of universal quiet made me uneasy, and I felt myself drawing back from it, though its appeal was very strong. It must have something to do with the quality of the light, I decided vaguely: the rich, golden afternoon light in which the sweeping crescent of the city was steeped, in which its bathers and the boat and the river itself—in spite of their motion—were fixed and curiously taken out of time.

"There's always something going on," said Miss Roper's dry voice in my ear; she, clearly, was not bothered by the quiet.

I roused myself on my elbows and shook off my mood. "That's certainly the least macabre funeral I've ever seen. Will they simply dump the old man when they get out to the middle?"

"Yes," said Martin Fenwick. "The holy men and small children are simply put into the water; the others are burned." Then he added, "I quite agree with you. There's nothing macabre about it—not even the idea of the happy crocodiles."

We had tea in the "garden," which was really a dense thicket in the midst of the courtyard. Bananas and plantains and bamboo cast speckled shadows over the little wicker table and Miss Roper's green-and-white Wedgwood service, and there were many flies buzzing around the milk pitcher and the shallow bowl of sweetmeats. Chained to a stake nearby, a young rhesus monkey entertained the company by his optimistic attempts to snatch flies as they buzzed past him; otherwise he chattered and whimpered to himself, chewed bits of mango skin, flaunted his sore-looking pink behind, searched for fleas, and played with his own excrement. Despite all the foliage, it was hot in the garden, and there was an unclean smell of gutters and rotting leaves. Pouring the coffee-colored tea and occasionally clapping her hands together for the bearer, Miss Roper told of her feud with one of the Indian doctors at the clinic and of his attempts —which she had triumphantly blocked—to have her removed from the staff. "Someday," she said, "I shall be able to *prove* what I perfectly well know—that he has made an absolute fortune by selling all the drugs he's stolen from us."

Later, when it had begun to grow dark, we left Miss Roper in her garden and walked along the Asi Ghat Road until we reached the thronged alleyways of the main chauk or bazaar.

"Glad to be here?" asked Martin.

"Very! Can't you tell?"

"How did you like old Roper?"

"I liked her. I wouldn't want to listen to her all the time, but for an afternoon it's fine. She's really very interesting. I've never met anyone quite like her before."

"Oh, the type's common enough. Send Betsey Trotwood to India and you'd have Ethel Roper. More or less. What interests me is the way she manages to live in Benares and wear a sari and speak very good Hindi and work with Indians day and night and yet remain totally untouched by all this." Martin waved his arm vaguely, as though calling on everything that surrounded us to come closer. "She sees a lot and knows a lot, but really, she might as well be handing out pills in the East End of London. I don't think she has a clue what Benares is all about."

What was it all about? We were now in the midst of the chauk, and the calm golden sweep of the river front had given way to a dark tangle of streets, most of them far too narrow for any vehicles larger than a ricksha. This was a dense underground world buried beneath six-story houses whose projecting eaves and balconies hid the blackening sky. The chauk was full of deep recesses and winding ducts and sudden flaring lights—an entrail world, slippery with fresh cow dung, daubed with red and ocher paint, cluttered with beggars who stumped about on whatever limbs remained to them, screaming for baksheesh. We pushed ahead in what we guessed to be the direction of the bazaar where brocades were woven and sold; but there was no real direction within this tangle—we could only surrender to it, follow its convolutions, and hope eventually to emerge into the special loop or pocket which we sought. For me this surrender was accompanied by a strong joy, an exhilaration that made me slightly drunk as I plunged about in the welter of beggars, sadhus, pilgrims, humpbacked little bulls, white cows, tradesmen, and naked children brawling in the muck. Every few feet we came upon a shrine breaking into the arcaded shop fronts—sometimes a small temple with a gold-leaf dome and walls painted a dull red, sometimes just a niche containing the black linga of Siva, smeared with vermilion, decked with a few wilted blossoms. For this was pre-eminently the city of the Lord Siva, the lord of destruction whose emblem was a stylized penis, the god also known as Biseswar and Mahadeva, the Lord of the Universe, the Great God, whose golden temple was the holiest spot in Benares. Siva's emblems were also the trident and the bull, and his consort was the lovely goddess Parvati, who, in another aspect, formed the destructive mother-energy known variously as Durga and Kali. Siva's linga was everywhere, and so were his followers—blear-eyed sannyasin with matted hair and bodies smeared with gray ash, wild-looking ascetics, who lurked in doorways or stumbled along the street, staring wildly into my face as I passed. These were the real images of nightmare and derangement, far more grisly than the red-shrouded corpses lying about on litters, their scarlet-painted feet sticking out, waiting to be carried to the river front for burning.

We reached the quarter of the brass-smiths, and the din of hammering was added to the clanging of temple bells, the cries of peddlers and shopkeepers, the whine of beggars. The little shops of the brass-smiths flared behind the black archways like the caves of the Nibelungs. I've reached the inside of the earth, I said to myself drunkenly. I turned to look at Martin, whose yellow face and eyes blazed in the sudden flash of lights.

"I know where we are now," said Martin. He led me into a passageway to the right; we climbed a flight of steps and found ourselves in a street—somewhat wider than the others—which was lined on both sides by shops offering brocades and saris. We went into six or seven of them, pricing the materials. At last Martin found what he wanted—an elaborate palm-leaf pattern closely woven in gold and silver thread on a wine-red base—the perfect present for Anila. I looked closely at the merchant as the bargaining began. He was just an ordinary Indian shopkeeper, slightly paunchy, dressed in an ordinary dhoti. There were sweat stains under the armpits of his collarless blue shirt and his black, pomaded hair shone under the naked light bulb in the ceiling. His commonplaceness was strangely comforting to me; there was nothing about this pouch-cheeked, alternately stubborn and obsequious shopkeeper to suggest that he lived deep inside the entrails of the earth. His long fingers flashed diamond rings as they waggled in the eloquent fury of bargaining. No longer disoriented, I watched this purely human transaction with relief. The haggling ended on the sum of one hundred and twenty rupees.

"That's too much, Martin," I said. "He's cheating you."

"I know, but I'm tired of the game."

Then, not to be outdone, I bought a brocaded evening bag for Dorothy, and we returned to the street. The weird night still rang all around us, but I was now safe from its spell. We found a tonga and drove back to Spencer's Hotel, which was in the cantonment, the European quarter, nearly three miles to the northwest of the city and the river.

Every day we made the trip, by tonga or ricksha, down to the old city. Martin had several acquaintances, British and Indian, in addition to Miss Roper, and we made use of the letters of introduction which Ramesh had given us to his friends at the Hindu University. We went to a concert of sitar and drums at the Theosophical Society. We took a boat down the golden river front, from Asi Ghat to Aurangzeb's mosque, and then re-entered the bazaar, where I shopped for brass plates. We had tea again in Miss Roper's rank garden, this time in the company of the two French Hindus, one of them homosexually sly and insinuating, the other very scholarly, with an ascetic's bad color and a shy, inward, reserved manner; both of them were wearing dhotis and sandals. And each evening we left the reeking old city of Siva and returned to the decayed hotel, to the bleached bones of the cantonment.

On the morning of our last day, we visited the temple of Durga. It was painted a dull red-ocher, the color of dried blood. Hundreds of big, gray langur monkeys were swarming along the walls and in the overhanging branches of trees. Everywhere there was a sense of wriggling, chaotic life, and yet the temple itself was consecrated to blood. From time to time a squealing goat would be dragged into the center of the courtyard and stretched out on a block of wood. There was no ceremony. A slovenly attendant, barely paying attention to his job, would strike off the head and then turn to chat with his fellows. Women and children daubed themselves in the bright blood, which looked like new red paint. Another attendant took the carcass off to be butchered and sold; there was a pile of surprised-looking goat heads at the foot of the block.

"Does this bother you?" asked Martin.

"The smell does. That's about all. The smell and the flies. It's too disorganized and messy to mean very much." It was very hot, and I wiped the back of my neck with my handkerchief. "Don't forget," I said, "I've already seen this kind of thing at Kalighat."

"Ah, so you have."

We watched the monkeys for a little while and then returned to the cantonment. Martin had some government business to transact at the Civil Courts during the late morning. After lunch he went to his room and stayed there, presumably writing letters. Left to myself, I lounged about the hotel, reading battered, months-old copies of the *Tatler* and the *Spectator,* absently watching the sweeper scrub the floor of the long veranda. My stomach was a little queasy, perhaps from the sun or the atrocious food of the hotel. I kept imagining I could smell the temple of Durga and this added to my queasiness. I didn't mind being left alone. Even when we were together, Martin had kept much to himself, friendly yet detached, often silent for long stretches. He had been a good and thoughtful companion but always remote; he knew a lot about all we had seen and he told me much of this with a kind of benign impersonality; even during meals we had talked almost entirely about *things,* never about ourselves directly. Thus I knew Martin no better now than I had in Calcutta; nor did I really know why Martin had wanted my company on this trip. All of this in no way diminished my liking for the Englishman. My regard deepened each day and I welcomed even the long silences, glad, after the arid noise of my life in Calcutta, to taste the clear, thin water of impersonality for a while.

In the middle of the afternoon I paid a visit to St. Mary's Church in the cantonment. Now, in the last week in March, the hot weather had really begun. The powerful, heavy light beat down upon white roads and inert white buildings; the trees were already bleached with dust, the grass dry and rapidly turning brown. I pushed open the creaking door and entered, grateful now for the sudden dimness that refreshed my eyes and face. The church had a cool, musty, cellar smell of brick dust and plaster and rotting wood. As soon as my eyes had adjusted to the darkness, I strolled down the side aisles, reading the memorials set in the whitewashed wall: memorials to forgotten officers and their women, to captains of the Bengal Army slaughtered at Kabul in 1842, at Meerut or Cawnpore in 1857, to wives who had died of cholera or childbirth here in Benares. The words "honour" and "gallantry" and "devotion" seemed to reverberate through the empty building like footsteps on the brick flooring. As I emerged, blinking, into the sunlight, I stood for a moment on the porch, immobilized by the echoes of old suffering and endeavor. Here, cast high and dry above the churning Indian sea, were the stranded wrecks, the skeletons, the empty shells of the nineteenth-century Raj, desolate and whitened, bleached in the strong light.

I walked slowly back to Spencer's Hotel, which stood like a crumbling Louisiana mansion—wide verandas, Doric columns, and unpainted shutters—facing across the unpaved road to a sun-cracked parade ground where sepoys and their British officers had once marched and countermarched to the blare of a regimental band. It was time for tea, but I went to my room instead and took off my clothes and lay down on the sagging brass bed. A sense of remoteness and unreality had already set in, a detachment from all that I had thought and done and felt in my life before. I was entirely isolated; the bedroom was a watertight box drifting quietly across the surface of an unruffled ocean. Even Martin in the next room writing letters or whatever he was doing was far beyond my call, almost beyond my imagining.

I had thought very little of Dorothy during all this time—no further, really, than the fact that she would be there for me on my return. The relationship could not last forever, but there was no reason, I decided, why it might not last a long time. I had the curious sense that the future was out of my hands; I was completely unable even to *imagine* a set of conditions beyond those of the present. Thus, I had not thought about it very much, but now, as I lay on the bed, an image came of our last evening together. With perfect clarity and detachment—as though I were looking through the glass wall of an aquarium—I saw her putting a record on the phonograph; it was "Paper Doll," and she had said, "That's your trouble. What you really want *is* a paper doll, and not a real live girl." And I remembered—but did not feel—the way in which she had begun making sexual overtures to me early in the evening, clutching my fingers under the table at Firpo's, making me stop to kiss her on the way to the car, and I remembered my annoyance at having the sexual initiative taken from me and also the guilt that forced me to hide my distaste beneath the rags of tenderness. As though watching a pornographic movie that couldn't arouse me, I saw myself pull away from Dorothy after we had made love, after she had clung to me with the persistence of her mouth and hands when I had spent myself. I saw her lying taut and desperate, her coppery hair fanned out dark against the pillow, her face, throat, and shoulders flushed brick-red in the lamplight, her blue eyes locked in desperation. And I remembered how, after dressing, I leaned over the bed to touch her rigid brow with my lips and how she turned violently away, as though I had seared her with a hot coal, and how I forced myself to whisper, "I'll miss you, darling. I'll miss you."

Then I tried to recall how Dorothy had seemed to me months ago, at the Mitchells' party, when I had first taken notice of her. She had imitated a Southern matron trying to entertain some roughneck Brooklyn G.I.'s at Sunday dinner, and I had laughed until I was choking for breath. And I remembered comparing her to the bread-and-butter English girl, Lucy

Denham, whom I'd been taking, *faute de mieux,* to tennis parties and Saturday Club dances ever since my break with Violet Hardy early in the summer. What was this clowning, good-looking woman from Macon, Georgia, really like? I knew that she was divorced, that she had "been around," liked a good time, and was very popular in both Jungly Wallah and Clive Street circles. How old was she—how much older than I? Would she go out with me if I asked her? Would she let me sleep with her, as Lucy Denham very clearly would not? And I remembered my feeling of leaping triumph when Dorothy, on our second date, dug her fingers into my back while I kissed her and I knew that the long months of celibacy had come to an end.

I was drawn to Dorothy's physical lavishness, her high color, her high spirits. I wanted to share in the vividness with which she wore her life, a vividness that even at the start made me feel a little pallid by comparison. I thought I might even fall in love with her. I knew I would never marry her. And I was certain that, unlike Violet Hardy, this heedless and experienced woman would never expect or even want me to. This was the margin of safety I needed—and it didn't seem to me in the least self-defeating. Someday, I assured myself, I'd find a girl to marry, but meanwhile . . .

I was, as far as I could learn, about twenty years younger than any of the British suitors Dorothy had had in Calcutta—and there had been a number of them. She was as quickly drawn to me as I to her, and at first her expectations had been as frank—and limited—as mine. "It's fun to rob the cradle for a change," she said. A few weeks later she added, "I've always been a sucker for the well-bred type. You're a kind of challenge to me. I haven't had too much luck with your type. Mostly I scare them off. But I keep trying."

After that, it seemed to me, vividness became more and more confused with willfulness, and a new wistfulness had also appeared. Nothing ever seemed quite simple again—neither Dorothy nor my need for her. But it was still possible to have a good time.

All this had taken place in another world. It had nothing to do with the room in Benares or with the bed that creaked as I turned on my side to go to sleep.

It was after seven when I awoke. I gave myself a sponge bath, pouring water from a pitcher into a battered tin basin. Then I put on my relatively clean seersucker suit and went downstairs. Martin was waiting in the lounge. "Are you feeling better?" he asked. "I looked in on you an hour or so ago and you were lying sprawled across the bed like a corpse. You didn't hear me knock or open the door."

"I do feel better. Well enough to drink a gimlet or two."

"I've already ordered one for you."

"What sort of day have you had?" I asked. It was Martin, I thought, who looked unwell—gaunter, more sallow, more yellowed than ever.

The Englishman shrugged. "I really can't say. I've scribbled a bit. Nothing much. Mainly I've been in sort of a funk. I can't think why, really."

We had dinner in the nearly deserted dining room, which was hung with faded brown photographs of the late-Victorian and Edwardian viceroys and of the King-Emperor George V and Queen Mary at the Delhi Durbar in 1911. Only three other tables were occupied. Afterward we decided to take one final walk through the cantonment.

It was now nearly ten o'clock; the sky was unseasonably overcast and the night so thick and dark that we occasionally stumbled against one another as we walked. Following the road by its feel underfoot, we found our way to the bridge that crossed a small stream called the Barna, nearly dry at this time of year. The road was familiar, leading as it did to the bank and to the Civil Courts; it was also the route which we had taken, earlier in the week, to the disappointing ruins at Sarnath. But now the darkness had inked out every trace of the familiar, and we stared into a blackness that seemed to press against our eyeballs like a hand across the face. The air was dense and oppressive, and there was no sound at all, not even the mad crying of jackals that we had heard in the distance as we left the hotel. With my hands spread on the gritty surface of the parapet, I leaned forward and inhaled the damp smell of mud and rotting vegetation; there was a fecal smell, too, for the Barna, at this season, was more sewer than stream.

Finally Martin spoke in a very low voice—as though we were near an enemy outpost. "Just now I've convinced myself that if I were to drop a pebble over the side, I'd never hear it land. We're leaning over a crack that goes straight to the center of the earth."

"I think I can smell the earth's insides," I answered, playing along with the fantasy.

"My theory is that the earth's crust is thinner in India than anywhere else in the world. And at Benares there's an actual puncture, a sort of crater leading all the way down."

"You enjoy looking over the rim, don't you? So do I."

"I must say I rather hoped you would. That's one of the reasons I urged you to come along." A moment later Martin added, "And I have to confess I was terribly curious to see how you'd take it."

"Take what?"

"Benares. I wanted to rub your American nose into it," he said in a suddenly mocking tone. "You have such a clean, nice, cautious American nose, you know. Such a beautifully controlled American nose. Very straight and neat."

"Is it as bad as all that?" I said, trying to disguise my hurt feelings. Martin had evoked an image of myself that I disliked.

"I never said it was bad. To the contrary, my dear John." He was laughing at me. "Anyway, most Americans find it quite hard to take, I believe. After all, Benares is the world's great drain. All the sores of India flow toward Benares. Tens of thousands of the diseased come here to die. You saw their bodies, lying around in doorways, waiting to be burned. This is the cesspool of the world. The place reeks of sour milk and blood and liquid cow dung. It's unhygienic. It's thick with death. This is the anti-West, and as a progressive, hygienic American, you should be horrified by it."

"I'm sorry I've disappointed you. I haven't found Benares so hard to take. There's even a tiny part of me that welcomes everything you've described."

"That's because you think you can escape it. You think you can lower yourself in, just for a minute, and then climb out again and wipe yourself off and be just as clean and hygienic as before. That's what you think."

"Thanks for reading my mind," I said with a laugh.

When we returned to the hotel, I suggested having a drink in my room. I had brought along a bottle of bourbon whisky, which, except for one nightcap I had poured myself, was intact. Taking off my shoes and socks, I sat on the edge of the bed, and Martin sprawled down into a large cane chair, his thin legs spread at a wide angle. We drank our whisky—mixed with a little bottled water, and quite warm—from two silver cups belonging to a leather-cased set of utensils which Martin had brought with him—a gift, he said, from a girl he used to know in Dacca. After more than a week of moderation—two or three gimlets before dinner—we found ourselves drinking rapidly, especially Martin, who had gulped down two drinks before I finished my first. For a while we talked aimlessly and were often silent for long stretches. But I was determined to break through the glaze of impersonality, and I finally said, "What made you come to India in the first place?"

Martin smiled down into his cup. "Mainly because I was at the time a very stubborn pacifist. Otherwise I should probably have gone off to the war in Spain with some of my Cambridge friends. I took the examination for the Indian Civil Service instead. Looking back on it, it seems an odd thing for a pacifist to have done." He paused. "Did I ever tell you about my first assignment?" he asked. "Pour me some more of this awful American whisky and I shall tell you all about my initiation into the service of Mother India."

And Martin, in a rather dry, occasionally ironic voice, described how he had been sent to an upcountry district of Bengal, near the Bihar border, where he had arrived just at the outbreak of a whole series of terrorist killings. After the arrests, it had been his job to sort out the unbelievably complicated and conflicting evidence and he had really believed that eventually he would see Anglo-Saxon justice done. On the basis of his reports, which he knew to be inconclusive, six men were tried, found guilty, and sent to the penal colony in the Andaman Islands. "Not six months later," he said, "I came across evidence—conclusive evidence—that four of the poor wretches were perfectly innocent. By the time the courts finally got around to ordering their return, two of the four were dead from cholera."

"But that wasn't your fault," I said.

"I never said it was," said Martin.

He went on, after a little while, to tell about his two-year assignment in Noakhali, in the delta country of eastern Bengal, where, in almost total isolation and loneliness, he had spent his evenings learning Sanskrit and systematically studying all of the Indian scriptures he could lay his hands on, not just the Vedic Hymns and the *Upanishads* and the *Bhagavad-Gita* and the commentaries of Sankara but the more esoteric *Tantras* as well. The only break in this routine had been an occasional trip to Dacca, where he knew an Anglo-Indian girl named Kate Walker —the girl who had given him the set of silver cups.

Then, during the war years, Martin had been sick much of the time with malaria and with amoebic dysentery, but it was not until early 1945 that he had taken six months' home leave. From this leave he had returned to his present job with the Labour Department of the Government of Bengal.

"And you were glad to come back—to India, I mean?" During the last quarter-hour, as the whisky began to take hold, I had come to look at the sprawling, yellowed Englishman with a feeling of intense awe: this man, I thought, has lived and acted and suffered on a level that I will never reach.

Martin did not answer at once. He seemed to be contemplating the mystery of his cup. Then he said, "Once when I was very young—a lad of three or four, I should think—my father was transferred from Derby, where we lived, to Nottingham for six months—he was a clerk with the Midland Railway —and my mother and I went with him, my older brothers and sister staying at home with my grandmother. We stayed in some sort of boardinghouse and I was ill nearly the entire time— colds, stomach upsets, bronchitis—so much so that the doctor was afraid I was becoming consumptive. Finally, after about four months, my poor mother decided to take me back to Derby. I was so weak when we arrived that I had to be carried into the house. Most of this was told me afterward, but to this day I can recall how I felt when I was taken into my old room, a dark little hole in the rear of the house, and put into my old bed— really a sort of crib. I touched the familiar wooden sides with the most extraordinary feeling of recognition—John, I can't begin to describe it—recognition and familiarity and relief, and then I began to cry. I remember what it was like to cry from sheer relief. And then I went to sleep and slept for nearly twenty-four hours. When I awoke, I was much better. The only time I have ever felt a comparable sense of relief and home-coming—I almost wept again—was when my ship entered the mouth of the Hooghly and I heard the men who had rowed out in their dinghies shouting to one another in Bengali."

I got up and poured each of us another drink; the bottle was now three-fourths empty. Sitting down again, I said, "Martin, I envy you more than anybody I know. In fact, you're the only person who *really* believes in what he's doing. While I spend my time explaining visa regulations to half-witted Anglo-Indian girls who think they're in love with half-witted G.I.'s, you're giving everything you've got toward creating some kind of order. . . . Now wait," I said, raising my hand as I saw the Englishman squirm, "now wait. I mean what I'm saying. I really do. I know what you're up against, too—the stupidity and apathy and all that. You're giving your life for a country that would like nothing better than to kick you out. They probably will kick you out before long, and you know that. And still you are committed to them. You want them to be able to stand on their own feet. No wonder you were so glad to get back. This is where you are committed."

I finished, breathing very hard. I saw that Martin was grinning.

"Your faith in me is very American, you know." Martin's voice was teasing. "Would you be surprised to learn that I am perfectly convinced of the futility of everything I am supposed to stand for—and indeed *do* stand for?"

"Are you serious?"

"Perfectly serious. Mind you, I have to do as I have done and try to believe in the things I work for. Yet all the time—and more and more—I am obsessed by the way things cancel one another out. Do you know what I mean?"

Martin leaned forward, nursing his cup in both hands. His open shirt showed the corrugation of collarbone and ribs against his yellow skin.

"One sweats to set up new conditions," he said, "to make things possible—things that seem good, that placate the moral hump on one's back. But every altered condition spawns a secret progeny—a sort of bastard progeny—that almost at once declares war on the legitimate offspring. You increase standards of health in this bloody country, you cut down infant mortality, the birth rate shoots up—in no time you have twice as many people to starve. The mothers may not die of childbed fever but the corpses of the grandmothers—so light that you can lift them with one hand—line the roads and clog the paddy fields. You must remember that I saw the famine of 1943— as you did not."

"Yes!" I shouted. "But that was because of the war. The Japanese had cut off the rice from Burma and Indochina. That was a very special situation."

"The war merely provided a foretaste of what will come, what *is* coming at this very moment. India is the one place where all the Western solutions have come along too late to do more than inoculate for one disease while rendering the body susceptible to five others. Don't think industrialization is going

54

to help; don't think that in twenty years you are going to find nice, planned families of four living in nice, suburban housing estates and buying refrigerators and cars."

"Don't worry, I don't think that. My picture of India's future runs more toward collective farms and concrete flats for workers."

"My dear John, don't talk like a fool. Socialism and Communism are just as Western as the little bourgeois scene I've been describing—and they will also come too late." He looked at me furiously for an instant. "Yet I as an Englishman," he went on, "and you as an American—both of us with moral humps on our backs and rational tumors in our skulls—we *have* to be in favor of public health and living wages and self-determination and the rest of it. We are children of the Enlightenment. We can't help ourselves, even when we *know* how absurdly pointless all these things are where India is concerned."

"Do we really know that?" I demanded. "Have you always been so pessimistic?"

"Call it pessimism if it pleases you," said Martin without answering the question. "Believe me, Benares will triumph over the refrigerator. Benares will, India will. India is the ravenous womb of the world. It devours the light. It spreads and absorbs —pulls everything to it," he added, drawing his closed fists up against his chest. "Its conditions are already those of most of Asia. You watch what happens in Japan and China. Technology and nationalism, even communism, are merely the procurers, the instruments, the tentacles—whatever you like—for this insatiable darkness. And this darkness will swallow, suck in, rather, the rest of the world. For its principles operate there, too. London and Paris and New York and Moscow are all built on the foundations of Benares. It is the oldest city in the world and it will outlive the rest."

In his excitement Martin leaped from his chair and strode about the room. His face was transformed; his sunken cheeks and lifted chin were those of a backwoods prophet, a beardless John Brown. He was very drunk. Sweat sparkled on his throat and chest.

"I'll tell you this," he said. "The temple of Durga will replace the skyscrapers. Siva will dance in Piccadilly Circus, just as he has in Berlin. His image will replace the statue of Eros. The blackness underneath those places will crack the pavements. It will suck in the light itself."

"God, but you're drunk!" I shouted. I had advanced closer to Martin's vision than I wanted to be. "And then, after all this —this cataclysm—what's the next stage? That's what I want to know."

"Stasis," he said. "Inertia, equilibrium. I don't know. Probably some sort of universal huddling together in the darkness, head lowered—knees drawn up—sexless—indistinguishable."

"Awaiting a new birth?"

"What difference would that make? The process is endless for all I know."

I got up to fill our drinks. I poured the last drop into Martin's cup. For a moment we stood facing one another. My hand trembled a little as I gripped the empty bottle.

"What does all this mean to you?" I demanded.

"My dear John," the Englishman began thickly. "I—I can hardly say. I only know that I have ceased to resist its encroachments—the darkness's, that is—though I shall still, I suppose, go through some of the motions of a child of light."

He looked out the door, his body twisted, his arms hanging like dead weights from his shoulders. Then he straightened himself and raised his cup chest-high so that the light flashed from its rim.

"I have put it too negatively. I am a hero—what the Hindus call a *vira*. I *embrace* the darkness. Kali or Durga or whatever you want to call the black goddess—Hecate, if you wish— anyway, she's never had a more ecstatic worshiper than I." Martin laughed as he lurched into the room and flung himself into the cane chair. "I seek the darkness with all the fervor of a bridegroom! I drink her health!" He emptied his cup and let it drop, clattering, on the floor.

I picked up the cup and placed it on the dresser. Steadying myself on that piece of furniture (for, in stooping over, I had become very dizzy), I looked down at Martin, whose chin was now resting on his collarbone.

"Go to bed, you crazy fool!" I shouted. "You crazy fool," I repeated, beginning to laugh. "You idiot, you crazy idiot."

Martin shook his head and opened his eyes. His face was very white but he was smiling. "There's no need to abuse me," he said. "None at all."

PART II

CHAPTER V ❧ WE came back to Calcutta on a Saturday, arriving at Howrah Station about noon, and were met by a car and driver from the Bengal Labour Department. The April sun was very hot; not so parching as in New Delhi, where we had spent the last five days, but still strong and glaring as we drove across Howrah Bridge and looked down at the yellow Hooghly swirling beneath. Martin dropped me off at Harrington Street as casually as if I had been a hitchhiker. This did not hurt my feelings at all, for ever since that final wild night in Benares, Martin had retreated into an even greater remoteness than before—a remoteness that was perfectly friendly and satisfactory as far as I was concerned.

The new chokra, Abdul, stared at me when he opened the door; he must have thought I had gone away for good. McClure Sahib was out for lunch, he informed me in Hindustani. I went straight to the bathroom, washed the dust and soot from my face, hands, and throat, and then telephoned Dorothy. I had written to her twice and had made a date with her for this evening, which I wanted to confirm. Her voice, a little hoarse but laughing and very Southern, sounded good to me over the phone. "What did you bring me?" she teased, and when I told her to wait and see, she replied, "If it's not something real nice, I'm going to send you right back to Benares. You've got to bribe your way back into my affections, Johnnie-boy." But just before hanging up, she said, in a slow, quiet tone that set me tingling, "I just cain't tell you how nice it is to have you back in town. I've really missed you, sweetie. I really have."

I slept all afternoon. Stretched across the sheets under the wheeling punkah, I plunged into a deep, down-groping sleep, as though I needed the purifying rites of total oblivion before taking up my Calcutta life. When I awoke, Dorothy's rich voice was humming through my mind. Thank God I had gone away! It had been the best possible thing for us to separate for a while. Now I longed to see her, to touch her; she loomed before me full fleshed and vibrant, miraculously easy, yielding, and warm —a dream woman to replace the nagging ghost that had whined over my bed in Benares. I was now aroused, aching and throbbing to touch her. And I also felt something very odd—that peculiar palm-sweating anxiety that, as an adolescent, I had sometimes experienced before a really "big" date. It was a sensation I had long since outgrown, I thought; to have it reappear at the age of twenty-seven, in connection with a woman as patent to me as Dot—this was something to puzzle me as I bathed and dressed.

Coming into the living room, I found Ralph just returned from an afternoon of tennis at the Saturday Club. Without basically liking one another, Ralph and I got along very well, and we spent nearly an hour talking over a couple of drinks. The only part of my trip that interested him was the five days in New Delhi; he had wanted to hear the latest news from the Commissioner's office. In turn, he told me about the arrival of "new blood" at the Consulate—the three long-awaited American clerks. Two of them, he said, were first-class bags, real beasts; the third—a girl named Julia Cobb—was good-looking but not his type. And then he moved on to Philip Sachs, who had raised a lot of eyebrows last week by bringing Diane Cummings to the Belgian Consul General's reception. "She had on a dress that was cut practically to the navel, and I'm sure she wasn't wearing anything underneath it. Philip was so pleased with himself I thought he was going to explode. I'll bet he told her to dress like that on purpose." Ralph gave me a challenging glance as he spoke; his large-eyed, rabbity face, usually so at odds with his weight-lifter's body and mien, could at times look fierce enough. He detested Philip and resented my friendship with him.

"He probably did," I answered with a smile. I no longer paid any attention to Ralph's feelings about our colleague, feelings which, in all fairness, Philip had gone a long way to provoke.

I drove off in high spirits to pick up Dorothy. I was cool and on fire at the same time, though no longer nervous; the gin-and-tonics had temporarily dried up the sweat on my palms. When we met in her living room, I caught her in my arms and held her with a long, searching kiss—something I had never done before in the presence of her bearer. Dorothy was delighted with the evening bag from Benares and also with a bottle of strong, oil-based perfume which I had bought in the bazaar at Lucknow; she immediately dabbed some behind her ears and then wrinkled her nose at the overpowering smell of jasmine. "This stuff is dynamite," she said, and I grinned with foolish happiness over the success of my presents. We gulped down a couple of daiquiris and set out for the Saturday Club, where I had reserved a table.

Feeling happy and flushed, I ordered a bottle of burgundy to drink with our roast mutton and then cognac with our coffee. Between courses we danced to the six-piece orchestra, which played at a very fast clip. All around us were British couples, mostly middle-aged, all in dinner clothes, all bouncing about heartily in a manner which I associated with World War I and my parents' generation. Dorothy and I moved in a discreet fox trot, our faces several inches apart in deference to the Saturday Club's ban against cheek-to-cheek dancing and other indecorous (i.e., American) practices, such as jitterbugging. Back at our table, we received "visits" occasionally from people we knew, including several of the paunchy Clive Street wallahs and their wives, who found Mrs. Eustace so delightful—and so very American.

Across the room I had spotted my "rival," Major Phipps, sitting with Sir Ronald and Lady McAllister, and I was not surprised when, later in the evening, he sauntered over to our table and, with a little nod in my direction, asked if he might dance with Dorothy. With amusement, I watched her go off with the straight-backed Phippsie, whose scalp shone a bright pink through the carefully combed strands of his silver hair. It was our convention to treat the major as both a joke and as a pretext for baiting one another. A retired soldier of about sixty, now working in Clive Street with the shipping firm of Dougald-Fletcher, he was the most faithful of Dorothy's British admirers, escorting her occasionally to parties at the Bengal Club or to the homes of such Clive Street magnates as the McAllisters, the Dougalds, and the McNabs. I had never thought it worth while to protest, though I sometimes made cracks about "fumbling old men" to annoy Dot, who in turn would accuse me of being secretly glad to have Phippsie and the others around. "They take me off your hands," she would jeer. "They keep me from making too many demands on your precious time." And she would usually add that I didn't have the guts to get really jealous, anyway.

They were back in five minutes. Phippsie gave me another military nod and a watery, blue-eyed twinkle as he went away. "Phippsie is a perfect darling," said Dorothy, sitting down, "but he jogs so when he dances. He's like one of those toys you wind up with a key and then set down on the floor."

"It's a relief to know I don't have to be jealous of Phippsie's dancing."

"It's a lucky thing," she said. "Damn lucky. I like good dancers. You're not bad, you know." She tilted her head appraisingly. "But you're not as good as Harry Eustace. He's a big man but he floated when he danced—I always thought I could lift him with one hand. We won second prize in a tournament in Atlanta. Back in thirty-eight, just after we were married. The prize was a two-year subscription to the *Reader's Digest*."

"Why do you always have to compare me with Harry?"

"Don't worry, sweetie, there's lots of things where I wouldn't think of comparing you."

About eleven, I suggested that we go back to Ballygunge. I was pleasantly high but not at all drunk. I felt alive and supple and I wanted to ride the crest of this mood straight toward the consummation of our evening. But Dorothy had her heart set on going to the Jungly Wallah. "This is a big night," she said. "We've got a lot to celebrate. Let's not quit while the going's good." She said this playfully, but her eyes glistened with the hard brilliance of her will.

I hesitated. I didn't want to go to the Jungly Wallah. All I had to do was refuse. But what, then, would happen to our evening?

"Please, John. We've got the whole night ahead of us." She lowered her eyes, then raised them, full and shining, seductive but still determined, and whispered, "And you won't have to leave at dawn. I told Kassim he could have the whole day off."

I gave in. "Fine. We'll look in on the Jungly Wallah but we won't stay long. Okay?"

"Won-derful!"

I felt very depressed.

When we reached the Jungly Wallah I tipped the head bearer to give us a table next to the dance floor and ordered champagne —a South African vintage at twenty rupees a bottle. I still felt depressed, but I was now determined to enjoy myself. My hands were beginning to sweat again.

"I've really missed you, Dot," I said, trying to convince myself that this was true.

"I ought to send you out of town more often," said Dorothy. "They must have fixed you up with monkey glands or something at that Monkey Temple."

I laughed and reached for her hand, knocking over my glass as I did so. Still laughing, I sopped up the liquid with my handkerchief and squeezed it into an ash tray. The room was swaying softly with the dancers; its cherry-red walls, painted to look like brocade, burned darkly beyond the pink-clothed tables, each fitted with a tiny, rose-shaded lamp; on the walls the gilt lighting fixtures were points of flame. Across from me Dorothy, too, seemed to burn: her skin was ruddy as cinnamon against the yellow silk of her dress; fake honey-colored topazes glowed at her ears and throat, and scarlet hibiscus blossoms had been carefully fixed in her hair.

"I missed you so much in Benares I could hardly stand it," I repeated with thickening emphasis, and I believed what I said.

"Keep on talking. I love to hear you talk," she said, rhyming "talk" with "squawk" and drawing out the sound.

"You think I'm kidding." I filled my glass to the top and smiled into the bubbles. You don't have to gulp it down, I said to myself as I felt the tickle of a dozen small explosions against my lips and nose. But I finished off the glass in three or four swallows.

A little later I said, "Right now, I'd rather dance than talk. I want to hold you." I stood up, reaching out both hands to Dorothy, and nearly fell across the table. "Hold on now," I said aloud, catching myself and laughing. "Take it easy, boy." I'm drinking too much, I thought, and vaguely wondered why.

The dance floor was crowded, so much so that we kept colliding with other couples. The dancers were a very different lot from the Saturday Club's staidly bobbing Scots and Yorkshiremen and their hefty wives, who, in retrospect, seemed all to have been wearing dresses of flowered cotton. Here the British element was in the minority. Brocaded Indian women, their eyes ringed with kohl, glided by on the arms of fat Armenian businessmen. Equally stout Indian men jogged up and down with the wives of the American Colony. American officers jitterbugged with Army nurses or WACS. Suzy Mitchell, her monkey face grimacing with delight, called out, "Hi, kids!" to us as she swept past in the embrace of the Nawab of Chittagong. It was fun to dance with Dorothy, who was light beneath my fingers, quick to follow the most minute shifting in my rhythmic mood. I was tight, but not so tight as to be clumsy. Still, before long, I wanted something to drink.

Instead of returning to our seats, I led Dorothy into the bar, where we were met by an uproar of greetings. Philip Sachs, looking very grand and lordly, was sitting at a table with Diane Cummings, an Indian couple named Doris and Kiwi Das Gupta, and the Maharaja of Berhampore. They all screamed and beckoned to us, and the Maharaja instantly grabbed two chairs—whose owners were dancing—from the adjoining table.

"How are you?" asked Philip. "I must say, Benares doesn't seem to have brought about any marked alteration in your appearance." Then he added, "I'm glad you've come along. Suds, here, has just been cooking up some plans for next weekend and they include you." Philip, speaking in the pseudo-British accent he sometimes affected, now turned with a kind of lordly ease toward the Maharaja, whose nickname, Suds, he had just used.

"Oh, yes," said the Maharaja, who was fat, owl-faced and very rich—the second largest landowner in Bengal. "Yes, we are cooking up jolly plans." And he explained that he was getting up a luncheon party for an American friend of his who would be staying at Berhampore next weekend. "I want you and our friend Sachs here to come—and you two young ladies, of course," he added with a gallant sweep of his pudgy hand toward Dorothy and Diane Cummings. "And would you be so kind as to ask Vice-Consul McClure for me? I'd rather hoped to see him here tonight but presumably he is enjoying himself elsewhere." The Maharaja laughed loudly at this, his eyes forming slits on each side of his sharply beaked nose; it was an open secret that he was the principal backer of the Jungly Wallah Club. He was also a notorious Americophile—even to the point of wearing a white Palm Beach dinner jacket (the British always wore black jackets and white trousers during the warm weather). Consequently, when he turned to the Das Guptas, who had been looking sulky and left out, it was natural enough that he should apologize along the following lines: "This is a purely American shindig I'm planning. You'd be bored to death by all the talk about the States. I would not submit you to it for the world." But the Das Guptas did not brighten up noticeably at this explanation, and unfortunately, after a few minutes the Maharaja so forgot himself as to mention to me casually that Ronny Powell would be driving up in a Government House car and could give us all a lift.

"Good show!" said Diane Cummings, who had long since drowned out her Anglo-Indian singsong with what she took to be the flutelike tones of Mayfair. "I must say, all this sounds great fun, doesn't it?" With her lovely, tapering, red-nailed fingers, she plucked a thread from the sleeve of Philip's black dinner jacket. He smiled down at her. The Maharaja was watching them closely.

"Your Highness, I think you're just as nice as you can be to include me," said Dorothy, countering with Southern sweet talk. Since Berhampore was merely a district of Bengal and not an independent princely state, the Maharaja did not legally enjoy the title of "Highness," but he was not at all displeased when someone chose to use it.

I looked at Dorothy with a flicker of annoyance: here was another middle-aged man for her to suck up to. But almost instantly my mood changed again. I was enthusiastic about the trip to Berhampore, and, after the Maharaja had bought us all a second round of Scotch, I heard myself, as though from a great distance, calling him Suds.

We walked back to our table through a blur of rosy light. I was fairly unsteady and I decided to have no more to drink. I did not want to lie in Dorothy's arms like a bag of wet sand. I figured I must have had at least two drinks for every one of hers—thus reversing the usual course. But at the table I was enraged to find the champagne bottle empty. "God damn it, there was at least half a bottle left," I shouted, and furiously I ordered the waiter to bring us another.

"Take it easy, sweetie," said Dorothy. "You're fairly looping already."

"This bottle's for you. I'm not going to have any."

"I can't drink a whole bottle all by myself!"

"Don't worry, we'll have company."

And we had plenty. The first to come were Jock and Suzy Mitchell, who had lived in Calcutta for twenty years; this made them the charter members of the American Colony. Jock, a dark, hulking, blue-cheeked man with the build of an aging boxer, had drunk and quarreled his way through a succession of jobs and was now merely an assistant engineer at one of the jute mills up the Hooghly, depending heavily on his poker winnings to supplement his income. I had once seen him smash a Norwegian sea captain's face into a bloody smear after flooring three of the men who tried to break up the fight. Tonight I loved him, and I loved his wife, Suzy, who had the face of an exhausted baby, a face that once must have been "cute" in the style of the twenties; she still painted her mouth in an exaggerated Cupid's bow that reminded me of photographs in an old movie magazine. My God, I thought, my eyes moist with drink and sentiment, what this woman's lived through! The next to arrive was the Nawab of Chittagong, with his begum, a hard-looking Englishwoman named Audrey; the Nawab, a wizened little man, took no notice of his ex-mistress, who was dancing with Philip not twenty feet away. I poured the Chittagongs a glass of champagne, then one for myself, and then loudly ordered another bottle. Willard Doney, of the Pittsburgh Machine Tools Company, and his wife, Connie, joined us, followed by Kiwi and Doris Das Gupta, who said that the Maharaja's table had broken up. "This is much more fun," said Kiwi, opening his cigarette case. "The other group was a little stuffy."

"It's surprising how stuffy Suds can be sometimes," said Doris Das Gupta, who was not Kiwi's wife but his sister. They were the grandchildren of the late Sir Sudhindrinath Das Gupta, who had been the most famous lawyer in India in his day; now in their late thirties and rapidly losing their looks, neither Kiwi nor Doris had married, much to the disgust of their fierce old mother, who had fought unsuccessfully against every inch of their "Westernization."

"You know, I don't think I've seen you since Ronny's party," said Kiwi, turning to me. His soft eyes were bloodshot and his mouth hung loose beneath his drooping mustache.

"Been out of town," I said indistinctly. Kiwi's remark was probably a rebuke—I had once seen a lot of the Das Guptas—but I was too fuddled to think of a good reply.

"Wasn't it the bloodiest party?" he continued. "Government House drinks have always been bloody—weak as water and hours apart. But I'm afraid it's too much to expect our distinguished new Governor to do much to improve them. I doubt if His Excellency's taste goes much beyond a half-pint of mild at his local." And Kiwi, who had spent a year at Balliol and knew all about the English class system, now took up what was currently the favorite topic of Calcutta malice—the fact that the new Governor of Bengal, a Labour appointee, had once been a railway porter before becoming an official in his union.

"I call 'em the Coolie and the Dhobi," he said, using the Hindustani words for porter and launderer—the latter an allusion to the widely circulated report that the Governor's wife was unused to servants and had always done her own wash. "I wondered just *who* they thought they were impressing with that kind of publicity?"

Kiwi's words floated toward me like motes through the hot fog of cigarette smoke. What a disgusting snob! All around me the red walls of the room were quivering. Suddenly depressed again, sweaty palmed, I put down my glass and got to my feet unsteadily. Saying nothing, I allowed everyone to think I was going to the men's room. Fresh air, I thought, lurching across the dance floor—*fresh air*. I lurched on down the hall, past the durwan, and into the mild Bengali night. The air seemed thin, unable to purge my lungs or to synchronize my legs. At last I found my car in the parking lot and climbed into the front seat, leaving the door open.

Slumping back, my nape resting on the top of the seat, I was dying, my chest riddled in a dozen spots, the taste of blood on my tongue. Why had I drunk so much? For the last two hours I had watched a monstrous baby rise from the depths and gulp down everything in sight, a horrible, insatiable baby, all belly and mouth, a usurping baby beyond my control. Then I heard a voice and the crunch of feet across the gravel. A man laughed. "That's Philip and Diane," I whispered aloud to myself. Suppose I called out to them? A car door slammed, headlights flared into the dark, a motor started up and settled into a rich hum. I can't call them now, I thought, as the Bentley pulled away. They're happy, they'll make love—and I saw Diane plucking the thread from Philip's sleeve. A few minutes later I told myself that I had to go back to Dorothy. But I did not move. The Jungly Wallah was a huge crimson flower, poisonous and hot, and Dorothy a red insect at its burning core. . . .

A hand touched my shoulder. "Are you all right?" asked Dorothy. "I was afraid you'd fallen in the john or something."

"Much better," I mumbled, thinking, She's just a woman— I'll kiss her—everything will be all right. Swinging my legs out of the car, I stood up and caught her by the shoulders to steady myself. "Want to kiss you," I said, pulling her close. The jasmine perfume struck my nostrils like chloroform and made my head spin. As we kissed, I suddenly felt miserably sick. Dorothy's mouth was intolerable, cloying, reeking of cigarettes. "I can't breathe," I said, tearing away, already gagging. I stumbled to the front of the car, leaned against the fender, and began to vomit helplessly.

Dorothy had to pay the club bill, stripping my wallet and borrowing the rest from Jock Mitchell, and then drive the car back to Harrington Street; there she had to get Ralph out of bed to help me upstairs. My mind was now perfectly clear but my legs kept buckling like a marionette's. Over and over again I murmured apologies, groping for Dorothy's cold hand. She wouldn't speak to me. They left me sitting on the edge of my bed, and Ralph offered to drive her home.

CHAPTER VI ☦ I was too sick all the next day to think very clearly about what had happened. Broken images came to me: clogged, stinging nostrils; the hopeless misery of retching; Dorothy's hand fumbling in my pocket for the car keys; the controlled savagery of her face as she and Ralph helped me into the lift. And I had wanted her so much! What had gone wrong? I should have insisted on taking her back to Ballygunge after the Saturday Club, I thought. Again I saw the glittering of her determination—and even now I shrank from it. I had allowed myself to be scratched by the diamond-sharpness of her will. But why should that tiny scratch have turned me into a monstrous, gulping baby? Our wills had clashed before; I had given in many times before. There was no answer. In the depths of my hangover it seemed to me that the conscious, willing part of myself was no more than a bit of foam riding on the crest of a stream.

I was guilty, I had to apologize; yet I shrank from telephoning Dorothy. The sharp crystal, the red insect . . . It was not until the next day that I forced myself to call, and then she was out. Thank God! But on the following morning my mood had shifted again, and I was relieved when she telephoned me at the Consulate. Laughing away my apologies, Dorothy said she'd never seen any human being look so much like a sick hound dog; it had made her realize I was human after all. I asked her to meet me that night, but she was going out. Since I was tied up for the next two evenings, we made a date for Friday. Then I reminded her of the trip to Berhampore on Saturday; she had not forgotten. I hung up, again full of wonder at Dorothy's resiliency. The *status quo* was still intact—no matter how precariously—and I did not want it otherwise.

Later in the day something else gave me satisfaction—a satisfaction that quickly went a bit lame: Miss Nellie Lawrence, whose hopeful, muddled face had peered across the desk into mine dozens of times during the last year, at last produced a document that would enable her to go to Tulsa to marry ex-Sergeant Leroy Latchford. This was an affidavit, sworn before a magistrate at Asansol, stating that Francis O'Connor, a retired stationmaster of the Bengal Nagpur Railway, had personally known Mrs. Florence McCarthy Da Susa of Ranchi, grandmother of Nellie Lawrence, and knew her to be of pure British descent, both her parents having come from Liverpool. There was no way of checking the truth of the affidavit—I had my doubts of it—but it was good enough, when added to the other documents, to get Miss Lawrence past the Immigration Service, despite her very brown face. The girl broke into a long wail when I told her that I could now cable the State Department for her quota number. Sobbing through a dainty pink handkerchief, she blubbered out her thanks, all the while apologizing for her tears. In all this profusion of gratitude there was no slightest sign of resentment toward the naked racism of United States policy, no hint that the humiliating research I had forced upon her was anything other than right and natural. I congratulated Miss Lawrence, telling her I hoped she wouldn't have to wait too long for passage. I was relieved and pleased, but all the time my thoughts kept plunging ahead. Would she thank me six months from now, when the sharp outlines of America had penetrated the haze spread before her vision by Hollywood and a soldier's talk, when the neighbors in Tulsa had stared long and hard at Sergeant Latchford's dark-skinned "English" bride? By approving the dossier I had made the girl weep with happiness; I had set up new conditions, made things possible, and for the moment, I had, in Martin Fenwick's phrase, placated the moral hump on my back. What responsibility did I bear for the "bastard progeny" (again to use Martin's term) which these new conditions were almost certain to spawn?

I did not have long to brood over this question. As soon as Nellie Lawrence left my office, Philip Sachs dropped in to waste a little time and to invite me to have dinner with him after the Hubbards' cocktail party on Thursday.

The Consul General and his wife gave three or four parties a year "just for the family"—i.e., the officers and American clerks of the Consulate. The party this evening was identical with the one held just after Christmas, except that we were now all wearing summer evening clothes and tended to spend more time on the veranda of the big house on Camac Street. Leaning against the veranda balustrade with Ralph and Morris Halpern, I casually watched Philip through the French doors leading into the brightly lit drawing room. We could see him stalking about among the other guests, giving orders to the bearers, and then returning, every few minutes, to his post beside Mrs. Hubbard. Philip always assumed the unofficial role of aide-de-camp to Mrs. Hubbard, a fact that intensely annoyed Ralph.

"It's too bad Philip's so rich," he said. "Otherwise he'd make a fine gigolo."

Knowing that Ralph was trying to provoke me into a defense of my friend, I refused to comment and after a while he left us.

Then Morris, who was assigned to the Consulate as an economic analyst, said, "You know Philip pretty well, don't you?" His voice was both nasal and glottal, the voice of his native Brooklyn.

"I suppose so."

"You understand him?"

"About as much—or as little—as I understand anybody else I know fairly well. Why?" I peered into the heavily pouched eyes and caught the half-smile that was hovering over the wide and drooping mouth of this Brooklyn Jew, who was probably the most intelligent man in the Consulate. Morris had the look of a melancholy frog.

"You know where he gets all this Anglo-Catholic stuff?"

"I think he was brought up an Episcopalian. I've heard him talk about going to church with his mother when he was little."

"Oh? I thought he might have picked it up at Harvard, along with his blazer and pipe and the rest of that crap."

Ralph rejoined us with a drink. "The new blood's here," he said, referring to the three American secretaries who had arrived in Calcutta only ten days before. "The Schneiders brought 'em. I guess Liz is adopting them, as usual."

"I'm not sure which is which," I said. I had been introduced to the girls on Monday and had not seen them since.

Philip came onto the veranda. "Well," he said cheerfully to

Ralph, "and how's the Junior Chamber of Commerce this evening?" He loved baiting Ralph, especially about the latter's passionate alliance with the interests of the American colony. To Morris he said, "Where's your wife?"

"Esther's got a touch of Delhi-belly. She wanted to come but I wouldn't let her." Morris answered slowly, as if examining Philip's simple question for hidden meanings. It was a rare thing for Philip even to notice the existence of the Halperns.

"I'm sorry to hear that. I haven't had a chance to talk with her in ages. Give her my best." His large face open and glowing with pleasure, Philip smiled warmly at the astounded Morris. No one knew better how to please than Philip; I had seen more of this side of him than anyone else in the Consulate except, of course, Mrs. Hubbard.

Just then I saw one of the new girls standing hesitantly in the doorway. "Come on out and join us," I called.

She turned out to be Julia Cobb, the only one of the three who was not, in Ralph's terms, a beast. Julia was, in fact, a fresh-faced, brown-haired girl, almost pretty, with a smile that indicated her willingness to like everything—and to be liked, too. "Well," I said, "what do you think of the family?"

"Everyone's been just wonderful to us. I feel right at home."

"What an insipid remark," said Philip. "Can't you make a more original observation about your first ten days in what has been mildly described as the armpit of the East? I can hardly believe," he continued, "that your home—humble though it may be—bears much resemblance to Calcutta."

The girl laughed uneasily. "I only meant—" she began.

"Don't mind Philip," said Ralph. "You'll eventually get used to his way of being friendly." Then, turning to Morris, he suggested that they get another drink, and the two of them went into the house.

"What have you seen of Calcutta?" I asked. "Have you been going out much?"

"What he's trying to find out," interrupted Philip, "is how many dates you've had since you arrived."

Julia Cobb laughed again, but in a relaxed way. "Only one.

You must give me time." Then she added, "We went to a place called the Jungly Wallah Club."

"Oh? When was that?"

"Saturday night."

"Did you see me?" I counted on the half-darkness of the veranda to cover the blood which I felt rushing into my face. She paused for a few seconds, and the light reflected in her eyes seemed to dance. "No, how could I? We hadn't been introduced then. But," she went on, glancing boldly at Philip, "I did see you. You stared right into my face without speaking."

"That's just my way of being friendly." Philip saw that he was being challenged, and for a second he looked as though he were about to raise his arm, cautiously, to swat a fly. "But tell me," he said, his fine teeth gleaming, "why have you come all the way out to Calcutta? Are things so bad in the States that you decided to join the Fishing Fleet?"

"The Fishing Fleet?"

"Yes. For generations the unmarried older sisters and spinster cousins of Englishmen in India were in the habit of coming out to spend the cool weather with their relatives. There was usually plenty of wifely or maternal pressure involved, I expect. At any rate, once the Fishing Fleet had arrived, the poor men had to put on their best behavior and put away their Anglo-Indian mistresses and introduce the hopeful ladies to all their bachelor friends. Since there's always been a shortage of eligible women—especially in upcountry posts but even in Calcutta— some members of the Fleet made really spectacular catches in a very short time. On the other hand, a withered few were known to make the long voyage out from England six or seven times before hooking anything. But I believe they always landed something in the end."

"I'm not sure I qualify for the Fishing Fleet. I haven't any brothers or cousins to look out for me, and besides, I've come at the end of the cool weather, not the beginning."

I liked the way the girl was handling herself under Philip's onslaught. With her head thrown back, her large eyes catching the light of the drawing room, she clearly did not need my help.

"Times have changed," said Philip. "How old are you? Thirty? Twenty-nine, perhaps?"

"I'm twenty-four. Does that disappoint you?"

"I'm sorry. Perhaps the light isn't as flattering as it might be. Still, I must say you look very nice. Your dress is unexciting but in perfectly good taste. You have that nice, virginal, upper-middle-class look. You are clearly the kind of nice Vassar girl who likes to romp on big green lawns with big woolly dogs."

"You certainly don't make 'nice' sound very nice."

Philip laughed, again flashing his teeth. Then, glancing over his shoulder toward the bright room, he said, "Mother Hubbard seems to be signaling in my direction. I'd better see what the old girl wants. Will you be ready to leave in about twenty minutes, John? I told Ala-uddin to expect us at quarter to nine."

Julia and I followed him into the house. As we parted, I invited her to have lunch with me and Ralph at the flat some day next week. Then, in the time remaining to me, I circulated among the other members of the Consular "family," talked briefly with Herbert Schneider, the executive Consul, and his wife, Elizabeth, both of whom I liked; avoided Andrew Wanamaker, the sour, whisky-soaked "commercial" Consul; chatted with Tom Berger, the agricultural attaché, and his wife, Sue; with Mary Buxton, who was a vice-consul; and with Mary Haakinson, who was my secretary in the visa office. Then I sought out Mrs. Hubbard, who, having dispatched Philip on some special mission, was standing, for a moment, with her husband. She was glad to see me, eager for the chance to talk about Philip and Diane Cummings. "I suppose you've heard," she said, fixing me with her handsome blue eyes, "that he brought her to Monsieur Grimm-Martin's reception. She was outrageously dressed. I must say she doesn't *look* particularly Anglo-Indian, but the touch of the tarbrush is only too clear the minute she opens her mouth. It doesn't bother *me* particularly," she went on, fidgeting with a strand from her graying pompadour, "but you know how the British feel about these things.

It simply doesn't do for an American vice-consul to be seen at official parties with such a person. I've asked Alfred to speak to Philip about it, but he absolutely refuses."

"Golly, Martha," protested Mr. Hubbard, who looked strikingly like General Eisenhower, "what in the world would I say to him? Besides, as long as he doesn't disgrace himself, I think it's the youngster's own business who he sees."

"Well, I shall have to speak to him myself, and I *hate* doing that. What's she like, John? I suppose you'll try to defend her."

"I don't really know her," I said evasively, still amused at the notion of the thirty-year-old Philip as a "youngster." I was rescued from further pumping by Philip's return to his post. From the affectionate glance Mrs. Hubbard turned upon him, I guessed that she was not so displeased as she made out; probably she found the affair a little shocking but suitably "spirited" and "dashing" for such a protégé as Philip.

After dinner Philip and I went into the living room to have coffee and a glass of the 1850 Madeira which he had procured from the Bengal Club. I settled into a red-brocaded armchair and, sipping the warm brown wine, gazed contentedly at what I regarded as one of the two pleasantest rooms in Calcutta—the other being the Chaudurys' tiny whitewashed parlor in Kalighat.

"I've never seen you in better spirits," I said. "You even seemed to enjoy your dinner," I went on, referring to Philip's habit of supplying his guests with sumptuous food which, usually, he merely picked at. "Is all this the effect of love?"

"You can call it that if you like." Philip smiled luxuriously. Sitting across the coffee table from me, he had removed his tie and opened the upper part of his dress shirt, laying bare the small gold-and-enameled cross which hung against the curling black hair of his chest. A bluish plume of smoke drifted upward from the flattened Egyptian cigarette between his fingers. "I'm very happy just now—happier than I've been in a long time."

"I'd like to know Diane better. She's very beautiful, but I don't really know what she's like."

"She's intelligent, and open, and extraordinarily subtle in her ways of pleasing me. Later on, I'll see to it that you get to know her, but just at this stage I rather enjoy keeping her in a sort of Oriental seclusion—as far as my good friends are concerned." Again he smiled, even more complacently than before. It was as though he had Diane concealed, at this very moment, in one of the upper rooms of the house. Then he said, "She's coming with us to Berhampore, you know."

A little later, Philip put a stack of records—the Bach *Magnificat*—on the phonograph. "Do you want some whisky?" he asked before turning on the machine.

"No, I think I'll have another glass of Madeira."

The music poured into the room. After a while I glanced toward Philip, who had closed his eyes. Seeing him now, peaceful and slack, I found it hard to imagine how formidable he could be. I remembered the ferocious delight with which he had insulted Ralph the first time they met, not an hour after Philip's arrival at the Consulate. Why had he set out to make so many people dislike him, especially Americans? I was almost the only younger American whom he tolerated—and who was able to tolerate him. With the older ones—the Hubbards and the Schneiders—he took the trouble to please, succeeding with them as he invariably did with Europeans and Indians. The Indians tended to find him more intelligent and cultivated, if not more rich, than any American had the right to be.

Perhaps half an hour later, as though speaking from the context of a dream, I said, "You know, I can understand your dislike for Ralph. You've behaved badly to him, but there was never any chance of your getting along—you're built too differently. But it puzzles me you've never given the Halperns a chance. In some ways Morris has more in common with you than anyone else in the office—certainly more than I have. Yet tonight was the first time I've seen you be even halfway polite to him." Philip was now eying me carefully and his full lips had begun the curving of a smile. I waited an instant for him to speak and then blurted out, "Is it just his Jewishness that puts you off?"

"I have no objection to his being a Jew—but he's a kike as

well, and I do object to that. I have no doubt Morris is as bright and all as you say but he's still a typical New York kike. You can tell the minute you look at him."

"He's not loud, he's not vulgar, he's not pushy, he'd never short-change you—he fits none of the stereotypes. And you know it."

Philip jeered at my indignation. "But *look* at him," he said, spreading his hands. "I'll admit Esther's a different case—but then she's a refugee. Besides, she's rather good-looking. I suppose—if you want the truth—my objection to Morris is more aesthetic than anything else." His cool smile proclaimed that I would be wasting my time to argue against the mere *irrationality* of such an attitude—I could like his perversity or lump it. Then he said, "Why did you bring this up? After all, you've lived with my feeling about Morris for a good while."

I hesitated. "I guess it's because you were fairly nice to him at the Hubbards'. Also"—I faltered again—"he was asking about you earlier."

"What did he want to know?"

"He wanted to know when you became an Anglo-Catholic."

"Aha!" Philip wheeled about. "And what did you tell him?" he demanded.

"That I thought you'd been brought up an Episcopalian. But then it occurred to me I wasn't really sure."

"Do you often discuss me behind my back?"

"No more than anyone else," I said, surprised by the violence of Philip's reaction.

"He's at his old game again." Philip was calmer now and had begun to smile. "I thought he'd given up. John, can't you see he was trying to get you to admit that someone named Sachs has no business calling himself an Anglo-Catholic?"

"That hadn't occurred to me."

"You're very naïve. You should have seen the look Morris gave me when Mr. Hubbard first introduced us. At last, he thought, here's another Jew. It was stamped all over his face. I could feel it in his handshake. And for the first few days he kept hinting—kept trying to get me to make some demonstration of brotherhood or something." Philip laughed, very pleased with himself. "I simply stopped speaking to him. It was as simple as that. The sheer arrogance of his assumption annoyed me, and I saw no point in explaining that Sachs happens to be a perfectly good German name and that my mother's maiden name was Schuyler."

"So that's why you really dislike him so?"

"Not at all. I've already given you my chief reason."

"The aesthetic reason?"

"Precisely," he snapped. Then, in an odd voice, he said, "Do I look at all Jewish to you?"

I laughed. "You have dark, curly hair—that's suspicious—but your eyes are yellowish—that's merely curious. Your nose is straight. The shape of your chin and the curve of your lips— suspiciously Mediterranean but they might be Italian or Greek."

Philip was amused. "Then I gather," he said dryly, "that you don't automatically think of Cruikshank's drawing of Fagin the minute you lay eyes on me."

We dropped the subject. Philip poured us each a third glass of Madeira and then put on *The Abduction from the Seraglio*. After a few minutes my mood softened again. No matter how exasperating—or even vicious—he might be, I found it impossible to stay angry with Philip for any length of time. He had an extraordinary knack for turning my outrage into something that struck me as merely priggish, leaving me with the feeling that I had just delivered a stern moral lecture to a grinning ape.

I did not concentrate on the music very long. Settling even further into my chair, I allowed the wine and the rich room and the sweetness of Mozart to ease me into a pleasant blur of consciousness that was just this side of sleep. Philip's living room was anything but a whitewashed cell. Having started with a good foundation of Georgian furniture and Persian rugs belonging to the elderly Scottish couple from whom he rented on a two-year lease, Philip had stocked the house with his own collection from America and with the new purchases he had made—and continued to make—in India. The John Marin water color of Deer Island, and the two Picasso ink drawings, the record albums, the Capehart phonograph, and most of the books had been shipped out from New York at the expense of the Department of State. To these had been added a Thomas Daniell lithograph of the Kutub Minar, three Kangra miniatures of the Krishna romance, and a South Sung scroll painting of a Zen monk conversing with a spidery-looking ape; the latter had been bought, together with three pieces of carved jade, from a Chinese merchant who had escaped from Penang with his collection at the time of the Japanese invasion in 1941. The latest purchase was by far the most extravagant: a Mogul chess set of elephants, horsemen, towers, and foot soldiers, all made of ivory and enameled gold, and displayed in a glass-fronted cabinet where the Scottish couple had once shown off their own kinds of bric-a-brac. By shifting my head slightly to one side, I could catch the burst of golden sparks that the chessmen threw into the subdued lamplight of the room.

More and more over the last year I had come to regard this house and this room as a kind of fortification, an outpost standing rocklike in the jungle. The late-eighteenth-century house, cream-colored and balustraded, was set back in its own compound, shut off from the rest of Alipore by high, cream-colored walls topped with broken glass and iron spikes. Philip's essentially Western, essentially eighteen-century taste was bold enough to make frequent raids into the alien countryside. The Indian and Chinese objects all around me were like hostages—greatly prized but well guarded by albums of Mozart and the stacks of novels and memoirs sent out each month by a New York bookshop. Furthermore, the Oriental trophies had all been plucked out of the past; there was nothing to suggest the desolate junkyard that Calcutta had become. I liked the security of Philip's fort, I enjoyed its well-ordered luxury, and from time to time my need to take refuge there was as sharp as a tired soldier's longing for sleep. I even enjoyed the lectures in connoisseurship that Philip occasionally delivered to me.

When the music was over, Philip said, "I'm glad for your

company tonight, John. This is always a difficult anniversary for me."

"Anniversary of what?"

"Of my mother's death." Turning his heavy face toward me, fixing me with his yellowish eyes, he said, "I'd like to tell you about it. Do you mind?"

It was late and I wanted to leave, but I nodded. "How old were you when it happened?" I asked, hoping to sound sympathetic.

"I was fifteen. We had been traveling together in Germany during the summer and she'd left me with a tutor in Baden-Baden—I was supposed to brush up on my French while she went to Venice for a month. What I didn't know at the time was that she'd gone there to meet a lover." Philip smiled at me. "I seem to be telling you all sorts of things tonight. Not many people have heard these things. I hope you realize you're in a rather special category."

"I'm glad of that." I didn't know what else to say.

Philip looked down, still smiling, at the elaborately arabesqued rug at his feet. His shoulders were stooped and his head lowered—the head of an exhausted boxer, a Roman boxer. "You may as well know," he said quietly, "that my mother killed herself in Venice. Slashed her wrists. I knew nothing about it until two weeks later when my father—who I thought was in New York—suddenly appeared in Baden to take me home with him. Mother was always terrible about writing, so I hadn't been worried."

"Good God, Philip!"

At last the heavy face was raised again. "There were many things I didn't learn right away. One of them was that I'd inherited a very considerable sum of money. Then, that Christmas, when I came down to New York from Andover, my father gave me a small, brown-paper parcel one evening, just before I was going to bed. He said, 'Look these over and if there are any questions, I'll try to answer them tomorrow.' I sat up until three in the morning reading and rereading what he had given me. They were letters—written in the most peculiar English you ever saw—and they were from my mother's lover. The fact that she didn't destroy them before she killed herself was absolutely typical: Mother was the most impulsive and heedless woman who ever lived." Although Philip was smiling again, his voice had become more and more hushed, as though he were talking under the influence of a hypnotic drug.

I shifted uncomfortably in my chair. From a dreamlike distance I could see the schoolboy in the New York bedroom, his head bent forward, shuffling and reshuffling the scrawled letters, his eyes wondering and tearful in the yellow light of a bedside lamp. The picture was remote but strongly lighted and very clear—yet it left me curiously unmoved. "What in the world did your father think he was doing?" I asked, as much to relieve my distress as to satisfy my curiosity.

The smile broadened. "My father is a very strange man. When I didn't speak to him the next day, he was terribly hurt. I can still remember the way he said, 'I thought you were old enough to accept the truth. I did it for your own good. I wanted you to see your mother as a real person—it's healthier to mourn for a real person than a goddess.' And all the time he was blubbering on like this, he had such a grip on my arm I couldn't break away."

"That's not a pretty story."

Philip merely shrugged. "Someday you must meet my father." Then, after pausing to light a cigarette, he said, "The lover was a German named Willi von Horst. He later became one of Goebbels' chief assistants; I used to find his name in articles on Germany just before the war. The letters were revolting, full of phrases like 'Your Willi kisses your little hand.'" Philip laughed. "Poor Mother. She had such atrocious taste where men were concerned. Though, I must say, Willi was a good-looking devil—there was a snapshot of him along with the letters."

When I finally got up to leave, Philip protested. "Don't go yet. I want to talk to you about my piece on the I.N.A.," he said, referring to a report that he was writing on the Indian National Army. For Philip, in addition to his work in the Shipping Office of the Consulate, had turned out several voluntary reports that had been well received by the Department. I weakly envied him this ability and sometimes made promises to myself about what *I* would do—when I found the time and energy.

"It'll have to wait. I'm much too tired and groggy. But I've had a fine evening," I added.

He looked at me narrowly. "You haven't got a late date, have you?"

"Good Lord, no! I'm heading straight for bed."

"I'm glad of that. I shouldn't like to think you rushed away from my house to go straight to Dorothy."

"What the hell—" I began. Then I got control of myself and said, "I know you don't like her. I'm sorry about that but it can't be helped. Anyway, it's got nothing to do with this evening."

"She doesn't do you justice, that's all."

"To hell with that, Philip." At the front door I held out my hand. His face was sulky. "Good night," I said firmly, "and thanks very much. I'm glad you told me about your mother." This mollified him, and we shook hands cordially enough.

As I pulled out of the driveway, I glanced back toward the house, which stood solid and graceful in its wide lawn—an elegant bulwark against the hot blackness of the Alipore night. Through the red-curtained windows I could see Philip moving across the living room; then he began to turn out the lamps.

Driving along Asoka Road, breathing in the warm, leafy smell of the suburb, I again felt the discomfort that had come over me as Philip told his story. And this distress puzzled me, for it clearly had nothing to do with Philip's suffering or pity for his mother. Then I realized, with a heavy thud of conviction, that the story itself was a lie. I couldn't account for this certainty; yet even as I was listening, some part of me must have sensed that Philip was playing a game, that he was working on my sympathies through some obscure need of his own. I had known for a long time that Mrs. Sachs was dead, and I could see no reason to be sure that she hadn't killed herself or that she hadn't had a Nazi lover named Willi von Horst; there was, in fact, no single detail that I *had* to reject. But the total remained heavy and inert—I simply could not lift it over the threshold of my belief. I felt no indignation toward Philip, no sense of betrayal. With a detachment that in no way lessened my friendship for him, I realized that while becoming more interesting, Philip had at the same time surrendered a part of his strength. He was less formidable. With my new insight, I had gained an advantage which I didn't really want. Furthermore—and the thought saddened me—it meant that in the future I would be less able to relax in his company, that I would have to strain to keep my awareness in sharp focus.

CHAPTER VII ✾ ALTHOUGH Dorothy had said that I reminded her of a sick hound, she didn't make me feel like a bad dog on Friday. All had clearly been forgiven. After a few laughing references to the fiasco, the incident was forgotten and we talked of other things—especially tomorrow's trip to Berhampore, which excited her. We went to Firpo's, her favorite restaurant, and then to a revival of *Rebecca* at the New Empire Cinema. Dorothy was at her best: gently bantering, humorously Southern, affectionate. Although my hands were sweating again, I held hers all through the movie; we were like a pair of high-school lovers. We'll make love again, I thought; then everything'll be the way it used to be.

But when we reached the house at Ballygunge, Dorothy wouldn't let me come in. I was too astonished at first even to protest—of course she was just teasing me. But as I tried to push past her through the open door, she said, "I'm *not* fooling. I mean it. I just don't feel in the mood tonight." She stood solidly in the doorway, her open palms resting against my chest.

"Now, Dot, come on, baby . . ." I tried to kiss her and she gave me a little shove and at the same time jerked back her head.

"I'm *not* fooling," she repeated. "I'm absolutely worn out, John. Really exhausted. So just give me a simple kiss and let's say good night."

"What the hell have you been leading me on for? You weren't exhausted fifteen minutes ago."

"I've been tired all evening, sweetie, but I tried to hide it. I wanted you to have a good time."

"So you could let me down now? To hell with that!"

"John, please lower your voice. You'll wake up the entire neighborhood. The fact is, I'm having cramps, sweetie. I feel rotten."

Lowering my voice, I begged her to let me come in anyway. "I'll just hold you in my arms. My God, it's been nearly a month since I held you in my arms!" But it was my will, locked with hers, that made me plead; desire no longer had anything to do with it.

Dorothy was not to be moved.

"To hell with you, then," I said at last, and turned toward the car.

I drove away angry and bruised. This was the first time, in all our months together, that she had ever refused me outright. I simply did not believe her sudden claim to exhaustion; she had never bothered to conceal tiredness before. And the claim that she had the cramps was clearly an afterthought. A complete lie, I decided after trying to reckon the time since her last period. She was obviously trying to punish me. But why in such an underhand way? This deviousness was not like her.

I didn't even try to account for the relief that had briefly flared up when I finally realized that she wasn't going to let me in.

As I reached the intersection with Lower Circular Road, I came face to face with another car heading toward Ballygunge. Only after I had nearly reached Harrington Street did I realize that the face and silvery hair glimpsed for a second in the headlights were almost certainly those of Major Phipps. With blood throbbing in my temples, I backed into the next driveway, turned the car around, and tore through the streets as furiously as ever Philip had driven. I slowed down only as I drew near Dorothy's house; then, turning off my headlights, I crept forward as silently as the quiet motor would permit. There was no car parked outside and the lights were off in Dorothy's second-story flat. I cruised slowly about the neighborhood to make sure, then drove back to Harrington Street in a far more exhausted condition than even Dorothy had claimed for herself.

The upholstery of the huge Government House Rolls-Royce was dove gray and very deep. Slouching in my corner of the back seat, I felt myself withdrawing, almost visibly, from all that surrounded me. I could hear the voices of Philip and the uniformed driver, and the contralto of the baby-faced Englishwoman sitting next to me. Her name, if I had understood Ronny's introduction, was Lady Griselda Seton; she was staying at Government House and Ronny had brought her along. Sitting just beyond her was Diane Cummings. They seemed to be talking about the Viceroy, but I couldn't make the effort to follow. Remoteness swept over me; I felt as isolated as I had in the hotel bedroom in Benares, when the very room had seemed like a box floating on the sea. The softness of the upholstery lulled me, and my thoughts slipped back to other outings in the solemn comfort of a high-roofed seven-passenger car. That had not been a Rolls but my Grandmother Wickham's Pierce-Arrow, in Baltimore, when I was a child. The old car, driven by Victor, the colored chauffeur, and carrying the old lady and a huge wicker picnic basket, would leave the house on Mt. Vernon Place and slowly proceed out Charles Street to our suburban house in Guilford. There my sisters and I would fight for the privilege of sitting on the "little seats" until Grandma, losing patience, said that unless we quieted down she would tell Victor to drive straight back to town and there would be no trip to Gibson's Island—or to Bel Air or out the Green Spring Valley or wherever we were going. These outings had continued until my grandmother's death in the early thirties, for she had kept the Pierce-Arrow and Victor even after my father had lost most of her (and his) money and we had been forced to sell the place in Guilford and huddle together in the dim row house on Bolton Street.

What an impact that move had had! At the age of twelve, in 1932, I had known perfectly well what was happening to my family—and to myself. My father, in fact, had made no effort to soften the blow for his children but had done his best, through his own lamentations, to wipe out whatever resiliency a boy of my age might have had. Thus the move from the large, neo-Georgian house in the North Baltimore suburb of Guilford came to mean more than the loss of big lawns and wooded vacant lots and a tree house and the steep, grassy banks of the Reservoir. The fact that other families were undergoing similar or even more drastic comedowns hadn't made the slightest difference to Father. Poor Mother tried her best to meet the situation with what she called "quiet dignity," but even she could only retreat into not-very-quiet tears on those horrible occasions when my father, weeping drunkenly, would fix us with his inflamed eyes and announce that the failure of the Charles Street Trust Company had ruined not only his life but ours and Grandma's as well. The very respectability of Bolton Street—that oasis in the general desolation of downtown Baltimore—was what galled him most; although he wouldn't have lived anywhere else downtown, the drop from the fashionable to the respectable—to the haunt of old ladies and other "quiet but well-connected people"—must have been harder for him to take than a plunge into some unimaginable slum.

I remembered how Grandma, who had been disappointed in both her husband and her son, once predicted that I would be the first Wickham to amount to anything since my great-grandfather (who made a lot of money selling shoes to the Union Army during the Civil War); she had embarked on this flight of prophecy when I won the lower school public-speaking prize at the Gilman Country School, for a speech on "Maryland, the Border State." Well, I thought, here I am: a vice-consul of the United States of America on my way, in a Government House Rolls, in the company of a peer's daughter, to have lunch with His Highness, the Maharaja of Berhampore. Could my grandmother's loving prophecy have envisioned so much?

Ralph, who was sitting on one of the jump seats, suddenly said, "What are you grinning about?"

I opened my eyes. "Oh, nothing much. I was just thinking how funny life is."

"Really, it's such a shame about poor Dot," said Ronny Powell for perhaps the fifth time. "She'd be such fun on a jaunt like this."

Would she? I closed my eyes again and once more, compulsively, went over the morning's decision.

I had awakened about five thirty with aching eyeballs and a heaviness of spirits so great that I could hardly lift my head from the pillow. My first thought was that I didn't want to see Dorothy, didn't want to go with her to Berhampore. I couldn't bring myself to go over the details of the night before. Either

Phippsie had come to her or he hadn't; either Dorothy and I would continue to be lovers or we wouldn't—it all struck me as equally pointless. Then I remembered her taunts that I was not man enough to be really jealous, and the thought bit me sharply. It was true: instead of being jealous, I was apathetic; where flame should have been raging, mud had settled heavily, as though dumped over me by some primeval shifting of the land.

I had lain motionless in bed, immobilized by apathy, until Ralph knocked on the door and told me I'd better get a move on if I didn't want to keep Ronny waiting. "Don't forget," he said, "we've got to allow time to pick up Dorothy, too."

At that instant I saw Dorothy smiling at the Maharaja, putting on her Southern-girl act, talking her sweet talk. "Dorothy's not coming," I said, raising myself on one elbow. "She got sick yesterday."

"Oh, that's too bad," said Ralph. "Nothing serious, is it?"

"Bad stomach cramps. Probably just a touch of Delhi-belly. Nothing serious."

I looked sideways at Lady Griselda, who was now talking about her stay in Jaipur. Philip was encouraging her to gossip about the princely household there; his accent had become almost as British as hers. I wondered just who Lady Griselda was. I had gathered only that she was in India on some sort of official business and was stopping over at Government House for a week or so. She was not bad-looking; her face, beneath the heavy mass of her dull-blond hair, was soft-featured and a little pouting. She seemed to be about Dorothy's age.

"You know, you've been terribly spoiled by Jaipur and Delhi," said Ronny from the front seat. "You mustn't expect Berhampore Palace to be *quite* so grand as the Viceroy's House."

"I dare say," said Lady Griselda, taking out a gold compact and adding more powder to her already dead-white face.

Am I really incapable of jealousy? I wondered. What do I really feel? I couldn't answer myself, but in the blank depths of withdrawal, I felt a sudden spurting up of resolution. But I *can* find out, I thought, shivering a little; I won't let the day pass without knowing where I stand and what I *really* want. Meanwhile, I decided, I might as well enjoy myself.

At Krishnagar, as so often happens in India, the road ended abruptly. We had to leave the car there and take a train for the remaining fifty miles to Berhampore. At the Krishnagar station we were met by the District Magistrate, a brisk Muslim named Mr. Dossani, whom Ronny had telegraphed to procure us a first-class compartment. Ceremonious but unservile, the D.M. urged us to come to his house for refreshments, but Ronny declined, saying it was almost time for the train. And in a few minutes the train did arrive, its open-slatted third-class cars bulging with dhotied travelers and their bundles; there must have been forty or more Indians in each stifling car. With profuse salaams, the Sikh stationmaster unlocked the door and ushered us into our compartment, where we sat down facing one another on hard wooden benches. No sooner had the train begun to move than clouds of dust and soot poured through the open windows, drifting down our necks and clogging our nostrils. Swarms of flies buzzed about our faces, which had already begun to tickle with rolling sweat. Having to some degree anticipated these unpleasantnesses, Ronny had brought along a large Thermos filled with iced gimlets. There was some attempt at conversation at first, but soon we were all sitting in a rather lumpish silence, sweating and ill-tempered, sipping the cool mixture of gin and lime. Finally, turning on my bench, I leaned out the window with my eyes nearly closed against the dust and glare. There were fewer rice paddies now and wider stretches of the scrubby grass and bamboo thickets called "jungle." The train stopped at every village, each the same with its mud walls spotted with pats of drying cow dung, its crumbling brick and plaster, torn posters, roofs of palm thatch or corrugated metal, and, always, the same gaunt, brown-black arms and straining faces and white loincloths and red-stained teeth of the small mob waiting to shriek and clamber its way into the third-class carriages.

My headache returned with a dull drumming in my temples. I now closed my gritty eyelids completely to keep out the glare.

We were met at the Berhampore station by two ancient Daimler touring cars from the palace. After passing through the cantonment area of the town, we drove for several miles until we came to a high stucco wall running for perhaps a thousand feet along the roadside, so close to the gutters that there was scarcely room for the pan wallahs and vendors of coconut milk who had set up their stalls along the way. Slowing down to a squeaking crawl, the two old cars followed one another through a high gateway surmounted by white plaster lions and guarded by two Gurkha durwans. We were now in a wide courtyard, and before us rose the palace—a buff-colored building, vaguely Italianate, with two-storied verandas and a Corinthian portico. At the far end of the compound were a number of smaller buildings, where I could see men and women going about the various activities of a large Indian establishment.

The Maharaja, accompanied by a shriveled old man, appeared on the front steps as the car drew up. Plump as a gourd, he was dressed in a blue seersucker suit—something I had never seen anyone but an American wear in India. After shaking hands all around, he suggested that the men go along to the guesthouse for a wash, while the ladies came into the palace, where his sister would make them comfortable and introduce them to the Maharani. "My wife has old-fashioned ways," he explained, "and prefers to remain in the zenana." After we had all reassembled, we were to meet his American visitor, Mr. Schill, and then have lots of jolly talk about the States. The Maharaja beamed at us like a happy owl; his hooked nose looked sharp enough to tear flesh, but his eyes were humorous and his little mouth as soft as a child's.

After the women had gone in with the Maharaja, the old man, who seemed to be some kind of steward or perhaps a poor relation, led the rest of us across the compound to the guesthouse. This turned out to be a low, classical pavilion in mud-colored stucco. The old man whispered instructions to the slovenly bearer waiting at the door and then, after a deep salaam, began to back away, shuffling and grinning as though he expected one of us to strike him at any moment. Inside we found three bleak white rooms, high-ceilinged and cobwebby; there were three brass beds, three teakwood wardrobes, and a few rattan chairs—no rugs, no curtains, no pictures except for one framed sepia photograph of Darjeeling. Tearing off our jackets in the dense heat, we searched in vain for some way to turn on the ceiling punkahs—they were obviously electric but there seemed to be no switches or cords. The bearer seemed as helpless as we. I sat down on one of the beds and nearly choked in the dust that rose up all around me. Just then Philip called out, "For God's sake, come look at the bathroom!"

It was spectacular. The architect must have had a Roman bath in mind, for in the center of the room was a sunken square pool, about three feet deep; at each corner stood a slender Ionic column supporting a canopy of wood, painted in red and green to look like a coffered ceiling. The pool itself was lined with speckled green marble; on one side, a flight of steps led into the pool from a low bench, also of green marble, on the rim. Along one wall of the room we saw two Victorian washstands with white marble tops and blue china pitchers and next to them a wooden rack from which hung towels as big as blankets.

"I can't resist this," said Philip. "I've got to have a bath."

The rest of us were content to take off our shirts and sponge our faces, necks, and chests at the washstands. My headache still bothered me, but I felt a slow renewal of strength as I rubbed the caked dust from my throat and cleansed my nostrils and ears. In spite of a kind of numbing remoteness, I was going to have a good time in Berhampore.

Philip, meanwhile, had undressed and sat naked on the marble bench, like the statue of a softened Roman boxer, waiting until one of us had finished washing and could pour water over him. Finally Ronny volunteered. He filled one of the pitchers from a huge earthenware jar—a real Ali Baba jar—and then, having mounted the bench, poured a stream of water over the dark, curly head of Philip, who was now standing in the pool just below. Philip yelled at the contact, hunching his shoulders and clasping his belly with both hands. Next he soaped himself with wide sweeping motions, and Ronny again and again doused him with fresh water, laughing like a schoolboy at Philip's flinching. After a good rubdown, Philip climbed out of the pool, holding the big towel draped around his shoulders like a chlamys. Then, striding around the room, he began to slap his chest and thighs noisily.

"If you're trying to look like a Greek god, or something," said Ralph in a savage voice, "you'd better pull in your belly." Standing next to me at one of the washstands, Ralph had gradually straightened his back as he watched the performance.

Philip stopped his strutting and stared, his head raised so that his pale eyes were focused on the top of Ralph's brow; his right hand clutched a corner of the towel over his shoulder—the gesture of an orator before a heckling mob. "Nottatall," he said, running the words together in the British way. "I assure you, I never felt less like a Greek god." He spoke slowly now, with a deliberate and infuriating drawl. "Nero's more my type, I should say, and for that I should rather think a slight paunch was *quite* appropriate." Turning away with a satisfied grin, Philip lifted his right foot to the bench and, resting one arm on his raised knee, his buttocks extended toward Ralph, he leaned forward to dry his toes with the towel.

Ronny laughed until his small, pinkish face had become purple, making his little mustache look yellower than ever. "Nero!" he gasped. "That's it exactly. I knew you reminded me of something Roman."

While Ronny was laughing with good-natured foolishness, Ralph glanced at me and said in a carrying whisper, "Wasn't Nero a fairy?"

"What did you say?" demanded Philip, swinging around so quickly that his towel whirled like a dancer's cape.

Ralph's bulging eyes, usually as soft and brown as a rabbit's, were now deadly; his snub face was pale, his recessive chin now stiffened with scorn. He was nearly as tall as Philip and much more thickly built. "I asked John if Nero wasn't an exhibitionist. God knows you are."

Ronny, who had been staring with alarm, cried out, "I say, don't let's row!"

Philip advanced two steps toward Ralph. His forehead and chest were streaming with sweat. Jolted from my remoteness, I quickly stepped in front of him and grabbed his arm.

"You needn't hold me back," said Philip. "I don't intend to pay the slightest attention to what is, after all, a rather remarkable exhibition itself—an exhibition of—"

"Shut up!" I said. "Shut up, both of you. Get dressed and let's clear out of here."

"Splendid idea," said Ronny.

Ralph gave a short laugh, picked up his shirt, and went into the next room.

"Come on, Philip," I said. "Get dressed and let's go." I had begun to shiver again. I felt suddenly as though I were holding up, singlehanded, a structure that might topple at any moment, and I longed to relax, to let go, to sink back into the pleasant distance from which I had emerged. At the same time I was struggling to get used to an idea that had hit me just now— the idea that Philip, despite the grand array of his manner, was ultimately defenseless against the onslaughts of someone like Ralph. This sense of his vulnerability frightened me; it was heightened by Philip's nakedness and the streaming sweat—perhaps also by my discovery of Thursday night. I suddenly felt very angry. Why must I be Philip's shield? Apathy was beginning to set in. Everything's too much trouble, I decided; nothing is worth it. I was now thinking of Dorothy as much as Philip.

"Lady Griselda is quite a gal," said Ronny with forced cheerfulness as we were walking across the blazing courtyard toward the palace. He explained that she had been making a semiroyal tour of India as the representative of Huntington Motors, Ltd., which was trying to push its new Felix VIII sports car. As the daughter of the Marquis of Blackpool, an old friend of the Viceroy's, Lady Griselda had come armed with an entree to all the government houses from Aden to Hong Kong and introductions to half the Chamber of Princes in Delhi. Although she had received some handsome orders from Jaipur, Gwalior, Baroda, Patiala, and Delhi, she had had no luck at all in Calcutta, despite a party thrown for her by the Nawab of Chittagong, to which many of the Jungly Wallah sports were invited. Her hopes, Ronny said, were now pinned on the Maharaja of Berhampore; he was just the man to need a Felix VIII and thus redeem her otherwise profitless stay in Bengal. "She's frightfully clever, you know," Ronny concluded. "Without in the least overdoing the snob appeal, she rather makes one feel that the Felix VIII and the Garter are roughly in the same class."

This account restored our good humor, and even Ralph managed a smile for the first time since he had stalked out of the bathroom.

A bearer met us at the main entrance and led us through a dark hallway thickly hung with the dusty heads of tiger, rhinoceros, and nilgai. We found the rest of the party already gathered on the garden veranda; these included Pria Rani, the Maharaja's sister, and a bald, large-framed American named Schill, who was wearing a blue seersucker suit exactly like the Maharaja's. The two women from Calcutta looked cool and freshly powdered, but I soon noticed that Lady Griselda seemed upset: her baby mouth was compressed into a thin scarlet ribbon against her white face and she was nervously twisting an emerald ring on her little finger.

"Ernie tells me he popped in on your Consul General while he was in Calcutta," said the Maharaja, "but he didn't have a chance to meet the younger gentlemen of the Consulate."

"It's a real pleasure," said Mr. Schill. "Nothing like meeting fellow Americans when you're about ten thousand miles from home." Then, fearing he might have been tactless, Mr. Schill quickly added, with an emphatic nod toward his host, "But I must say nobody's ever made me feel more at home than the Maharaja."

"How did you happen to come to these parts?" asked Ralph, who had automatically slipped into what I thought of as his chamber-of-commerce pose—body thrust forward, hands on knees, head slightly cocked, and a look of eager intelligence in his earnest brown eyes.

"Greatest luck in the world. Met His Highness a month or so ago at a party our Bombay agent gave at the Taj Hotel. I think I can say we hit it off right from the start, didn't we, Suds?" Mr. Schill turned modestly toward the Maharaja, who said, "You bet."

"So when I came to Calcutta this week, it was already fixed up for me to spend the weekend here at Berhampore."

"Damn lucky for all concerned, I should say," said Ronny, who seemed anxious to remind the company of its British members. "If I'm not being too inquisitive, sir, would you mind telling me just what sort of business you represent?" Ronny's pink little face with its blond mustache and parted lips was as eager as Ralph's had been.

"Not at all. I'm with the overseas division of Studebaker. We've gone into full peacetime production and I'm trying to drum up a little interest in our new models. And I don't mind telling you the results have been more than gratifying. The people of India have a real eye for styling." Mr. Schill smiled at the Maharaja, who smiled back, his tiny mouth almost disappearing under the cruel point of his nose. "Of course dollar permits present quite a problem, but there are ways of meeting the difficulty."

"But I say," cried Ronny, "what an extraordin'ry coincidence! Did you know that Lady Griselda here—"

"Ronny, darling," she interrupted in her throaty-sweet voice, "you simply *mustn't* give Mr. Swill the idea I'm the *least* interested in a Studebaker. *I* haven't got a dollar to my name."

"But that's not what I mean!"

"Never mind. Do let's keep it our own little joke, shall we?"

"What will you give me to change the subject, Lady G.?" asked Philip with a malicious grin. But she ignored him, and turning to the Maharaja, said she was simply dying to see the rest of the palace.

But it was Diane Cummings, not Lady Griselda, who stuck

close to our host during the tour. Falling into a role which made me think, suddenly and guiltily, of Dorothy, she went into elegant raptures over the Durbar Throne, which was made of ruby-red glass with silver mountings. She held us all up in the gallery by asking questions about each work, most of which turned out to be blackened copies of paintings in European galleries. There was, however, one spectacular original, "Diana Bathing with Her Maidens," by Bouguereau; here Diane commented professionally on each of the figures, suggesting diets or new hairdo's, much to the Maharaja's delight. And when we moved into the Gothic Library, she exclaimed, "What I love about all this is that it's terribly impressive without being in the least *stuffy*. It has such a lived-in feeling."

I noticed that Philip seemed determined to have as little as possible to do with Diane. He stayed close to Lady Griselda and grinned when the latter, in a loud stage whisper, said, "I do believe that extraordinary creature is trying to *make* the Maharaja."

Meanwhile we had come to the Crimson Drawing Room, which was furnished with a single suite of gilt furniture, elaborately carved and upholstered in red velvet—all of it designed from a model that had caught the eye of the Maharaja's grandfather at the Crystal Palace Exhibition in 1851. Large portraits of all nine of Queen Victoria's children hung on the walls.

"It's simply breath-taking," said Diane Cummings.

"I keep wishing Mrs. Schill could see all this," said Mr. Schill.

We returned to the Gothic Library to drink gimlets and then filed into the dining room. I was still having a good time, but I had absolutely no appetite. Tasting my mulligatawny soup, I knew that I would have trouble finishing it. My mouth seemed coated with paste; I moved my tongue heavily and swallowed. Glancing across the table I saw that the Maharaja was talking to Philip and that the latter had taken on a special role: he was now very much the suave young political officer, replying deferentially to his host's questions about American foreign policy but making it clear that he was holding back much more information than he chose to reveal. Ralph was watching him closely.

The talk veered around, at last, inevitably, to India. The Maharaja was scornful of the British Cabinet Mission which was currently trying to work out an agreement between the Congress Party and the Muslim League in New Delhi. Contemptuously, he referred to its head, Lord Pethick-Lawrence, as "Pathetic Lawrence." The Mission, he said, was consulting every group in India except the zamindars—the landowners. What else could you expect from a group representing the Labour Government in England? "I do not speak as a zamindar myself," he insisted, "but as one who knows the Indian people. The Indians look to their natural leaders—to those who are representative of the best in the past—and who are also most up-to-date and modern in their ideas. They are the ones who must lead India very gently by the hand into the modern world. I warn you," he continued, narrowing his small eyes, "if the zamindars, who have been the natural leaders of India for centuries, if they are expropriated, then this country will fall into the modern world in the worst way possible. I assure you it will fall through the trap door of communism. This is a truth I'm not sure the present British Government understands. That is why I hope Britain will attempt no final settlement of the Indian question until a Tory government is back in power. There now," he concluded, "does that sound sufficiently reactionary for you? My enemies call me a reactionary. What do you say to that?"

"Sir, do you consider Gandhi and Nehru to be natural leaders?" asked Philip with a show of innocence.

"Ah, Mr. Sachs, let me counter your question with another. What do you, as a representative of the most modern, up-to-date country in the world, think of Gandhi?"

"Gandhiji is unquestionably the greatest human being since Christ." Philip gave me a mischievous glance.

"Dear God, d'you really think so?" asked Ronny with blue-eyed astonishment.

All of the old fury had poured back into Ralph's face. "That's the most irresponsible statement I ever heard," he said.

"Mr. Sachs," said the Maharaja, "I should have thought that you, as an American with modern, up-to-date ideas, could have spotted the danger in Gandhi's position. He is unquestionably, as you say, a very great man, a most remarkable person, but he mistrusts the modern world. He mistrusts modern science, modern industry—and modern medicine, too. He is the real reactionary. What India needs is machines, not spinning wheels. Iron and steel, aluminum, know-how!"

I began to pay closer attention, remembering that the Maharaja was not merely the second-largest zamindar in Bengal but also the principal owner of the All-India Steel Works in Brindalpore.

Then the voice of Lady Griselda—the first woman's voice since the political conversation had begun—rose in its subtle contralto across the table. "I simply can't understand what earthly good it will do for *us* to pull out of India when all it means is that you Americans will take over with your cars and dollars and all that sort of thing."

"The American Way will save the day," rhymed the Maharaja with a giggle.

Lady Griselda arched her thin brows. "And I suppose the British dog—or lion—has had its day?"

"I'm sure the Maharaja didn't mean that," cried Ronny, looking acutely unhappy. "You're putting words into his mouth."

"I haven't the slightest desire to put *anything* into the Maharaja's mouth, Ronny, dear."

Tapping his plate with his fork, the Maharaja interrupted them. "There's one further question I want to bring up," he said in a commanding voice. "What do you think about Partition? Tell me what you think of Partition."

This was a subject on which I held strong views. The idea of dividing the country between Hindus and Muslims filled me with despair, and I was half-convinced that the British had stirred up the whole issue of Pakistan as an excuse for delaying Indian independence. But in my present remote and muffled state I felt unable to argue or even to listen as Philip, Ralph, and Ronny all had their say on a subject on which, as I now thought, there was nothing new to be said. But I couldn't sink back into complete apathy, for I was called on from time to time to answer whispered questions from Mr. Schill, who was sitting next to me. He was vague about the meanings of "Partition" and "Pakistan," uncertain just who Mohammed Ali Jinnah was; he had heard of Gandhi and Nehru, of course, but wasn't sure whether they were on the same side or not. I did my best, whispering in turn, and Mr. Schill jotted down notes on Studebaker business cards which he took from his wallet, hiding his action behind a large napkin. "Thanks a million for the briefing, John," he said at last with warmth. "Ever since I got to India I've been waiting for a chance to get all this straightened out."

Straightened out—I echoed the words. A five-minute briefing, then on with the job.

Then, hardly believing what I heard, I realized that the Maharaja was speaking in favor of Partition, though not in a way that would have pleased the Muslim League. He felt that there might be definite advantages in the breaking-down of India itself into its old provinces. An independent Hindu state of Bengal, he suggested, might best serve the cause of progress and modernization, unhampered by a greedy democracy in Delhi. Perhaps the people would turn at last to those who really understood them, who had their interests at heart.

The American Playroom, where we went for coffee, was, as the Maharaja had promised us, "completely unstuffy—very much in the modern taste." Paneled in what looked like plywood, the room was crowded with billiard tables, slot machines, and pinball machines that flashed in all the colors of the spectrum. And one entire wall was lined with distorting mirrors of the kind I had seen as a boy in the Fun Fair at Ocean City. "Come along, everyone," cried Suds, who had changed into a carnival barker. "Everyone must take their turn. Don't be shy. It's great fun." Laughing, clapping his hands, he led the way to the largest of the mirrors, where he began to posture with his thumbs in his ears, his cheeks puffed out. Instantly his spread fingers were like the antlers of a moose and his face became a set of enormous, pinkish-brown buttocks ballooning outward on each side of his nose; his body, meanwhile, had shrunken into a pale-blue carrot dangling beneath the monstrous head. It was very funny. We each took a turn, stretching out our mouths with hooked fingers, sticking out our tongues, pulling down the corners of our eyes. Dropping her Mayfair pose, Diane Cummings put her hands on her hips and began a slow shimmy in front of a mirror that changed her into an hourglass, four feet high and four feet wide at the bust and hips. Watching her I again thought of Dorothy—how she would have loved this! I could almost see her prancing and cavorting, could almost hear the raucous Southern laugh.

Then, all at once, I felt very dizzy. The room was like a surrealist movie. All around me was a crazy jumble of performers, dancing and gesturing, and I seemed to be watching from outside, like a god. I'm outside of everything, I thought. Even my own body was just a performer—as separate from me as everything else in the crazy show. None of it made any sense. My excitement increased, and for a moment I was trembling with a new, thrilling, terrifying perception: I had merely to flip over my mind—by a little trick that I would master in the next second—and then everything, including my own body, would vanish. None of it was real—there would be nothing left! Just one more tiny effort, just one more little push . . .

But I drew back, scared of the thunderous and irrevocable *click* that I was about to hear. My head was aching again. I mustn't get sick, I thought. Mustn't get sick . . .

Stumbling against one of the metal folding chairs with which the room was littered, I sat down at once, leaning forward with my head in my hands.

"Are you all right, John?"

I looked up at Ralph, who was bending over me. "I'm a little dizzy."

"It's this frightful heat," said the Maharaja. "You must drink some hot coffee. Heat on heat—that's what the modern doctors tell us, isn't it?"

CHAPTER VIII ❧ THE party broke up just after coffee so that we could catch the four-ten train to Krishnagar. The Maharaja urged us to stay, promising an elephant ride, a trip to the Dilkusha or summer palace, and beds for the night—all of which had to be refused as politely as possible. The rail journey was again hot and dusty, but I felt better, knowing that I could fall asleep once I had settled into the soft back seat of the Rolls. I wondered whether I was really physically sick; sometimes it seemed to me that I had a fever in addition to the ever-throbbing headache, but then the heat of the afternoon was so savage that I couldn't be sure. In any case, I held on, determined not to give in before reaching some kind of settlement with Dorothy.

I did sleep in the car, lulled by the hum of the motor. The rest of the company had fallen into a sticky and morose silence, which was not broken until Ronny ordered the driver to stop at the Willingdon Bridge. "Thought we might all enjoy stretching our legs before the final sprint into Calcutta," he explained apologetically as I was jerked into wakefulness by the sudden jolting of the car on the shoulder of the road.

With heavy legs I climbed out of the car. We walked down to the riverbank near a large Saivite temple whose steps led down to the Hooghly. Under the metallic sunset, the river water was as iridescent as an oil slick.

"Quite a fish down there, or whatever it is," said Ronny, pointing to an odd shape—about three feet long—on the yellow mud flat below. Two gray crows were picking at it.

"That's not a fish," I said. "It must be the spinal column of a dog or something." Then, despite the thick sludge of mud, I made out an unmistakable shape. "Let's go," I said. But I was too late. My stomach had already begun to heave when I heard Ronny exclaim, "Dear God, it's human! It has a human skull!"

A few minutes later, sitting on the running board, I said weakly, "Something must be wrong with me. I didn't think there was a sight left in India that could make me sick." And to myself I kept whispering, the chokra—it's the chokra.

"Oh, for heaven's sake, *do* come along," called Lady Griselda

105

from the inside of the car. She, too, had become sick when she saw me vomiting.

"Are you quite sure you're all right?" asked Ronny.

I nodded and we got into the car. Raging over this final humiliation, Lady Griselda sat in her corner, whiter than ever; she had rinsed her mouth with what remained of the gimlets in the Thermos and now kept biting her lower lip. Then Philip said, "The extraordinary thing, of course, is that the priests bathe within just a few feet of that corpse. Presumably they don't even notice it. Perhaps for them it doesn't even exist."

"*Must* we continue to discuss it?" said Lady Griselda. "Surely there's no point in trying to account for anything in this bloody country."

When we reached Harrington Street an hour later, I took a long, hot bath and put on clean clothes. I'll feel better once I've had a drink, I thought. But the drink didn't really help, and when Ralph and I sat down to dinner, I could hardly touch the food. My hand trembled so violently when I tried to lift a spoonful of soup that I was afraid Ralph would notice. In a few minutes he said, "You look terrible. You ought to go to bed."

"I'm all right."

"You shouldn't go out. Where are you planning to go?"

"I'm going over to Dorothy's awhile. I—I want to see how she is." The thought filled me with dread, but I was determined not to give up.

"Why don't you just telephone? She'll understand if you're not feeling very well."

"No, I want to see her."

But when we got up from the table I had another dizzy spell and had to sit down quickly to keep from falling. "John, don't be a fool," said Ralph. "Your forehead's hot as fire. You're running a temperature."

I did not protest. I had given up. Ralph brought a thermometer from the bathroom and I looked on passively when, two minutes later, he held it to the light. "One hundred and one degrees—that's not too high," he said, "but I think I'd better call Dr. Harlestoun. Since I'm going out, I want to be able to enjoy the evening with a clean conscience. You go on to bed." I obeyed and I was glad when Ralph was unable to reach Dr. Harlestoun: now I would not have to hold myself awake until he came.

My sleep was troubled, and after a while I woke up to find a light burning in the room. Dorothy was standing in the open doorway. She was dressed in green pajamas—women's pajamas with short, puffed sleeves. "What the hell are you doing here?" I said.

"I just had to see you. I couldn't let the day pass without apologizing for last night."

I stared at her. She had not mentioned Berhampore. She was so filled with her own guilt that she didn't resent at all what I had done! She thought that she deserved every bit of it! Drunk with relief, I got out of bed and came toward her. "Dot, I'm sorry about going off without you today. But I don't want to talk about it. Let's dance."

She nodded, and I led her into the living room, where I put a stack of records—beginning with "Sentimental Journey"— on the phonograph. I felt much better; I was light-footed; my fever had gone. We began to move slowly to the soft beat of the record. Dorothy held herself rigid in my arms, as if every movement she made was unwilling. I tried to put my cheek against hers, but she pulled away, as though I had touched her face with a hot coal. Damn you, I thought, and catching the back of her head with my hand, I forced her face against mine. Slowly we swayed together. I could feel her body beginning to soften in my arms. "Ah-h-h!" I moaned in triumph as I slipped my hand under the pajama coat, sliding my fingers down her back and under the elastic band of her trousers. For a moment I touched the heavy, silken flesh of her buttocks. "My wife," I whispered, unable to stop myself. "My wife, my sweet wife, my sweet wife." Then I kissed her forehead, her closed eyelids, and her lips. "Oh, my sweet Dot," I moaned. "My sweet wife." She frowned slightly, without opening her eyes. My fingers pressed into her soft upper arms. I undid the middle button of her pajama coat and moved my hand up the rib cage to her breasts, catching one of them from below and gently resting my thumb and fingers on the nipple. "Now," I whispered, "now," and I felt her fingers dig into the flesh of my back.

Then, as we were lying together on the ground, a maddening thing happened. The elastic band of her pajama trousers had tightened—I couldn't bare the lower part of her body. I struggled frantically, becoming very hot, but I still couldn't move the tight band—I couldn't even insert my fingers beneath it. And all the time I felt my desire slowly draining away. If I'm not quick, I thought, it'll be too late—I'm losing my erection. . . .

Exhausted and very hot, I raised myself on one elbow and tried to catch my breath. The rice paddies stretched on all sides, as far as I could see. I was now kneeling at the rim of a tank full of cool water—clear and drinkable, not like the usual scum-mantled pool. My heat was intolerable. I knew that I would die if I didn't plunge into the water. But just as I was about to leap in, a shadow passed over the sun. Looking over the paddies, I could make out a small black cloud in the sky. "As yet it's no bigger than a man's hand," I said, watching it intently.

The black cloud moved swiftly toward me. "Locusts!" I shouted. They were like birds, great waves of crows or starlings. They'll strip the paddy fields, I thought. Now they were whirring over my head, forcing me to my knees on the riverbank, which was flat and slimy with yellowish mud. My fingers sank into the muck.

A large bird perched on my chest, so heavy that I couldn't breathe. It was a vulture with a scrawny purple neck that protruded from a ruff of black feathers. Slowly moving its head in a circular motion, the huge bird stretched its beak toward my face. It came closer and closer until I was staring into the horrible bird's eyes, which were clouded with a network of tiny red veins. Heavy and sharply hooked, the beak was within inches of my own eyes. Violently, I twisted my head back and forth, but I knew that I couldn't save my eyes merely by closing them. Stricken with a fear worse than any I had ever known, I was unable to scream or even to breathe. And far beneath the fear I was aware of disgust, too, for I knew that vultures vomited up carrion on their enemies. "No!" I yelled, suddenly finding my voice, and I grabbed the bird by its neck and wrung it savagely, hurling the dark form from my chest.

I flung myself into consciousness. After my heartbeat had steadied, I became aware of a violent headache. Stumbling into the bathroom, I took some aspirin; then I changed my pajamas, which were soaked with sweat. I was hardly back in bed before another sweating fit drenched me through, and the sheet underneath. I dozed a little, but some great, crashing image of terror kept hurling me out of sleep. I now began to feel sharp pains through my back and legs and convinced myself that I had polio. Finally, early in the morning, I dragged myself out of bed to telephone Dr. Harlestoun.

The doctor arrived in about an hour. He examined me briefly and then announced in his Scots-gruff way that I had dengue fever and would be laid up for at least ten days and maybe as long as three weeks. Judging from the usual incubation period, he guessed that I had received the mosquito bite in Benares, though it could just as well have been in Calcutta. Dr. Harlestoun prescribed a diet largely of tea and broth and promised to come back later in the morning with some drugs to cut the fever and deaden the aches. "It's not called 'backbreak fever' for nothing," he said. "But you won't die. I think you might get better attention in the Presidency Hospital. How about it?"

I mumbled that I'd rather stay where I was—Ghulam and Ralph would take good care of me. The doctor nodded, snapped shut his bag, and left the room.

CHAPTER IX ❦ THE aches would start in the small of my back, then spread across the pelvis and branch out into my thigh bones and shins; they came with a rhythmic build-up, and at their height I couldn't lie still but would thrash my legs about until I had kicked off the covers. The pains would go away after I had swallowed one of my white pills, but, being limited to six of these a day, I tried to hold off taking one as long as I could, often waiting until my legs were twitching like a galvanized frog's. Between these bouts I lay fitfully, weak from fever and boredom, unable to read, my eyeballs aching.

What little energy I had went into fighting off sleep, for it was in that realm that the worst terrors lurked. I had only to close my eyes to become a living bait for such nightmares as I had never known, not even in early childhood. When I complained to Dr. Harlestoun, he told me there was nothing unusual about such dreams when one was running a high fever and he gave me some pills, pink ones this time, which, he assured me, would put an end to this nonsense. If anything, the sleeping pills only increased the fantastic proliferation of the nightmares and made it harder for me to obtain the unspeakable relief of waking up. As I felt sleep coming on I would brace myself, digging my fingers into every handhold of consciousness, clutching at roots and leaves to stave off the inevitable plunge, certain that this time I would lose my mind, that I would never be able to climb out again. Of course I could never record the exact moment when the subtle, then accelerating, slip into violence began. Many of the dream stories were old ones, but there was now something grotesque and primordial in their detail, as if they had erupted from some ultimate pool of terror. I no longer fell from cliffs or bridges but through some fantastic moon pit, whose walls were decked out with fatly succulent plants and lava flows that had hardened into thorny tangles far below. I would wake up, finally, into a swaddling of wet sheets, my chest heaving to catch the breath that had exploded from my lungs during the fall.

After a few days my beard grew to a dirty stubble and my hair became matted and gross, as though my scalp had been sweating gum. The dry blast of fever tightened the skin of my forehead and jaws, cracking my strained lips. Refusing to use a bedpan, I would stagger to the bathroom to relieve myself, but I lacked the strength—and the wish—to shave or to do more than mop my face and armpits and chest with a damp cloth. My body had berayed me—it revolted me—and I submitted with a kind of feeble assent to its indecency. Thank God there was no nurse to fuss over me. Ralph stuck his head in the door several times a day to ask how I was, and Ghulam and the chokra came only when I rang for them. Even Dr. Harlestoun, after prescribing a variety of drugs, left me alone, saying there was nothing else to do but let the sickness run its course. My mind, too, had become unkempt. I could seldom pull together the shreds of thought that flickered past during those long afternoons when the shutters let through a dry pallor from the white blaze outside; and when I woke up at night, the seething images were almost as rank as those of my dreams.

Opening my eyes one white afternoon—the fourth or fifth of my illness—I saw Dorothy standing by my bed. This was no dream but I couldn't bring myself to say a word. My eyelids were granulated and the light hurt my pupils.

"You look like you'll live," she said. "But right now you better get up and sit in that chair while I make your bed. I never saw such a God-awful tangle."

"Don't bother." I could hardly hear my own voice.

"What did you say? Speak up, you're not *that* weak." She was already rolling up the sleeves of her blouse, determined to play the nurse.

"I said don't bother."

"Now look here, for once in my life I'm going to have things *my* way. Now get up like I say."

But I wouldn't move. I felt utterly incapable of making the effort, even if I had wanted to. Finally I compromised, letting her fluff the pillow and tug at my sheets and then rub my back with alcohol. Ordinarily I would have welcomed the back rub as one of the best of life's minor sensualities, but on this day my body shrank as though every stroke of her long fingers were part of a spell that would paralyze me forever.

"I didn't learn you were sick until this morning," she was saying. "I'd already sworn I'd never speak to you again."

The glide of her fingers speeded up, as if to chafe a response from my unyielding shoulders.

"What ever made you do a thing like that? I waited around half of Saturday morning before I phoned and found out you'd already been gone for hours. Were you still sore about Friday night? Is that why you did it?"

The Southern voice hummed in my ears, the firm hands ran up my back and across my shoulders, coaxing me into speech. But what could I say? I was much too abject and miserable to show fight, to make accusations about Phippsie, much too weak to endure the scene that would follow.

After a while she said, "I reckon you must have already been sick and delirious to do something as mean as that."

"I reckon so," I murmured into my pillow. She had forgiven me and I didn't want to be forgiven. I wanted to be left alone.

Finally the cool hands were lifted and I heard the top being screwed onto the bottle of alcohol. "Better put on your pajama top," Dorothy said. Obediently I rose up and stuck my arms through the sleeves and then lay on my back, buttoning up the jacket. She stood by the bed, rolling down the sleeves of her blouse. When she had finished, Dorothy shook her head slowly. "There's something sort of nice and pitiful about men when they're sick," she said. "I remember the time Harry Eustace walked into an empty swimming pool outside of Atlanta. He was stoned, which is probably the only reason he didn't kill himself. All he did was bust his leg. Anyway, I sometimes think it was the happiest time of our marriage. He really needed me. Harry was just like a baby—a great big helpless baby." Again she shook her head. "I had to do everything for him. It means a lot to a woman to know she's needed."

For the first time I managed a smile. "It means you've got him where you want him," I mumbled.

"What did you say?"

"Nothing. Thanks a lot for coming." I could see that she was dissatisfied with the results of her visit; though she kept up a show of sickroom breeziness, her tanned face was heavy with disappointment. I felt sorry for her but there was nothing I could do. Finally Dorothy said, "You'd better get some sleep now. I'll be back one of these days. Tell Ralph to phone me if you need anything." She pressed her lips for a second on my hot forehead and then left the room. She'll never touch me again, I thought. This conviction brought no relief or joy or sadness with it; it was simply there, as dense and immovable as the earth's center.

By Friday my fever had let up a little and I was no longer so driven by the hags of sleep. But now boredom and a black heaviness of spirit weighed upon my chest where nightmares had perched. "Dengue always makes a chap feel like blowing out his brains," Dr. Harlestoun said. Still, knowing that depression was one of the regular symptoms didn't really help. During the long, pale reaches of the afternoon the sheer paltriness of my life overwhelmed me: there was every objective reason why I *had* to be depressed. Again and again I reviewed my last six months with Dorothy, trying to make some sense of the affair. What had I really wanted from her? Or felt about her? I had wanted someone to sleep with, someone who would make it easy for me, someone who would keep me company. I had never seriously thought of marrying her. What else? I had wanted to share in her grappling with life, and the result was that I had come to feel more pallid, more swaddled and blanketed than ever. I had never really loved her.

The fact was, of course, that I was incapable of falling in love. Though it wasn't new, this realization now hit me like a blow in the stomach. I can't fall in love, I thought; I can't even really *care*—about any woman, any friend, about my parents or my job or India or anything. I saw myself wrapped up like a living mummy—bound, swaddled, able to see, unable to move. It had always been this way, always would be. Why had I never seen it so clearly before? For a while I lay stiff as a corpse, my hands clenched at my sides. The room was airless and white, and finally I had to close my eyes against the meaningless revolving of the slow punkah.

I thought of Betty Kinder, the girl I had known at Swarthmore in 1940, during my junior year. For a little while I had been able to pretend to myself that I loved her. And for a long while afterward I had used her as a proof to myself that I *could* fall in love. I could still summon up the round face, the full lips, the black hair worn so long that its curls fell about her collarbone. A pleasant girl, always wearing that enormous tan sweater that hung like a sack over her small breasts and waist. Always smoking a cigarette—I remembered how the chain-smoking used to get on my nerves. In some ways it was easier to recall these things than the details of that night in the early spring when I finally persuaded her to go with me to a tourist camp outside Valley Forge. We were both very nervous and it hadn't worked out very well, though we both pretended that it had. We considered ourselves practically engaged. But by the first of May I had withdrawn so much—and she had grown so hateful to me with her hurt look and tobacco-stained fingers—that I could hardly go through the motions of a campus lover; we had already, without ever bringing it into words, ceased to be actual lovers after a second visit to the tourist camp. The good times we had had together were all gone: only the pain and distress were real for me now.

Most painful of all was the weekend when I took her to meet my parents in Baltimore. Betty was nice-looking, well-dressed without being stylish, pleasant in her manner, but, as a Midwesterner and the daughter of a dentist, she was just different enough from the girls I had grown up with in Baltimore to cause my parents to give her what I thought of as "the full treatment." My father had been lively, sardonic, heavily gallant. Jockey-sized, wearing his dark banker's suit and Ivy Club tie, his small shoes carefully but not too brightly polished, his brown eyes threaded with tiny red veins—I could still see him as he danced attendance on Betty, preening before her, occasionally half-turning to catch my eye. Warmed up by his whisky, he reminisced about Princeton, where he had been cox on the famous 1912 crew, and about his experiences in France, where he had been a first lieutenant in the Field Artillery and aide-de-camp to General "Hooty" Blair of the Maryland National Guard. Always he spoke directly to Betty, paying her the compliment of never explaining the special references with which his conversation was laced; if she didn't know who "Whitey" and "Spoff" and "Twitch" were, or the distinctions between the Bachelors' Cotillion and the Assembly, or between the Gold Cup, the Maryland Hunt, and the Preakness, it couldn't make less difference, he implied. I had seen him carry on this way before some of my high-school friends—the "new" friends I'd made after Father's financial collapse had forced my withdrawal from the Gilman School; he managed it all so skillfully that only I could catch the faint sarcastic theme which trilled high above the rich flow of his politeness. Apparently he felt that places like Toledo (Betty's home) and the less fashionable sections of Baltimore were obscurely to blame for his retreat into the dim little parlor on Bolton Street, and in this way he got his subtle revenge. After Betty's departure he said, "Well, son, you sure know how to pick 'em," and grinned so that his brown eyes, dark and long-lashed like a Spaniard's, glowed through their fiery network of veins.

Mother was much less devious, and less malicious, too. I saw her in the kitchen with Betty after dinner, removing her rings before washing the dishes and saying, for the third or fourth time, how put out she was that the cook, who usually came when they had company, had failed her at the very last moment. "With just Mr. Wickham and myself here," she explained, "we really don't need anyone full time." And later she told me, in her permanently resigned voice, that Betty seemed like a nice, wholesome girl, *very* Midwestern in the way she had been so helpful about the house; she supposed that girls from even quite substantial families in Toledo were more used to that sort of thing than "the kind of girls we know in Baltimore."

Even in the wretchedness of this memory I had to smile, cracking my fever-dried lips. What would they have made of the others? Of Violet Hardy, for instance? Or of Dorothy!

Then it struck me that my true motive for joining the Foreign Service had been purely snobbish. All the other reasons—the passionate interest in international affairs which I had developed at Swarthmore, the encouragement of my departmental adviser, the prospect of travel—all these had only masked the shameful reality. Bound and immobilized in the white emptiness of the afternoon, I was now convinced that the retreat from the wide lawns of Guilford to the row house on Bolton Street had alone determined my choice of a career. How pathetic! So this was the career that was to make up for Bolton Street! I signed passports and laid down the law to visa applicants, and in thirty years, if I was careful about detail, I might end up as Consul General in Sydney or Bordeaux. What had happened to my ambition to write political reports, to try to work myself into the diplomatic side of the Foreign Service? I now knew better. I couldn't really see myself escorting visiting senators or standing behind the Secretary of State's chair, slipping him memoranda, at an international conference. I'd leave the writing of political reports to people like Philip. I'd never be more than a good consular hack. At any rate, my life would play itself out a little more entertainingly in Calcutta or Sydney or Bordeaux than behind a desk in Baltimore.

My fever has gone up, I thought, feeling the hotness of my breath against the rough skin of my lips. Suddenly I had to thresh my legs. The tangle of sheets was intolerable. I rolled from one side to the other, then stretched out my arms and legs and lay spread-eagled, staring at the white ceiling.

It wasn't until the next Tuesday that I felt strong enough to take a bath. By that time my temperature had been normal for two days. I had shaved once before and had sponged myself a number of times, but my hair was foul as a gluepot. I rang for Ghulam to light the geyser and also to bring some hot water for the basin, so that I could wash my hair.

Standing in front of the mirror, I rubbed my chin and cheeks, rasping the skin of my palm against the five-day stubble. Each bristle was black and distinct, and my hair and eyebrows, because of the extreme pallor of my face, were darker than I had ever seen them. I badly needed a haircut: the dull hair hung over the tops of my ears and down the nape of my neck. The brown and white of my eyes were dull, too, and the pupils enlarged. I must have lost fifteen pounds, I thought, feeling very shaky all at once. With strengthless fingers I soaped my hair, ran my nails over the thickened scalp, and lowered my head to rinse it in the hot water. As I leaned forward, the water suddenly blackened and I felt a sharp blow on the chin.

When I came to, I was lying face down on the tile floor, and in front of my mouth was a small pool of blood, not yet dry. I lay quietly, knowing that I had fainted and would probably do so again if I tried to stand up. My lip was puffed up and hurting, but I hestitated to touch it or even to move my tongue, fearing to discover that I had broken a tooth. I had no idea how long I had been lying there.

The temptation was to stay where I was, crumpled on the floor, never to move again. After a few minutes, however, I gripped the rim of the bathtub and pulled myself to my feet. I was extremely weak and felt nauseated, too. Reaching slowly forward, I was able to grasp the wash basin, which, to my surprise, was full of barely tepid water. Then I looked into the mirror and nearly fell backward in terror. A dead man had assaulted my eyes, a corpse with a brownish, swollen, bloodied mouth, and hair that was bunched and matted and gray. I stood paralyzed with revulsion, as though I had encountered some hideous double that had rounded the earth to meet me there. Holding the basin with both hands, I stared into the image of my own dissolution. Finally, after the echoing of my heart had died away, I very gently touched my extraordinary hair; it was stiff with soap that was almost dry.

Another wave of terror and disgust broke over me, and feeling very dizzy now and afraid of another fall, I groped my way back to the bed. I lay with my face in the pillow, crying with weakness and disgust, my lip throbbing with pain. I was overwhelmed by the reality of what I had seen. That corpse in the mirror was the ultimate fact of my existence; my own ultimate corruption had been revealed to me as brutally as if all the layers of flesh had been peeled back from my forehead and cheeks. This was no distorting mirror like the one in Berhampore. There's nothing to be done about it, I thought; I can't change it—it's *there,* it's *there!* My God, how I hate it!

An hour or so later I heard the doorbell ring and the sound of voices. Ghulam came to the door. "Sahib see Fenwick Sahib?" he asked.

I mumbled *"Tik hai"*—yes—without looking up. Then I rolled over. I must have fallen asleep.

Martin Fenwick came in. "Hallo, John," he said. "I've been wanting to drop by. How's it going?" Then he exclaimed, "Dear God, what on earth's happened to you?" He strode over to the bed and leaned over, his yellowish face screwed up with concern.

"Cut my lip," I said thickly.

"Best have a look at it, I think. Hold on a minute." Martin went into the bathroom and returned with a damp washcloth. Switching on the lamp, he again leaned over the bed and with the cloth gently wiped the blood from my chin and the circumference of my mouth. "Do you have some sort of antiseptic?" he asked.

"Mercurochrome. In the medicine cabinet."

When Martin had finished dabbing the swollen lip with a cotton swab soaked in Mercurochrome, he said, "You still look perfectly frightful, but it's not such a bad cut. Won't need stitches. Now tell me, what on earth happened? The bathroom floor is simply covered with blood."

I suddenly felt very much better. "I had a vision," I said, propping myself up on one arm. I wanted to laugh out of sheer high spirits.

"What are you talking about?"

"A vision of your goddess. In the bathroom."

"My goddess?" Martin's expression became so absurd in its puzzlement that I had to laugh in the face of my friend. He thinks I'm delirious, I said to myself.

"Yes, your goddess. I had a vision of Kali. I saw her black

face and the red tongue sticking out. And the necklace of skulls. Everything. I saw her in the bathroom mirror."

Now Martin laughed. "Don't blaspheme. She's no joking matter. Sooner or later, we all furnish trophies for that necklace." Then he added, "It looks to me as though you must have kissed her."

"Oh, no. She struck me across the mouth. I have no desire to kiss her."

"I see." Martin was silent for a moment. "Now tell me how you are. Dengue's no fun, is it? Still, it's high time you caught something. You've been so disgustingly well since I've known you. I feel one hasn't really lived in India until she's drawn a bit of one's blood."

We talked on for about half an hour. I had Ghulam bring a gin and tonic for Martin and some tea for myself. I was feeling decidedly better. I asked for news of the Chaudurys. Ramesh had dropped by two days before but had found me sleeping and had gone away, leaving a box of sweetmeats which Sujata had made for me out of honey and curdled milk. Then Martin told me about a particularly difficult case that had come up in the Bengal Labour Department; it had to do with the arbitration of a tramworkers' wage dispute and had taken up a lot of Martin's time.

He got up to leave. "You look as though you'll live. Now I must tell you something that may interest you. Anila and I have decided to get married."

"Martin, that's wonderful news! I'm very pleased to hear it." I sat up in bed. "When's it going to be?" I asked, conscious of more enthusiasm in my voice than in my feelings. I was struck by the curiously drawn look that sabotaged Martin's broad smile.

"Sometime this summer. Depends on when my brother can get away from Singapore." His smile broadened still further. "So you think it's a good idea, do you?"

"Of course I do."

"We made up our minds just a few days ago. Saturday, I think it was. I've been thinking about it for a long time, as you've probably guessed. She's the one person in the world for me, John. And I'm the only man for her. Really, it's as simple as that."

"I'm very pleased."

"I'm glad we have your blessing. We must see a lot of you as soon as you're up and about."

When Martin had gone, I continued to sit up in bed, hands clasped in front of my knees. Martin's news had saddened me. I didn't like Anila, despite my admiration for the way she looked; she struck me as affected and capable of really biting malice. Even more, I was disturbed by the expression I had caught behind Martin's smile. What sort of look was it? Resignation? No, it had seemed more defiant than that, more humorous, and at the same time more despairing. My thoughts went back to that last evening in Benares, and I could hear Martin's drunken voice shouting, "I seek the darkness with all the fervor of a bridegroom! I drink her health!" For all her faults, poor Anila was hardly the principle of darkness. She was merely a rather improbable mate for my somewhat battered English friend.

CHAPTER X ❧ CLOSELY shaven now, my scalp clean, I sat in an easy chair in my bedroom, reading—or rather skimming—a fat novel called *Gallant Are My Sons,* by Marijane Packer Aldrich. This book, a present from Mrs. Hubbard, dealt with the turbulent lives of a rich and "colorful" family of Auburn, New York, in the early years of this century. On the table were other presents: *The Unquiet Grave* and Lord Berner's memoirs of his school days at Eton, both from Philip, and two back numbers of the *Partisan Review* from Morris Halpern. After some two weeks of illness and another of convalescence, I was now eager for both books and company.

I had especially enjoyed Philip's last visit. He had been very social lately and was full of talk about a number of people whom I knew only from a distance. One of these was Lady Maitland, the wife of a justice of the Bengal High Court and a tireless giver of parties—parties to which Philip was now beginning to be invited. Lady Maitland, it seemed, had recently taken a young Indian under her patronage—a youth named Mirza Ali Khan, who was somehow descended from the Mogul emperors of Delhi. "You should see him," Philip had said scornfully. "The stock of Tamerlane has produced its finest flower. The boy's half-monkey and half-devil, and he and Rosa Maitland giggle together like a couple of schoolgirls. They're inseparable."

"And what does Mr. Justice Maitland think of all this?"

"I doubt if he's even aware of Mirza Ali's existence. The old boy never comes to his wife's parties."

Philip also told me about a new voluntary report he was writing—a report on local reaction to the British Cabinet Mission's visit. I listened patiently to his summary of it.

No mention was made of Diane Cummings, and I decided not to ask.

When Philip had gone, I found myself thinking once more about Dorothy. She had not come back since that first visit at the beginning of my illness. She had not even telephoned to find out how I was. Although I had known when she left my room—and still knew, with the same stony conviction—that the affair was over, that I would never touch her again, I nonetheless was puzzled and, unreasonably, a little hurt by her neglect. Of course I'd behaved to her in a way that even my sickness couldn't excuse, but in the past she'd always been so quick to forgive me. Even now I was sure I could have her back if I wanted; nothing was irrevocable—except my own conviction that I would never touch her again.

There was still the job of telling her about this conviction—or decision, whichever it was—and I didn't look forward to that at all. I wished it had already taken place, preferably during a quarrel, when anger was blazing up on both sides. I hated the thought of hurting her. Maybe it wouldn't be too bad; after what had already happened, she ought to be prepared for anything. And I would let her tear my face in rage if she wanted to. Still, though part of me was hurt by her neglect, I was mainly grateful for every hour that postponed the ordeal.

I heard the doorbell, and moments later Elizabeth Schneider was standing at the door of my bedroom. This was her second visit. "I've got Julia Cobb with me," she said. "She won't come in till I've inspected things. We both mistrust bachelor quarters. Your pajamas look clean enough. Put on a bathrobe and I'll bring her in. I assume you're in the mood for company?"

"Of course," I said, happily shoving *Gallant Are My Sons* aside. "This is a real treat." I was always entertained by Elizabeth's way of beginning things with a rush of words, as if to batter down any obstacles to whatever might follow.

The girl entered, smiling, and held out her hand. "I'm glad you're feeling better. Liz and I were having tea together and I happened to ask about you and here we are."

"I had a dreadful time getting her here," said Elizabeth. "She was sure you'd think I was trying my hand at matchmaking or something."

"That's not fair! After all"—and Julia looked straight at me —"you practically invited me to lunch the last time I saw you. Only you didn't name a date."

"And then I got sick," I said with a laugh. "Anyway, you're both more welcome than you'll ever know."

"There," said Elizabeth. "I told you so." Evidently she had adopted Julia—the fact that the girl was already calling her Liz indicated as much. Elizabeth tended to be very enthusiastic about new people if they were at all her type. She kept her protégés close only until they could fend for themselves; after that, although she remained a good friend, they were definitely on their own. It was predictable enough, in view of Liz's mild snobbery, that Julia, alone of the new arrivals, should be a candidate for adoption.

"Tell me what it's like having dengue," said Julia. "You've had a bad time of it, I hear. You do look pretty thin."

"It's uncomfortable at first. Then mainly depressing because you feel so weak."

"God knows how I hate being sick," Elizabeth broke in passionately. "It's such a miserable waste of time. It's hard enough anyway to keep a good grip on life, and when I'm sick I have the awful feeling I'll never really get my hands on it again. I feel just like a rider who's lost the reins."

The three of us talked on, with Elizabeth doing most of the talking. I had always enjoyed her company. Her eye for people and situations was sharp but on the whole kind, and she was just snobbish enough to be amusing without being boring. I must see more of the Schneiders, I thought—as I did whenever I was with them. They made a good couple, though a typically childless one. Herbert was hard-working, a little dry, taciturn, and at the same time surprisingly tolerant of people who didn't share his energy or ambition; Elizabeth, beneath her rattling, was intelligent as well as smart—and a skillful hostess who would come into her own if Herbert ever got the really good diplomatic post he deserved. The Schneiders were extremely popular in Calcutta, far more so than the Hubbards, whose approach to entertaining was as dutiful and official as churchgoing. I noticed how tired Elizabeth looked. Both she and Herbert had caught amoebic dysentery in Kabul, their last post, and they had been sent directly to Calcutta, without home leave. Herbert's dysentery was now under control, but hers continued to flare up from time to time, making her look sallow and drawn, older than her thirty-eight years.

Elizabeth told us about the new French vice-consul, Frédéric de Croye, whom she had met at the French Consul General's the other night. "He must be at least fifty-five and he's still just a vice-consul. It seems he was demoted—something to do with Vichy during the war. Monsieur Fouquet explained it all to Herbert on the veranda—practically *apologized* for his presence, Herbert said. De Croye's terribly distinguished-looking—a bit like De Gaulle—very tall and high-nosed—and he's terribly sullen and resentful-looking. I don't suppose you can blame him. In some ways. And on top of everything else, the poor man's stuck with a crazy wife. Hungarian, I think. When we were leaving, she clutched my arm with the most painful grip and said something in very bad English—so bad I had to ask her to repeat it. Can you imagine what it was? She said, 'I vant to sank you for beink so beau-ti-full.' Those were her *exact* words —can you *imagine?*"

"You'd better watch out," said Julia, laughing. "She sounds dangerous."

"She is! Just *look* what she did to my poor arm." Elizabeth pushed up the short sleeve of her dress and pointed to a faintly bluish smear on the white flesh above her elbow. "*She* did that —I'm not joking!"

"Serves you right," said Julia, "for being too nice to people you don't like."

"Oh, dear, she's starting to preach at me, John. This girl has the most implacable standards of conduct. She's always rebuking my frivolity. Thinks we do nothing but waste the taxpayers' money on an endless round of parties and gossip."

"That's not fair," Julia protested. "I only said that before I came to Calcutta I never would have dreamed people could spend so much time thinking and talking about parties. That's all."

124

"Don't let any congressman hear you say that," I said. "The Foreign Service has a hard enough time getting Congress to give us a cent for 'representation.' "

"I must say I love parties," said Elizabeth. "At least when I'm feeling well."

"I like parties, too," said Julia. "When I like the people."

I glanced at her. There was nothing severe or implacable about her looks. Her eyes were bright, almost flashing, light-brown and clear. I liked the oval of her face and the way her small chin, after starting to recede, quickly and firmly reasserted itself. Her eyebrows were straight, much darker than her eyes, and there were chestnut flashes in her brown hair. Her mouth was well-formed but very young-looking—the mouth of a school-girl, a promising mouth that would ripen nicely. In her white blouse and madras-print skirt, she was almost too much the clean-limbed schoolgirl—this despite the filled-out breasts and the easy, slow curve of her hips and legs.

Suddenly Elizabeth looked down at the tiny band of diamonds on her wrist. "My God, I'd completely forgotten!" Jumping up and brushing out the wrinkles in her skirt, she explained that she had promised to go to a meeting of the Bengal Home Industries' committee at Mrs. Sinha's.

"Julia doesn't have to go," I said quickly, turning toward her. "Why don't you stay awhile, and then Ralph could drive you home when he gets back."

"Do you really want me to stay? Aren't you tired?"

"Of course he wants you to stay," said Elizabeth.

"I wouldn't ask you if I didn't."

When, with the wave of a white glove, Elizabeth had gone, I said, "Now then, tell me something about yourself. What with my leave and being sick and everything, I haven't had much chance to talk with you."

"What do you want to know?"

"Oh, where you're from, where you went to school, what sort of family you have. Since I don't know the first thing about you, anything at all will be news." Realizing that I had given her a tall order, I tried to make my voice sound encouraging. "Start with your family. If you're at all like me, you'll find that an easy topic."

But she wasn't abashed in the least. "There's nothing very interesting about my family," she said. "Just big." And she told me that besides her parents she had three sisters, all of them older, and a younger brother, now a freshman at Cornell. They had all grown up in Plainfield, New Jersey, and she had gone to the public schools there before going away for college. Her father was a lawyer, who practiced in Newark. He was ten years older than her mother but still very active at seventy; he went fishing in Canada every summer and still played golf with his clients.

"Have you always lived in the same house?" I asked, wondering if she had ever had a childhood uprooting comparable to mine.

"Oh yes. It's a big old brown-shingle house. Mother and Dad moved into it the year I was born. It looks more like a beach cottage than a regular house—have you ever seen those monstrosities on the Jersey shore? Well, that's what it's like. Built around nineteen hundred."

Julia was perfectly relaxed. Except for my questioning, we might have been old friends or even lovers. I liked the way she put herself at ease.

"So you went to school in Plainfield. Was Vassar much of a change for you?"

"Why Vassar?" She raised her dark brows.

"You went there, didn't you?"

"No, I went to a small girls' college called Wells. Did you ever hear of it?"

"I think so. Isn't it somewhere near Cornell? But I could have sworn you said you went to Vassar." Had I dreamed it? Had I sent her off to Vassar to satisfy some obscurely snobbish impulse? "I can't account for it," I said, shaking my head. "In any case, was college—Wells, that is—much of a change for you?"

"In some ways. I liked it fairly well, but it was no great

revolution—no eye-opener—the way college is for some lucky people. All girls, more athletics, maybe better teachers. And then the war started in my sophomore year and we all felt very isolated."

"Look," I said after a pause. "I hope you don't mind being pumped this way. I mean it as a compliment. Most people in Calcutta don't have any past at all as far as I'm concerned. I'm content to take them entirely for what they seem—whether they're good company or not, whether they're helpful or not—that is, if their jobs have any connection with mine. I suppose a foreign colony has to live more in terms of the present than any other group of people. The past is wiped out—it just doesn't exist as far as most of the people I meet are concerned. You'll see what I mean after you've been in Calcutta awhile."

"So you're complimenting me by being interested in my past?" The irony in Julia's voice tapped me softly, like a cat's paw.

"Exactly." I smiled back at her. "Look, how about a drink? I feel like one; it'll be my first in over two weeks."

"You poor boy."

Ghulam brought us each a Tom Collins and some cashew nuts. I was enjoying myself: I liked the girl and I liked playing the part of the old India hand, as I now began to do, telling her at length just how her feelings and attitudes toward Calcutta would change after she had been here a year. "Well," I said finally, "we've talked about the past and the future. How about the present? Are you having a good time in Calcutta? How is your social life?"

Julia laughed suddenly. "I believe you're trying to find out about my luck with the Fishing Fleet."

"Well?" I asked, smiling, and at the same time blushing, for I now realized that my question hadn't been completely disinterested. I *did* want to know whether she was going out with other men, and I was ashamed at my lack of subtlety.

"I'm having a very good time, if that's really what you want to know." Then, after this mild rebuke, which made my blush redden, Julia's eyes became teasing and she said, "Calcutta's a marvelous place for a single girl. Much, *much* better than

Washington. I'm out fishing every single night. I've already hooked and thrown away dozens of the *yummiest* fish."

"All right, I asked for it."

Just then the doorbell rang. I was expecting Ralph, but he would have used his key, not rung. Then came the sound of Dorothy's voice, speaking to Ghulam. A moment later she strode into the bedroom.

"Well," said Dorothy, staring hard at Julia. "*Hello* there."

"You've met before, haven't you?" I asked.

"I don't think so," said Julia and added, before I could introduce her, "My name's Julia Cobb. You're Dorothy Eustace, aren't you?"

"That's me all right. I think maybe I've seen you around." Dorothy remained standing. From my chair she looked unnaturally large, glowing like a sunburned Juno, her tan skin burning against the jade green of her dress.

"Sit down, Dot, and have a drink."

"I hope I'm not interrupting anything."

"Of course you're not. Sit down."

"I wouldn't interrupt anything for the world," Dorothy persisted, with a heavyhandedness that maddened me. I could sense, too, Julia's embarrassment.

"For God's sake, Dot, sit down."

"I just dropped by to see if you were still alive." She took the chair that Elizabeth had occupied and crossed her bare, shining, glossily tanned legs. "I thought you might be just in the mood for a back rub," she added, swinging her red-sandaled right foot in a little arc.

At the intimacy of this remark, Julia stirred uncomfortably in her chair and murmured something about having to leave in a few minutes.

"You don't have to go yet. Finish your drink and have another." I was furious at Dorothy for discomforting the girl.

"For goodness' sake, honey, don't leave just because *I'm* here. *I* haven't any monopoly on John. We're just personal friends—old acquaintances, you might say. I rub his back and sometimes he does as much for me. That's all. I'm sure he finds your company a welcome and stimulating change."

"Shut up, Dorothy!"

Julia got up. "I really do have to go. You're not driving me away," she said, holding out an uncertain hand to Dorothy. "Nice to have seen you."

"Look, Julia, wait until Ralph comes. He can give you a lift home." My God, I thought, she looks a thousand years younger than Dot. She's just a schoolgirl.

"No, I really do have to go. Great Russell Street isn't very far. I can walk or take a ricksha." Julia smiled, at ease again—as if she'd caught my comparison. "It's been lots of fun talking to you. Good-by." She left the room.

CHAPTER XI 🏵 **DOROTHY** laughed. "I didn't know you were collecting mice these days."

"Shut up, Dot. I'm in no mood for this sniping."

"Okay. I'll be good. Now can I have a drink?"

I rang for Ghulam and ordered two gin-and-tonics.

"Well, how are you, anyway?" said Dorothy. "You look pretty bright-eyed and bushy-tailed, if you ask me. Much too healthy for a back rub."

"I haven't asked you to rub my back."

"I expect you've had enough stimulation already for one afternoon. Young miss looks like she'd be real stimulating company. Who is she, anyway?"

"She works at the Consulate. She came by with Liz Schneider and stayed on for a while after Liz left." I had no sooner spoken than I hated myself for this explanation. Dorothy was grinning at me. I've got to do it, I told myself. I can't let her leave without telling her. And I felt my skin go hot and wet at the thought.

Ghulam brought our drinks. My hand was trembling as I took my glass from the tray. The tremor was an inheritance from the dengue; my wish to hide it from Dorothy only made it worse. I set my drink down with a clatter on the table next to my chair.

"You look like you've been getting along without me all right," said Dorothy. "It's probably just as well." She flashed a quick, sharp glance at me, then smiled at the rim of her lifted glass. "Because that's how it's got to be from now on."

She's beat me to it! I thought, half-relieved, half-alarmed. She's going to tell me to go to hell! But I was not prepared for what came next.

"Phippsie wants me to marry him. And I've decided to do it. We're going to get married in Bombay just as soon as I can clear out of this place. I've already resigned from my job."

After I had found my breath, I asked, foolishly, "Is it all settled?"

"Absolutely."

"Then you're out of your mind!" I felt sick with helplessness and rage. Phippsie—the wine-colored Phippsie—thin hair, silver hair, pink scalp shining through, pink freckled scalp. Blurred eyes, blue running into pink . . . "You can't do that! You're just trying to spite both of us. My God, he's thirty years older than you. He's a drunk, fumbling old man. You can't do it."

The raw, challenging face drew back into a scream. "You've no right to say that! No right at all! You're out of my life. You haven't a God damn thing to say about what I do. You're out of it!"

"I do have some say in this, whether you like it or not. You've meant too much to me, we've been too close for me to—"

"Close!" She shut her eyes and laughed, rocking backward and forward in her chair. "Close!" she repeated, gasping, almost sobbing. Now she raised her blazing face, her eyes and teeth flashing with hatred, deadly as a knife. "So you think we've been close. We've never been closer than ten thousand miles. Not even when you've been in my bed. Not even when you've been inside my body. *And you know it."*

"That's ridiculous!"

But the indictment had just begun. For a while I listened silently, listened to what I shrank from as a horrible travesty of my motives and feelings. This was a raving whore, a drunken actress, not a real woman with a real and deep grievance against me. Yet I remained silent, unable to point to any detail and say, You lie—there's not one jot of truth in this.

"My God," she was saying, "how many times have I seen that high-class look of disgust come over your face? That pompous, smug, snobbish, high-class face of yours all twisted and tight with disgust like I was a bad-smelling animal or something you had to hold at arm's length. My God, whatever made me think you looked like a nice guy? That's what I thought the first time I met you—that you were probably a kind of snob but a nice guy all the same. A real gentleman. Nice brown eyes and a pleasant smile. But it didn't take me long to find out. You never really wanted or needed me—you just pretended to. All you wanted was a playmate—a convenience." Dorothy paused, her tanned face pulled taut with fury, her bright lips quivering.

"All you wanted," she said, "was someplace to dump your garbage."

"Shut up!" I yelled, half-rising from my chair.

"I know what you're thinking. I can see it in your face. You think I sound like some old whore. Well, if I do, it's because you've always treated me like one."

Then Dorothy accused me of always having been ashamed of her, of having kept her in a compartment, away from my real friends. This was unfair—here I could really protest. I reminded her how often she had complained that she had nothing in common with the Chaudurys and Martin and Philip, how often she'd said they bored her to death.

For a while she didn't answer. Then, in a subdued tone, she said I'd never given her a real chance to know them. But she didn't press the point.

I was now very tired, weak as a sick child, too weak to try to answer all that she had said. "Do you really hate me as much as all that?" I finally asked.

Dorothy's eyes had burned out, cold and dull. "No," she said, shaking her head, "you aren't that different from all the rest of them. I don't hate you." There was another pause, during which we both stared at the space of flooring between our feet. "No," she repeated, "you're not that different. You may have a little more spit and polish and background, but basically you're just one of a series, and the Lord only knows how sick and tired I am of the whole business. It's been the same old story ever since I was fifteen. Lots of men chasing after me and all of 'em the wrong kind. Some wanting me for this, some for that. None of 'em really wanting me for myself—for *all* of me. But I'd pretend to myself they did. And I'd face hell and high water for them. I reckon I must have had one of the worst reputations in Macon." Dorothy began to smile. "My dad must have threatened he was going to lock me out of the house a hundred times, but I never paid any attention. And you know, the funny thing is some of 'em just wanted somebody fairly cute to wear on their arms when they went to a dance, so people would think he was a hell of a fellow—one of the boys. You'd be surprised how many

132

never even made a pass at me except in public. Of course a lot of 'em just wanted what was between my legs and that was all." Here she gave me a look, but it was unchallenging, unbitter. "Harry Eustace wanted me for that all right, but I swear I think he mainly wanted somebody to fry his bacon and wash his socks and open a quart of beer for him in the evening. It's always been the same in the end."

"Why do you think you've had such bad luck? Why have you always found the wrong kind of man?"

Dorothy shrugged. "Lord knows I'm tired of it."

I saw my opening. "Do you really think that marrying Phippsie is going to break the circuit?"

She didn't flare up at this, as I had expected her to. "You don't know anything about it," she said quietly. "Not one damn thing. What you don't understand is that Phippsie loves me— he really does—and he needs me. The Lord only knows how I need to be needed by someone who loves me. None of the others have ever really needed me."

"I'm sure he needs you. He needs a nurse."

"You've no right to say that!" But Dorothy calmed down almost at once. "Fifty-eight isn't so old. After all, I'm thirty-five."

"You're thirty-two!" I almost shouted.

"No, I'm thirty-five." She faced me steadfastly. "Now that you know that, you'll think I'm a worse whore than ever."

"No," I answered wearily. "I don't care if you're forty-five. He's still much too old for you. He's a worn-out, whisky-soaked old India hand who wants someone who'll look after him. And let him run his paws over her whenever he feels up to it."

"Don't say that! You haven't any right!" Tears had sprung to Dorothy's eyes, but she held her face together, refusing to cry. "He has a lot to offer me. You just don't understand, John, how much it means to be loved and needed and to have a chance to settle down for once in my life. Phippsie's had a good job with Dougald-Fletcher ever since he left his regiment and now he's been shifted to Bombay with a good promotion. He's due for home leave next year and we're going to England to see his daughters. And in case you're wondering, they think it's just fine he's getting married again."

And you'll be cheating on him in six months, I wanted to say, but a fresh welling up of hopelessness and sadness made me hold my tongue. Instead, I asked when she'd decided to take this step.

Dorothy seemed uncertain how to answer or how much to answer. Finally she said, "He's been wanting me to marry him for months. I finally told him I would about ten days ago. But I've been pretty sure of it ever since you went to Benares and dead sure after the last time that I walked out of this room."

And how much of this time have you been sleeping with him? That was the question I wanted to voice, but I lost my nerve: I was afraid of the answer. After a moment I said, "Would you have stopped seeing Phippsie—stopped having anything to do with him—if I'd asked you to?"

A touch of the old bitterness came back into her face, and with it raised eyebrows and a smile. "But you never did. You felt safer with him around. It meant you and I couldn't get too close for comfort—for your comfort, that is."

"We won't argue about this theory of yours, but if I *had* asked you?"

"You haven't any right to ask me that. It's none of your business any more." She stood up.

I let out my breath. "All right," I said, and I stood up, too, and followed her out of the room. "How soon will you be leaving Calcutta?"

"In about a week, I reckon. Soon as I can get away."

"I don't suppose there's any reason for us to see each other again."

"I don't see any point to it."

When we reached the front door of the flat, I expected her to turn, to come to me, to give me a farewell kiss. But she stood with her hand on the knob, not looking at me, her face solemn beneath the suntan and the lipstick. A sharp spasm of pity and love wrenched my chest. I went to her, caught her by the shoulders, and spun her around.

"Now listen, Johnny," she said after we had kissed. "I'm doing the right thing. It's the only smart thing I've ever done in my whole life. Like you said, I'm going to break the circuit of my bad luck. And I don't want you to worry about me."

"Of course I'm going to worry."

"Please don't. And stop looking like you've been the accidental cause of my death or something." Her lips, only inches from my own, parted into the familiar insolent, challenging grin. "I ain't dead yet. So stop acting like I was. All right?"

"All right."

"Take care of yourself," said Dorothy. "And good luck. Sometimes I think you need it even more than I do."

Do I? I wondered, as I returned to my bedroom. I had never really thought of my life in terms of luck. But I was overwhelmed now by the realization that my plans and conscious wishes had almost nothing to do with the course of things. In deciding to break with Dorothy, it was as if I had taken a small step and had then been snatched up and planted many feet ahead and to the side of where I had expected to find myself. This perception compounded my sadness, a terrible sadness which was not depression but which extended beyond Dorothy and myself and reached out like a fine net thrown over the whole world. In such a context, the idea of personal luck, whether good or bad, seemed almost beside the point.

I nearly stifled in my room, and after a little while I put on some clothes and decided, weak and rubber-limbed though I was, to take a walk.

My strength held out better than I had expected, and when I reached Chowringhee, I crossed the street and entered the Maidan, that great expanse of field and park in the very center of Calcutta. Now, in the late afternoon, it was still extremely hot, but the heavy blue-green shade of the banyan trees bordering the path gave at least the illusion of coolness—enough to make walking bearable if done slowly enough. Or so I thought. Actually, I had not gone a hundred yards, sweating and kicking up puffs of dust with each step, before I had to sit down in a kind of saddle made by the coiled roots of one of the old trees. Across the Maidan—now mostly yellowed grass—I could see mounds of cloud, thunderheads, piling up against the intense blue of the sky; in an hour, perhaps, they would reach the setting sun and blacken it. This was the season (as the hot weather began to anticipate the approaching monsoon) when occasional storms broke over the Bengali paddy land, often with violent wind that flung dust in every direction before the hail and rain could wet it down. Just now the upper air was still, broken only by the lines of enormous bats—flying foxes—that always at this hour left the banyan groves and flew toward the south, flapping their wings with the steady deliberation of herons.

I felt deflated, emptied, very sad, but not depressed. I knew what real depression could be, and I knew that I was free of it for the present. I didn't try to account for this assurance, but I was grateful for it—and glad to be out of my room, glad to be sitting in the cradle of roots, breathing in the delicate smell of bark and dust and dry grass, absently crumbling lumps of dust between my fingers. All around me were the aerial roots of the banyan, dropping like ropes from the branches around the central trunk; some of these had already fixed themselves in the ground and would eventually become trunks, too, sending out their own branches and trailing roots. I thought of the smooth, cylindrical stones, sacred to Siva, which I had often seen nestled in the roots of such a tree, and of the childless women who daubed those stones with red paint and sprinkled flowers around them. Poor Dorothy! I remembered the story she told me, after we had first slept together, of her abortion at the age of nineteen. Since then, she had never been able to carry a child beyond the fourth month of pregnancy; she had had a total of five miscarriages during the eight years of her marriage to Harry Eustace. But, so far as any gynecologist could tell, the abortion had not been bungled; there seemed to be no physical reason why she couldn't have a child. My God, I thought, how little our lives have to do with what we want—or think we want! I saw Dorothy now plunging like some distracted mare toward a cliff. All through her life she had been plunging this way and that. What drove her? What drove me? I had a crazy vision of some dark rider—a rider who didn't straddle the back but crouched inside, black and very powerful but unable to see, lashing and spurring the poor beast from within. The poor beast could see well enough to sidestep a few rocks and jump a few ditches but still couldn't avoid the steep drop-off ahead. Broken leg, slow mending, stiffness, another break, writhing, limping, lurching, a new start—with maybe a brief rest now and then, a chance to browse in the meadow before a new start over rough ground, perhaps toward the final cliff . . .

It occurred to me that even when I had been most anxious to preserve the *status quo* with Dorothy, some part of me had already vetoed that project, had already changed my course. Toward a pasture or toward even rougher ground? I didn't know, and the little control I had seemed very weak. Despite all the desire that I had felt for her physically—or thought I felt? —I had not made love to Dorothy since my return from Benares; and it now seemed to me that even if we had gone to bed, I would have found myself impotent. Yet I didn't feel completely helpless or driven. If the rider was inside me, it was then, in some sense, a part of me, perhaps even my ultimate self, not to be separated from its vehicle and its feeble conscious eye. Dogs and riderless horses don't seem driven against themselves; there's no split between themselves and their wills. They never fight their wills—they express them. And they don't destroy themselves. Why should I be less whole than a dog? Why should Dorothy plunge toward a cliff, something an unridden or unpursued horse would never do?

A faint sound—distant shouting or cheering—broke into my awareness. I opened my eyes. Across the level Maidan in the direction of the white-sugar Victoria Memorial, I saw a group of British soldiers playing soccer. Sighing, I pressed my head against the tree trunk and let the warm light filter through my half-closed eyes. In a little while I would have to get up and leave the sheltering tree and walk back through the hot sun and dust toward Chowringhee. And then what? I couldn't really think of the future, which seemed to lie outside the present circumference of shade. Illness had cut back my life, trimming the branches and shoots. I seemed to have no energy and no desire. There would be time enough for the undiminished knot of life inside me to uncoil. I could wait.

I tried to summon a picture of Julia Cobb. She interested me, I liked her, I knew that I would want to see her. After Dorothy, she seemed easy, restful—undriven. It occurred to me that I had never been involved with an easy and uncomplicated girl. I wondered what my chances were with Julia; there didn't seem to be any serious rival as yet. But in my present mood Julia's image was strangely bodiless; it stirred nothing and soon drifted away. One of the effects of the dengue had been to leave me completely without sexual feeling. There hadn't been the slightest stirring, either in body or in fantasy. This blank celibacy of mood didn't bother me; it wouldn't last and for the moment I was rather glad of my freedom.

Ahead of me I saw only a white emptiness, the blank, undemanding world beyond the shade of the banyan. Even the scene with Dorothy had now been bleached of its angry coloring. Only a thin wash of sadness remained.

PART III

CHAPTER XII ❦ "SINCE it's on our way, why don't we stop by Kalighat?" I asked. It was a Sunday—a scorching, humid day with a milky-white glare—and I had suggested to Julia that we drive into the country, toward Diamond Harbour. Just now we were on the Bhowanipore Road, following the route which I regularly took to the Chaudurys'. "You haven't seen Kalighat, have you?"

"No," said Julia. "I don't think I could stand it."

"You really ought to see it." I smiled at Julia, who looked very fresh and uncrumpled in her green cotton dress. Her wind-blown hair was freshly washed and very soft. "It's the holiest place in Calcutta," I insisted. "And it's certainly the most completely Indian."

"I'm sure it is, but I don't want to see it. I can live without watching goats having their heads cut off. I have no desire to watch little boys and old women smear themselves with blood. That's what goes on there, isn't it?" She puckered her mouth slightly as she glanced at me. "Why should you want me to watch goats being beheaded?"

"I'm not being sadistic, if that's what you're implying. Besides, the sacrificing isn't really horrible or even very interesting. Just messy and disorganized. Lots of beggars and wilted flowers and scraps of paper. A bell clangs for no particular reason. Nobody pays much attention when a kid is brought to the block. It's like killing poultry. The only really positive things are the smell and the flies, and even they're much worse around any garbage heap on Chowringhee. The temple itself is fairly small and dull. They won't let you go inside to look at the goddess."

"Then why do you think I ought to see Kalighat?"

"As I said, it's a very holy place. It was there long before Calcutta was founded. And it's very Indian," I repeated, uncertain how to get across my idea of the spot. "Kali's the goddess of destruction, but that's not quite the impression you get at Kalighat. In spite of her black face and the necklace of skulls and all the chopped-off goat heads, you come away with the feeling that she's really the goddess of mess and disorder and loose ends."

But I could see that Julia's reluctance was deep, and after a while I said, "Well, you're safe now. We've passed the turnoff to Kalighat."

"Thank goodness. Little goats are much too nice to have their heads chopped off, even if Kali is the most important goddess there is."

I laughed. "The chopping goes on, whether you care to look at it or not. And I suppose Kali exists whether we choose to worship her or not. My friend Martin Fenwick believes in her."

"Is he serious?"

"Partly. You'll have to meet Martin soon. You'll like him."

"I doubt it."

"You will. He's a thoroughly nice person."

After this, I drove on in near silence, concentrating on the potholes in the road and the children, the chickens, the pye-dogs, and the goats who were likely at any point to scurry in front of the car. Often a bicycle-ricksha would take up nearly the whole road. Calcutta, like other large cities, straggles on far beyond its boundaries. The openness of Tollygunge is deceptive and soon gives way to an ugly congestion of stucco and corrugated metal and bullock carts; then there are paddy fields—real country this time, you think—and again a squalid outcropping of the city. Julia spoke occasionally, but mainly she, too, looked straight ahead, her eyes and nostrils alive to all that the straggling, mean, crowded, no man's land of the suburb thrust in our way.

I was very happy to be with her. After four or five dates together, we had passed beyond the tentative, exploratory phase and now accepted each other's company as a natural part of our lives. Neither of us was in love with the other, and one of the pleasantest aspects of our relationship was that neither felt any pressure to pretend to a larger degree of feeling than actually existed. Still, we had already begun to build up that structure of shared allusions and shared humor and shared gesture in which true lovers can live at their ease. I was acutely aware of her presence, her physical presence, though as yet there had been little intimacy between us; it was not so much that she held me off, but rather that I was content to relax in the bounty of God's time. The promise seemed immense; we moved together gently forward and I felt no need to rush matters. Some of this slowness probably had to do with the sexual quiescence which followed my illness and which, after a month, had not entirely broken down. But more than that, I felt burned out and exhausted by the affair with Dorothy. There was a need to be physically uninvolved for a while, and there was also a trace of fear, a fear that the old pattern would repeat itself, and a great reluctance to start something that might end with the old disappointments and all the flaying and rending of emotion that I had known before.

I had heard nothing from Dorothy except for a brief note thanking me for my wedding present and saying that she and Phippsie were comfortably settled into their duplex apartment on Malabar Hill in Bombay; it was a dully conventional note, in which I could find no trace of Dorothy's voice or style, and its very deadness renewed all my misgivings about the marriage. My own life during these weeks had been very different from anything I had known in Calcutta before. I worked late in the visa office every night, cutting through the tangle left by Mary Buxton, who had taken over during my illness. And in the evenings I read a lot and went to bed early. With a kind of happy ruthlessness I turned down most of the invitations which, despite the hot weather and the slack season, continued to clog my mail. This need to isolate myself stemmed partly from continued physical weakness and partly from a reluctance to meet all of those people who, for half a year, had thought of me and Dorothy as a couple and who now (as I rather conceitedly imagined) would all demand explanations. Ralph had, in fact, reported that the Mitchells and other members of the Jungly Wallah set were asking him how in the world I had ever let an old-timer like Phippsie snatch Dot away from me. I didn't mind their talking, but I didn't want to hear—or to account. I even avoided any private meeting with Philip, whom I knew to be pleased by the break, for Philip would want to finger all the details of the relationship and try to bully me into confessing that the whole thing had been a sorry mistake from beginning to end. I was in no mood to do battle on that issue.

Meanwhile, I was glad to be able to read for a change. Gandhi's autobiography and Nehru's *Toward Freedom* had been lying around the flat for a long time, and yet, having once begun, I charged through each of them in a matter of hours. More slowly I read Ferguson on Indian architecture and Coomaraswamy's *The Dance of Siva* and *History of Indian and Indonesian Art*—each of these borrowed from Martin Fenwick. I even made an attempt at Stella Kramrisch's *The Hindu Temple* but was driven back by the bristling of untranslated Sanskrit on almost every page. One whole Saturday afternoon was spent in the deserted library of the United Services Club, from which I emerged carrying all four volumes of William Hickey's *Memoirs,* together with *Jude the Obscure* (left unfinished at Swarthmore five years before) and Linklater's *Juan in America* (once recommended to me by Ronny Powell as the funniest book he knew). I read haphazardly, letting one book suggest another, and had a very good time.

I continued to see Ramesh and Martin, meeting them once a week for lunch at the Chung-Wah, mainly talking politics. Sometimes Morris Halpern would join us and set about tearing down Ramesh's political castles as fast as the Indian could build them; Morris had acquired a wonderful bludgeon of tough-mindedness from the Stalinist-Trotskyite debates of his undergraduate days at New York University during the Depression.

I was able to take Julia, on our second date, to the Chaudurys' for dinner. She had never been before in an Indian home to eat an Indian meal, and I had enjoyed watching her curiosity and enthusiasm as much as eating my own curry and rice. I was immensely relieved—far more than I could justify to myself—that Ramesh and Sujata seemed to share my good opinion of the girl.

.   .   .

"John, we've simply got to get out and walk for a bit." Julia had lowered the window on her side and was leaning out to look at the little village we had come upon. During the long drive we had only sporadically talked and then rather listlessly. Now, as she pulled her head and shoulders back into the car and turned toward me, I was struck by the difference which even the merest spark of animation brought to her face. "Do you realize," she said, "that this is absolutely the first time I've been out of Calcutta? I *hate* that city!"

We left the car parked in an open space near the village tank and strolled through the main street. Although the full monsoon was not due for probably another week, a number of heavy rains had left the roadway spotted with yellow puddles. The afternoon had freshened a little, lifting the white glare of steam and deepening and cleansing the blue of the sky. We were soon damp with sweat but comfortable enough to keep going and to enjoy what we saw. It was a village of the simplest, oldest, most primitive kind: two lines of mud hovels, baked to a pale yellow by the sun, each with a single opening and a palm-thatch roof. Inside we could see the beaten earth floors with mud fireplaces in the center, braziers, iron pots, clay jugs, straw mats, and an occasional charpoy with a printed cotton cloth thrown over one corner. Everything looked clean: the mud walls, the straw, even the pats of cow dung, each marked with a handprint, drying on the sunny clay. The smells, too, were clean and warm, smells of wetness, dryness, heat, steaming rice, spices, cow dung, damp wood, goats, and smoke. Old women leaned out to watch us, most of them widows with sunken mouths, their dark skin dry as paper, their withered breasts visible beneath their scrappy white saris. Soon a monkey troupe of naked children had surrounded us, grinning, jumping, and some of them holding out their palms for baksheesh. They looked well fed; some of them had protruding stomachs but none of them had the horrible potbelly that goes with the chicken-bone arms and legs of starvation. In the hot cleanness of the day we could see no lice, no filth that seemed filthy, no hunger; nor could we, in the strong sunlight, sniff the taints of malaria, dysentery, or cholera; whatever cripples, lepers, or tub-legged victims of elephantiasis the village possessed, none was stumping along the street.

Julia caught my arm to point out a shaggy black kid staring up at us with bland yellow eyes, vigorously chewing, wiggling its ears, and wagging its tail like a dog. "Isn't he *divine?*" she said, squeezing my arm. "Every inch of him is alive. And so greedy! Look at the way he tosses his head." And a moment later she was laughing at a tiny girl—brown and naked except for an immense silver nose bangle—who was tugging at Julia's skirt and murmuring, "Baksheesh, mem-sahib, baksheesh, mem-sahib, baksheesh, mem-sahib," in a barely audible voice. "She can't be more than two, do you think?" said Julia, searching her purse for an anna. "Three at the most. Give her something, John. I'm out of change." I did as I was told and the other children pushed and jostled to get close, raising their voices, thrusting out their hands. "Gives you a kind of God complex, doesn't it?" said Julia as the children shoved past her to get at my largesse. I handed out what few coppers I had, then turned out my change pocket and spread both empty hands. The children grinned up at me and some good-naturedly continued their pleas for baksheesh but merely from habit, with no real hope in their piping voices.

We stopped to watch the potter slapping clay against his wheel. Then we moved on to stand in front of the smithy, watching the orange sparks fly out. Feeling thirsty, we bought two green coconuts and drank the sweet, tepid, sap-tasting water from holes which the vendor punched through the husks with an awl. Catching Julia's eye as we were emptying the coconuts with heads tilted back, I winked at her out of sheer pleasure and she, winking in return, laughed and almost choked and then had to wipe the sap from her chin with a handkerchief.

We tossed the husks into the heap under the vendor's stand and walked on through the outskirts of the village. We were now following a path that led through a thicket of bamboo and glossy banana palms.

"I have never seen any of this before," said Julia, "and yet everything is completely familiar. The potter is *exactly* the way I knew a village potter would be. Do you know what I mean?"

I nodded, smiling at the fervor in her voice; yet I, too, was almost trembling with a sense of *déjà vu*. The mildness of the village had settled over me like a blessing. Though I had no pastoral illusions about the place, the fact that everything around us could have been set back a thousand years into the past with no recognizable change, this quiet fact sang its own spell, and I was in a mood to listen. "Both of us," I said, "must have lived in a village like this during one of our previous lives."

"Speaking of such things, is this a Hindu or a Muslim village?"

"Hindu."

"How do you tell them apart?"

"That whitewashed building we passed is a temple, not a mosque. But the quickest way to tell is that the little boys in a Hindu village are uncircumcised."

"I'd never have thought of *that*," said Julia with a faint blush.

Our path had now turned into a dirt road, so muddy in places that we had to watch our footing. The thicket gave way to a grove of coconut palms and this brought us to the open paddy fields which stretched into the distance on both sides of the raised roadway. For the first time in months there was water standing in the paddies; after a few weeks of the monsoon these fields would change into shallow lakes, soon to become green with new rice. I took Julia's hand and we strolled along together, subdued by the stupendous monotony of the watery blue sky and the watery plains broken only by far-off marching lines of coconut and toddy palms. Ahead was a single tree, a banyan that seemed to be growing from a mound of rubble—the remains, probably, of a small temple reduced to ruin by the tree itself as it grew from a single seed dropped into a fissure by a passing bird. The tree was now large and shady, with many rooted streamers dangling from its branches. Drawing near, we could see a lot of movement among the leaves and then Julia cried out, "Oh, look! That tree is alive with parakeets." Releasing my hand, she dashed ahead, gracefully side-stepping the ruts and bogs of the road. Hundreds of little parrots, green and bright as jade, with spots of vermilion on their wings, were fluttering, climbing, and screeching in the big tree.

From a distance, I watched Julia slowly walk around the outer circumference of the banyan, her face turned upward, her bare arms and clasped hands behind her back. I saw her disappear behind the main trunk, next to which was a pile of grassed-over brick still high enough to look like a wall. Then I heard a short scream, and Julia darted back into sight and stood holding one of the tree's aerial roots as if tugging on a bell rope.

"Are you all right?" I called, terrified by the thought of a cobra. A few seconds later I was gripping Julia by the arm. "Are you all right?" She nodded, but her face and lips were bloodless.

I followed her gaze to the point where the crumbling wall reached the trunk of the banyan. Not ten feet in front of us a bony man, his body a deathly gray-white and naked except for a scarlet G string, stood with his shoulders against the tree. In one hand he carried a small trident with narrow, wirelike prongs, and in the other a brass bowl. Witch hair—black, matted, filthy—hung in tangles across his shoulders, and his forehead was daubed with patches of red and yellow paint. Across his chest he wore a kind of rosary of amber-colored beads.

"He's a sannyasin, a holy man," I whispered. This apparition had startled me, too, but I immediately recognized what I saw. Letting go Julia's arm, I laid the palms of my hands together in the Hindu greeting and bowed my head. There was no return of this greeting: the chalky body, smeared over with the white ash of cow dung, remained rigid; the bloodshot eyes continued to stare; the red saliva and blackened teeth of a betel-nut chewer showed through the half-open lips.

"Come on, let's go back to the car," I said, catching Julia by the hand as if she were a child. Her face was still blanched with fear. Skirting the snake knot of banyan roots, we made our way back to the road and were soon beyond the shade of the tree and the chattering of the parakeets; once I looked over my shoulder—the sannyasin hadn't moved. Then, noticing that Julia was limping, I glanced down and saw that her right foot was covered with mud to a point well above the ankle. "You've hurt yourself. Let me look."

She bit her lower lip and shook her head. "No," she said after a moment, "it's all right. Maybe—I don't think I twisted it." Her voice was strained and flat. She gazed at her yellow-caked foot with a kind of loathing.

Taking out my handkerchief, I squatted and gently rubbed off her moccasin-like shoe, cleaned it out, and then wiped the sole and toes of her foot. "That'll do for the moment," I said, standing up. "Now see if you can wiggle your ankle." Julia obeyed with a blank face. "Does it hurt much?" She shook her head. "Now try putting some weight on your foot." She did so, grimacing. "That hurts?"

"Not really. I can walk all right."

"I don't think you've actually sprained it—just a slight twist. Now put your arm over my shoulder," I said, "and put most of your weight on your other foot. We'll walk very slowly."

We moved ahead cautiously, both of us watching the ground and the offended foot. "Good," I said, "that's the way." Then I looked up suddenly, appalled to find that she was crying. "Oh, Julie, it really must hurt! Here, maybe I'd better—"

She shook her head, her eyes tight-closed. "No, my foot's all right. I'm sorry, John, I'm so sorry!" And she pressed her face against my chest, clinging and sobbing.

"Is it the sannyasin? He must have given you a bad scare. They're weird-looking all right—but hadn't you seen one before? You sometimes see them in Calcutta." I talked on, not knowing what else to do. I could understand her being startled, shocked, but I wasn't prepared for such a storm of tears.

Julia pulled away. "I know," she said, her face wet and streaked. "I know. I've seen them before. It's just—" Tears again brimmed in her eyes. "Oh, *why* did it have to happen? Everything was so perfect, just perfect." She caught her breath sharply. "You must think I'm the world's biggest fool. I'm sorry."

We walked on for a while, Julia still limping a bit. "Everything had seemed so clean and fresh and alive. And I felt the same way. The children, the goat, the coconut—I was breathing everything in, just drinking it in. And then the parakeets! They were the biggest treat of all, just like a tree full of jewels. . . ." She paused, her mouth faltering. "I was full of happiness and excitement, and I guess I just wasn't prepared. That skinny body, all that awful black hair. Those awful red eyes!"

"He did look pretty wild. He scared me, too."

"There was something awful about him. Everything had been so clean—clean and peaceful. And then he popped up, leaning against that wonderful old tree."

"For a moment I was afraid you'd stepped on a cobra."

"And almost the same instant I saw him, I must have stepped back and my foot sank right into the puddle. It was too much!" Julia gave a little laugh, a strained laugh, and ran her fingers through her hair. "What are those people, anyway? I know they're supposed to be holy, but what *are* they?"

"They're wandering ascetics, sort of yogis. I think this one was a follower of Siva: he was carrying that trident." I paused, realizing that this guidebook account of the sannyasin probably had little to do with Julia's question. "I frankly don't know what they really are. Ramesh Chaudury tells me that lots of them are fakes as well as fakirs. He says many of them are half crazy or hopped up on opium or hashish and that they eat their own filth. They wander around begging food and visiting all the holy places. Ramesh says some of them extort money from people who are afraid of their curses. I really don't know enough about them. I suppose some of them must be real mystics—yogis who've cut themselves off from the world."

"But why should he upset me so? That's the real question."

"He startled you. God knows he looked wild enough. Beyond that, I can't answer you."

I had to leave it at that. I didn't understand the sannyasin or his effect on Julia—or on me. Perhaps opium or insanity was the best explanation for that glow of total uncontrol that made his eyes so disturbing. The man's presence under the tree had been like an eruption of Benares into the flat, placid, rice-paddy world of Bengal—a hideous explosion, scattering mud and filth over the landscape. I shrank from it, and in my own shrinking I could sense some of the fear and disgust that had produced such a violent reaction in Julia. I felt a sudden strengthening of the bond between us. We were alike, we both drew back from the vision of the uncontrolled. Glancing into Julia's still face, on which the tears had now begun to dry, I wanted desperately to take shelter with her against the world's outrage, and I silently cursed the holy man who had spoiled our day.

But in an instant I hated this shrinking of ours. I had to fight down an impulse to abandon her there on the muddy path and to go back, to stare down the red glow, to grapple with those lithe bones until I had wrung the ugly mystery from them.

A cold drop of rain struck my forehead. Above us watery white clouds were beginning to coalesce, their centers darkening. "If your foot will let you walk a little faster," I said, "it might be a good idea. There's going to be a real downpour in about ten minutes."

Julia looked into the sky and nodded. We increased our pace almost to a run.

CHAPTER XIII ❧ DESPITE our hurrying, we both got soaked, and by the next morning Julia had a vicious summer cold. "I'm paying for all the fun I had yesterday," she said when I saw her that evening.

"Maybe the sannyasin put a curse on you."

"Oh, don't bring him up. I'd almost put him out of my mind."

Julia's cold hung on stubbornly, and she had to stay home from the office for a couple of days. Meanwhile, during that week and for the next two, I worked harder than at any time since the end of the Japanese war, nearly a year before, when hundreds of starved Americans had been flown into Calcutta from Japanese prison camps all over Southeast Asia and I had had the job of registering them, cabling for money, and arranging for transportation to the States. Now, each day, the visa office was thronged by hundreds of nervous Indian students, Anglo-Indian brides and fiancées, and American civilians, all of them due to sail for San Francisco aboard an army transport on July third. Since my staff needed help with the extra paper work, I arranged for Julia to be assigned temporarily to the visa office, along with an Indian clerk. Under my supervision she typed out visa forms, fingerprinted the scared and recalcitrant students (who regarded the process as a gross indignity), and stamped passports for returning missionaries. It was fun to look up from my desk and see her there, though we had little time for anything but the demands of the job.

Finally, to my great annoyance, the day of sailing was shifted from July third to July fourth, which meant that I had to give up my holiday. Julia and I sat for ten hours beneath a shed at Garden Reach Jetty while nearly nine hundred civilians—among them Nellie Lawrence, who cried when she saw me—filed past for a final inspection of their papers. There was absolutely no need for this additional red tape, but the commanding officer of the *Marine Wolverine,* who was panicky at the thought of transporting so many aliens, had demanded it before he would consent to take them aboard. I became hoarse trying to make myself heard above the constant screeching of Indian voices and the intermittent but deafening clatter of the monsoon rain on the tin roof. Afterward, drenched with sweat, I went aboard to visit the troop decks, far down in the ship, where all male passengers had been quartered. There I entered a half-lit and already stinking hell of three-tiered bunks into which G.I.'s, oil-drillers from Burma, palsied old missionaries, and some four hundred Indian students had all been promiscuously tumbled. A furious sergeant came up to me and shouted, "Who the hell's responsible for billeting us with these God damn wogs? One of them has vomited all over the passage, for Christ's sake!" I had hardly pushed past him when a group of students, remembering me from the visa office, pressed toward me, wringing their hands in an agony of fear. "Oh, sir, this is outrage!" one of them cried, and instantly a soldier called out, "For Christ's sake make those fucking wogs shut up!" An old missionary, sitting on a bunk in his undershirt, looked at me and shook his head; his throat and arms were like the skin of a boiled chicken. Barely able to breathe, hating my own countrymen, exasperated by the shrill panic of the Indians, I tried hopelessly to reassure the students. At last I emerged and made my way back to Julia through the steam bath of drizzle.

When I told her what I had seen, her eyes flashed and she said, "Americans are nice people. Why do they have to be so awful? It makes me sick."

"They're no worse than anyone else," I said. "Just more ignorant." We drove home together, too tired to say anything else.

The Fourth of July celebrations—the Consul General's annual reception and the American Club party—actually were scheduled for the fifth in order to take advantage of a Friday evening. When I called for Julia that evening, I thought she had never looked better. She was wearing a bright orange-red silk dress, printed with a black design; it was low cut and tightly fitted around her waist, showing off the high roundness of her breasts and the rounded slimness of her arms and body. Her fragrant hair touched my face like a breeze when I kissed her.

My God, she's beautiful, I thought. Why hasn't she married before now? Julia was in high spirits too, eager for the parties ahead of us.

We went first to the Hubbards' reception, where we stayed only as long as we had to. It was very formal and rather dull. They had invited the European consular people, twenty or more officials, both British and Indian, from the Government of Bengal, the top military people, and perhaps fifty of the "nicer" Americans, who could be counted on to act as though they had been used to parties of this sort all their lives. Mrs. Hubbard had called in Philip to help make out her list, and he had been ruthless in his exclusions. Thus none of the Jungly Wallah crowd like the Mitchells were to be seen among the ambassadors of banking, oil, and engineering. Philip was charging about, flushed and elated with his role as aide-de-camp. He barely took note of me and Julia, and at one point, with a maximum of insolence, he broke into a conversation between Morris Halpern and Brigadier Leith-Symington, shutting Morris off in midsentence, and led the astonished soldier off to introduce him to Lady Maitland.

The American Club party was, by contrast, a real brawl. As soon as we entered the hall of the Jodhpur Club, we were sucked into a swirling mob who greeted us with shouts of welcome— as if only our arrival could make the party a success. Julia squeezed my arm, and I grinned at her. "Let's get really drunk," I said, knowing that I was going to have a good time. "We've never been drunk together."

"I'm game. But I warn you, I always get sick first."

I steered her through the crowd toward the bar, where bonded bourbon whisky, furnished by Colonel Kelley of the U.S. Army Graves Registration Unit, was being served, together with Martinis and Manhattans—no gimlets or other "limey" drinks being allowed. I ordered two highballs, and then we started making our rounds. Moving from group to group, I hailed people whom I hardly knew, laughing and joking with them like old friends. Julia laughed, too, keeping a tight grip on my arm. I was already a little high from the two gimlets I had had at the Hubbards', but mainly I was happy now, reveling in the pressure of Julia's hand, proud of the way she looked, delighting in the way she kept turning to look into my face with an easy smile. We advanced into the heart of Dorothy's old crowd—Jock and Suzy Mitchell, Al and Florence Doyle, the Lindsay Krauses—and then moved on to join Ralph McClure and his girl, Marcia Brennaman, whom we'd promised to have dinner with. We were loudly hailed, and Ralph assured us there was plenty of time for another drink or two before dinner, which couldn't begin until the Hubbards arrived. He was clearly swimming through the evening, blissful among shoals of his own kind, and he had put aside that truculence which so often hardened his eyes. Marcia, an Army nurse now attached to the Graves Registration Unit, giggled a lot but less nervously than usual, and the gaze she turned on Ralph showed, for once, more confidence than fear. Filled suddenly with love for them both, I wanted them to get married. I wanted everybody to be married and happy. Like Dorothy, I thought, and I felt my smile sink with a little irony.

The Hubbards finally arrived, Philip accompanying them, and a few minutes later the whole mob surged upstairs, with much yelling and waving, to the ballroom, where card tables had been set up. Seizing a table near the door, we sat down and immediately began firing off the crackers found on our plates and putting on the paper hats which were colored red, white, and blue, as were the streamers dangling from the ceiling. All around us people were blowing horns and whistles at the scared-looking bearers who were trying to pass around the shrimp cocktail. Afterward we ate American ham baked with cloves and served with rings of canned pineapple, corn on the cob, which was greeted with cries of delight and nostalgia but which turned out to be tough, candied sweet potatoes, green peas, and, for dessert, apple pie with vanilla ice cream—the latter provided by the Sunflower Dairy Company, where Jock Mitchell was now working. Except for the shrimp and ice cream, all the food, even the apples for the pie, had come from American merchant ships, which also furnished several enormously drunken skippers and mates for the party. I tore into my food as though I had been condemned to a milk diet for months. Food, alcohol, and sentiment sloshed around inside me. I felt a suffusion of love spread outward beyond Julia and Ralph and Marcia until it enveloped the room. They're good people, I told myself: open, friendly, hospitable, generous, and really democratic— the last in a way that no Englishman could really understand or be. The Californian was indistinguishable from the Kansan, and the Alabaman differed only in his accent. This fused wave of America was not only sweeping across the matchstick fortresses of Boston and Baltimore and Charleston but flinging its spray into the farthest reaches of the world. And my own father, steeped in alcoholic snobbery, brooding in his dark corner of Bolton Street—he dared to turn his back to this great surge!

And then, just as I was reaching the crest of this vision, I was struck by a sadness that filled my eyes with tears. "Look at them!" I said, interrupting Ralph, who was explaining the fraternity system of the University of Nebraska, his alma mater, to Julia and Marcia.

"Look at who?" said Ralph.

"All these people," I said with a sweep of my arm. "My God, they're nothing but children! They're just babies. What are they doing so far from home?"

"What on earth are you talking about?" said Ralph.

"They're all lost," I continued fervently. "They have no idea where they are. All around us—outside these walls—is the strangest and most desperate country in the world, and yet they —we—all sit here and have our birthday party and never doubt for a moment we can find our way back—safely back to the front lawns of America."

"Just what would you have us do?" asked Ralph irritably. "Take all this ham and give it to the beggars out in the street?"

"You're missing the point, Ralph," said Julia, her face shining with the glow of my revelation. "I know *exactly* what John means."

I loved her for this loyalty—was it more than that?—but already I was beginning to be embarrassed by my outburst.

"I don't feel like a child," said Marcia Brennaman. "I think we're all pretty mature. At least at this table."

"I'd still like to know just what John wants us to do about it," persisted Ralph.

"I—I'm not sure." Then the scene in the troop decks of the *Marine Wolverine* came back to me and I said, "We should know more, we should be more aware of other people. Less ignorant. My God, we're the most ignorant people in the world!"

"That's ridiculous." Then Ralph added, "I suppose you're one of the enlightened few?"

But before I could answer, I became aware of a ringing sound —someone was tapping on a glass. Willard Doney, who was the Calcutta representative of Pittsburgh Machine Tools and this year's president of the American Club, was standing at the main banquet table, his face purple-red beneath wavy gray hair. "Quiet, everybody! Quiet, everybody!" he bellowed across the uproar. Finally the room quieted down enough for us to hear him say he was sure everybody was enjoying themselves as much as he was and how great it was that this party had been organized and what a fine spread the ladies of the Entertainment Committee had provided and how great it was to be with such a fine bunch of Americans—"no reflection," he added, "on our esteemed friends the British or for that matter the Mookerjees and Chatterjees and Bannerjees, not to mention all the good baboos, past, present, and future." Waving aside the sputter of laughter, he said that he was sure everybody present esteemed the British and the Indians as much as he did, but it was still a relief to be with such a great bunch of Americans and now he wanted to introduce to them somebody they all knew already, the head of the American community in Calcutta and one of the greatest guys it had ever been his privilege to know: Mr. Alfred Hubbard, the American Consul General.

Leading the applause, Willard Doney took his seat, and the

C.G., looking startled and unhappy, his bald head gleaming like a pink bowl, made a short, jerky speech about the Consulate's readiness to serve the American community in every possible way and concluded by proposing a double toast—to the President of the United States and to the Republic of the Philippines, which had received its independence yesterday, on the Fourth of July.

There was a loud scraping of chairs as everyone stood up. Mrs. Hubbard smiled over the room as graciously as if her husband had, singlehanded, bestowed independence upon the thankful Philippines. Beside her stood Philip, the tallest man at the table, conspicuous in his black English dinner jacket (all the other men were wearing white coats), his face frozen with boredom. I had my own reasons for toasting this Fourth of July. Along with the independence of the Philippines had come other evidence of American bounty to the Orient: India had at last been given an immigration quota of one hundred per year—a fact which, to a microscopic degree, would make my life in the visa office less embarrassing.

In one corner of the card room, Jo-Ann Doney was singing the song which she always sang at this stage of a party—"The Old Apple Tree in the Orchard"; her husband, worn out by his duties as m.c., leaned over a table nearby, his face buried in his folded arms. Overhead, the punkah was churning gray spirals of cigarette smoke. In the center of the room, three card tables had been brought into a jerry-built T, and around them ten of us sprawled, our elbows propped up in little clearings among the evening's rubble: ash trays heaped and spilling over, whisky bottles, match folders, bits of cellophane, glasses empty and half full, glasses with cigarette butts floating in liquid the color of strong tea. It was now past one in the morning, but the general noise was louder and hoarser than ever. Groggy but not sodden with whisky, my eyes stinging with smoke, I reached over and whispered to Julia, "Let's go out and get some air."

She nodded, her face brightening. For the last half hour she had been trying to focus, through sagging eyelids, on the sporadic conversation and hilarity of the table.

But before we could leave, Florence Doyle, known to the Jungly Wallah set as the Atomic Blonde, lurched toward us, put down the empty whisky bottle she was carrying by the neck, and announced that she was sick and tired of her husband. "You can have him," she said, indicating the company at large with a sweep of her white arm. She tried to sit in Jock Mitchell's lap, but Jock, leaning back in a red-eyed, slack-jawed stupor, paid no attention, and Florence kept sliding off his sloping, unco-operative knee. "You can have this son of a bitch, too," she said as she recovered her balance; then, picking up her whisky bottle, she moved away with the careful delicacy of an offended queen while everybody laughed. I got up and held out my hand to Julia.

The lawn of the club was wet from a recent shower. From all sides came the rustle and drip of water, and the air smelled of soaked earth and the damp greenness of new leaves. We walked to the edge of the tank and stood watching the shreds of mist rising from its black surface. We could hear the ragged chorus of "Roll Out the Barrel" from the club.

"I feel better," said Julia, leaning her face against my shoulder.

"You're not enjoying this, are you?" I said a little thickly. But my head, too, was beginning to clear.

"Not at this point. But I had a good time earlier."

Something stirred in a bamboo grove to our left. Probably a mongoose on the prowl. I could almost taste the sweet wetness of the air. "Julie," I said, pulling her closer, "I'm a little drunk, and what I'm about to say will probably sound pretty crazy, but I'm more alive tonight than I've ever been. And I have to talk about it. I guess I've already made a fool of myself—in that outburst just before dinner—but I don't care! There's so much to see and feel in this world. So much to know. It horrifies me how little we can know—or feel—at any one time. And there's not much time and our lives are so small and cramped and shut in. So limited—" I broke off and looked down intently at Julia, whom I could just see in the faint light that came from the club windows across the lawn.

"Julia, what was your impression of me when we first met? What sort of man did you think I was?"

Julia laughed and snuggled her head like a burrowing rabbit against my shirt front. "I thought you were a most attractive drunk. You were at the Jungly Wallah. With Dorothy Eustace. You were very suave-looking but staggering just the same."

"Julie, be serious."

"I am. Then the next time, at the Hubbards', you were nice to me, so naturally I liked you."

"I didn't strike you as being like a smug young banker—like a young banker interviewing someone about a loan?"

"Good Lord, no!"

"That's how someone who knew me pretty well once described me. And a lot of it's true. But it's not the whole truth."

"I wouldn't be here with you now if it were even partly true."

"You don't know me very well," I said, pressing her head against me, feeling the warmth of her cheek through my shirt. "The fact is, Julie, I don't know what I am. I'm like an adolescent all over again—I swing this way and that. The old shell's been cracking up for several months now, and I still don't know what's ahead. I'm tearing off bandages and I'm not even sure I'm well underneath. I feel exposed and vulnerable and at the same time almost hard."

"I felt something hard in you the first time we talked. Something almost ruthless."

"Did you? That's strange, because I almost never feel that way about myself. But I'm less cautious than I used to be. I am changing. I think India has a lot to do with it. Everything's so exaggerated in this damn country. It's like an enormous distorting mirror, and if you let yourself look into it, the old image of yourself and the world around you begins to go crazy. Of course all of this might have happened to me anyway, even if I'd never left Baltimore. Possibly not. How will I ever know?"

I paused, breathing heavily with excitement. Then I kissed

Julia hungrily on the mouth, on her forehead, her cheek, her throat, her mouth again, holding her body very close to mine, aching to share with her everything I felt. "I'm in love with the world," I whispered. "And I want to make love to life—I want to dig all the way to the very heart of it before I'm done. And yet sometimes it scares me to death. This is what you've got to face with me, Julie. I warn you right now that I won't be the same person for two days straight. But I'm on the move, and the main thing is you're with me. That's my great luck— that's what gives me confidence now, even when I'm scared. The fact that I've found you—that you're with me."

For a long time she said nothing but kept her arms around my waist, her head once more lowered, quite heavy now, against my shoulder. Still breathing hard, I raised my eyes, staring into the vague mist over the tank.

"I'm glad you want me to be with you," she said in a voice that startled me by its closeness to tears. "And I'm glad you found me. But John, you mustn't hope for too much from me. Not right away."

"What do you mean, Julie?" I kissed her forehead, which was very hot.

"Things aren't as easy for me as they may look. That's what I mean."

I laughed, reassured. "You're more at ease with life than any girl I've ever known. There's no sense of strain with you, there's no—" Then, suddenly remembering the sannyasin, I broke off. People were never fully at ease, fully simple. It was silly, even insulting, to insist on it.

Julia had drawn away from me. "That's not true. Life isn't that easy for me. I'm changing too, John. I hope I am. I'm trying to, and I've learned to make a good appearance, but sometimes the effort leaves me so exhausted and worn out that I'm just a shadow. And a shadow can't make a very full response."

"But that's ridiculous. You're responsive and natural and spontaneous."

"Sometimes. When I'm not tired or afraid. John, you've

warned me about yourself. Now I have to warn you. In spite of all appearances, in spite of the fact that I'm twenty-four, I'm really a girl and not a woman. And I don't mean that I am a virgin. I mean that I despair of ever being able to think of myself as a woman."

She said this with a dull finality that blew through my heart like a cold wind. I caught her by the shoulders. "Now look here," I said. "You've got to stop talking like that. I can't tell you how much it upsets me. Of course you're a woman. I wouldn't be drawn to you if you weren't."

"It's kind of you to say so, especially since you've been used to the real article in the past." Her laugh was short and joyless, but I felt the tension loosen in her body. "I'll try to think of myself that way. I want to very much—you've no idea how much."

"You mustn't worry about it, Julie." I had already begun, doggedly, to reassemble the fragments of my high hope. I knew that I could reconstruct it, but I also knew that it would never again look simple or unflawed. Every hope in life has to fall, be smashed, and then be put together; it doesn't become real until it's been mended.

There was a shriek of drunken laughter from the club. "Now there's a real woman for you," said Julia. "I'll tell you something if you promise not to laugh at me. I'm in awe of Florence Doyle. I wish I could let myself go the way she does."

But I did laugh, and in a moment Julia was laughing, too. The black storm had broken up. We kissed again, feeling more subdued but very tender, and then we strolled back toward the club, ready now to go home.

CHAPTER XIV ☃ ALTHOUGH it had jolted me, the revelation of Julia's misgivings had the effect of grappling me to her more closely than ever. I felt challenged, not discouraged, by the shattering of my dreams of simplicity. And curiously, her very denial of womanhood had the immediate effect of making her more womanly, less girlish, in her response to me. Just in the way in which she greeted me at the door of her flat two days later, I felt the impact of firm and joyous but troubled strength radiating from her level eyes; her voice seemed richer to me and her body more solidly fleshed beneath her crisp linen dress. We had an easy good time that evening, deepened but unhaunted by our new awareness. From then on I knew that I loved her.

Meanwhile, after the sailing of the *Marine Wolverine,* the visa office slumped back into its old routine. I began to expand my social life again, though on a much quieter scale than before. For some time I had avoided any real intimacy with Philip for fear that he would want to probe the wounds of my relationship with Dorothy. But I had missed his company, and now, secure in my new love, I sought him out in the office and joined him for lunch whenever there was an opportunity. He didn't seem to have noticed my partial withdrawal. The next invitation to dinner at Alipore was phrased no differently from any of the others, and I was delighted not to have to find excuses for declining it.

But on the day before this dinner something happened which made me feel as though a layer of skin had been suddenly peeled from Philip's face. I had had lunch with Morris Halpern, and when we returned to the Consulate, he asked me to drop by his office for a minute. "I thought you might like to see this," he said, holding out an envelope. It was an air-mail letter from New York. This is what I read:

545 W. 111 St., July 6, 1946

DEAR MORRY,

Your letter came as a surprise after such a long time, but still it was good to hear from you. The account of your work in Calcutta gave me a slight twinge of envy, tied down as I am to this narrow strip of rock. India ought to be the perfect spot for someone with your instincts and training.

You are right in thinking that I might have known Philip Sachs at Harvard, though I have to add that our acquaintance was fairly slight. He tended to shy away from the Jewish students—even the rich and social ones of the Warburg-Lehman variety. Still, he tolerated a few of us he regarded as intellectuals. What can I tell you about him? He used to give a lot of parties in his rooms at Eliot House, which were talked about a good deal. I recall hearing about one for which he hired both a harpsichord and a visiting harpsichordist to entertain the few guests who could still squeeze into his living room. He also gave dinner parties at the Ritz in Boston; I was never invited. I can't remember exactly who his special friends were—I have an impression of young men who scorned Shelley and worshiped Pound, but that's all. He also played around with some of the bachelor faculty and a few grad students and used to go to concerts with one of the rich old ladies in Cambridge who liked to have students at her parties. In spite of all this, he had the reputation of being a kind of undergraduate Don Juan. I think he majored in art history, but he must have taken a good deal of classics, too—he had a big part in some play put on by the Latin Club. As I say, our acquaintance was strictly limited. In addition to my Jewishness, I was also interested in the natural sciences, a field he had nothing but scorn for. Still he did have me to his rooms a couple of times (for sherry, yet!). I remember lots of paper-backed French books and some good drawings, too. He was definitely bright and could be very pleasant and funny when he wanted to be. I guess I envied him in certain ways, though I resented him, too.

After your letter came, I called up Marvin Kraft, who had also known Philip and knew his family, too. The father is a Wall Street broker—though not connected with Goldman-Sachs. Philip is an only child. His mother died quite a while ago after a long period of paralysis. She was the daughter of a dress manufacturer who left her about two million bucks, according to Marv. Philip grew up on Central Park West and they had a summer place on the Cape. He went to the Fieldston School in Riverdale before going to Harvard.

That's about all I know. He was 4-F during the war (some kind of heart murmur) and hung around Harvard. I think he started some kind of graduate work before going into the Foreign Service in the fall of '44. Since you were pretty vague as to why you wanted this info, I can't be sure I've given you what you need, but it's the best I can do, anyway.

My own news is nothing special. I'm still producing lots of fine microbe cultures for the Institute and wishing that biochemistry paid better—esp. since our second child, a boy named Norman, was born last winter.

Let's keep in closer touch from now on. When are you due for home leave? Lillian joins me in sending regards to you and Esther.

All the best,
Bob.

I replaced the letter in its envelope, noticing that Bob's surname was Feder, and handed it to Morris. "How did you happen to write to him about Philip?" I asked.

"A little background always makes me feel better about someone who might want to damage me. It helps me handle the situation."

"Do you think Philip might want to damage you? Apart from being rude and that kind of thing?" I remembered the way he had interrupted Morris at the Hubbards' reception.

Morris twisted his mouth into a drooping grin of almost comic sadness. "I can stand almost any amount of snubbing," he said, "but I don't want it to go beyond that. Who knows what Philip has been pouring into Mrs. Hubbard's ear? The man seems to be getting more out of control all the time; who knows what he might do or say? As a Jew, I obviously represent a very special kind of threat to him."

"I suppose you must. It's funny, but I don't feel I've learned anything I didn't already know. And yet most of what your friend says is completely new to me."

"Weren't you taken in by the Anglo-Catholic upbringing and all that?"

"Oh, certainly. But for quite a while I've had the feeling it wouldn't do to question Philip too closely." We looked silently at each other for a moment. Then, puzzled, I said, "How did you guess that your friend Bob knew Philip?"

"When I first knew Philip and learned he'd been at Harvard around thirty-eight, I asked if he remembered Bob. He denied it at once, but in such a way as to make me suspicious later on —after I knew Philip's habits a little better."

I felt very uncomfortable. Philip had been stripped naked again, and his vulnerability scared me, just as it had in the bath at Berhampore. As I got up to return to the visa office, I said, "What are you going to do with this letter? You're not going to show it around, are you?"

"No," said Morris, sliding the envelope into his desk drawer. "No, the letter exists for my own satisfaction. I've let you see it only because we've talked about Philip before—and I know you're his friend. Now that a few things have been cleared up, I can afford not to bother too much about Philip."

When I arrived at Alipore the following evening, I found that Philip had invited the new French vice-consul, Frédéric de Croye, to come by for a cocktail; he couldn't stay for dinner. Philip's manner was somewhat mysterious from the first, and after we had each been served a gin-and-tonic, he led us to the corner of the living room behind the piano and switched on a lamp. Then, from the lower shelf of a bookcase, he lifted a shallow box, about ten inches long, made of dark and heavily carved wood and inlaid with ivory plaques; this he laid carefully on the table under the lamp. M. de Croye and I drew nearer, leaning forward, still holding our drinks. The plaques consisted of shields and crests, deeply cut, framed by twisted columns and scrolls. After fumbling with the clasp for a moment, Philip opened the lid and then drew back with the movement of a jewel merchant revealing his wares. Against a ground of red velvet, threadbare and stained, I saw an ivory crucifix, almost as dark as amber; the gaunt body was twisted, the eyes turned upward, the mouth open; the hair, thorns, beard, and loincloth were made of gold.

"It's rather nice, isn't it?" said Philip, shifting his yellowish eyes quickly from me to the Frenchman.

M. de Croye leaned over still farther. His face, distinguished by its proconsular nose and hairline mustache, was pale and expressionless, almost waxen—the face of a middle-aged man in slow but constant pain. "Portuguese, I should think. Baroque. About 1625?" He spoke in a flat, emptied voice with an almost perfect English accent.

"That would be my guess," said Philip as he shifted the lamp to throw a more direct light on the crucifix. "It's probably from Goa. I like to think that some Portuguese viceroy or Inquisitor brought it out to adorn his meditations."

I ran my forefinger lightly over the agonized figure, which had a slick, greasy feel to it. "Where did you find it, Philip?"

"A dealer got hold of my name somehow—he's from Bangalore—and we settled the whole thing very quickly over a drink at the Great Eastern. All very civilized." He snapped the lid shut, as though our eyes had feasted long enough on the relic. "I must say it cost rather more than I can afford. But then, I never regret my extravagances." After restoring the box to the shelf, Philip led us back across the room and refilled our glasses. "Someday I shall trace the coat of arms and try to identify the original owner. Meanwhile I shall think of myself as his heir."

"The heir of a Portuguese Inquisitor?" I asked.

M. de Croye fixed his sorrowing eyes upon me. "You must not mock those old friars, Mr. Wickham. Along with the missionaries, they nearly accomplished something very great. You must not mock them. Have you ever thought what a Christian Asia would have meant to the world? At one time the heart of Catholic Europe was beating firmly and regularly in Asia, at Goa, and its pulsations reached as far as Japan and the Indies. Only think what a Christian Japan would have meant to the world, or a truly Christian China."

"Do you *really* believe such a thing might have happened?" I asked.

"Certainly. Most assuredly," he said in his dead, meticulous way. "But God, in His inscrutable way, saw fit to replace the followers of St. François Xavier with those *incomparable* missionaries, the Dutch and the English."

"And the French," said Philip delightedly. "You mustn't forget the French."

"My dear Sachs, I have no desire to forget the French. I can only say that by the time they arrived to take up the shield of the Portuguese, it was already too late. The English and the Dutch—those devout missionaries of commerce—had already had their way in Asia. We inhabit the results of their triumph today."

"Are you suggesting that the Portuguese and the French were *not* interested in commerce?" I stared at the older man, trying to detect the spot of humor or irony which I felt must be lurking in that unbelievably dignified face.

"But of course they were. And sufficiently ruthless, too, I have no doubt. But behind it all was the idea—the truly great and saving idea—of Christian Asia. And that idea finally died when Clive triumphed at the field of Plassey and put an end to any role which France might have played in the destiny of India."

"Oh, come now," said Philip jocularly. "You still have Pondicherry, you still have Chandernagore, the tricolor still flies gloriously over the French Empire of India."

Frédéric de Croye ignored him and addressed himself to me. "Quite seriously, I feel this has been a most unfortunate development. You must believe that I am speaking not merely as a Frenchman but as a European. The English have brought nothing to the East except techniques—no saving idea, no yeast of the spirit to leaven the inert mass of their conquest. Indeed, the accidents of their own history have prevented them from doing so, and the result is—well, you see it on all sides." He gestured with a sweep that embraced the room and all of Alipore and the vast reaches of Asia beyond. "It is a well-known fact," he continued, "indeed, it is one of the sublime paradoxes of history, that the Catholic mind has traditionally possessed a unique understanding of the Oriental mind, a real sympathy for it which is beyond the comprehension of our English friends. We have done the Orient the honor of taking it seriously. We do not condescend to it, we do not merely patronize its quaint manners and customs. We smoke its opium. Our colonials have married its women. In short, we pay the Orient the supreme compliment: we desire to convert it."

Not once during this speech had M. de Croye smiled; he had merely lifted his tufted eyebrows higher and higher, deepening the wrinkles of his white forehead. For a Frenchman he had a remarkable control over the trickier sounds in English; only his *r*'s, together with a special deliberateness in his enunciation, gave him away.

"By 'we' do you mean the French Republic?" I asked.

M. de Croye crossed his long legs and brought the tips of his fingers together before answering. "Your question is undoubtedly malicious," he said at last in his carefully sheltered voice, "but I will reply to you in all seriousness. By 'we' I do mean France, the real France, not the stricken, divided, and humiliated country that bears her name. I do not conceal the illness that has afflicted my country. In her weakness she has at times forgot her great mission, she has laid down the shield of Catholic European civilization, she has sought to apply to herself the fashionable quackeries of modernism, the secular and so-called progressive nostrums. Now, in her pitiable delirium, she even dangles before her bosom the dagger of communism."

M. de Croye paused and spread the palms of his hands. "The thought of what my country must endure before God restores to her a new awareness of her inescapable role in Europe and in the world—this thought fills me with the most profound grief. And now," he said, lifting the superb banner of his profile, "I must apologize to you, my dear Sachs, for this outburst. And you must forgive me, Mr. Wickham, for giving way to my emotions on this auspicious meeting between us, a meeting which our friend Sachs was so very kind to arrange." Now standing, Frédéric de Croye shook hands gravely with Philip and me.

"I have kept my poor wife waiting too long already," he said when Philip urged him to stay for another drink.

Philip talked about the Frenchman during most of dinner. Although he didn't insist upon his title, Frédéric de Croye was, Philip said, a vicomte, and his wife, who was a first-rate pianist though mad as a hatter, came from a Magyar family that had crusaded against the Turks for centuries. "He is *très catholique,* as you can see," said Philip. "The last time he was here he talked for three hours straight about the Knights of Malta and the various papal titles and about the organization of the Vatican court. He was stationed at the Vatican during the thirties. Needless to say, I ate it up."

"I'm sure you did," I said, returning Philip's smile.

"De Croye liked you. I could tell."

I said nothing and picked at the last scrap of *boeuf-en-gelée* on my plate.

"I gather you don't reciprocate the feeling?"

After a silence I said, "I can see why his colleagues might be a little unhappy about him."

"They *hate* him," said Philip vehemently. "They hate him, and his poor wife embarrasses them to death. It isn't enough that he's been reduced to a vice-consul. They want to humiliate him every way they can." Then he added, "De Croye's situation moves me very much. I find him a deeply tragic figure."

"Tragic or pathetic?"

"Tragic!"

Gliding in like an aged hawk, Philip's bearer, Ala-uddin, brought us our dessert. I ate in silence, aware of a strong emanation of hostility from my host. Then all at once I thought of Kalighat and said to Philip, "You know, I think the temple at Kalighat would make a fine test to show up the difference between the French and the British approach to things. Especially in their attitude toward the East."

"What on earth are you talking about?"

"Just this: the British, while holding their noses, would tend to leave Kalighat strictly alone; whereas the French—or at least the kind represented by de Croye—would want to remodel it along classical lines—turn it into something like the Madeleine."

"And what would the Americans do?" demanded Philip. "I suppose you would scrub it down with Rinso and then install a conveyor belt for sacrificing the goats. And put Ralph McClure in charge."

"Perhaps," I said, laughing. I could see that Philip's mood had improved.

Back in the living room, we talked for a while about the members of the new Interim Government for India, which had just been announced, and then both fell silent. Philip picked up an old copy of *Art News* and began turning the pages. I stirred my coffee, sipped it, and looked around me. The room had become more enriched, more encrusted, since my last visit. Philip had taken up the landlord's perfectly good rugs and replaced them with two fine Bokharas, designed in arabesques of deep red, mahogany, and black; the red curtains had given way to heavy, wine-colored brocades; and on the mantel stood a new bust, a fat bodhisattva in red sandstone with a topknot and a curiously drooping mustache. I wondered whether the Portuguese crucifix would take its place on the walls along with the Marin water color and the Picasso drawings or whether it would be kept in its box, the relic of a private cult to be shown only to rare and selected guests.

Philip clattered his cup. I turned and found that he was slumped back in his chair, staring at me through narrowed eyes. "John," he said, "why have you been avoiding me?"

"I haven't really, Philip. It's just that since my sickness I've been leading a very quiet life, waiting for my strength to build up. That's all." This was only partly true, and I knew that Philip was not likely to leave it at that.

"So that's why you've turned down three or four invitations from me?"

"Yes. But I'm very glad to be here again. I've missed Alipore a lot."

"I've often wanted you here. I thought I might be of some

help to you after the breakup with Dorothy. It must have been very hard on you."

"Perhaps it wasn't as hard as all that." I didn't want to talk about Dorothy.

"In any case you seem to have pulled through all right on your own." Philip looked away. "John," he began, "I really wanted you here for my sake. Whether you needed me or not, I needed you." And when I didn't answer, he said, "I've been going through hell. Absolute hell. Shall I tell you about it?"

"If you feel like it."

"It had to do with Diane. I expect you know I don't see her any more."

"I'd guessed as much."

"But I'm sure you haven't guessed the reason." Philip now lit one of his Egyptian cigarettes with almost as much deliberation as if it had been a pipe. He had already loosened his tie and unbuttoned the top of his white silk shirt, revealing the tiny enameled cross lying against his matted chest. "John, I had to order her out of this house. I caught her in the act of stealing."

And Philip told me how he had begun to miss various objects —studs, cuff links, a gold penknife. He suspected one of the servants but didn't want to make accusations until he had proof. Then one night, while Diane was asleep, he had found her purse in the bathroom—a purse of Benares brocade which he had given her. Acting on an impulse which he couldn't account for, he had rummaged through the purse and discovered his penknife. Then he went straight into the bedroom, turned on all the lights, shook Diane awake, and demanded an explanation. "I had her red-handed," Philip said, "and all the while she was denying everything and accusing Ala-uddin of having planted the knife, I just stood over her and said nothing. Finally she burst into a flood of tears and confessed."

I shifted uncomfortably in my chair. I hated the story, I didn't want to picture its details, and I was upset by the relish with which Philip told it. Was he lying again?

"I watched her dress," said Philip, "and then rang for Ala-

172

uddin and told him to find mem-sahib a taxi or a ricksha or something. I haven't seen her since."

I shook my head. "Why would she have done something so stupid? Was she in debt or something?"

"Apparently. John, I can't possibly tell you how much the whole episode revolted me. I'd been excessively generous with her. I loathe being taken advantage of, I simply can't stand it. It's the common failing of a rich man, I suppose." Then, in an altered voice, he said, "Do you think I was too harsh with her?"

I shrugged and avoided a direct answer. "When did all this happen?"

"Weeks and weeks ago. While you were ill, I believe. It shows how out of touch we've been."

After a while Philip got up to mix us each a highball. He did not sit down again but moved restlessly about the room before coming to a halt in front of the fireplace. There he stood, one arm resting on the mantel piece, the plump bodhisattva peering over his shoulder like an owl. Philip's Roman face scowled darkly at me across the room and he said, "I can't tell you how upset I was by the whole sordid business. It plunged me into the blackest kind of depression. You were the one person who could have helped me, John, and you were much too absorbed in your own affairs. I dislike saying it, but you let me down rather dreadfully."

"I'm sorry. I didn't realize you were going through a time of troubles."

"It's not really your fault. You weren't aware how desperately lonely I was—and am. Besides, I shouldn't have expected too much from you in the first place. I ought to be hardened by now to the idea that every human relationship is finally disappointing—especially those on which one builds the most. My expectations always outrun the reality, and even the possibilities, in such a relationship."

Philip's tone angered me. "You're being very unjust," I said.

"Am I?" In a little while he said, "You know, John, I really think I find the greatest satisfaction in those friendships that are limited to start with—the ones that remain completely on the surface and never sink into deep water. Take my friendship with Martha Hubbard. We're a couple of old buddies. We gossip over the telephone almost every day and we write each other little notes. I flatter her and she knows it and loves it. She consults me about dinner parties and things and I make myself very useful to her. We're very affectionate and easy together—rather like Disraeli and Queen Victoria. Or take Lady Maitland. She's a fat, nasty piece of business beneath that thick paste of gentility, but she gives very amusing parties, and we get along beautifully, with no illusions whatever. I try to explain modern art to her and she encourages me to make wicked remarks to her little boy friend, Mirza Ali. I'm genuinely fond of her. But then, I don't expect real loyalty or understanding from her. She *can't* let me down or disappoint me."

"Did you expect real loyalty or understanding from Diane?"

"I suppose not," he said at last. "But she was terribly important to me in other ways. I've felt utterly deprived ever since. I haven't even tried to replace her."

Philip returned to his chair. "So much for my human relationships, such as they are. I have almost reached the point where I dread a new friendship—a real, below-the-surface friendship. Does that surprise you?"

Philip's massive and sorrowful countenance was brought to bear, and I felt myself shrink beneath its demand. "In a way," I said. "Though you've just finished accounting for it."

"I think Frédéric de Croye is going to become such a friend, which is one reason I wanted you to meet him and like him. And I rather dread it. I long for it and I dread it. Do you understand?"

I nodded slowly.

"I'm feeling very sorry for myself tonight, John. Everything human seems to be failing me. I suppose that's why I cling so desperately to the nonhuman things about me—the things I buy—objects made by humans but not quite human in their constancy. And in their solace. It's inconceivable that my Portuguese crucifix will ever disappoint me. Or that superb

Gandhara head," he added with a glance toward the mantel. "They're like points of steady flame. I keep adding more and more points of flame to keep out the darkness. Do you remember the end of *The Wasteland?* There's a line that goes 'These fragments I have shored against my ruins.' That's the way I feel about these objects. They're shored against my ruin."

Tears had come into Philip's eyes, and I retreated from them in a sweat of panic and distaste. But beneath all the maudlin and whipped-up emotion, I could make out a real cry of pain: Philip was in real need, and there was nothing I could do for him. In a white brillance of insight, I realized that the kind of friendship I could offer Philip was not enough; if, at this moment, I were to stretch out my hand in sympathy, he would try to seize the gesture in such a way as to pull me violently off base—he couldn't possibly return the grip and then let go. Thus, marking time but feeling compelled to say something, I picked up the word "darkness." "You know, Philip," I said lightly, "you're just the opposite of Martin Fenwick. You want to keep out the darkness. He wants to embrace it."

"It looks to me as though that's just what he's about to do, quite literally." And for the first time the settled gloom of Philip's expression began to break up. But then he blurted out, "Oh, John, it's meant so much to have you here tonight. You must never desert me again."

"I'm glad to be here again." Oppressed, weighted down, vaguely threatened by Philip's appeal, I stood up to relieve my feelings. "But I have to go now. I'm still trying to get to bed at a reasonable hour."

Philip also stood up. He was now smiling at what he was about to say. "John, I have to confess something. In the past, when you used to leave, I always felt depressed. I had the fixed idea that you were always impatient to get away, to hurry off to someone I disliked—someone I felt to be unworthy of you. It's very selfish of me, but I'm delighted Dorothy's no longer here for you to go to."

I laughed. "You never did Dorothy justice. But we won't argue about that."

"You're not really serious about Julia Cobb, are you?"

My face must have shown my fury, for in an instant he said, "I'm sorry. I seem to have touched a nerve." Then he added in a dull voice, "I only wish you'd find someone who does you credit."

"Let me be the judge of that." I turned away from him sharply.

"I'm sorry. I won't mention it again. Good night, John."

CHAPTER XV   ✿   O N E result of my evening with Philip was that he promptly invited Julia to have lunch with him at Alipore—just the two of them. He was very nice to her, Julia told me—much pleasanter than he had ever been before. This was the beginning of a whole series of courtesies to Julia. From now on, I was never invited to Alipore without her, and the invitations—for drinks or dinner—came two or three times a week. We didn't always accept them, but when we did, Philip tended to single out Julia—no matter who else was present—as the special object of his favor, drawing her into the conversation, encouraging her to shine. All this was done with great subtlety and charm, and Julia flowered under the steady warmth of his attention. I was suspicious at first, but within a week or two Philip convinced me that his liking for the girl had become real enough. In any case, I decided not to interfere with the ripening of a friendship which no longer struck me as curious. I enjoyed Alipore, and it was convenient to be able to share it with Julia as I had never been able to do with Dorothy.

Meanwhile I was with Julia every day. Although she didn't stay on in the visa office after the sailing of the *Marine Wolverine,* I often went to the Great Russell Street flat for lunch with her and her roommates, Ellie Myers and Mary Haakinson; even when I planned to be with Julia later in the evening, I would drive her home from the office and stop off for tea or a drink. I persuaded her to take Hindustani lessons with me, so that we spent two hours together each week with our munshi, a wizened old Muslim named Habib Khan, who came to Julia's flat at five-thirty. He was not a very good teacher, but he was full of political gossip, and I liked to pump him about events like the current telephone strike or the Muslim League's new policy of "Direct Action" and the possibility of civil war. Julia developed a strong attachment for the munshi; afraid to hurt his feelings, she studied her assignments and vocabularies so conscientiously that she soon outsripped me and won elaborate praise from the old man, who was astonished to find such ability in a mere woman.

We enjoyed doing things together, and by the end of July she was able to say what her look and touch and voice had already told me: that she loved me. I now discovered for myself that loving someone was rather different from being in the state which I labeled "in love." I loved Julia, very tenderly and physically, but I couldn't deceive myself that I was in the classic state of romantic infatuation. This worried me at first, but after a while I didn't care: what existed was richer and far more pervasive than anything I'd ever known before. If the other came, fine; if not, what was already here was more than enough. Julia, on the other hand, was "in love." She became enslaved to the minutest fluctuations of my mood; any sign of detachment or withdrawal or any flicker of irritation on my part could cause her a sleepless night. The most elementary kindness or thoughtfulness flushed her with pleasure. The sense of my power over her scared me a little, and made me very careful not to abuse it. As our intimacy increased, Julia began to worry more about her unwillingness to let me sleep with her. "If only I felt moral or religious or virginal about it, it would be so much easier," she once said. "You'll just have to be patient with me for a while. I'm not ready for you yet."

I could be patient. Each meeting brought her closer to me. I could afford to wait. I knew that she had had a first, brief affair shortly before she came out to Calcutta, and I gathered that it had been, for some reason, very painful; neither of us wanted to talk about it. There was a ban, too, on discussing marriage. Julia had forestalled any proposal by saying, not long after the American Club party, that she would need a long period of loving a man without commitment—a chance to test herself very deeply—before she would ever have the confidence to marry. This need struck me at the time as wrongheaded, but here, too, I could afford to wait. I had never before found it so easy, so rewarding, to live in the present. Besides, I wasn't yet ready to commit myself.

One Friday evening near the first of August, we had dinner with the Halperns and then came back to Julia's flat. We had the place to ourselves—the roommates had gone to bed—and

I stretched myself out full length on the sofa, my collar and tie loosened, my head resting in Julia's lap. She was reminiscing about her life at college and at the same time stroking my hair and occasionally tugging at my ears. I felt lulled, comfortable, drowsily excited by the smell of her body which reached me through the laundered fragrance of her cotton skirt and the mildewed staleness of the sofa cushions.

"At Wells," she was saying, "I was stamped as a typical 'girl's girl.' I had almost no dates. Wells is isolated enough as it is, and with the war on, there were almost no men around except for those in the midshipman program at Cornell, and I never got to meet any of them. I found myself belonging to a group of what the British call 'splendid gels'—all of them first-rate hockey players, members of the student council, that kind of thing. I think of them as being always sunburned, clear-eyed, and honorable. And with a good sense of humor—that is, they were always telling funny stories in which they were the butt of the joke. *Terrible* things were always happening to them, like missing the last bus back to Aurora or discovering at the last minute that they had packed saddle shoes instead of high heels when they arrived for an out-of-town wedding."

"I know the type. But you certainly don't fit."

"Oh, but I did. Don't underestimate the need for protective coloring. I blended in perfectly—on the outside at least. We seldom talked about men, and when we did, it was chiefly about brothers and fathers. It was the style to be devoted to your brother or father and at the same time to laugh—very affectionately of course—at what absurd creatures they were. None of my friends had many dates, and when they did have one, the boy was usually someone they'd played tennis with the summer before or gone riding with in the Adirondacks. In any case, he was always a wonderful sport with a fine sense of humor and he could usually be counted on to be content with a brisk, sporting good-night kiss."

I looked up into her face, laughing. Julia's eyes were shining, almost mischievous, and a lock of brown hair had fallen over her forehead as she tilted her head to one side. "My God," I said, watching the soft rise and fall of her breast, "I've never seen anyone who looked less like a girl's girl."

She grinned at me. "But that's what I was. And that's what I was brought up to be." More pensive now, she said, "My parents are fine people—I love them very much—but they were too old to have a daughter as young as I. My father was very strict with me. He nearly had a fit the first time I put on lipstick for a dance—and I must have been nearly seventeen at the time. Mother was more easygoing, but she always backed him up. For some reason, Father couldn't stand to see me grow up."

"Did you go out much with boys in those days?"

Julia shook her head. "I wanted to. But . . ." She paused, her fingers resting lightly on my scalp. "When I was about fifteen I developed some kind of rash or eczema on my arms. It wasn't very noticeable, but it made me terribly self-conscious. I acted as though I'd been disfigured for life. I'd make a date and then at the last minute I'd think I looked too horrible and I'd find an excuse to break it. Then I'd cry for hours in my room. Oh, John, I really was a mess in those days! I've come a long way, believe it or not."

"I believe it," I said quietly, unable to imagine *this* girl sobbing in her room.

Julia smiled. "The eczema went away during my last year in high school, but I didn't have a really serious beau until my last year at Wells."

"I don't want to hear about him. Tell me some more about life at Wells."

"All right. I'll tell you about Miss Nottingham, our hockey coach. She was an Englishwoman, and she used to go all up and down the East Coast arranging tournaments and hockey conferences. Everybody adored her, called her The Nott. Before the war she used to take a few of her favorites on bicycle tours through England. To be asked to go was the highest honor that could happen to you—it showed you'd really measured up."

"What did The Nott look like?"

"She had a face the color of rare beef and bright blue eyes—

real china blue—and corn-colored hair, very straight, which was beginning to go a little gray. And she had the best sense of humor in the whole world."

"I'll bet she did," I said, lazily raising my arm to touch the softness of Julia's cheek. She leaned over to kiss me and then I shifted my position and we made ourselves comfortable on the sofa.

That night I went home balked by the sudden wrenching with which Julia had cut short the flow of our pleasure, but still jubilant, hardly daring to believe the great forward leap in our intimacy. For a few moments, before the fearful turning away, I had actually held her warm, naked, and slightly trembling body in my arms. I went to bed as edgy and restless as a chained dog, knowing that I would lie awake for long hours, my hands still remembering the contours of her body, its smell still clinging to my fingers. But almost at once I fell into a happy and compensating sleep.

On the next day, when I called for her to go to Martin and Anila's wedding reception, I found Julia dull-eyed and listless. Having looked forward to the sharing of my quiet jubilance, I was hurt by the flatness of her greeting. I pretended not to notice, and in a few minutes her face brightened and her mouth became less drawn.

I had hardly started the car when a sudden downpour rattled against the roof, so blinding that I could barely see ten feet ahead. I inched my way to Chowringhee, where the rain, instead of slackening in a few minutes as I expected, beat down in such a torrent that I had to stop the car. The merest crack in the window let in a flood of water, and the air inside was heavy as a wet sheet. A rash of prickly heat began to tingle along my chest and back. Beyond the streaming glass I could just make out three ricksha wallahs huddled under their tipped-up rickshas. Conscious of the sweat tickling down my arm, I said, "I doubt if even those ricksha wallahs are much wetter than we are."

"That 'not much' makes all the difference," said Julia sharply. And in a minute she added, "You know, John, you're the last person I'd expect to make such a remark."

I stared at her with astonishment. "What do you mean?"

"I mean that you sounded callous and indifferent. Full of that awful indifference people get after they've been in this country awhile. I'd thought you were different—much more sympathetic and aware of things. It scares me to hear you make such a remark."

"I don't think I was being callous," I said as mildly as I could. This outburst stunned me; it was our first real clash, and I couldn't imagine how my innocent and offhand comment had produced it.

"Yes you were. I catch the same thing in myself. People out here—the white people, that is—get so that their imaginations dry up. They can't imagine what another person—somebody completely different—is feeling. The voices they use toward their servants get louder and harsher. They start yelling at beggars in the road who hold up traffic."

"Are you accusing me of all this?"

Julia looked away, her face slightly petulant, and did not answer my question.

Nettled by this attack, I was now determined to batter down her charge. "Can you imagine what it's like to be a ricksha wallah in a monsoon downpour?" I demanded.

"I can! I can imagine what it's like to be wet and miserable and eaten up with envy. I can put myself in their place."

"But can you imagine what it would be like if you'd never known anything else? If you had no basis for comparison, no bright patches to lay against the dark. Can you imagine what it's like never even to think that life could be different from the way it is?"

"No," she said slowly, "I suppose not. But what makes you so sure they never think things might be different or better?"

I wasn't so sure. Shifting my ground, I said firmly, "Look, Julie, on any day of the week I can walk from Harrington Street to the Consulate and on my way see things so horrible that they'd turn my stomach if I saw them in Baltimore or New York or Plainfield. But I can't be sick every time I walk to work. I still don't enjoy seeing running sores and deformities and children who've been kept in baskets until their spines are curved like a snail shell and then put out to beg; but I don't retch, and I suppose that means my imagination *has* dried up to some extent. Well, I'll admit it. I've had to become callous just in order to survive and function as a human being in this incredible city. But that doesn't mean I've become indifferent."

"It's a hateful city!" Julia cried. "And I hate myself for becoming used to its hatefulness."

I let out my breath. Julia's attack, clearly, had come to an end with this turning of the fire upon herself. The rain, too, was letting up. I started the car and we moved slowly down Chowringhee just as the ricksha wallahs were beginning to leave their shelters.

Martin and Anila had been married privately early that afternoon by an Anglo-Indian justice of the peace at his Dhurrumtolla Street home. Their reception was held at the Calcutta Club, which was a replica, for exclusively Indian membership, of the Bengal Club and the United Services Club. Its wide lounges were now crowded as a theatre lobby with several hundred guests, European and Indian, whom old Mohan Chatterjee had summoned to his daughter's wedding. I steered Julia through the main lounge toward the receiving line. She was quiet and rather pensive, but her expression continued to brighten as she recognized people she knew. "But I don't see Philip anywhere," she complained.

"Hallo, you darlings. How lovely to see you here," said Anila when we reached the wedding party. Draped in a raspberry-colored sari with wide bands of gold brocade, her eyelids blackened with kohl, her dark-ivory arms heavy with gold-filigree bracelets, her throat glittering with seed pearls and rubies, Anila looked more than ever like Hollywood's dream of an Eastern beauty. Next to her stood Mr. Chatterjee, the Brahman landowner and speculator, stoutly jovial, pumping hands like a Rotarian, and Martin, gaunt in his white linen suit—two low-comedy actors flanking the radiant star. Anila's three younger

183

sisters also stood in line; they were shy girls with braids and downcast smiles, looking like masquerading children in their overelaborate saris. Their mother, I assumed, was dead or divorced.

Martin shook hands with the embarrassed affability of any English bridegroom. "Hullo, John. Hullo, Julia. Ask the head bearer for whisky if you can't stand the rum punch. I suspect it's much too sweet for hardened American tastes." Martin's eyes were haggard and glittering—the eyes of a desert prophet.

We wandered into the dining room, where long tables were heaped with mounds of sandwiches, curry puffs, kabobs, Indian sweetmeats, and Viennese pastries from Trinkler's. At the bar were pitchers of lemonade, bottles of soft drinks, red and yellow and chemical green, and, for those who wanted alcohol, the punch Martin had warned us against. It was indeed very bad— sweet and rosy with grenadine—but it seemed easier to drink it than to ask the harassed bearer for whisky. Clustered near the bar was the group which Philip always referred to as the Good Mixers, each couple consisting of an English husband and an Indian (usually high-caste) wife.

"Old Mohan has st-st-staged a real show, hasn't he?" said Harold Porter as we joined them. With his beard and snub nose, he looked like a picture I had once seen of D. H. Lawrence. "Exactly the kind of d-d-display one would expect from an Indian businessman of his p-p-particular sort. M-m-must say I rather enjoy the openness of his vulgarity."

Mira Porter giggled. "You rather enjoy eating and drinking everything in sight, vulgar or not, don't you, dolling?"

Afterward, while Julia talked with Mira Porter and Khuku Bloodworth, I asked Harold whether he thought there would be trouble on Direct Action Day, which the Muslim League had scheduled for August 16, just two weeks in the future. But Harold, though a communist, was much too excited by the wedding to talk politics. He wanted to speculate about how big an allowance Mohan Chatterjee would give to Anila and whether he was as pleased about the marriage as he pretended to be. Soon the other Good Mixers had drawn close and were making their own contributions of gossip and guesswork. Charles Bloodworth, who, like Harold, was a schoolmaster, had heard that Martin planned to resign from the Indian Civil Service; this rumor I could confidently deny. Then Usha McViddy said she'd heard that Martin wanted to have their children raised as Catholics, to give them a sense of security, but that Anila was opposed. I was about to deny this, too, when her husband, Duncan, who worked for the *Statesman*, said she was talking like a perfect fool. Finally, Harold Porter, after glancing around to see that no outsiders were listening, announced, in a loud, stuttering whisper, the report which had reached him through a cousin of the Chatterjees: the only reason old Mohan had consented to his daughter's marrying a European was that she had some kind of "g-g-g-g-g-gynecologic m-m-m-m-m-malformation" and couldn't have children at all.

At this point, Julia, who had been listening in smiling silence, caught my eye. As soon as we were able to break away we went off to search for the Chaudurys. They spotted us first and came toward us—Ramesh waving both arms and Sujata, now eight months pregnant, walking behind him like a deep-breasted pigeon. "We must go find a chair for Sujata," said Ramesh. "I've already suggested to her that she might add to the general hubbub by giving birth. Don't you think that's an excellent suggestion?"

"That would certainly put Anila's nose out of joint," said Julia.

"And who would want to do *that* to such a lovely nose?" said Sujata, who had just sat down in a wicker chair. She folded her plump hands, the color of caramel, over her belly, which ballooned upward beneath her purple sari.

Ramesh's long stallion face was suddenly convulsed with pleasure. "Here comes our dear Philip!" he cried. "Welcome, welcome! Now we are complete. Now we are a little enclave of good folk in this mad and terrible world. Let it dissolve! Who cares?"

But Philip was not alone. With him came an elegant young Indian, looking no more than eighteen, dressed in a long black achkan, which reached below his knees, white jodhpurs, and slippers with turned-up toes. "I'm very proud of myself," said Philip as he performed the introductions. "I persuaded Mirza Ali to crash the party."

The Indian's hand was boneless as wax in my grip. He stood swaying like a mantis, his head too small for his long body. "I adore crashing parties, but I so seldom have the courage," he said with a perfect Oxford accent. "Anila should have invited me anyway, just for old time's sake. Her mummy was my mummy's favorite chum at school." His voice was light and insinuating, the kind of voice that underlines even the most direct statement with hidden laughter.

"You look very chic and fetching this afternoon," said Philip as he turned to Julia.

"And you look full of the devil," said Julia, beaming at him with the affection of an old friend.

There was a sound of shouting and clapping near the doorway. Martin and Anila had left the receiving line and were making their rounds among the guests.

"Isn't she lovely?" said Sujata as they came into view.

"Quite," said Philip. "But she shouldn't dress herself up like a Christmas tree."

Mirza Ali Khan touched Philip's sleeve. "Don't you think," he said, "that this might be the *tactful* moment for you and me to sample the goodies in the dining room? Then we can rejoin these delightful friends of yours once the goddess and her poor mortal have passed this way."

"Coward, coward!" said Philip, laughing. He caught my eye, as pleased with himself as if he had brought a golden phoenix to the party.

"Just who is this Mirza Ali Khan?" asked Ramesh when they had gone.

"He's the last of the Moguls," I said. "The descendant of Tamerlane. Philip discovered him at Lady Maitland's."

"I think he's awful," said Julia. "He's like a precocious little boy. I can't see why Philip finds him so amusing."

The bridal party came toward us. "Oh, here you are, you darlings," cried Anila, who was drawing Martin along by the hand. She smiled at us and then back at him, as though she, too, were leading a phoenix.

Martin was now more pale than yellow, but he still managed a kind of strained affability. When I asked him how he had spent the morning, he replied, "I spent it in literary endeavor. I was trying to compose the most brilliant possible letters of resignation from the Bengal Club and the Saturday Club."

Somewhat later the question of the wedding trip came up. "I can take only a week now," said Martin, "which we'll spend in Darjeeling. Then in January we'll go to England for six months' leave."

"Yes," said Anila. "He's going to take me to visit his mother. She now lives in Newcastle." She paused, looking adoringly at Martin. Then, when she was sure we were all listening, she said, "I warned Martin that he should think twice before carrying coals to Newcastle."

There was a round of nervous laughter. Martin grimaced and then tried to smile. "Oh, dear!" cried Anila. "I'm afraid I've said something rather wicked. Darling, you must forgive me."

"You're upset, aren't you?" said Julia as we got into the damp car.

I sat with my hands on the wheel, making no effort to start the motor. "The whole thing saddens me," I said. "It really saddens me very much."

"I think Martin is very much in love with Anila. Maybe it'll work out."

I nodded. "Maybe it will. But you know, the thing that worries me is that he doesn't seem to take her seriously. He treats her like a beautiful, willful, clever, difficult child. I'm sure he loves her, but I'm also sure he isn't blinded by passion. He must know that she's affected and vain and selfish."

"Anila's *so* beautiful. She's really breath-taking. Maybe she's nicer than we think."

"A mixed marriage is so difficult to start with. And yet—"

"And yet what?"

I hesitated. "For some people it must be the easiest kind of marriage. Maybe the only kind possible."

"I don't think I follow you. I think a marriage like that would take a lot of courage. Much more courage than I have."

I turned toward Julia, whose face was as still and serious as a praying child's. "I'm not sure I'm making much sense."

A little later I said, "I found myself hating the Porters and the Bloodworths and the others. They're so God damn pleased. Martin may have been a friend of theirs before; *now* he's one of them. He's an Englishman with an Indian wife and all the difficulties and disabilities that fact implies. Now he's a member of their half-world. Any child he fathers will be an Anglo-Indian and it's no joke to bring an Anglo-Indian child into the world. In India such a child will always be a half-caste and an outcast, too—rejected from both sides. I suppose it won't be so bad if they live in England—but bad enough, even there. These people—the Porters and the others—have had to face the problem, and most of 'em have ducked it by not having children. Now they're waiting around to see what Martin will do."

"I think you're being unfair to them."

"Perhaps. In some ways, you know, they're the most interesting group in Calcutta, and in some ways I admire them a lot, but I hate that ingrown, gossipy, spiteful quality a lot of them have. They're almost like a homosexual clique in that way. And they're so gleeful when someone else is forced to join their clique. To get a good man like Martin is enough to make Harold Porter rub his hands with glee for months to come." I had really worked myself up now, and I could hear the growing insistence of my own voice. "Even Martin's beginning to play the expected role," I continued. "Did you notice all this business about composing his letter to the Bengal Club and the Saturday Club?"

"But he *had* to resign, didn't he? It seems to me that's the main fact to keep in mind."

"Of course. It's just that he made such a point of telling us. It made me feel very sad, that's all."

Julia reached out her hand to mine and said, "Poor John, it really *has* upset you. I'm sorry, darling."

The word "darling" touched my ear like a kiss.

CHAPTER XVI ❧ ON the evening before Direct Action Day, Julia and I went out to Kalighat for dinner with the Chaudurys. There we found a Muslim journalist named Syed Huq, who had just arrived from Lahore to cover Direct Action Day for his paper. He was an old university friend of Ramesh's and was planning to stay with the Chaudurys over the weekend. We also met an American couple named Evans. They were Quakers, associated with the American Friends Service Unit on Wood Street. I had seen Evans briefly in the visa office, where he had come to have his passport renewed, but had paid little attention, dismissing him quickly as merely another missionary. I knew of course that the Quakers did some "good work" and were much more respectable than the Seventh-day Adventists and the various pentecostal sects, but I so resented the presumptuous notion of "Christianizing" India that I had never bothered to find out just what the Unit was trying to accomplish. I was surprised to meet the Evanses in Kalighat, but not nearly so surprised as Ramesh was to learn that I was unacquainted with these fellow Americans. "Just because they don't go to your everlasting cocktail parties and American Club lunches and all that kind of rot," Ramesh chided, "you consular people have missed knowing the most important group of Americans in Calcutta!"

But the real event of the evening was the arrival of Martin and Anila, who were making their first social appearance since their honeymoon. Ramesh ushered them in like an impresario, loudly calling on everyone to stand up and applaud. Martin scowled with a mixture of embarrassment and fury at this reception, while Anila managed a fitful and demure smile. When I finally got a chance to ask Martin if they'd liked Darjeeling, he said, "Oh, yes. Quite." Then he added that the weather had been bad and changed the subject.

Once dinner got under way, the conversation turned to Direct Action Day. Syed Huq was the most hopeful, insisting that the Muslim Chief Minister, Mr. Suhrawardy, would find himself in serious trouble if he allowed the demonstration to get out of hand. "He wants lots of noise but no bloodshed," said Huq. "He knows the Governor will sack him in an instant if there's serious rioting."

"*Surely* you're a member of the Muslim League?" said Martin in an almost supercilious voice. He had been listening with an expression of contemptuous disbelief on his haggard face.

"Oh, no!" cried Huq, gleeful at the chance to refute the scornful Englishman. "Oh, no! In fact, sir, I was a member of the Congress Party until a year ago. Then my editor gave me an ultimatum and I had to quit. I still haven't joined the Muslim League and perhaps I never shall. Perhaps I shall be fired—who knows?—though I doubt it. Would you hire me for *Amrita Bazar Patrika,* Ramesh? Couldn't you use a Muslim spy?"

I was delighted with Syed Huq. This spruce, lively, mustachioed Punjabi was like Ramesh in his enthusiasm and his love of verbal extravagance. He was also the only Muslim I'd ever met who thought the idea of partition was wrong.

Only Martin thought there was likely to be serious rioting. I had never seen him so aggressive in his arguments, so quick to contradict the rest of us. Once, when he had pounced on one of Huq's remarks with open rudeness, Ramesh caught my eye with a glance of dismay. But Huq was all good nature, refusing to take offense, laughingly and forcefully stating his case. Ramesh and I backed him up, Walter Evans looked on, interested but troubled, and the women remained quiet. I was puzzled and upset by Martin's tone even more than by his prediction, and I looked toward Anila for some clue. If Martin was more aggressive than usual, she was unnaturally subdued; her lovely face was downcast, madonna-like, almost, in its perfect stillness. Much to Sujata's consternation, Anila had barely touched her food.

After dinner I made a point of talking to Walter Evans. I learned that he was co-director of an experiment in co-operative farming at a place called Nasirghat, some forty miles to the east of Calcutta, and that his wife, Helen, was working with a training center for midwifery in Barabazar.

Martin, who had wandered over toward us, drink in hand,

interrupted. "May I ask how many converts you average per year?"

Evans did not seem to notice the hostility lurking in the question. "None," he replied. "The Friends have never been interested in proselytizing. My co-director is a Hindu. Our schoolmaster is a Muslim. They go their own way where religion is concerned. Our only common tie is the aim of service."

He blushed as he finished speaking. With his large ears, his slicked-down hair and sandy mustache, and his slow, twanging voice, Walter Evans had an oddly hayseed quality about him; his bashful earnestness suggested a Midwestern farmer who was also a lay preacher on Sundays. So strong was this corniness that I had trouble taking him seriously at first. But after he had described to Martin and me the preparations which the Quakers were making for possible trouble on Direct Action Day (laying in supplies of cholera and typhoid vaccine, organizing a motor pool, and storing quantities of milk for children), I felt a new and somewhat reluctant respect for both him and his organization.

The party broke up early to spare Sujata, whose face was stretched tight with the fatigue of her pregnancy. Syed Huq, more jovial and energetic than ever, pumped my hand and cried, "Perhaps we shall meet at the barricades! Who knows?" As we walked through the dark hush of Kalighat toward our car, Julia told me that she had had a long conversation with Helen Evans and had promised to visit the training center for midwives.

The Consulate was in a holiday mood the next morning, for Mr. Hubbard had, with his usual caution, decided to close the office at one o'clock. There being almost no customers for the visa section, I wandered down the corridors to the shipping section to chat with Philip.

"I gave a party last night. Perfectly ghastly," he added, with a happy grin. "Frédéric monopolized the conversation at dinner. Talked for hours about the Dreyfus *Affaire*. It seems that during the war some important documents came to light which were distinctly unfavorable to Dreyfus. Frédéric says the whole case would have been reopened if the Communists hadn't got hold of the papers during the *Résistance*. They destroyed them. Actually, Frédéric was quite interesting, but since no one else except me knew anything about the *Affaire,* it wasn't a very happy table."

"It's too bad his superiors from the French Consulate weren't there. They'd have been interested, I expect."

About three thirty, Ralph and I walked to the corner of Harrington Street and Chowringhee, where we found a high-spirited, excited crowd of Indians milling about. There had been a mass demonstration of Muslim Leaguers in the Maidan; having begun at noon, it was just now breaking up. The Indians, mostly young Hindus who looked like students, were laughing and joking, horsing around, embracing, shoving one another, holding hands in the Indian fashion, shouting and gesturing. A few carried sticks or soda bottles which they from time to time brandished at the heads of friends.

"Is there going to be trouble?" I spoke to a young man in European clothes who looked as though he knew English.

"Oh, yes," he answered with a happy flash of teeth. "Perhaps it has already begun in the Maidan. Who knows?" Still grinning, he shrugged his shoulders.

Just then two jeep-loads of police rushed by on Chowringhee, headed for the Esplanade. Beneath their khaki-colored topees, their bronzed faces were keen-eyed and set, the faces of young men in a recruiting poster. The bystanders yelled and cheered. But nothing else happened. The crowd increased and flowed idly along the sidewalks and in the street (there were no cars in sight), and for a while Ralph and I walked with them, caught up in the carnival spirit, wondering at the general good humor, the strange lack of menace. When we reached the corner of Lower Circular Road, we stopped to watch a squad of British soldiers drilling in the courtyard of the barracks there; then we turned around and strolled back through the mob to Harrington Street.

Later, when I went to Great Russell Street for our Hindustani lesson, I found Julia restless and excited. Leading me into the living room by the hand, she said, "I was worried about you—you're half an hour late. And Habib Khan hasn't shown up. Is there going to be much rioting?"

"It's too early to tell, but I doubt it. I telephoned Martin a little while ago. He'd had lunch with the Chief of Security Control—Captain Burton—at the United Services Club. Burton's called up all available police forces and they're certain they can handle anything that comes up without calling in the army."

Julia brushed back her hair with her right hand as she often did when she was keyed up. "Just the idea of street fighting makes me ill! There's nothing on earth as repulsive as a mob."

"Have you ever seen one?"

"No, but I once saw about half a dozen soldiers fighting in a bus station. I couldn't bear to look, and yet everyone else was standing around yelling and cheering. I was afraid I was going to faint."

"I enjoy watching a good fight."

"Oh, John, don't say that!" Julia made a face. She was exaggerating, of course, but I could feel the real loathing which the mere thought of violence aroused in her, and I hesitated to tease her about it.

We waited in vain for our munshi. I was just as glad to be alone with Julia. We drank a couple of cans of American beer and had a good time. I could tell that the tide of her love was flowing toward me, more strongly than it had since the night before Martin's wedding. Then her roommates came in, and after a polite fifteen minutes, I got up to leave.

Julia followed me to the door. "You don't suppose that feeble old man is actually out in the streets slashing Hindus, do you? Remember when he told us about that scimitar of his, the one that had been in his family ever since they fought in the army of the Moguls?"

"He's old and feeble, but the blood of the Prophet runs strong in his veins. If he can lift that scimitar, he's sure to use it."

194

"The very thought makes me want to cry," said Julia with a laugh. Then, after we'd kissed good-by, she said, "None of this is going to make any difference about tomorrow night, is it? You're still planning to come here for dinner, aren't you?"

"Nothing's going to interfere with that. And be sure to mix a sleeping potion in your roommates' food."

Ralph and I had asked a young Indian doctor, Ravi Dass, to have dinner with us at the flat. We waited for him until nine thirty, then tried to telephone, but could get no answer at his number. After we had eaten, we tried again; still there was no answer. Feeling let down, apprehensive, and thoroughly talked out, we took our coffee out to the veranda and sat down on the concrete balustrade, six stories above the street. The night air was dense and very black—the cool, moist, closed-in air of a tunnel. Having speculated about all the possible results of Direct Action Day, we sat now in perfect silence, welcoming the hush of the city. There seemed to be no cars at all moving down Chowringhee; even the ricksha wallahs who usually gathered under the street lamp at the corner of Harrington and Camac Streets had disappeared. From the railing I scanned the horizon of the city in a sweep that took in the far reaches of Ballygunge, Bhowanipore, and, still farther, Kalighat and Tollygunge; I saw the expected line of street lights along the length of Chowringhee and the Ballygunge Store Road, a scattering of house lights, equally expected, in the European quarters, and then the great darkness beyond, broken only by two or three spots of orange light in the direction of Syed Amir Ali Avenue.

I looked for a long time, relishing the quiet and the coolness. There were no stars; probably the clouds were building up for a shower. Then I said, "What are those spots of light out beyond Ballygunge? They seem to be flickering."

Ralph stood up and leaned over the railing. "By God," he said, "I think they're fires."

I felt a tremor of intense pleasure. It was like watching a newsreel in which an enemy plane, a mere speck amidst the puffs of ack-ack smoke, suddenly begins to trail its own black plume and arches across the sky toward the ground; it was a pure excitement, distant and uncontaminated by the pilot's agony—and shameful for that very reason.

"So they've decided not to wait until morning," I said in a voice that carefully padded both my excitement and my shame. I, too, stood up and leaned over the rail. It was like standing on the ramparts of a great fort.

"Look," said Ralph. "There's another fire over toward Kalighat."

In an instant both the purifying distance and the excitement had collapsed like a struck tent. I could think only of the Chaudurys and their Muslim guest. I could see Sujata's tired and smiling face, her plump hand resting on the great bulge of her belly. I could see Syed Huq as he threw back his head to laugh at Ramesh's joke.

About an hour later we heard a faint crackling that might have been gunfire; it was as faint as the sound of someone crumpling a piece of paper two rooms away. By this time exactly ten fires ringed the horizon and the low clouds had begun to glow with a dirty grayish-red.

For a long time I was unable to get to sleep. Probably they're safe enough, I assured myself, thinking of the Chaudurys as a family stranded on a rooftop during a flood. Still, it might be a good idea to get Syed Huq out of the way. Or perhaps Sujata and the children would feel more comfortable at Harrington Street until the rioting was over; it would mean doubling up, and Ralph might object, but that could be handled. Or they might even stay with the Fenwicks in their large new flat on Wood Street. Now that I was full of these schemes, I became even more sleepless, restless with impatience. In the morning I would try, as a "nonbelligerent," to get through to Kalighat; perhaps I could arrange for a policeman to accompany me if the fighting was still going on. For one sweet, improbable moment, I thought of going at once, right now, in the middle of the night, but an instant later I calmed myself. When I did get up, at nearly 3 A.M., it was only to get a drink of water and to take a couple of aspirins.

Perhaps half an hour later I saw Julia's face and the look of promise in her clear eyes. I'll ask her to marry me, I thought. Then I smiled into the darkness of my pillow and shortly afterward fell asleep.

CHAPTER XVII ❧ MY plans to go to Kalighat the next morning were exploded by a telephone call from the Consul General, which woke me up at eight. He was sorry to disturb our Saturday morning, he said, but he would like for me and Ralph to come to the Consulate with him to help send out dispatches to the Department on the rioting; he would pick us up in his car at nine. "How do things look from your place?" he asked.

I didn't want to admit that he had awakened me, so I said, "Very quiet, Mr. Hubbard. We could see some fires last night, but there's nothing now. No smoke or anything."

"My bearer's brought his whole family into our compound. Wife and about ten kids and an old grandfather. Most of 'em are in the kitchen right now. My wife's about to lose her mind." Sad and nasal, the Consul General might have been describing an infestation of cockroaches back home in Milwaukee.

As it turned out, there was little for us to do once we got to the Consulate General. The center of town was deserted, all the shops closed; steel shutters, which I had last seen during the February riots against the British, had been lowered like metallic eyelids over all the shop windows along Chowringhee. The Maidan, too, was empty; only the litter of rain-wet scraps of paper remained as evidence of yesterday's demonstrations. At Esplanade Mansions we found the Consular bearers barricaded behind the main door of the Consulate, sleepless and unshaven. Although there had been no invasion of the compound, they had heard rumors of wild slaughter in the back alleys and didn't dare venture beyond the protective door with its brass plate and the great seal of the United States. It was impossible to get through by telephone either to the Government of Bengal or to the police commissioner for news, and so, as the morning wore on, we had to resign ourselves to our isolation. All of us sat around in Mr. Hubbard's office while he fussed over the wording of a dispatch which merely said that some disorders had occurred but that the central part of Calcutta was quiet. Quiet was hardly the word: from the balcony of Esplanade Mansions, the city looked like an abandoned movie set, its façades more than ever like false fronts, streaked and peeling from the rains. I was bleary-eyed from lack of sleep and felt restless and caged in.

But shortly after noon, Herbert Schneider and Morris Halpern, who walked over to the National City Bank to deposit some Consular funds, returned saying that they had nearly stumbled over the body of a sanyassin lying across a doorway on Hare Street. He had just been clubbed to death by a gang of hoodlums (called *goondas* in Calcutta) whom the Consular men had seen running toward the Strand Road a little earlier. An Englishman and an Anglo-Indian had watched the whole thing from a building across the street; they had telephoned the police and been told that all available forces were already deployed all over the city—there was nothing to do except wait for the burial squad.

Mr. Hubbard wrinkled his pink brow. "Golly," he said, "I guess this is more serious than we thought. Wonder what the poor fellow was doing in the European section of town?"

"Obviously he had been chased a long way," said Morris in a disrespectful tone that made the Consul General blink.

Mr. Hubbard then gave orders (hardly necessary) that the bearers should sleep within the locked doors of the Consulate. He instructed the rest of us to return to our homes and stay there—there was no need to stick our noses into trouble and, besides, he might want to reach us by telephone. He would cable another dispatch to Washington in the afternoon; if any of us heard any news, we were to get touch with him at once.

As I walked to the lift with Morris, he said, "I can't tell Esther about the sanyassin. Her brother died the same way on the Ring Strasse in thirty-nine."

Toward the middle of the afternoon, after several hours of brooding, I decided to try to reach the Chaudurys, even though it meant disregarding the C.G.'s orders. I asked Ralph to come with me, but he refused, disapproving strongly of the whole idea; he promised, however, to cover up for me in case Mr. Hubbard called. I then telephoned Philip, who agreed in an instant.

Driving toward Alipore, I found the streets still quiet and empty but now guarded at the main intersections by British troops lounging in front of their jeeps; this meant that the Governor had called out the military arm. Following a hard rain, the sun had at last come out and was riding, pale as the moon but white-hot, behind a gauze screen of dirty-white cloud. The sweat salt on my throat and chest had set off my heat rash, and I cringed under the blaze of itching. I was uneasy, too, struggling under a heavy reluctance that seemed to coat my tongue with the taste of mud; the flouting of authority always affected me this way. On the other hand, there seemed to be no real danger: this was, after all, a purely communal struggle between Muslims and Hindus; an American, clearly identified, should be able to pass unmolested.

I found Philip standing at the door of his house. He waved and called out, "Did you bring a pistol?"

"Of course not." I got out of the car and started across the lawn. "May I come in and get a drink of water?" I asked.

"Wait there!" Philip ordered in a peremptory voice. "I'll be right out." And before I could answer, he dashed into the house.

I waited under the unhelpful shade of a flame-of-the-forest tree. Philip was clearly in a highly-charged, stallion mood, and I both welcomed and feared his exuberance. But I can handle him, I thought, gazing blankly toward the classically well ordered and clear-eyed façade of the house. There was a slight movement at one of the claret-colored curtains of the living room, and a face showed itself for an instant and then ducked out of sight. It was the face of an Indian child, whom I pictured, with some astonishment, as standing on a chair to look out of the window. I glanced back toward the car, turned my head quickly, and saw the face just as it disappeared again. But this time I also glimpsed a long, bare throat and the shoulder of a gold-brocaded Benares dressing gown which belonged to Philip.

Then I realized that Mirza Ali Khan was inside the house and that Philip didn't want me to know it.

Before I could reflect on this, Philip returned, followed by Ala-uddin, who was carrying a glass of iced water on a silver tray.

"I'd have asked you in," said Philip, "except for the fact that I've got a visitor who'd have to dash out of the living room to keep you from seeing her *en deshabille*. I've no intention of telling you who she is, so you needn't ask."

Feeling suddenly very bleak, I handed the glass to Ala-uddin and turned toward the car without saying a word—a fact that seemed to annoy Philip, who was waiting for some reaction to his bait.

Just as I put my hand on the door handle, Philip said abruptly, "I'd rather take the Bentley."

"No. It's too conspicuous, Philip." I didn't want him at the wheel.

"Nonsense. It looks more official." He walked straight past my car toward his own, which was parked under the carriage porch.

"Philip, I'd prefer my car if you don't mind."

He spun around. "I *do* mind. Do you want to come with me or shall we go separately?"

I had often found it easier to give in to Philip than to argue. "What the hell," I said, and walked toward the Bentley.

We drove down Alipore Road and along Lower Circular, past the Presidency General Hospital, where a number of military trucks and ambulances were pulled up in the driveway. I was still angry about the car, but more than that I kept thinking of the face in the window. Don't leap to conclusions, I warned myself, but of course I already had, and I felt a kind of dull hopelessness. Poor Philip!

When we reached the junction of Lower Circular and Chowringhee and tried to turn right toward Bhowanipore, we were halted by a picket of British soldiers.

"Sorry, sir," said a rosy-faced young Scot. "Civilians are na allowed past this point."

"We are not civilians," said Philip. "We are officials of the American government. We have every right to pass. See here," he continued, taking out an Army identity card from his alligator wallet.

"Sorry, sir, it canna be helped."

"This is ridiculous. I insist upon speaking to an officer. Where's your lieutenant?" Philip gave the word its British pronunciation of "leftenant."

"Wot seems to be the trouble?" A sergeant with teeth like blackened pegs stood beside the car.

"You're not an officer," said Philip roughly. "I demand to speak to an officer."

"None here, sir. If there was, he'd tell you the syme thing—no civilians allowed past this point."

"You're insolent, damn you. I shall report this."

"Come on, Philip," I said. "There's no use arguing. Back up." He did so, and I then suggested that we try the Ballygunge Circular Road and approach Kalighat by the back route—though probably we'd run into barricades there, too. I had no intention of giving up the expedition.

There was no picket at the main intersection—so far so good—and we tore along the deserted road at a fast clip. "Take it easy," I warned. "We have to turn right at the next corner."

Philip ignored me until the last minute, slowing down just enough to avoid turning over as he swung sharply into the narrow street.

"Watch out, Philip!"

Ahead of us, in the middle of the street, was a band of perhaps a dozen Indians in flapping shirts and dhotis, all of them armed with the narrow, sticklike clubs called lathis. They waved good-naturedly as they forced us to stop. "It is impossible for European gentlemen to proceed," said a pockmarked young Hindu, pushing his head into Philip's window. "Please, kindly turn around, sirs." A strand of blue-black hair, shining with grease, fell across his forehead; his eyes were red-rimmed and feverish, and his pitted cheeks bristled with a three-day growth of beard. The car was instantly filled with a smell of sweat and pomatum.

Philip leaned a little toward my side of the car but managed to smile. "You men look as though you're enjoying yourselves. My friend and I—and by the way we're American, not British—we're on our way to see some very dear Hindu friends in Kalighat."

"Oh, sirs, I must beg of you to turn around. This is no place for Europeans." The young Indian was friendly enough, but there was something hurried and shrill in his voice, and he kept jerking his head to the side as if with a tic. Meanwhile the rest of the band had gathered on each side of the car and were talking in high-pitched Bengali, very excitedly, and with much waving of the arms. One of them tapped the hood of the car with his lathi.

"I'd prefer you didn't do that," said Philip politely, "You might dent the bonnet."

The crowd laughed with extravagant good humor, and the lathi-wielder stopped his tapping and looked up with a grin; he said something in Bengali to his companions and touched off another explosion of laughter.

Craning out of my window, I could see clumps of men idling in the street ahead. The gutters on each side were heaped and overflowing with garbage and litter. One of the four-story tenements—a building of pink stucco, with latticework balconies—had all its windows broken, and in front of it, spilling partly into the street, rose a crazy pile of charred furniture and bedding. There was a lot of broken glass in the street. I drew in my head and said, "Turn around, Philip. Things look pretty cluttered ahead."

The pocked face again appeared in Philip's window. "Oh, yes, you must turn about at once. It will not do to go ahead. This is communal fight. This time there is no anger for Europeans, but they must not interfere."

"Look here, this is nonsense," said Philip. "My friend and I have no intention of interfering. We leave that to the police.

But neither have we any intention of turning back. Kindly tell your companions to stand away from the car." And he began to race the motor while holding the clutch to the floor. As the engine roared, the Indians immediately in front began to back away, but I could see that the stragglers down the street had drawn together, watching.

"Turn around, Philip. *Turn around,* I said!"

I shouted out my last words, for Philip had pressed his thumb against the horn. The muscles in his jaw tightened. Then, just as he began to release the clutch, I reached over and pulled the hand brake as hard as I could. The car jolted, bumping my forehead against the dashboard. At the same instant several lathis banged down on the roof and fenders of the car. The long blast of the horn stopped.

"Are you crazy?" I yelled. "Do you want to kill us?"

Philip, still holding the steering wheel, looked straight ahead, his face rich with blood, his eyelids quivering.

Outside there was a lot of shouting. Pock-face leaned into the car. "We will teach Americans how to respect the youth of India. If you do not turn around we will burn you with the car." His once grinning face was now like a raging skull.

"My friend was only joking," I said. "He's going to back up."

Without a word, Philip put the car into reverse and both of us leaned out of our windows as the car edged backward. The Indians watched us in silence until we reached the corner and turned once again into Ballygunge Circular Road.

I waited until we were headed along the route we had come before I said, "Why did you do that? I believe you were deliberately trying to get us killed."

"Nonsense. Those people in front would have scattered like chickens."

"Like hell they would!" I was beginning to tremble with the sense of what we had just escaped.

For a while Philip said nothing else. Then, as we were approaching Lower Circular Road, he said, "Is your life really so good, John, that you'd be reluctant to lose it?"

I was very tired. The day had seemed interminable, and I

could think only of getting away from Philip as fast as I could. I was too tired to argue or to be angry. After a while I said, "Good or bad, I'm in no hurry to give it up."

Suddenly, the car began to bump and lurch toward one side of the road. The rear left tire was flat. There was no way of getting help, and it took us a long time to figure out how to use the English jack, which had been rusted by the monsoon.

"You look ghastly," Julia said. "What on earth's happened to you?" She led me into the living room. The blinds had been shut, and the lamplit, threadbare room, with its faded cotton slip covers and shaggy cotton scatter rugs, seemed dim and inviting after the garishness of the day. Mary Haakinson and Ellie Myers looked up, smiling, as we came in.

I sat down on the badly sprung sofa and said, "I didn't get much sleep last night and I've had a pretty rough day. Right now I'd love a drink."

The day had indeed been rough. The holiday mood with which the rioting had begun had now turned ugly, and I was sick with worry about the Chaudurys. From time to time the image of charred bedding, heaped into a gutter, flashed through my mind. And there were the other images, too—the second-hand but utterly real image of the sanyassin lying face down in a pool of sticky blood, Morris' brother-in-law dead in the Ring Strasse, Philip's look as he gunned the motor of his car, the face of the sinister child in the window at Alipore, the pock-marked Indian leaning into the window. These ghosts haunted my fatigue, making it hard for me to keep my attention on Mary Haakinson's account of the food shortage. Only Julia, sitting across the room from me, seemed completely real as I sipped my whisky and sank lower into the cavernous sofa. She had said little but watched me closely, her face glowing in the dim light, filled with tenderness and concern. She was my one refuge from the clangor of the day, and I yearned toward her like a hungry child.

Our dinner consisted of canned chicken and canned corn— the cook hadn't dared go to the market, which was, from all accounts, empty to begin with. I told them something about what I had seen and done and heard, but I felt like a sleep-walker or someone who had been hit over the head. After dinner we turned on the radio and listened to the Governor's rather grumpy Midland voice announcing his intention to restore order at all costs with the help of the army. The number of dead was estimated at 250 and the property damage in the millions of rupees. A strict curfew was to be enforced, starting at once.

"It sounds as though you have a visitor for the night," I said, turning to the three women. "I've no intention of having to explain myself to the police. I'm much too tired to make any sense."

"I expect a jail cell would be lots more comfortable than that sofa of ours," said Julia. "But you're welcome to use it."

"I'd better telephone Ralph," I said. But when I tried, I was unable to get the operator.

After a while, Mary and Ellie tactfully left the living room to Julia and me. Drugged with sleepiness, I lay on the sofa, my head in Julia's lap. Vaguely remembering that I'd asked her to mix a sleeping potion in her roommates' dinner, I opened my eyes and smiled. "This isn't the way I'd expected the evening to be," I murmured. "But my God, Julie, I'm glad to be here. Stay with me; don't leave me. I'm going to sleep for a few minutes. I can't help it. Then I'll be better. Don't leave me."

Her fingers touched my forehead, light and tickling as feathers. "Shut your eyes, John. I'll be here."

Her hand began to move across my brow and through my hair. In a moment I let go of the fragment of consciousness I'd been holding; it floated away from me like a balloon.

I awoke into complete darkness. For some moments I was baffled by the roughness of the cloth under my hand and against my face; this was not my bed. I could hear the sound of heavy rain and the splashing of gutters outside. Then I thought, I'm still at Julia's. As I turned to try to read my wrist watch, I saw something glimmering like a white curtain just a few feet in front of my face. I rose on one elbow.

"Did I wake you?" Julia's whisper filled the room. "I thought you might need a sheet over you. The rain has cooled things off."

My hand groped toward the whiteness and touched nothing. "You've come back," I murmured.

"Don't you want this sheet?" The white blur moved closer, and I felt my fingertips push into the dry and yielding cloth of the sheet. "Lie still. I'll spread it over you."

"What time is it?" Waiting for her to come closer, I lay coiled and unmoving, hardly able to breath.

"About two thirty. The rain woke me up." Her voice was now directly above me. "Do you feel all right?"

"Yes." I sat up quickly, reaching out both arms. "Julie—oh, there you are!" I caught her behind the knees and drew her to the side of the sofa. "My sweet Julie!" The strangeness had gone: she was now fully embodied, her legs very firm and warm beneath the sliding silk of her nightgown. Her fingers brushed the short hair at the back of my neck.

"My dearest John."

She was trembling, shivering, but still very warm. I brought her forward and down so that she was kneeling on the sofa cushions. Then I rose up on my knees and felt her warm breath against my face in the instant before we kissed.

Later, when we were both naked and she clung to me, breathing heavily, I whispered, "I'll be very careful, darling. I won't take any chances."

Her breath came into my ear. "We're all right, John. I'm prepared for you."

Afterward, Julia said nothing but lay completely still as I continued to pour out my whisperings and to kiss her, touching my lips to every part of her body, unable to believe what had happened, loving and incredulous and a little sleepy. My happiness continued to break like waves against the dark. In a little while my sexual feeling mounted powerfully again, and it was only then that I realized how still and rigid she was. I held her very close for a long time, making no effort to take her again, wondering what she thought and felt and not daring to ask. Her breast moved with her breathing, and I could feel and almost hear the beating of her heart. I knew that she was awake. Finally I whispered, "Are you all right, Julie? You've been so quiet, darling. Julie, I want you to be as happy as I am. I want that more than anything else in the world."

She still said nothing, but let out her breath and then kissed me on the shoulder. I continued to hold her, very sleepy now, no longer worried but a little sad. Everything will work out, I told myself.

When I opened my eyes, Julia was standing by the sofa. "I'm going back to my room," she said. In the grayness of the living room I could see that she was wearing her nightgown. "It'll be light soon. Go back to sleep." She turned away and left the room before I could rouse myself to touch her. Groggily, I straightened the damp and tangled sheets and then found and put on my underwear before settling back into sleep.

CHAPTER XVIII ❦ ELLIE Myers awakened me. She was clomping about the room in slippers and a loose, sacklike wrapper. Raising myself on one elbow, I said, "Good morning."

"Oh, hi there, John. I thought I'd get the eight thirty news." Then, in perfect innocence, she said, "You must be black and blue from that awful couch."

I pulled on my trousers, and together we listened to the bland English voice announcing on the radio that the fighting was now under control and that all the major streets were now open; casualties were estimated at about one thousand killed and wounded, and the property damage at over a million rupees; His Excellency the Governor had scheduled a meeting with the Chief Minister, Mr. Suhrawardy, at eleven this morning.

Then I washed, and by the time I had finished, Mary Haakinson was in the living room. There was no sign of Julia.

"We'd better wake her," Mary said. "Breakfast is ready."

"No, let her sleep," I said. "We were up pretty late."

The two roommates exchanged smiles, and the three of us went into the dining room. Breakfast was meager—tea, toast, and bacon—for the cook had been afraid to go in search of coffee and eggs. Afterward I again tried to telephone Ralph and this time got through. Assuming that I had stayed over at Philip's or Julia's, he had not been worried. Mr. Hubbard had just telephoned; he wanted all the staff to meet at the Consulate about eleven to help him compile another dispatch. Ralph had managed to conceal the fact that I was not at home.

As I tiptoed into Julia's dark room, I heard her voice from the bed say, "I'm awake, John. Make all the noise you want to." Leaning over to kiss her forehead, I could see, even in the shuttered dimness of the room, that her eyes were wide and staring, and that the skin encircling them was dark as a bruise. *She's ugly,* I thought, shocked by the change in her face.

"Haven't you slept, Julie?" I took her hand, which was damp and hot inside mine.

"Not really. But it doesn't matter." Then, turning her head away from me on the pillow, she said, "I wanted so much to be with you last night, but when the time came I'm afraid I lost my nerve. You must have thought you were making love to a piece of wood or something."

"That's nonsense, Julie. Look at me." I caught her under the chin and turned her face toward mine. "This is the happiest morning I've ever known. Last night was the happiest night. And this is only the beginning for us, darling. I can't stand for you to be depressed about it, Julie."

For the first time she smiled. "John, you're going to have to put up with a lot of nonsense from me, I'm afraid." And she added, "I hope you're right about what's to come. But just now I feel so awful it's hard to imagine I'll ever feel better. But I will."

"Of course you will. Try to get some sleep. There's no reason for you to get up now. I'm going home to shave and shower and then I have to put in an appearance at the Consulate. The news is much better this morning. I'll come back about six, darling. Try to get some sleep."

I kissed Julia again and then left without telling her that I was going to make another attempt to reach the Chaudurys.

At the Consulate we found the office bearers in a state verging on panic, for they had exhausted their small supply of rice. Luckily Ralph remembered having seen several cases of condensed milk in one of the storerooms; these were dragged out and distributed to the grumbling bearers with the promise that rice would be obtained for them in the morning—from the grain reserves of the Government of Bengal if necessary. Then we all pooled whatever information we had and another long dispatch was sent off to Washington. Before we broke up, Mr. Hubbard repeated his instructions that we were all to stay within the European section of the city.

After lunch, I went to the United Services Club, hoping to find Martin there. The dining room was deserted except for one table, where old Mr. Justice Maitland and Colonel McPherson of the Forestry Department were finishing their meal. The

Colonel, with whom I had once had drinks in the bar, recognized me and beckoned me to their table.

"Well," said the Colonel, "I dare say, Wickham, you'll agree with Maitland and me that this is indeed a sorry business, a frightful business. You Americans must be jolly glad India's not your baby, as they say."

"What's the latest report?" I asked.

"Captain Burton from Security Control was here earlier. Poor chap, his right arm's in a sling. Some *goonda* broke his wrist with a lathi. Hasn't slept a wink in twenty-four hours. Dreadful business. Well, Burton thinks everything's under control for the time being. But he fears trouble will break out again after dark in the back streets. Estimates at least three thousand have been killed already."

"Good God!" I said.

"Frightful, isn't it?" said Mr. Justice Maitland.

"The Governor, I fear, is very much to blame," said the Colonel, who, before transferring to the Forestry Department, had served thirty years in the Indian Army. "He should have called in the military at the first sign of trouble. Still, I don't suppose one can really expect an ex-railway porter to know how to cope with something like this," he continued, referring to the fact that the Governor, a Labour appointee, had begun his career in this humble position. "Poor chap, I've no doubt he's doing his best."

When I reached the Fenwicks' flat on Wood Street, I had to ring a long time before anyone came to the door. Finally a harassed-looking bearer let me in; his white coat was stained as though tea had been spilled down its front. I stood for a few moments in the entrance hall, listening to the hubbub from the inner rooms. Then Martin appeared.

"Ah, John, the more the merrier. Do come in and join the happy throng. You'll find us in some disarray, I fear, but you're an old friend—you won't mind." Martin's voice sounded odd, as though he had a mouthful of food. "Do come along," he said, grasping me by the sleeve. "You see, my dear father-in-law has moved in with us for the duration—he and Anila's three sisters and five servants. He found things a bit too hot for him around Park Circus. The Muslims in that neighborhood were making too many sacrifices to Kali to suit him, though he's a very devout man, so he cleared out, bag and baggage, and here they are."

I stopped before we reached the living room. "Martin, I came to see if you'd come to Kalighat with me. I want to see if the Chaudurys are all right." I broke off and looked hard at Martin. He was leaning against the wall, so drunk that he could hardly keep his balance.

"Ah, the Chaudurys." Martin rubbed his forefinger across the reddish bristles of his mustache. "Yes, the Chaudurys. Yes, John, I'll come with you. I'll just tell Anila and be with you right away." He turned, swaying a little, toward the living room, but before he could take a step, Anila rushed toward us.

"What is it now?" she cried. "Oh, John, it's you. What do you want?" She looked at me fiercely. Anila, whom I had never seen without lipstick, without kohl, without jewelry and a brocaded sari, was now wearing something that looked like the cheapest calico, and her face was naked of make-up.

"John here wants me to come to Kalighat with him, my dear." Martin's speech was still slurred, but he had straightened himself.

"No, no!" Anila screamed, raising both hands to her face. "No, John, you don't know what you're asking. Please go away. Martin can't possibly come. Please go away."

"She's right, Martin. I'll let you know what I find out." I backed toward the door. "I'll get in touch with you this evening."

I took a very different route from the one Philip and I had tried yesterday. Syed Amir Ali Avenue, which I chose as the widest and probably the most open approach, was destitute of both cars and people. In the gutters and along the sidewalks I again saw the piles of charred furniture, bedding, and torn clothing that marked the total destitution, if not massacre, of some wretched family. British pickets, together with tanks and searchlight batteries, had been stationed at every major inter-section; they made no attempt to interfere with my passage. The city, as the radio had announced, was under control. It was also dead—a brick-and-plaster and broken-glass shell of a city laid out beneath a hot sky which, suddenly cleared of monsoon clouds, was the color of milky-blue glass and speckled with thousands of wheeling birds. As I drove along, I felt increasingly nervous and jumpy, though not really afraid, and longed for the presence of someone—even the helplessly drunken Martin—in the seat next to mine. The loneliness and desolation of the street seeped into me like a slow poisoning.

How far away and unreal Julia seemed. Our love-making in the dark hours of the morning had taken place a hundred years ago in another world. But it *had* taken place—I clung to that fact, depending upon it like a magic token to lead me back into the reality of that world again. More real to me, less dreamlike, was the white, staring face in the darkened bedroom after break-fast, but even Julia's distress, though painful, was only an ugly mask, a temporary disguise which I could easily rip away from the radiance underneath. For the first time in my life, I thought, I am in love and I've made love to the person I love. I want to marry her. . . .

And Martin is drinking, I thought. And Philip is sodomizing —or is he? And I am driving through the dancing ground of Kali. An image of Kali came to me as I had once seen her in a lurid oleograph hanging on the wall of a brass-seller's stall in the Hogg Market: the Black Goddess, with blood-dripping tongue and necklace of skulls, dancing, many-armed as a spider, over the prostrate corpse of Siva. Yet, though she dances over his corpse, Kali is the consort or divine energy of Siva, who is himself immortal—the terrible God of Destruction who is also the Creator. And even the Black Goddess has her loving aspect: she is the Divine Mother from whom all things proceed and who lovingly gathers all things together in death for the next in the countless creations (and destructions) of the world. I had read, or been told, all of this, and once again I felt the frustration which every Westerner experiences when he tries to gain a foot-

213

hold in the swamp of Hinduism. Sooner or later every principle slips into its opposite. Contradictions are swallowed up, rational distinctions ignored; nothing is excluded. Was this perhaps the final validity of Hinduism—that even Kali and Siva, though all-powerful, are ultimately no more real or unreal, meaningful or meaningless, than the tiniest drop of spray cast up by the ocean of God? Everything cancels out in the end, I thought, suddenly hating the formlessness of the system, and made uneasy by the tug of its mystery.

I turned away from Syed Amir Ali Avenue to the right and drove along the Dhakuria Lake, past the deserted wards of the American Army Base Hospital, toward the intersection with Russa Road. Drawing near the place where I would have to leave the main road, I spotted a British picket and searchlight battery and decided to park my car well within their firing range. I would go the rest of the way on foot.

"What's going on in there?" I asked one of the soldiers. I pointed toward the thicket of tenements and alleys that lay just beyond the row of rather pretentious apartment houses fronting on the lake. "I want to get in touch with some people there. It's quite important."

The corporal looked me over carefully before answering; he had a wily, snub-nosed, suspicious little face, but his tone was friendly enough. "Last patrol that came out said all's quiet. Likely to start popping again tonight, though. Are you thinking of going in alone, sir?"

"Yes, unless one of your men would care to come with me."

"Can't do that, sir. But my guess is it's safe enough just now. You'll be out well before dark, won't you?"

"Oh, yes. Thanks very much."

The first passage I tried was so full of rubbish I couldn't get through. I backtracked, turned to the left, and followed another road leading in what I took to be the direction of the little square and tank. I had never approached the Chaudurys' from this side before. Clouds were beginning to pile up, tufted clouds with dark, pregnant centers. No one was in sight, but with the approaching rain a dimness fell over the scene and an even heavier silence, in which I began to pick up tiny sounds that had escaped me before—scratchings or mutterings faint as mouse sounds, coughing, the click of shutters parted half an inch as I passed by. I kept my eyes on the ground to avoid as much of the muck as possible, but I was intensely aware of the thick life crowded behind every peeling wall. Then I caught the smell of death, the indescribable dead-dog, dead-rat taint suspended like an oily vapor in the motionless air, mingling with and cutting across the prevailing miasma of damp brick, burnt cloth, urine, frying fat, and uncollected garbage. I couldn't guess its direction.

I rounded a corner and was almost knocked down by a rush of black wings. The narrow passageway was dancing with enormous vultures. Crowding toward the center, they leaped into the air and onto one another's backs, their naked heads bobbing and dipping, frantic with greed. I turned away instantly, but I was too late: my eye had already caught and fixed the image of something yellowish and swollen, nearly buried beneath the jerking wings.

I took a long detour and once or twice thought myself completely lost. The sky darkened. I looked at my watch and was astonished to see that only fifteen minutes had passed since I had left the car. Then it began to rain in straight, needle-like shafts, very silently. The water was warm as it rained down my forehead, quickly plastering my hair; I walked on, keeping close to the walls, the collar of my jacket turned up. The day's unreality enveloped me—a strangeness composed of mist and universal wetness and the varied silences of dissolution, subsidence, and sprouting. I heard the steady drip of water, the squelching of my shoes, and a kind of sucking or perhaps sighing, barely audible, from the refuse mounds that choked the alley. Hundreds of birds—kites and carrion crows—wheeled over my head with little cries, suddenly swooping to the ground for scraps of offal too small to interest a vulture.

There was a noise behind me, and I spun around to see that two men carrying huge black umbrellas had come out of one of the houses, their white dhotis held high to avoid the filth.

My racing heart slowed to its normal beat. What could be less menacing than those two clerks with their umbrellas and pompous, mincing steps? I wanted to laugh as the warm rain splashed in my face; I must be drunk, I thought. Still, I was glad to see that they were walking very slowly, that they had fallen behind.

Some impulse steered me to the right at a crossing, and a minute or so later I came into the familiar square and saw its green tank shimmering in the rain. I began to run toward the passageway leading to the Chaudurys'.

After I had knocked, off and on, for over five minutes, I paused, now very much alarmed. The house was dead, a hollow block of concrete, echoing to my knock. Then there was a low wail, a child's cry, which was suddenly cut off, as though a hand had been clamped across the child's mouth. I pounded again, and this time I heard the drawing back of a bolt. The door opened; Ramesh stood there, his face ghastly and streaked with tears. "You'll rouse the whole neighborhood," he gasped, clutching my wrist with his bony fingers and pulling me into the house. "Oh, John, why are you here? You should not have come. You must go away at once!"

"I've come to see if I can help. For God's sake, what's happened, Ramesh?"

"You should not have come. They will follow you here!"

"There's no one outside. Everything's perfectly quiet. The British are patroling the whole area."

Calmer now, he led me into the little whitewashed living room, which was littered with dirty clothes, tangled bedspreads, unwashed dishes, and wooden toys. We sat facing one another on hassocks; for some moments Ramesh did not speak but sat stooped over, his elbows on his knees, his face covered by his fingers.

Then he told me that on Direct Action Day, Syed Huq had awakened with a slight fever and diarrhea and had not been able to attend the rally in the Maidan. They had all stayed quietly indoors, the children and the servant having been warned to say nothing about the Muslim visitor. But that evening, about nine o'clock, a group of neighbors came to the door and demanded that the Muslim spy be handed over to them. "Can you imagine our terror?" said Ramesh, raising his long face which, sunken-cheeked with exhaustion, was more horselike than ever. "They cried, 'Give us your wife's lover! She sleeps with the English and the Muslims. Give us your wife's lover, who is a Muslim spy!' " And Ramesh went on to tell how he had stalled them at the door, denying Huq's presence, while Sujata hid their guest under the bed—where, of course, he would quickly have been found if a real search had been made. But just as the intruders were about to come in, another group in the neighborhood discovered a Pathan moneylender—the most hated of all Muslims—hiding in a shed and a great outcry went up. The men at Ramesh's door had all run off to be in on the kill.

"Oh, what a din they made, those babus!" cried Ramesh, lifting his spread hands in an appeal for my belief. "Those worthy, peaceful babus with their fat bellies and their mean souls! Ah, John, the hatred of those respectable men, the hatred and bloody-mindedness of those eaters of vegetables and drinkers of goat's milk! And I would wager that all of them have pictures of Gandhiji above their family shrines. Nonviolence, indeed!"

All of that night and all of Saturday the Chaudurys and their guest had huddled in terror, listening to the roaring and the shooting all around them, waiting for the mob to return to their door. Then, this morning, Sujata's labor pains had begun. In a kind of panic Ramesh had run out of the house and halfway across Kalighat to get the midwife, who refused to come. Finally he thought of an old widow who lived in a single room two houses away. She was fearful, but at last he had bullied and bribed her into coming; she was with Sujata and the children in the bedroom now. "She's very weak and ignorant," concluded Ramesh, "but she does know something about midwifery."

"How is Sujata?"

"The pains are very slow and irregular. It will be a long time."

I sat for a minute or two in silence, shivering in my damp jacket, listening to the rain, breathing in the vaguely fecal air. "What can I do to help?" I asked.

At that moment, Syed Huq came into the room. He recognized me with a wry cocking of his head and sat down next to Ramesh. His brown European suit was as full of wrinkles as a crumpled paper bag. "I was under the bed again," he explained, shamefaced and ill-looking, too. There was still some diarrhea, he said, but his fever was gone.

"I think," I said at last, improvising, "that it would be unwise to try to move Sujata. My car's too far away; it would be too risky. But now while everything's quiet, I can take Mr. Huq with me—"

"Oh, no!" cried Ramesh. "Syed will be torn to pieces the minute he steps outside! He will be recognized. You will both be killed!"

"There's no danger now," I said. "But there may be tonight. We'd better get him out while we can. Then all of you will be safe."

"Yes, that is best," said Syed Huq to the still unpersuaded Ramesh.

Then I suggested, more to reassure Ramesh than anything else, that Huq disguise himself as a Hindu just to be on the safe side; Ramesh could lend him a dhoti. The Muslim agreed at once, though, weak as he was, his manner had a kind of dull, bled-white passivity about it, as though he were waiting to be carried from the house on my back. I went on to say that once Syed Huq was safely accommodated at Harrington Street, I would get in touch with Elizabeth Schneider, who was on the board of a charitable organization that provided midwives for indigent mothers; perhaps she would be able to find someone better than the old widow to see Sujata through her delivery. To all this Ramesh raised objections, always taking the blackest view, until at last I had to control my exasperation through clenched teeth. But finally he came around.

While Syed Huq was transforming himself into a Hindu, I went with Ramesh to the door of the tiny bedroom. Sujata was lying on an old brass bed, covered to the throat with a printed cotton spread. The two children were squatting in the corner with the toothless, crop-headed old woman, who closed her palms and bowed in the gesture of darshan; the immense black eyes of the children followed every movement that their father and I made. How strange Sujata looked without her silver-rimmed glasses! Their absence further softened her face, but curiously this softening made her look suddenly much older, as though there had been a general collapse of muscle and tissue. Her black hair, parted in the middle, had been drawn into two braids on either side of her throat instead of into the familiar bun.

"I am glad you are here, John," she said. "This is very good of you."

"I'm glad to be here."

And I told her very briefly about my plan to find a decent midwife. She nodded sideways, smiling, but said not to worry—she could tell it would be an easy delivery. Then, as if in contradiction, she closed her eyes for a moment and her body stiffened under the covers.

We found Syed Huq a perfect Bengali Hindu. He had put on a collarless shirt, striped blue and white, which hung, tails out, over his dhoti; he had even taken off his socks, wearing only a pair of soft black shoes. Embarrassed, he smiled wanly as Ramesh examined him, making a slight adjustment in the length of his dhoti. Only the hairline mustache still contained a hint of the warlike Punjab, and this was a detail which any sportive Bengali might affect.

"It's nearly stopped raining," I said. "Let's leave before the next shower."

The monsoon shower had dissolved into a white mist by the time we stepped out of the door. The passageway was an inch deep in slime, and we had to pick our way over wide puddles. We were in a world of dripping silence. Neither Syed Huq nor I spoke as we walked at a moderate pace toward the square.

No one was in sight as we rounded the corner, keeping close

to the built-up side of the opening, away from the tank. But then we heard the padding of feet behind us, and I saw about six men hurrying toward us, all of them carrying lathis. I caught Syed under his upper arm and we quickened our pace slightly. My impulse was to run, but I was afraid that the Muslim, drained by his illness, would not be able to keep up; this being the case, we had best walk ahead as calmly as possible. My mouth had become dry as chalk. I did not dare look around again, nor did Syed. We had nearly reached the nearest road leading out of the square when another four or five men stepped out of a doorway and blocked our way. In an instant those behind us had caught up, surrounding us.

"Why are you here?" asked the oldest man in the group, a well-fleshed, honey-colored Bengali with gray hair, whose manner suggested that he was more than a clerk or shopkeeper—perhaps a doctor.

"I am the American vice-consul," I said, summoning all my will to keep my voice steady. "This gentleman and I have been to see some Indian friends."

"You call upon friends in such time of rioting? That is very odd." He smiled at his companions and said something, very quickly, in Bengali.

"The lady is expecting a child very shortly. We were afraid she might not be able to get the proper kind of assistance, because of the trouble." I felt a little calmer now. There was nothing hostile in the faces—mostly middle-aged—that encircled us. And, I thought, my statement sounded plausible enough.

"Your friends are Chaudury family?"

I nodded.

Then, abruptly, my questioner spoke to Syed Huq in rapid Bengali. Huq cocked his head to the side several times, as though in agreement, but then he said in English, "I come from Bombay side. I do not understand Bengali very much. Speak to me in Hindi if you like."

Again the gray-haired man consulted with his friends in Bengali. There was much whispering and cocking of heads. "But why," he said, addressing Huq, "if you come from Bombay side, are you wearing Bengali-style dhoti?"

I held my breath, my legs suddenly numb with fear, but Syed Huq, whose eyes and posture had lost their dullness, answered promptly, "My suit was very wet. My friend Chaudury kindly lent me a dhoti." He looked fearlessly into the group, which, in a matter of minutes, had increased to at least twenty men. I could see others coming out of all the tenements on the square.

After another consultation, the leader said to me, "We have no quarrel with American friends. We are fighting only Muslims, who are killing poor Hindus all over Calcutta. Please do not interfere while we investigate if this man is Muslim." Again he spoke in Bengali and instantly several men pushed in between me and Syed Huq, jostling me backward several steps.

"No!" I yelled, pulling at the shoulders of the man just in front of me. "Leave him alone! He's ill. Stop this!" Suddenly I was shoved violently to the side. Before I could regain my balance, someone who was rushing forward bumped into me from behind and I fell forward on my hands and knees in the mud. Everyone was pushing forward now, shouting. I was knocked down once again before I could get to my feet. Then there was a loud uproar which was partly a cheer, and I realized that Syed Huq had been proved a Muslim by the simple test of his circumcision.

"Leave him alone!" I shouted, out of my mind, running forward with the rest toward the jostling mass of backs and shoulders. "Leave him alone! He's ill!" Everyone was bumping, shoving, screaming, to get to the center. And then the bulk of the crowd wheeled fantastically to the right, just as a flight of birds will abruptly shift its course, and we were all running, much more in the open now, toward the tank. The uproar sharpened into a choric yell. They're going to drown him, I thought. As I flung myself into the turmoil of bodies, there was a sudden break in the mass and groups of men began sprinting to the right and left to surround the tank. For an instant there was an opening just in front of me. I could see the green tank, and I could see Syed Huq standing up to his waist near the middle of it, his back toward me, his arms folded, green ribbons of algae hanging from his hunched shoulers, his unwound dhoti trailing behind him in the path which his body had cleared through the scum. He stood quietly as a statue rising from an ornamental pond. A trickle of blood like bright paint was running from the back of his head down his torn shirt. He's broken away from them! I thought with a wild, crazy leaping of hope. "Syed!" I shouted. "Syed Huq!" Then the crowd closed its ranks and I could see nothing but the heads, necks, shoulders, and flailing brown arms of the men in front of me.

I should have run to get the British, I thought, now weeping at my own stupidity. Turning around, head lowered, I plunged frantically against the oncoming shock waves of screaming men. In the deafening noise I felt the ripping of my jacket as a straining hand closed over the rim of the breast pocket. I struck out with my free arm, ramming my fist into the man's paunch. His yell blasted my ear as he surged past me, pushed ahead by the charging mob. Someone crashed into my shoulder, spinning me around. I turned again, grappling with both hands to part this squirming wall of chests and bellies, blue shirts with gold studs and wet armpits, white dhotis, brown arms, contorted mouths. A blow in the stomach knocked out my wind. I can't breathe, I can't breathe, I thought, closing my eyes in an effort to shield a tiny nucleus of myself from the black storm of panic. I knew that if this nucleus vanished, everything—my life itself—would go with it. I clung to it, thinking with a weird calm, it will vanish if I don't draw another breath soon. How can I hold onto anything if I can't breathe?

When I opened my eyes, I was staggering in a nearly clear space of ground, gulping air. Bengalis armed with lathis and bottles continued to race past me, staring and shouting at me but without changing their stride. The roar behind me was louder than ever; it came in bursts like the organized cheering at a football game. Then I saw that the men were breaking away from the main crowd and running to a collapsed wall where they picked up bricks and ran back, brandishing them, toward the tank again. They're stoning him, I thought with a terrible spasm in my chest. Can he still be alive? For a second I felt an impulse to return to the Chaudurys', as if I could hide myself there forever, but I kept repeating: The British, the British—I must reach the British. And I wondered why they hadn't come; surely they must have heard the noise by now.

I turned into the main road leading out of the square—not the one by which I had come. Sobbing for breath, I ran for several blocks before my legs all at once gave out and I had to lean back against a wall while my heart pounded as though it were trying to escape the confines of my rib cage. Three Indians rounded a corner and sprinted toward me like trackmen straining for the final ribbon. Unable to move, I watched their grimaces of surprise as they came abreast. Then one of them—whom I suddenly recognized as Pock-face—cried out, "Ayeeee! Amedicanni sahib!" and swung his lathi at my head as he tore past.

It was a glancing blow, partly deflected by my raised arm, but it knocked me out for perhaps three minutes. I was already standing up, dripping with mud, and inching my way along the wall, when two jeeps full of British soldiers drove up. The first one honked its horn but kept going; the second stopped, and a lieutenant came over to where I stood. After a quick examination, he ordered one of his men to walk back with me to the searchlight battery. Then the jeep, with its red-faced, sweating, grim-eyed men, drove on. Although I was stunned and groggy, I managed to keep walking and even to answer some of the soldier's questions. The pitch of the crowd's roar had now changed, and we heard a number of shots.

At the battery, I sat on the running board of an armored truck while the corporal whom I had spoken to early in the afternoon applied first aid to my scalp. He mumbled his comforting clichés as he wiped the dried blood from my forehead. "Looks a bit narsty but it moight be worse, you know; don't think it'll need stitches. There, now, that's more like it."

Aware only of my aching head and the subdued nausea that

might rise at any moment, I sat very quietly, as though the slightest movement would send all my bones rattling to the ground in a heap. Syed's dead, I thought.

Another jeep roared up and stopped. I lifted my head just enough to see a man in khaki jump out; his right arm was in a sling. When he heard what had happened, Captain Burton strode over to the truck and stood before me, his legs apart, his uninjured hand on his hip. "Why can't you Yanks mind your own bloody business?" he asked in a weary, level voice. "Don't you think I have enough to do without having to stop and wipe your bloody damn nose when you've stuck it into someplace it's no right to be?"

I looked up at him, unable to say anything. But I could see that his face was red beneath its smearing of dirt; his blue eyes were fixed, almost bulging, the china eyes of an angry doll. His words fell around my head like the thudding of bricks.

"You'd best sit here till you're well enough to drive your own car," he continued. "I can't possibly spare one of my men to go with you. I must say I find this outrageous, Wickham. You'll get no sympathy from me, I assure you. In fact, I fully intend to make an official complaint to your Consul General."

He turned on his heels and sprang back into the jeep, which roared forward almost before he had his leg over the side.

CHAPTER XIX ❧ EXCEPT for isolated stabbings at night, the rioting was over by Monday. But the city still lay helpless, with its back broken. All public transportation had stopped. The markets were closed and most of the food stalls had been destroyed. Thousands of workers had fled from Calcutta, and tens of thousands of refugees, foodless and shelterless, had streamed into the Maidan, where whole families squatted on the grass, hunched beneath the showers and the watery sun, waiting dumbly for the government to think of some way to help them.

Most of this I learned from Ralph, for I had not attempted to go to work on Monday. I was still sore and bruised and subject to dizzy spells whenever I stood up suddenly. Dr. Harlestoun ordered me to stay quiet for several days. He didn't think there was any concussion but he couldn't be sure; perhaps fatigue and the general emotional shock were enough to account for the continued headaches and dizziness. So I slouched around the apartment, feeling caged in and blackly depressed, worn out with the hourly reliving of everything that had happened in Kalighat. Curiously, it was Captain Burton's voice that rang loudest in my ears. When Ralph at last came home, he was more shaken than I had ever seen him before. He and Herbert Schneider had driven around the Barabazar quarter that afternoon. "You just wouldn't believe what the destruction's like," Ralph said, forgetting for the moment that I had good reasons of my own for believing it. "We counted over fifty corpses in less than a mile along Chittaranjan Avenue." And a little later he said, "After this, the British won't have any choice. They'll have to stay here forever just to keep the Hindus and Muslims from exterminating each other."

"The British presence didn't do very much to prevent this bloodshed," I answered, knowing that Ralph's statement was one which I would hear from a number of predictable sources in the future.

"That's because they've already given the Indians too much freedom."

225

Martin paid me a visit on Wednesday. He had just come from Kalighat, where he had seen Ramesh. Sujata's baby, another boy, had been born dead.

When I flinched at this news, he said, "Look here, I hope you're not reproaching yourself for anything."

I shrugged, then said, "How is Ramesh? I suppose he's feeling rather bitter toward me."

Martin nodded. "Yes, but at the same time he knows it wasn't your fault and he's tremendously relieved you weren't hurt very badly. He'll get over it. Just now he's so stunned and grieved he can't think about anything very clearly. For instance, he's sure the noise and terror caused the baby's death. Actually, from what I could gather from the old woman, the baby was strangled by its umbilical cord—Sujata's terror probably had nothing to do with it. Still, it must have been unspeakably horrible for them, huddled there in the house, hearing all the uproar, knowing that Huq and probably you were being butchered, expecting their own turn to come at any moment. Poor Ramesh. Just now he's trying to compose a letter to Huq's family. He's torn up about twenty drafts already. I begged him not to think about it for a while. But of course he will. He feels terribly guilty that his own guest—a man who had eaten his food and slept under his roof—should have been killed. He blames himself far more than you—and just as irrationally."

"You asked if I reproach myself. I don't think so. I acted according to the best information available to me at the time. I don't think I did anything unpardonably stupid—I don't think so." Hesitating, I then said, "Maybe I should have foreseen something like this. I don't know."

Martin rubbed his forefinger slantwise across his gingery mustache. "As you know, I wanted to come with you and would have, except for—for being much too drunk. To that extent I share in your expedition—and its consequences. It's perfect nonsense for you to reproach yourself."

Martin then told me how he had been working with a squad of European volunteers that had been organized to clear the city of corpses. This job was made necessary by the fact that all the Indian scavengers—members of an untouchable Hindu caste called Doms—had fled to the country, leaving Calcutta in acute danger from pestilence. Since caste Hindus shrank in horror from touching any corpse and since the Muslims would handle only their own dead, the main task of cleaning up had fallen to the Europeans. Thus a group of civil servants, including Martin, had joined with Scottish businessmen and a disgusted detachment of British soldiers to help the vultures, jackals, and rats finish their work. Meanwhile, European wives were kept busy making gauze masks which, when soaked with chemicals, enabled a man to withstand the stench, if not the sight, of human offal. Martin now reckoned that at least five thousand had been killed in three days. The butchering and atrocities were beyond belief.

"Sometimes it's so grotesque, it's almost funny," Martin said. "Yesterday we came across about a dozen Sikh cab drivers lying in a semicircle around their burned-out cabs. The cabs were on their backs, like gutted metal beasts with their wheels in the air. The Sikhs were on their backs, too, grinning like idiots and puffed up to about twice their normal size; they had been stripped and their bellies were swollen and even their penises were stiff with gas, so they looked rather like bloated Roman voluptuaries having erotic dreams about their next orgy."

"And this struck you as funny?"

"Yes. Rather." He grinned at my disgust. "You think I'm being revoltingly callous, don't you? That I haven't a spark of decent human feeling?" Martin's smile widened, deepening the sunken lines of his face. "That I'm heartless—or perhaps gutless —and incapable of nausea?"

"Of course not," I said, much too weak to enter the bantering. "But I do think there's something in you that needs to be disgusted. Needs it badly."

"Aha!" Martin smacked his lips. "That's really very clever of you, my dear John," he jeered. "Frightfully clever. It's quite true, too. And you might add that there's no disgust like self-disgust. It's much the most potent kind."

I looked down, shrinking from Martin's yellow-toothed grin and the obscenity of his self-revelation. "Is your tour of duty finished?" I asked, hoping to turn the focus back to the world outside.

"No, I promised I'd help out again tomorrow afternoon. We've still got to get the bodies out of the canals and sewers. Which means," he added with a smile that bared his yellow-stained teeth, "that I shall be rather out of sorts in the evening. And *that* probably means that I shall have a bit too much to drink. Somehow gin seems to be the only thing that can muffle the universal noise these days. Anila will be furious and her dear father will deliver himself of another lecture on the intemperate and unspiritual British. Well," he said, standing up, "so be it."

For some time after Martin left, I sat in a kind of stupor, listening vaguely to the splash of rain on the terrace outside. The heavy shower had darkened the living room, but I made no effort to turn on a lamp. I saw Martin's face shrunken into a kind of skull with yellow-stained teeth. I know why he needs India, I thought: the mud's thickest here. Then, loosening myself from this image, I summoned my remembrance of his gentleness, of the kindness and tact and wisdom with which he had urged me against self-reproach. He's probably the best person I know, I decided, thinking of his dedication to the land of his need; this dedication might feed on disgust, but it also flourished like a bright flower in its own right. I saw a bright flower, a marvelous red poppy, bright as new paint—and with a shudder I had come back to Syed Huq standing in the tank. I tried to think of Julia, calling on her to come like a good angel to my aid. She was in fact due shortly—to have an early dinner with me before the nine-o'clock curfew closed down—but I couldn't even rouse myself to shave or change my shirt. I barely heard the ringing of the doorbell.

Philip stood before me, a jaunty yachtsman in his Harvard blazer and white duck trousers; a red-and-white polka-dot scarf was stuffed, British-style, into the open throat of his shirt.

"Well," he said, "how are you feeling? I must say that enormous plaster on your head looks rather glamorous."

"I'm all right." I got up—there was the merest trace of dizziness—to turn on a lamp.

"You've had rather a bad time of it, haven't you?" His voice was more sympathetic. "Any word of the Chaudurys?"

"Sujata lost her baby."

"Oh, no! That's really too much."

For some time we sat facing one another, our glances deflected carefully as if there would be pain in their meeting. Then Philip probed a little. "Have you heard anything from Mr. Hubbard?"

I shook my head. "Not directly. Herbert came by to see me last night. The C.G.'s very upset, but Herbert's managed to calm him down a little. The fact that nothing reached the newspapers is a big help. I don't think there'll be any special report on me to Washington—unless Burton carries out his threat to make an official complaint. All I expect now is some kind of reprimand from Mr. Hubbard—and probably a medium-black mark on my efficiency report."

"I wouldn't worry about it too much."

"I can't worry about it much at the moment; there are too many other things. But it'll come in for its share later on."

"Of course."

I was glad to see Philip, but I wished that he would leave. The cost of giving my attention—of talking—was more than I wanted to pay. But he was not done with me yet and finally I roused myself enough to get him a drink. Then, with an air of not yet having come to his real subject, he asked me about Julia. "Someone told me she's been sick," he said.

"She's had some kind of cold or flu. But she's better. She's coming here for an early supper."

"Ah, then maybe I'll see her. I must try to make a date for lunch sometime next week. You're *not* invited. I want to pry into the present state of your relationship."

"Help yourself. If you can find out, I wish you'd let me know."

"I can tell that you're feeling better." Philip took off his shoes and stretched out on the sofa. For a while he stared at the punkah. Then he said, "John, you are my most valued friend. I've something important to confide in you. Will you hear me out before you say anything?"

I felt like crying out, Leave me alone, I don't want your confessions! I don't give a God damn about Mirza Ali!

"Well?" said Philip impatiently.

"I won't say a word until you've finished."

He told me that he had decided to become a Roman Catholic. It was a step he had been contemplating for a long time, he said. Finally, something over a month ago, he had gone to see Father Bernier, a Belgian priest at St. Francis Xavier's, and had persuaded him to conduct his instruction in the Faith. It was proceeding faster than usual—they met about three times a week—and Philip hoped that the Archbishop would permit his confirmation in a month or two. "I'm an apt pupil," Philip concluded. "On some points I know more than the good Father himself."

I didn't know what to say. In my own numbed state, I had no strength to grapple with what Philip had told me; it seemed as remote and meaningless—or meaningful—as if he had announced his intention to join the Rotarians.

While he waited, his eyes bearing down upon me, I struggled to find some response other than a negative shrug. Finally I said, "I guess I'm not really surprised. It must have been a pretty big decision for you, I guess. Though maybe not."

"All of this mumbling means you disapprove. I expected that. You have never taken my religion seriously."

"I always thought of it as a kind of game. Your Anglo-Catholicism, that is."

"Of course it is! Don't be so obtuse. You know perfectly well one can be playful and deeply serious about the same thing at the same time. I enjoy playing with genuflections and incense. I always have. If Anglo-Catholicism is a toy box of such things, the Roman Church is a whole toy shop. I now have a supply of dogmas, saints, feast days, bulls, orders, rituals, pious beliefs, traditions, and other articles that will last me a dozen lifetimes. Now, does that satisfy you? Are you properly shocked by my playfulness?"

"I suppose I would be if I took you seriously."

The belligerency faded from his pale eyes. "That's precisely what I want you to do," he said. "To take me seriously. This is the most important step I've ever taken. Nothing less than my soul is at stake. I want the real thing, John. By comparison to *that*, Anglo-Catholicism is a tinsel sham. I've known it for a long time. Compared to the real thing, Anglo-Catholicism is a kind of Pre-Raphaelite imitation, a revolting valentine full of rosebuds and paper lace. It lacks the discipline and the fire and the authority of the real thing. *That's* what I *must* have. I've known it in my heart for a long time. Only inertia—and a ridiculous fear of what people like you would think—have kept me from it."

"I suppose I'd argue with you if I had the energy. Maybe I will later." Then something struck me. "How much," I asked, "has Frédéric de Croye had to do with your decision?"

"Nothing at all!" Philip shouted, sitting up on the sofa. "Of course Frédéric has encouraged me—I'll admit he's the one who put me in touch with Father Bernier—but I reached my decision months ago." He picked up his drink from the coffee table and finished it off in a couple of swallows, his eyes closed, like a child taking medicine. "Why do you want to deny me this sanctuary?" he demanded when he had put down the glass and wiped his mouth. "John, you know what my life is like. Why do you, of all people, want to deny me the one thing that will make sense out of my existence?"

"I wouldn't deny you anything, Philip."

"But you do. You look on my conversion as an intellectual surrender, as a kind of abdication. I know you do."

I couldn't deny it. I merely said, "Your solution isn't mine. It might be a surrender for me. Perhaps it isn't for you."

"Of course it's a surrender, you fool! It's a surrender and a victory all at once. For me the Church is like a circle of fire on a dark night. I'll surrender the darkness to anyone who wants it. I'll crawl on my hands and knees toward that fire. I mean that —precisely that! John, you will simply have to accept the fact that I have come to believe, completely and fervently, in the teachings of the Church. And there's nothing you can do about it," Philip added with a sudden burst of ferocity. "Nothing whatever."

Looking into the pale and sweat-streaming face, I could only nod. I knew that more was demanded of me, but I felt empty and pumped out. There was nothing I could give. Philip's words had barely reached me through the din of Kalighat. I waited desperately for the ringing of the doorbell to release me.

Philip was standing up. "We'll talk about this later. You look dreadfully tired."

PART IV

CHAPTER XX ❊ AS I look back now, after nearly fourteen years, on the period following the riots, I see myself as a tired swimmer gasping for breath, at times gulping water as the waves broke over me, but somehow managing with a sort of blind, desperate instinct to keep on my course toward shore. It was a bad time. With my head lowered, I moved forward slowly, riding out the worst depression I had known since my bout with dengue. The city, with its continued acid-throwing and anonymous stabbings on crowded buses, was hateful to me; the sight of the pacific babus swarming toward work in the morning filled me with bitterness. My ears still rang, too, with Mr. Hubbard's embarrassed reprimand. In all this I found little comfort from my friends. Although no word of reproach was ever spoken (or even left unspoken), I still shrank from the Chaudurys' grief, and my two or three visits to Kalighat were as awkward as any visit of condolence could be. Philip, absorbed in Catholicism and (I supposed) in Mirza Ali, had little time for my sorrows; nor did I have much patience for the way in which he had now begun to flaunt his conversion. Martin kept out of sight, hardly ever emerging from the burrow of his marriage; from a few signs I guessed that the drinking had increased.

But it was Julia, of course, who at first compounded my distress and who later put an end to it. Our night together had set the mysterious wheels of her own inner panic into violent motion. She became tense and withdrawn, and her spasmodic, frantic attempts to reach me in my withdrawal only made things worse. I couldn't begin to understand the causes or the depths of her trouble; I dreaded it, and although I wanted to be sympathetic, my own depression and self-pity made me feel a kind of betrayal in her inability to help me when I needed her most. We were almost like polite but embarrassed strangers forced to share the same compartment; and for nearly three weeks Julia invented all sorts of excuses—half frantic, half apologetic—to avoid sleeping with me again.

What really kept me afloat and on course during this time was the writing of a detailed report on the riots, a voluntary report designed to supplement the Consul General's dispatches. I undertook it with the vague but powerful feeling that the only way I could stop the flow of Syed Huq's blood (and my own) was to capture the assailant in the net of my understanding. I simply had to *know* more. Herbert Schneider, who, like Philip, had been urging me for a long time to try my hand at a report, now encouraged me and arranged with the Consul General to have Mary Buxton take over some of the routine work at the visa desk. I did a lot of reading and a great deal of interviewing, even paying a visit to Captain Burton of Security Control Headquarters. It was this process of informing myself, of *tying things down,* that proved therapeutic; the writing itself, once I began, was merely arduous.

Then, after several weeks, I suddenly found that I could reach Julia again. Almost overnight her panic had drained away, she was fully there, moving toward me, full of love. But when we had made love together once more and I asked her to marry me, she refused, pleading for time, not yet trusting her new strength. This time, however, there was no panic or withdrawal. Instead, she suggested that we take a trip together as soon as my report was finished. Before she could feel free to marry me, Julia said, she wanted to see how it would be to live together for a while, in full intimacy, day and night, as we couldn't possibly do in Calcutta.

"You crazy woman!" I exclaimed, laughing and nearly crazy myself at the thought of going away with her. "Do you mean that you want your honeymoon first, before your wedding?"

She smiled and nodded. "It's time you understood how perverse I really am."

"All right. Let's both apply for leave. But on the condition that it's a real honeymoon and not some sort of test situation."

Again Julia nodded.

We decided to go to Darjeeling. There was no trouble about getting leave: we both had two weeks owed to us. And although Philip reported to me that Mrs. Hubbard questioned the propriety of our going away together, nothing official was said on that subject. Thus, two days after I had submitted the final draft of my report, we found ourselves at Sealdah Station, waiting for our traveling bearer to finish loading our baggage into the compartment; and on the next day we were in a car (hired at Siliguri, the last outpost of the plains) and climbing along the twisting road which led upward through the dense rain forest of the Terai, through the rhododendrons and oaks of the still higher foothills, across the ridge at Ghoom, and finally into Darjeeling itself.

"I'm numb with cold and I'm very hungry," said Julia as she sat down at the table in the dining room of the hotel. "It must be below freezing in my room." Wearing a navy-blue wool dress and a bright-red cardigan sweater buttoned to the throat, she flashed with color in the winter-edged light of the huge window.

"This will warm you up." I handed her a steaming cup of mahogany-colored tea which I had just poured from a green china teapot. I had been waiting at the breakfast table for perhaps five minutes. Having already finished a half cup of tea, I felt warm and wide awake, comfortable in my tan sweater and Harris-tweed jacket. "Did you manage to get back to sleep?" I asked, rejoicing in the brightness of her face and eyes.

"Of course I did." Julia poured milk into her tea, stirred it, and raised the cup carefully to her lips. "It's scalding," she said, replacing the cup on the saucer in such a hurry that she spilled a little tea. As she stirred vigorously, Julia gazed over my shoulder into the morning beyond the window. "When I woke up and saw the sun shining, I was absolutely sure we'd see the snows today."

"It's just possible we won't see them at all. The monsoon hasn't completely broken up yet."

"Don't be such a damned pessimist."

For breakfast we had oatmeal with sugar and warm milk, scrambled eggs, thick English bacon, and toast; I also ordered kippered herrings.

"I don't see how you can stand them," said Julia, wrinkling her nose at the kippers.

"You're just like all the women in my family. None of them can stand kippers."

"If I weren't so hungry, the smell would make me sick. It's a good thing for you I'm so ravenous."

"You've become acclimatized," I said. During our first few days in Darjeeling, we had both felt a little queasy, and we attributed this, as well as our short-windedness, to the altitude, which was seven thousand feet above the sea-level plain of Bengal. "We've become acclimatized in more ways than one."

Julia, whose mouth was full of toast, met my look and nodded.

A few minutes later, after glancing around the enormous dining room, she said, "I don't see the Craigies anywhere." The Craigies were a young Scottish couple with whom we had played bridge the night before.

"Oh, they probably ate hours ago. It's quarter to ten, you know."

"It can't be!"

"It is." I'm very happy, I gloated to myself. For the first time since we had loved each other we could meet for breakfast and know that we would be together all day; and this knowledge made the events of the night seem less isolated, made them click into the natural order of our life together.

After breakfast we walked down the steep road from the hotel and along the ridge to the center of town and then down the side of the ridge to the bazaar. A savage wind was blowing; it stung our already windburned faces, bringing water to our eyes but making us feel clean, as though we were being aired and dried after months of stale damp on the plains. Just overhead the sky was a light morning blue, but toward the north, a mass of gray-white cloud mounted up in heavy ridges stacked one above the other like rolls of cotton padding until they blocked off the whole view in that direction. The market was crowded and noisy but very northern in its openness, very different from the entrail tangle of the bazaar in Benares. Here the tin-roofed stalls were set on the hillside, jutting out at crazy angles and at different levels, sometimes on stilts, with wooden duck walks, and with rickety ladders propped against the sides.

And the faces, too, were northern, Mongolian, un-Indian, belonging really to the high, sparse world beyond the padding of cloud. These were the grinning, slant-eyed faces of the mountain people, the broad faces of Lepchas, Sherpas, Bhutias, Gurkhas, and Tibetans; only a scattering of Kashmiri merchants showed, beneath their caps of curling gray lambskin, the gaunt features and sad eyes of the Aryan.

We wandered among the stalls, looking for some Tibetan cups we had seen—and not bought—the day before. "I could kill myself for not buying them," said Julia.

"We'll find them. A peddler doesn't travel over a twenty-thousand-foot pass one day to sell copper cups and then go back the next."

There were plenty of Tibetans about: strange, blanketed people with bronzed skin and braided hair, startling in their resemblance to American Indians, the women even carrying their babies like papooses. Julia examined the copperware—mainly ewers and trays—which they were selling, but she couldn't find the cups. They had been small teacups of an unusual design: copper with a silver lining on the inside and a silver base hammered into a vaguely Chinese pattern. The merchant had asked ten rupees for each cup and, defying the tradition of the bazaar, had refused to bargain. Thus Julia had not bought the half dozen she wanted and was sorry, and I was sorry I hadn't made her a present of them—something I intended to do this morning when we returned to the bazaar.

"It's dreadful to want things this way," said Julia after we had given up the search. "I *hate* that part of me which wants things so badly. Here I am—I won't ever be happier than I am right now—and all I can think about are those damn cups!"

"You're too hard on yourself," I said, laughing into her frown. "Why in the world shouldn't you want the cups?"

And even the cups were forgotten in a few minutes. The day was fast becoming hot; the sun cut through the wind, beating hard against the tin roofs and glancing from the ignited copperware and brass. I carried my jacket on my arm, more than warm enough in my sweater, and Julia took off her cardigan and put it over her shoulders, tying the arms in front; the bright scarlet wool cast a rosy light on her throat and under her chin. Hand in hand we walked through the stalls of the grain-sellers and the spice merchants, standing in front of the latter to breathe in the pungency of turmeric, nutmeg, cumin, ginger, coriander seeds, cinnamon, mustard seed, saffron, cardamon seeds, and cloves. Later, when we were thoroughly hot, we went like good American tourists to the terrace of the Magnolia Dairy Company, where we could drink cold, fresh milk, guaranteed absolutely pure—a commodity unobtainable on the plains below; the milk was thin and faintly blue but at least it had that "stateside" flavor which boiled or dehydrated milk could never have.

"Isn't it funny," I said, "the way the senses begin to sharpen each other once they've had a good start. Do you know what I mean?"

Julia nodded. "Yes, I think so, but I have the feeling we shouldn't talk about it. We shouldn't try to put *everything* into words."

Cooled and rested now, we climbed to the Buddhist shrine at the top of Observatory Hill before returning to the hotel for lunch. The Craigies joined us at our table, and afterward we played two rubbers of bridge in the lounge. Alan Craigie, the young manager of a tea plantation in Assam, was a driving, skillful, silent player who slapped his cards down in fierce triumph and who looked on in agony, his teeth clenched down on the stem of his pipe, whenever his wife, Margaret, who was as new to bridge as she was to marriage, had to play a card. This was really their honeymoon, for Margaret Craigie had come out from Scotland three months before to marry Alan at a time when he could not leave the plantation. I enjoyed the mixture of exasperation and affection which they showed toward one another, each in turn, for Margaret was humorous and unabashed and showed a fine Scottish resistance to bullying from her husband or anyone else. They're a good pair, I thought; and I realized, with astonishment, that I had none of the feeling toward them that I usually had for married couples whom I liked or admired—the feeling that they were superior beings, sharing a secret which illuminated their lives, a secret which I would never discover. I know everything they know, I said to myself, and this idea so bemused me that I lost track of the game and had to be called up sharply by Alan, who was then my partner.

Julia and I had never played together in Calcutta, where there never seemed to be time for bridge, and her skill astonished me. Her game was as good as Alan's, considerably better than mine. There was no room for shyness or hesitation in the way in which, toward the beginning of the second rubber, she bid and then deftly picked her way through the intricacies of a grand slam.

"Well done, gir-r-l!" said Craigie when she had picked up the final trick. He turned toward me, his black eyes flashing, his face rosy with excitement. "Look, man," he said, pointing with his pipe, "even if everything else were against it, you should mar-r-ry a gir-r-l who can play a hand like that!"

This was the first allusion to our situation, and I saw Margaret Craigie blush for her husband and look down at the table.

"No offense meant," he said quickly.

"None taken," I said, smiling at Julia.

"I'll never marry a man I can beat at bridge," Julia announced, returning my smile. "I want to be able to respect the man I marry."

When the game was over, the four of us strolled up to the Chowrasta, the hub of Darjeeling, where we had tea and Dundee cake and listened to a military band play "Waltzing Matilda" and airs from *The Student Prince*. Returning to the hotel about five thirty, Julia and I went to our separate rooms—for Julia, in agreeing to come to Darjeeling, had insisted upon this propriety. I took a short nap and then got up to conclude the letter to my mother which I had begun the day before. This was not easy, for I felt thoroughly dishonest in trying to describe the scenic wonders of Darjeeling without mentioning what really counted, the one thing that my mother could never understand or approve.

After washing I went downstairs to wait for Julia in the hotel's "American" bar. We had two gimlets apiece and then went into the near-freezing dining room for an enormous English dinner—clear soup, gristly and overcooked mutton, boiled potatoes, vegetable cutlets, Manchester tart with boiled custard, cheese savouries, and coffee that had a burnt-rubber taste; we consumed all of this with enormous appetite. Then followed a drowsy hour or two in front of the open fire in the main lounge, where we glanced at ancient copies of *Punch* or the *Tatler* and occasionally joined the flickering, waning talk of the other guests. These were Calcutta shipping agents and jute wallahs and their sweatered, heavily shod wives; civil servants and convalescing army officers; and managers of tea plantations, like the Craigies, from the districts of Darjeeling and Assam—all of them as windburned and drowsy as we. Even Alan Craigie was too sleepy to suggest bridge. Side by side on a deep sofa, Julia and I lost ourselves in the spectacle of the cavernous fireplace. Occasionally a red-glowing log would break in the middle, sending up a swarm of yellow sparks, and then a turbaned bearer, his dark face dyed brick-red by the light, would struggle with the enormous, clumsy tongs and the five-foot poker and finally lay another log into place.

"I'm groggy with sleep," Julia whispered. "I think I'll go up now."

I walked with her to the door of the lounge, both of us shivering with the cold that struck us as soon as we left the fire. We kissed briefly and then I returned to my seat for another half hour before the slow-footed climb to my own icy bedroom. No one, of course, was likely to be fooled by all this, but the little game had to be played carefully, step by step.

Some two hours later I opened the door of my bedroom and looked up and down the half-lit corridor. There was no sign of any of the hotel guests, but, all along the hall, traveling bearers were sleeping, swaddled in blankets, on straw mats outside their masters' rooms. Wearing only trousers and a sweater, I tiptoed thirty feet down the corridor, deftly stepping over the bearers, until I came to Julia's door; there our own bearer, a South

Indian Christian named Thomas (whom we had hired through Cook's for the trip), lay sprawled on his side, fast asleep.

Julia was waiting for me, wide awake and obviously tense, though less so than on the previous nights when I had come to her. "Thomas didn't wake up, did he?" she asked, reaching up through the blankets to take my hand.

"He's dead to the world."

"If only he weren't a Christian, it wouldn't be so bad, somehow."

We both laughed, and I sat down on the bed beside her and stroked her forehead. "Did you get any sleep?" I asked.

"Oh, yes. Until about half an hour ago. Then my built-in alarm clock knew that you were coming and woke me up." She turned over in bed, exposing the top of her shoulder above the covers. "Darling, I'm getting better at this kind of thing, but I still have the awful feeling that bells are going to ring all over the hotel the moment your hand touches the doorknob."

When, seconds later, I was lying beside her under the blankets, I could feel the trembling of her body. This is the way it had been each time, and now began the slow wooing back of love and confidence and desire itself from the dark places where they had hidden. The process this night was not so long; she was readier, the half-strangling gasps of pleasure came sooner under my touch, and a new playfulness, a kind of shy teasing, sent us both into half-smothered bouts of laughter as we began to move together into the exploring, quickening rhythms of our embrace. Afterward we lay together quietly, my heart still pounding, our legs entwined, my hand on her indented stomach, which moved gently with each breath, her head pillowed on my right arm, her hair tickling my shoulder. We were wet and naked, completely exposed to one another, suddenly very simple and childish in our intimacy.

"You mustn't say anything," she whispered after a long time. "Everything is getting much easier for me, but I won't stand for *one single word* of encouragement. Promise me you won't say anything."

"All right." I laughed, kissing her. "I won't say a word." And almost at once I plummeted into sleep.

Several nights later I dreamed that a crowd of Hindus had caught me swimming in a sacred tank. They were lined up on the ghat above the tank, and they shouted at me until they were hoarse and waved their lathis. "We'll stone you," they yelled. Then one of them stepped forward from the crowd and walked slowly down the steps toward the water. Very gently he broke the mantle of green scum with one foot. It was Syed Huq. . . .

Someone was gripping my shoulders, pinning me down, a black form in the gray light of the room. I lay gasping in fright, my eyes wide open, until at last Julia's voice broke through the wall of my consciousness. She was leaning over me, shaking me. "Darling, you've been having a bad dream. You're soaking wet!" She kissed me on the forehead, and I wanted to cry from sheer relief.

"What time is it?" I mumbled, reaching for her hand.

"It's just about daybreak." She was climbing out of the bed. "I think I'll lower the window some. It must be about zero."

I turned on my stomach, face down, already subsiding into sleep. Then I felt Julia's hand on my arm. "I hate to do this to you," she said, "but it's so beautiful you've just got to see it."

I rolled over. "See what?"

"The mountain. The clouds have broken up. It's absolutely clear." Julia handed me a blanket from the foot of the bed. "Here, wrap this around you. It's absolutely freezing."

The room was only faintly gray and intensely cold. Shivering as the chill air struck my wet shoulders and chest and finally my bare legs, I pulled myself out of the warm black nest of a bed and accepted the dark toga from Julia's hands. With my feet I groped for my slippers on the icy floor.

After we had stood for a few silent moments at the window, I said, "I was beginning to be afraid we'd never see it."

Beyond the terraces of the hotel the ground fell away abruptly into a ravine from which wooden shacks stuck out, propped on stilts; here the night still held its own, its shadows unbroken even by a lamp. From the dark bowl immediately below, a sway-backed ridge heaved itself up, slate-colored in the predawn, beaded with strings of electric lights; this was the main part of the hill station—the Chowrasta, the church, Observatory Hill, and finally, at the farthest point of the spur, the white block of the summer Government House. Then came the great falling off, the two-thousand-foot drop into the great valley of Sikkim, which stretched thirty miles in darkness before reaching the upward thrust, the final piling of range upon range, the muscled and knotted torso of the High Himalayas. Here the view stopped head on against the black wall which in turn disappeared into a ledge, perhaps two miles high, of iron-gray cloud. That was all there was—the black wall and the gray ledge—unless the eye looked up and up, looked to a point higher than any mountain could ever have risen, and then saw the fantastic peak of Kanchenjunga riding in the steely air. Already its double pyramid of snow was flushed to a warm rose color by the sun, which had not yet appeared over the hills in the east. A jet of snow blew horizontally, like a pennant, from the very top.

I drew my blanket closer. Even the modest seven thousand feet of Darjeeling had seemed almost stratospheric after the dead level of Bengal, and now this sudden image of terrifying isolation, this rose-pink, cruelly sharp mass (was it the second or third highest mountain in the world?) that dominated the whole northern sky somehow made the air that I breathed even thinner, colder, and less nourishing.

"Do you see the plume of snow at the peak?" I asked, moving closer to Julia, who nodded slowly, her lips parted, her hand still clutching the robe at her throat. "The wind is probably blowing over a hundred miles an hour up there," I added, rather awe-struck by this possibility.

"Isn't it strange?" said Julia. "That enormous pile of rock and snow has been there all the time behind the clouds. It just kills me to think we might have gone back to Calcutta without ever seeing it."

"Well, we've seen it now and we'll see it again. The monsoon's definitely breaking up. Let's go back to bed." There was too little comfort in the beauty of Kanchenjunga; it was too arid and remote, too frozen in its grandeur, and I resented its power.

As we settled back into the warmth of the bed, I held Julia in my arms, our toes, knees, and bodies touching lightly, our faces close together. We did not make love again but lay together in gentle intimacy. In a little while I would have to get up, pull on a few clothes in the cold air, and return to my room down the corridor. But for the moment I could stay where I wanted—more than I wanted anything else in the world—to be, and I drew in a deep breath of triumph.

"We've come a long way," I whispered.

"I know. I can hardly recognize myself."

I released my hold and lay back, with one hand closed over hers where it nestled by my hip. Moving my feet, I touched the silken wad of her nightgown at the foot of the bed. The room was becoming lighter, despite the curtains which we had closed at the window. Soon I would have to go. We've come a long way, I repeated to myself. It was hard to imagine Julia as she'd been during that agonizing period following our first coming together. And I've come a long way, too, I thought, remembering my nights with Dorothy, my restlessness, and the relief with which I had returned to the narrow haven of my bed.

CHAPTER XXI ❖ O N the last day of our two weeks in Darjeeling, we hired ponies and a Sherpa guide and went a thousand feet down to the cantonment of Lebong and then to a village of the hill people known as Lepchas. Our way down led through groves of moss-bearded trees on which orchids grew like ornaments of purple tissue paper. We jolted through thickets of rhododendron, past abrupt waterfalls, and along paths that threatened at any moment to disappear over the edge of a cliff. Far below we could see the tea plantations—small squares of bottle-green velvet sewn onto the rougher texture of the hills. I had been right: the clouds had stayed parted, and Kanchenjunga continued to fill the northern sky with its haughty thrust of snow.

But by this time we were both rather jaded with fine views. We concentrated instead on our ponies, who had the terrifying habit of walking as close as possible to the outer rim of every ledge; furthermore, our downhill journey forced us to lean all the way back in our saddles with our feet thrust forward, knees unbent, against the stirrups—a miserably uncomfortable posture. Still, the day was high and clear and for the most part we enjoyed ourselves. Coming back was much more difficult. Unused to riding, we were both very tired, and each step that the ponies took jolted through our straining legs and hips. The climb took much longer than we had expected, and by the time we reached the hotel, Julia, who had slept very badly the previous night, was so sore and exhausted that she could hardly move. She went upstairs at once to lie down for a couple of hours before dinner. I then went to my own room and ordered the bearer to prepare a hot bath which, I hoped, would take away some of my soreness.

As soon as I had dressed, I went downstairs to the bar for the drinks that I counted on to take away the rest of the soreness. There, sitting with my burra peg of Scotch, I stretched out my still aching legs and thought, I'll ask her again tonight, I can't hold off any longer. A few minutes later, as I was beginning my second drink, I heard a high English voice pierce the general hum of the room. "By God," it said, "you're quite right. It is John Wickham. Hallo there, John!" And through

247

the smoke I saw Ronny Powell, in his Guardsman's uniform, advancing toward the table. Just behind him, struggling to keep up, was Diane Cummings. "I say, how lovely to find you here!" cried Ronny, gasping for breath, his small face scarlet, his blue eyes watery. "Wonderful luck for us, isn't it, Diane? John, why the devil didn't you let us know you were coming to Darjeeling? That's no way to treat an old chum, is it, Diane?"

The fact was that I—without really meaning to—had seen much less of Ronny in recent months; somehow he belonged more to the era of Dorothy than of Julia. Still, Ronny's comment carried no hint of rebuke; gregarious and enjoying people rather than individuals, he was genuinely glad to see me and probably unaware that such meetings were no longer frequent. And I immediately felt the full glow of my old liking for the Englishman. Drinks were ordered and the round of explanations begun. The Governor and his staff had just come up to Darjeeling the day before, Ronny said; they'd be there a fortnight—the last visit of the season. There was going to be a cocktail party on Friday; I simply had to come; had I signed the visitors' book at Government House yet? And when I said I had to return to Calcutta tomorrow, Ronny cried out, "Oh, no! You simply mustn't. We can't possibly allow that, can we, Diane?"

"It would be *such* fun if you could stay," said Diane. She had been taking genteel little sips of her gin-and-orange while Ronny and I talked, and watching us with a kind of blank benevolence. Then she added, "When I first looked into the bar, I said to Ronny, 'Now there's a friendly face but I can't for the life of me think who it is.' Isn't that funny? Imagine not recognizing *you*."

"As if anyone could forget John's mug," laughed Ronny. "But seriously, old boy, we can't possibly allow you to go back to Cal before we've had a bit of fun here at the top of the world."

"Can't you two stay for dinner here at the hotel?" I asked. "I'm having dinner here with an American girl, Julia Cobb. She'll be along in a little while and I know she'd love to have you join us."

"Thanks awfully, John, but I'm afraid we can't possibly.

We're committed to a dinner party farther up the hill. We just popped in here to catch our breath and have a quick one along the way."

"It's such a pity," said Diane.

Then Ronny excused himself to go to the lavatory. "Be back in half a sec," he said, dashing off. Diane and I smiled at each other for a few moments, aware of some constraint. Finally she said, "Are you still the visa officer at the Consulate?"

"I still am—unfortunately."

"You know, I once thought of coming to see you. A friend of mine was urging me to visit the States. He had some important contacts there. And well, you know—he thought he might be able to arrange a screen test for me. Something like that," she concluded with a flurry of modesty.

"What happened? Why did you change your mind?"

She gave her genteel little laugh. "Oh, you know how life is. Also, I heard it's rather difficult for an Englishwoman to go to the States if she happens to have been born in India. Still, I was rather tempted, I must say."

"I think you'd do very well in Hollywood," I said with complete honesty.

"Thank you. That's very sweet." She moved slightly in her chair, a movement of pleasure and complacency, a movement in response to a caress. Diane was very beautiful, and despite the fool's-gold sheen of her long hair and the knife-edge demarcation of her lipstick, she looked healthy rather than artificial; the whites of her eyes were clear and her eyelids merged without a wrinkle into the clear, luminous, faintly olive skin of her face. Here, I felt, is a woman who never lets drink or love or ambition interfere with her eight-hour sleep.

She took another delicate sip and said, "How's Philip Sachs these days? I sometimes think of him, you know."

"He seems much the same," I said rather cagily.

"I *liked* Philip, you know. He's such a kind, generous person. But terribly deep. I could never tell what he was really thinking. Or," she added with a trace of a smile, "what he really wanted from me, if you know what I mean."

"Philip's not an easy person to understand," I began, wishing that Ronny would come back. Then I saw Julia standing in the door of the bar. "Excuse me," I said, leaping to my feet. "My friend's just come in."

As we walked back toward the table, Julia said, "My legs hurt so much I couldn't sleep. So I thought maybe a drink would help. But I don't want to butt in on your conversation."

"That's absurd," I said sharply.

We reached the table and introductions were made. Both women said they'd seen each other before but hadn't actually met. Then all three of us fell silent. I twisted in my seat, trying to catch the attention of the bearer to order a drink for Julia. I could sense the tension in Julia's hands and in the way her shoulders were set.

Then Diane said, "It's so nice to come across unexpected friends in a strange place."

Ronny rushed up to the table. "Well, the party's grown. The more the merrier. Hallo there, Julia. It's been absolute centuries since I've seen you. How have you taken to hill-station life?"

But Diane wouldn't let Ronny sit down. "I'm afraid we simply must run along. Such a pity."

"Oh, do let's have another drink here. One needs just a drop for the final push up that bloody hill." But he made no effort to take his chair.

As they left, I suddenly remembered that there was only one real building up the hill from the hotel: it was the large chalet referred to in the guidebook as Mountain Lodge—the summer residence of the Maharaja of Berhampore.

After dinner, instead of sitting in front of the fire in the main lounge, we decided to take a last walk to the top of Observatory Hill; walking, I said, would be good for our leg muscles after a day of riding. There was a bright three-quarter moon, so bright that we didn't need the flashlight I'd brought along. Julia remained quiet, as she had during dinner. She was still tired from the ride; furthermore, I suspected that her period was about to begin.

Reaching the top, we sat on the whitewashed wall of the Buddhist shrine. Behind us were long bamboo poles, to which cloth and paper streamers were tied, each representing a Buddhist prayer to be carried by the winds to the elements of the universe. But even at this height the Hinduism of the plains had begun the process of swallowing up its most famous offspring, for little figures of Ganesh and Hanuman and the linga of Siva had nestled up against the white stupa shrines of the Buddha. Just now the wind was blowing savagely, whipping the prayer streamers. The sky was cloudless, moon-washed, pure as a glacial lake, and to the north the stupendous snows of Kabru and Jano, Kanchenjunga, Pandim, Narsingh, and Siniolchu gleamed with a kind of arctic fury; the night was brilliant but too windy for that sense of stillness beyond depth which the frozen moonlight can sometimes give. I put my arm around Julia, drew her to me, and pressed my raw, burning cheek against her forehead. We're mammals, I thought, defying the mineral beauty that surrounded us.

"You've made me happier than I ever thought possible," I said; and I thought, Now I'll ask her—now she'll say yes. Under my arm she felt very warm, very soft, and very solid.

"Have I? Haven't you felt this way before?" Julia rubbed her forehead slowly against my cheek.

"Never."

"Weren't you this happy with Dorothy? Didn't she make you just as happy?"

"No, Dorothy and I never made each other very happy." I was annoyed that the name had come up, annoyed that she wanted to pick at my statement.

"John, tell me about Dorothy. What was she like? What were you like together?" Julia lowered her head, pressing it against my chest. "Why don't you ever talk about her?"

"Because I don't like to think about it. And also because you'd misinterpret everything I said, to your own disadvantage."

"Stop treating me like a child. I want to hear about the two of you—what you did, what she was really like. I can stand anything you tell me about her and about you."

"You can stand anything except the truth!" I nearly shouted. "You can't stand the fact that my relationship with Dorothy was limited and not really happy. And that what I've shared with you makes everything else in my life seem paltry by comparison. That happens to be the truth and that's all I'm going to say on the subject." Her insistence, more brutal than the wind, had slashed across my mood, cut deeply into my happiness. I drew away, half-turning, so that I couldn't see Julia. "Why did you have to bring up Dorothy?" I demanded. "What in God's name reminded you of her? What has she got to do with us?"

Julia was a long time in replying. "I think," she said at last, "it must have been seeing you with Diane Cummings."

"What has *she* got to do with Dorothy?"

Again there was a long pause. "I'm not sure. Somehow I think of them together."

"They're very different."

"I know. But they're both women in a way I'll never be. I dried up inside when I saw you with Diane, and I do the same thing whenever I think of Dorothy."

"Stop talking like that!" I grabbed her roughly by the shoulders.

"I'm sorry. You're perfectly right."

She leaned against me and put her hand into the pocket of my coat; a minute later my hand followed hers and closed over it. We sat for a long time without moving or talking, huddled lumpishly together on the white wall, hearing only the constant flapping of the prayer flags in the wind. Gradually my anger trickled away, my anger and my bitterness. I've won, I thought. And I felt triumphant, full of love and confidence. Pressing her to me, lowering my own head, I whispered, "Please say you'll marry me, Julie. Please say you will."

She stiffened, then drew back. Her face and eyes caught the full blaze of the moon. "You don't mean it," she said. "You're just trying to build up my confidence. You don't really want to marry me." She stood up abruptly. "You're just pretending. You say these things so I'll go on sleeping with you."

"For God's sake, Julie!" I reached for her but she was already walking away from me, away from the Buddhist shrine and toward the path leading down the hill. I rushed after her and caught her from behind, my arms around her breast, my lips at her ear. "If you ever say such a thing again," I whispered, "I'll —I'll beat the living hell out of you!"

I caught my breath, deeply shocked by what I had just said. And I felt Julia's sharp intake of breath as her body stiffened within my arms. Then, frightened, I quickly said, "Julie, when I said I wanted to marry you, I meant it more than anything I've ever said in my life. You've got to believe me."

"I believe you," she answered, crying. "What I said just now was horrible—I didn't mean it—I don't know why I said it. I know you want to marry me but I don't know why you do. Oh, John, I should never have come here with you! I don't know what I'm doing here! I've been deceiving you, I've been leading you on, raising your hopes."

Turning in my arms, she broke into a wild frenzy of sobbing. I held her tightly. "No, no," I muttered, patting her shoulders, stroking the back of her head, trying to throw some sort of bridge across the abyss of her despair—her despair, and now almost mine as well. "No, Julie, there's been nothing false about these two weeks. We've been our most real selves, our best selves. Now we know how high we can go—we've been there, and we can get there again. And even higher. That's the thought we've got to cling to—we've been there and we can get back. You're upset, you're scared by your own happiness, but we'll get back!"

She was calmer now, jolted by only an occasional sob. Gradually my hope regained its footing. "I feel better," Julia said as we started down the hill. "You've been very patient with me, John. Be patient with me just a little longer. Please give me time; don't press me. Maybe everything will work out, if you'll just give me time."

"As much as we need," I said, holding fast to her arm while we lurched and stumbled ahead down the rocky path.

CHAPTER XXII ❧ I N the morning Julia looked pale but said that she felt much happier about everything. We packed, had an early lunch, and then, in another hired car, began the descent to Siliguri. Julia looked out of the window most of the time, absorbed in the fantastic sweep of scenery. She was still subdued and a little preoccupied, shifting about restlessly in her seat, from time to time scratching her wrist or her throat. But we had fun together at dinner in the station dining room, talking about the Craigies and the other people at the hotel. The racketing, noisy train to Calcutta allowed only wispy fragments of sleep, and I was as dull-eyed as Julia when we arrived at Sealdah Station early the next morning. A car and driver from the Consulate were waiting for us, as I had arranged by telegram, and we drove straight to Julia's apartment. We sat for a few minutes in the living room with her roommates, who were just finishing their breakfast coffee. When I got up to leave, Julia followed me to the door and then threw herself into my arms.

"I'm so glad I came with you," she murmured into my shirt. "You may not think so, but I am."

"Of course you are. That last night was just a miserable dream. We've already shaken it off."

"I hope so. Just be patient with me. I'll be all right again."

At Harrington Street I found that Ralph had already left for work. In no hurry to make my own appearance at the Consulate, I decided to have a hot bath and some breakfast first. While waiting for Ghulam to prepare the bath (this involved lighting the geyser and having the sweeper bring in pails of water from the kitchen), I thumbed through the stack of mail on my bedside table. There were letters from my mother and one from my sister Alice; they could wait until the leisure of breakfast. I first tore open what was obviously an invitation, engraved in an elegant script, and read:

Philip Gerald Sachs requests
the Honour of your company at a Rout

to be held on Saturday evening,
Twelfth October, at eight thirty o'clock.

R.S.V.P.

7, *Asoka Road*

And at the bottom of the card Philip had added in his own scrawling hand: "To meet Mr. Sachs in celebration of his Christening."

Then I picked up the only post card in the lot. "Dear John," I read, "Phippsie has to make a business trip to Assam and I'm coming along as far as Calcutta for four or five days beginning Oct. 10. Staying at Great Eastern. Get in touch with me and lets have lunch or a drink. Lots of news. Love, Dot."

On the back was a picture of the Taj Mahal Hotel in Bombay.

I read it through again. God damn her, I thought, why must it be just now? Ordinarily I would have been happy enough to spend a couple of hours with Dorothy, answering or evading her questions, hearing all about the unstuffiness of life with Phippsie on Malabar Hill. But now, after Julia's outburst in Darjeeling, I wanted Dorothy to stay clear of us, out of our sight, out of our thoughts. In my mind, she had become a kind of witch, lurking in the twilight of my past; this of course was unfair to poor Dorothy, but I didn't want to be reminded of her for a long time to come. I tore up the post card and dropped the pieces into the waste basket.

As the week went on, I felt more and more encouraged about Julia. She had unusually severe cramps but then felt immense relief once her period started. I saw her every day. She still seemed rather nervous and jumpy, still scratched her wrists and brushed back her hair every few minutes, but she was in good spirits and her whole face broke into full life whenever she smiled. She was excited over the prospect of Philip's party, talking several times about the new dress she was going to wear.

There was a lot of work to be done in the visa office: once again, Mary Buxton had left a fantastic tangle for me to hack my way through. Even so, I began to make plans for a new

255

report. While writing about the riots, it had occurred to me that I ought to know more about the role of the labor unions in the Hindu-Muslim conflict. There wasn't time then for me to follow up the few leads I had, but I now decided it would be interesting to study the whole Bengali labor movement in its relation to political action. I talked over the idea with Morris Halpern, who knew more about the subject than anyone else in the office; he encouraged me, his tragicomic face working with excitement as he leaped at my ideas and tossed up many more of his own. Then I had lunch with Martin, who, because of his job with the Labour Department, would be indispensable to my project. He lacked Morris's Jewish enthusiasm—in fact he seemed amused and a little ironical at my wanting to undertake such a study—but he promised to help where he could. Although perfectly friendly, Martin was more remote than I had seen him since our trip to Benares; his gaze kept wandering away while I talked, as though he were watching some hidden play in the farthest corner of his mind. But then, smiling slightly, he would give a reasoned and precise response to whatever I had been saying. I noticed that he didn't take his usual drink before lunch.

I saw Philip several times at the office. He seemed more interested in talking about his party than the ceremonies which would precede it. I felt fairly detached about the whole prospect; nothing about it seemed in the least real to me.

But at breakfast on Thursday, Ralph suddenly broke his morning silence and said, "You should have been at the American Club cocktail party last week. You'd have been proud of Philip's performance." His voice and look were portentous, and I had the conviction that he'd been waiting to bring this up ever since my return from Darjeeling.

"What happened?"

Ralph's answer shocked me. Philip had brought Mirza Ali to the party, which was traditionally an all-American affair. "Well, he waltzed right in with him," said Ralph, "as pleased with himself as if he'd brought along Rita Hayworth. And I swear to God, he was wearing eye make-up."

"Philip?"

"Of course not. That damned Indian fairy. Most of the time they stood in a corner with a drink and giggled at everybody. Like we were a God damn circus or something. Don't think there wasn't plenty of talk about it. You ought to have heard Jock Mitchell sounding off in *my* hearing about all the fairies in the State Department. You can imagine how I felt."

That fool! It was the worst place possible to have pulled such a stunt. The image of the flaunting and giggling made me sick. And yet, in spite of all my dismay, Ralph's look of bug-eyed indignation made me want to laugh; in it I could see the concentrated outrage of the entire American Club, and for a second I wished I had been there to cheer Philip on. Of course I would have done nothing of the sort: the possible consequences for Philip were much too serious to allow that kind of flippancy.

After an abashed silence I did manage to suggest to Ralph that he and his pals were taking the whole thing too seriously, that Philip had always loved to show off, that he was just trying to shock everyone, that the whole thing was a joke. I had no expectation that this line of argument would carry much weight with Ralph; I knew myself that it contained only a partial truth.

Ralph was scornful. "A joke? Like this conversion business?"

"No, you're wrong there. I'm convinced the conversion is absolutely serious." And suddenly, I *was* convinced.

"Are you? If you ask me, the whole thing's just an excuse for this party he's going to give."

There was no point to arguing. "Well," I said at last, "when are you going to sick the hounds on Philip?"

"Sick the hounds on him? What are you talking about?"

"I don't know. Maybe you're going to complain to Mr. Hubbard about it; tell him Philip's a dangerous homosexual who ought to be dismissed from the Foreign Service at once."

"That's unfair!" Ralph looked like a sulky rabbit. "What do you take me for? Do you think I'd do a thing like that?"

"I'm only kidding," I said. And I felt that Philip was somewhat safer than he'd been a few minutes earlier.

Still, driving to work, I was very worried. I had assumed until now that only I knew about Mirza Ali, that Philip was being discreet. I wondered what had provoked this flaunting. Why should it break out just before Philip's entry into the Church? Had Mirza Ali insisted upon some kind of public display? While I had found the Indian distasteful before, I now hated and feared him as I would the first sign of cancer on Philip's body.

What, if anything, should I do? The idea of confronting Philip openly with the subject—of warning him—filled me with embarrassment and dread.

Heavy with these thoughts, I managed to avoid Philip at the office all that day and the next. Then, on the night before the party, he came to see me. Julia and I had planned to go to the movies, but she had phoned me to say she'd had an extremely tiring day and wanted to go to bed right after supper. "So I'll be in really good shape for tomorrow night," she explained. "I want to be able to dance until sunrise. I've never done that before." I agreed to this, telling her that I could use a little extra sleep myself. Thus, at ten thirty, I was at home when the doorbell began to ring so insistently that I thought it was stuck. Philip was standing in the hall, tieless and coatless, his shirt front drenched with sweat. "I feel like talking," he said. "Will you come for a drive with me?"

Instead, I urged him to come into the apartment. And when I saw him hesitate, I added that Ralph had gone out for the evening.

"My house is a wreck," he said, entering the living room. "Everything's turned upside down for the party. The damn workmen are still hammering away on the dance pavilion. That's what one gets for planning something rather Edwardian." He slumped into a chair. "As you know, everything takes place tomorrow. I'm in a ghastly frame of mind."

He indeed wanted to talk, and his face brightened as he began to explain all the preparations for the ceremony. By special permission of the Archbishop, all the necessary sacraments were going to be administered on the same day. His sponsors were to be the Belgian Consul General and Frédéric de Croye—a selection that had gratified the Archbishop, who had even agreed to make a brief appearance at Philip's party. Then, without warning, the cheerfulness vanished, and Philip's forehead broke into a beading of sweat. "I've got the most horrible stage fright," he muttered. I must have raised my eyebrows at this term, for he immediately added, "Not that I'm merely playing a part. Far from it. I almost wish I were."

After a moment's misgiving I blurted out something that had puzzled me. "Weren't you baptized before? Baptized as an Anglican?"

Philip shook his head. "No, the Anglo-Catholic business started at Harvard. And I was never baptized." We sat silently for some time, and when Philip spoke again, his voice had a kind of leaden hopelessness. "I've told you a number of lies in the past. Tonight I want to tell you a few things that are true."

Now I shook my head. "Don't confess to me. Save these things for the man who ought to hear them."

There was a lightning flash of scorn. "Ha! Are you afraid I'm going to blast your ears with revolting stories of my private life? Are you scared to know me as I really am?"

"No, it's not that—at least I don't think it's that." I didn't want to tell him that nothing he might say about himself or his background or his private life would come as a real revelation. However much I might have guessed of the larger outlines, I preferred to remain ignorant of the details.

Philip watched me narrowly as he spoke. "Do you know, for example, that I'm homosexual?"

There was nothing to do except nod.

"How long have you known it?"

"I've only been sure—well, since I heard about the American Club party." Then I added, "You must have been determined to make it clear. To everybody."

"But you guessed something earlier?"

Again I nodded, deeply relieved that I had not had to raise the subject.

"Doesn't the fact bother you?"

259

"Only if it causes you pain or trouble."

"In other words, you don't have any moral objection?"

I hesitated, trying to push through toward what I really felt. "None at all. As long as it's a private affair."

"Doesn't the idea disgust you?"

"No, I don't feel any disgust. I used to—or at least I thought I did. But that was mainly a conditioned reflex. No," I continued, fumbling ahead, "there's no disgust. Maybe even a little curiosity. And I don't think I really feel superior about my own sexual orientation. Maybe luckier—given the social view of things—but not much at that." I paused, bemused by the distance I had come, shivering a little, as though I had caught the sound of cold waves breaking over a tiny strip of sand. "It's such a joke," I went on. "We all have to hobble through life, the sprinter as well as the cripple. We all limp, one way or another. It hardly seems to matter very much in the long run." I fell silent. Neither of us looked at each other, but I could sense that Philip had sunk into his own well of meditation.

"Thank you," he said at last with grating irony. "That's all rather comforting, I suppose. But let's turn back to the short view. Wouldn't you have been disgusted with me at the American Club party? Wouldn't your face have registered some such emotion?"

"Yes, that's true. I don't like the public part—the flaunting and smirking and all that. But mainly I am worried—"

"I know, I know!" he interrupted. "You want me to be careful. You don't want me to jeopardize my career. Isn't that what you were going to say?"

"More or less."

"As if *that* mattered, really!" There was a long pause. "So," Philip began, "you say you feel no disgust. For the private act, at least. No moral outrage. I envy you. I wish I could take such a liberal view. I wish it could be that easy for me. John, you disgust *me*. You and your nice, easy, unstrained tolerance."

"You're being unfair to me. Whatever tolerance I have hasn't been won quite *that* easily."

But Philip wouldn't listen. "Your broad-mindedness sickens

me! John, if you only knew what an unspeakable loathing I feel for my whole situation; if you only knew how foul my existence has become, how I stink in my own nostrils!"

"Now you're being unfair to yourself. You're being *really* perverse."

"No," he groaned. "I think I really see myself. . . ." Philip's voice trailed off and he lowered his enormous head, gripping his clasped hands between his knees. Again the sweat had come; it began to streak down his face like small tears.

I sat speechless before this posture of gigantic despair. The self-dramatizing element was there all right, but so were the beads of anguish on Philip's gray forehead. Drops of real pain and real terror. There's no way I can help him, I thought.

"I believe in God," he whispered. "And in the fountain of His mercy. I've got to reach it. I haven't yet; perhaps I never will. I can't imagine my cleansing, but I've got to believe in its possibility. I've *got* to. Maybe I'll know the answer by tomorrow —or at least part of it."

I was deeply moved. "I believe it will work for you," I said. "It wouldn't for me, but we're very different. I believe there's a good chance you'll find what you need."

"I believe it, too," said Philip in a stronger voice. Taking out his silk bandanna, he wiped his forehead and cheeks and throat. Then he smiled secretly and inclined his head to one side. "Life is very strange," he said. "Isn't it curious that I had to come to India before I could become either a practicing homosexual or a Roman Catholic. I should never have dared to become either at home, and yet, even though these things are in conflict, they're both in a sense my manifest destiny. What is it about India that could bring this about?"

"There's so little cushioning in India. We're forced back on ourselves. It may be as simple as that."

"That's not very simple." Again Philip gave his secret smile, which was followed by a long sigh. "One of my old cushions or props or whatever you want to call him is pretty unhappy just now. I had a letter from my father yesterday. Naturally, being a good Reformed Jew, he's quite upset about my conversion."

My God, I thought, Philip's come through; he'll be all right! I met his eyes, smiling at him, and nodded. The hour of truth!

"You don't seem very surprised," said Philip, "to learn that my father's a Jew."

"I'm not. But, Philip, I'm very glad you told me."

He looked down for a long time, his smile playing and fading on his full lips. Then he broke into a laugh. "It's extraordinarily funny. It's a marvelous joke, really." His voice had become thickly Anglicized all at once, very snotty. "I seem to have some trouble surprising you tonight. But what will you say when I tell you that Arnold Sachs is not my real father?"

"What do you mean?"

"Precisely that. My mother was pregnant when she married him. He was aware of it, and he was always very kind to her. And to me. John, I've never told this to anyone before—except for Father Bernier. Actually, though not technically, I'm illegitimate."

"For Christ's sake, Philip!" It's a lie, it's a lie, I groaned to myself, stunned by the crashing of my hope. In my distress I couldn't say anything more; I didn't even dare to meet his gaze.

Philip misunderstood my reaction. "I knew it would come as a shock to you," he said. "But I've lived with the fact so long it doesn't pain me any more. Shall I tell you who I think my real father was?" His voice was glossy and eager.

Without answering, I got up and walked into the dining room, as though to get us another drink. Instead, I leaned out the open window, trying to steady myself with draughts of cool air. I saw the glare of headlights moving down Harrington Street; then the car turned into the compound.

I walked back to the dining-room door. "Ralph's coming," I said, glad to be rescued from Philip's tale.

He looked up. "Oh, is he? That might be a little awkward. You know, I haven't invited him to my christening party."

This, of course, I knew. Ralph had told me he considered it an honor not to have been invited.

"You know," continued Philip, "I think I'll invite him. It might be amusing to see if he accepts at this late hour."

CHAPTER XXIII ❧ ALTHOUGH I was now badly worried about Philip, I fully expected to enjoy his party. A christening party or a damnation party—it would give me a chance to dance with Julia again, to dance outdoors on a soft night under a twinkling swarm of lanterns. We hadn't danced together in a long time. This would be *our* party, our celebration.

On that evening I dressed early, planning to stop by the Great Eastern Hotel before I called for Julia. As the week passed and Julia recovered her spirits, I felt more confident about a meeting with Dorothy. Why not? I'd even tell Julia that I'd seen Dorothy—that would be best. Since I had been unable to reach Dot by telephone, I decided to leave a note at the hotel, asking her to have lunch with me on Sunday. This errand done (Dorothy was still out), I drove on to Great Russell Street in a charged and gleeful mood.

Julia met me at the door. She was wearing her blue flannel dressing gown and slippers. "Where have you been?" she demanded, hurling the words into my astonished face. "I've tried to phone you a dozen times in the last half hour." Then her voice became less frantic and she said, "I'm afraid I can't come with you."

"*What?*"

Julia's eyes were wide and glittering and the skin around them was the color of dish water. Her face had that pinched, colorless quality that I had inwardly named her "ailing-orphan look." Even her hair, usually so soft, seemed to hang drab and lifeless over the turned-up collar of her dressing gown. "I'm sorry," she said, "but I just don't feel up to it. I'm not at all in the mood for a party."

"But Julie, are you sick or something?"

"No, but I feel tired and out of sorts. I'm sorry to let you down like this, but I'm not fit company for man or beast tonight." Then, seeing the look on my face, she said, "John, don't be angry with me."

At first I couldn't speak; I felt as though I were smothering in my own blood. Finally I said, "So you've waited until now to tell me?"

"I *tried* to phone you. And earlier, I kept hoping I might feel better."

"There's no excuse for this. Go to your room and get dressed."

"Please don't press me, darling. It's out of the question to-night—you'd hate my company." She backed away from me into the hall, holding both white, clenched fists just under the bosom of her dressing gown. "Please give Philip my love and make my apologies. We're supposed to have lunch tomorrow. Tell him to phone me first. . . ."

But I was listening to none of this. "If you say you're not sick, then you're going to come with me. I won't put up with this craziness."

"All right then!" Julia cried. "Look! Look at *this!*" And she pulled up her left sleeve. "And look at *this!*" she wailed, opening her gown at her throat.

At first I could see nothing but the bare flesh. Then, staring more closely, I could make out a faint, rough-looking, pinkish-gray rash along the underside of her forearm and down the side of her neck. "What is it?" I asked stupidly.

"It's the eczema. It's come back. *You've* made it come back!"

"Oh, Julie, sweetheart! You mustn't say that, darling." I felt like crying as I caught her arm, dragging her toward me. "Sweet-heart, I can barely see it. It's hardly visible. You mustn't worry about it. Get dressed, darling. Put a little powder on your arms and neck if you want to. You'll feel much better. Nobody's going to notice anything."

Julia pulled away from me, weeping. "Oh, John, I didn't mean what I said! How could I? Of course it isn't your fault. Please go on to the party and let me go to bed. Please leave me now."

"Julie, sweetheart, you must come with me. You'll feel much worse if you don't."

"I can't! I can't!"

"Then I'll stay here with you. I'm not going to leave you like this."

"John, you've got to go. I don't want you here. It'll only

make things worse." Again Julia backed away; then she turned toward her bedroom, hunching her shoulders as if she were very cold. When I followed, she swung around in the doorway to face me. "You must be sick of hearing me ask you to be patient," she said. "But what else can I do? I can't bear to give you up—that's what I ought to do, but I *can't*. So if you still want me—I—I really don't know why you *should* when I'm like this—then, John, you'll just have to be patient and help me and keep on hoping and give me time."

As Julia spoke, she was gently scratching the inside of her wrist, and I cringed as if the next stroke would bring blood.

"I can be patient, but you've got to help, too," I said, looking away from those gentle, horrible fingers. "Julie, please, sweetheart, put on your new dress and come to Philip's with me. You can't give in to this, to whatever it is that's causing all this trouble."

She shook her head, tightening her lips. "Don't ask me to do that tonight. I'll try to be stronger another time, but not tonight."

I let out my breath. "Well, that's it, I guess. I'll drop by sometime tomorrow. You'll be better," I said, fearing the deadness of my own voice. Then I kissed her and walked away.

I was almost running by the time I reached my car, and I hurled myself awkwardly into the front seat, brushing my dinner jacket against the doorjamb as I did so. For an instant all my rage was concentrated on the black grease that had sprung up like a welt across the white cloth. God damn it! God damn her! I slumped back, unable to make the effort of starting the motor. A sack of bitterness had broken inside, and my heart and tongue were drenched in its bile. I mustn't despair, I thought, I can't give up now. But for the first time I tasted the prospect of total loss. What was wrong with her? What did all this mean? Ah, the poor girl! I felt as if I could only bruise my fists against a rough door that some witch had slammed between me and everything that I loved and wanted in Julia.

I drove home, not knowing what else to do, and spent a miserable hour or so. Finally I got up from the sofa, cleaned my jacket as well as I could, splashed my face with cold water, and drove on to Philip's.

On my way to the bar I encountered the Hubbards and had to stop to pay my respects. "Great party," said the Consul General. He had just lit a cigar and was looking about in his benign way. Ever since he had been forced to reprimand me, Mr. Hubbard had gone out of his way to be cordial. Mrs. Hubbard was less sure about the party. She was afraid Philip had gone a little far: after all, a junior officer didn't ordinarily entertain people like Sir Duleep and Lady Mitra or Brigadier Leith-Symington or the big Clive Street tycoons.

"I wouldn't worry about it," I said. "After all, an American can always get away with something like this. They expect it of us."

"I know," said Mrs. Hubbard sadly. "That's just the trouble." She looked fondly toward the veranda, where Philip was talking and gesturing with the Belgian Consul General and Madame Grimm-Martin.

The Consul General flicked his cigar. "For Pete's sake, Martha, stop worrying. Everybody's having a swell time. The Clive Street wallahs like a good party just like everybody else. So does a British general."

"*Brigadier,*" said his wife, mildly correcting him.

I set out again for the bar. This time I was intercepted by the Schneiders, who were with Andy Wanamaker, Mary Buxton, and Ralph. Liz quickly took me aside and said in an anxious whisper, "Where are the Halperns? I haven't seen them anywhere."

"I expect Philip didn't invite them."

She frowned. "Damn Philip! If he's invited everyone else in Calcutta and left them out, I'll never forgive him. Philip's simply asking to be taken down a peg."

"He didn't invite Ralph either until last night. And then only as a joke."

"Ralph can take care of himself. It's the Halperns I care

about. I thought Esther looked a little blank the other day when I mentioned the party."

"I expect they're tougher than you think."

Liz shook her head. "No one's ever tough enough not to feel this kind of thing." She edged back toward the others. "Where's Julia? Not sick again?" And when I said yes, she gave me a piercing glance. "What's the matter with you two? You look a bit sick yourself. I won't ask why, but I warn you, John: if you let that girl slip through your fingers, I'll whip you all the way back to Baltimore."

I forced a smile. "I'll keep that in mind," I said. Moving on, I managed this time to reach the bar.

On a raised platform at the far end of the canopied dance pavilion, Bela Szabo and his Budapest Ensemble (violin, tenor saxophone, upright piano, bass fiddle, and accordion) were thumping out Viennese waltzes, polkas, and very fast fox trots. Occasionally the violinist would play a solo, a *zigeuner* piece filled with all the melancholy of the Central European past, and then the other performers—aging men with gray shocks of hair —would look upward as the thin strains of music rose and quavered, and would rub their chins, as if meditating on the complex fate that had brought them from second-class hotels in Kraków or Bucharest or Innsbruck to strum and scrape for their living at a christening party in Calcutta. And the dancers would stop, too, looking bored, waiting for the next fox trot. I stood watching and listening, squeezed into a corner between the dance floor and a large tree, making a trip now and then to the bar, unwilling just yet to swim out into the crowd, unwilling to make smiling answers to the inevitable "Where's Julia?"

Finally my longing for her touch on my arm became unbearable and I wandered away. New couples were still separating themselves from the swirl of nearly five hundred people and moving toward the pavilion. As the guests sauntered about the lawn, formed clusters, strayed off in pairs, regrouped, ate, drank, or danced, they had the look of extras in a vast Technicolor spectacle—as if a director skilled in crowd effects had carefully arranged the spots of color: the black and white of the men's clothes, the flowered prints worn by the British and American women, the crimson, green, and gold of the saris. Even the black shadows had a stagy quality as they fell across grass which, under the lanterns and the strung-up lights, glowed with a soft, chemical green.

I found myself face to face with Diane Cummings and Kiwi Das Gupta. "What on earth are you doing here?" I blurted out in my surprise. "I mean, I thought you were still in Darjeeling."

"How lovely to see you again," she said in her elegant, piping way. Then she answered my question: "Wasn't Darjeeling lovely? But one can't stay there forever, can one? Especially if one's a working girl."

It had always been easy for me to forget that Diane's "official" job was that of running a beauty salon on Park Street. She went on to explain that she'd returned to Calcutta only yesterday, had found Philip's invitation ("So sweet of him to remember me"), and had prevailed on the Das Guptas to let her come with them ("I do so loathe coming alone to a party"). Then, of course, she asked where Julia was and her lovely face puckered into a mask of tragic concern when I answered that Julia was a bit under the weather. Kiwi led her off to the pavilion, and I continued to thread my way toward the spot where the Fenwicks and Ramesh were chatting with a little knot of Good Mixers. The presence of Diane set me laughing. Good old Philip!

Once the questions about Julia were over, I began to enjoy my new group. Martin was already a little drunk and argumentative. "You arrived too late for the procession," he said accusingly. "Terribly impressive." Then he described to me how the Archbishop had been led among the guests, like visiting royalty, flanked by Philip and Frédéric de Croye and followed by Father Bernier.

"None of us was grand enough to be presented," said Ramesh gleefully.

"I *adored* the Archbishop," said Anila in her most honeyed voice. "Such a spiritual-looking old dear. The most penetrating gray eyes I've ever seen."

"The spiritual-looking old dear honored the company for a very short time," said Martin, with a twisted grin at his wife. "Then he was whisked back across the lawn and through the house and into his waiting car. Or perhaps it was his waiting palanquin. Isn't that what archbishops travel in?"

"Perhaps even a s-s-s-sedia," put in Harold Porter.

Ramesh was ready to leave; Sujata was unwell and had stayed at home. Martin and I went along with him while he said good-by to Philip.

"It was good of you to come at all," said Philip with elaborate politeness. He looked well: robust and florid, his yellowish eyes alive and dancing with pleasure. Then, spotting Martin and me, he said sharply, "You're not leaving, too, are you?"

"Never fear," Martin said, lifting his glass.

When we reached the front lawn, Ramesh spread his arms and cried, "Ah-h-h, at last we can breathe the clean air of the night without drawing in all those poisonous fumes! Our friend has been lavish, magnificent, but he is determined to poison his guests with all that food and drink. You may laugh," he continued tragically. "Someday you will admit that the whole system of Western nutrition is disastrously wrong. Not to mention the drinking of spirits."

Outside the front gate, cars were parked up and down both sides of Asoka Road. There were also several rickshas, and Ramesh hailed one of these, despite the fact that Martin and I both offered to drive him home. "Certainly not," he said. "Go back in and enjoy yourselves. I shall take the ricksha to Belvedere Road and then get a taxi."

The ricksha wallah pulled up and stood waiting patiently between the hand traces while we took leave.

"Unless," Ramesh went on, "I can persuade you to leave this party altogether and come back to Kalighat with me. Oh, Martin, do dash back and get Anila right away! Sujata will be delighted. She'll give us all some freshly cooked sweatmeats and a wholesome cup of tea."

"You're so subtle, Ramesh," said Martin.

"I know, I know! It will never do. Only fiery Western spirits will console you tonight. Good-by, my friends!" He shook hands again with each of us and climbed into his ricksha.

Then, just as we were about to return to the party, an immense car—a polished black whale of a Daimler—drove up and stopped. An Indian driver in khaki jumped out to open the back door, and I heard a woman's voice, rather hoarse and very Southern, exclaim, "Well, look who's on the welcoming committee!" And Dorothy got out of the car, followed by a middle-aged British couple whom I recognized as Sir Ronald and Lady McAllister, old friends of Phippsie's.

I strode forward, holding out my hand. "Well, for God's sake! How are you? Did you get my note?"

"What note?" She came toward me, clutching her sequined evening bag and pulling at the white stole across her shoulders.

"I left one at your hotel this evening," I said after briefly kissing her held-up mouth. "About lunch tomorrow."

"I've been out. I wondered why the hell you hadn't called."

"I tried to. Several times."

"Never mind. Hello, Martin, do you remember me?"

"How could I ever forget you?" he said with a little bow.

Then Dorothy introduced us to the McAllisters, who had now extricated themselves from the ministrations of their driver. "Dear me, it does sound jolly, doesn't it?" said Lady McAllister, nodding toward the music and the hum of voices from behind the house. "We hardly know Mr. Sachs. Wasn't it kind of him to invite us? I'm afraid we're frightfully late."

"When I heard the McAllisters were coming," said Dorothy, "I thought 'What the hell' and phoned Philip and invited myself. Actually he was sweet as pie about it. Delighted to hear my voice and all that."

We moved slowly toward the house. I told Dorothy that she looked well.

"You haven't really seen me yet," she replied. "Wait till I'm in a better light."

And when Martin and I left them at the front door and started around the side of the house, Dorothy called out, "I'm going to be furious if you don't dance with me."

As we were about to re-enter the party, Martin and I stood for a moment and looked across the crowd toward the red-and-yellow tenting over the dance floor at the rear of the garden. "It's quite a gathering," I said. "Especially when you realize Philip's been here only a year."

"What's that got to do with it? Calcutta's a city of easy conquests. And quick departures. If Philip were to try to give this same party five years from now, he'd find that two-thirds of these people had vanished—most of them without leaving so much as a memory. Calcutta society's about as permanent as the sandbars of the Hooghly. About as permanent as the British Raj."

"Still, it's a fine party. I wish I were in the mood for it."

Martin gripped my arm. "Something's wrong, isn't there? You've been looking down in the mouth all evening. I don't want to know what it is, but I'm awfully sorry. Life's so unfair at times, isn't it? So terribly complex. I'll bet there's not one person in all that glittering mob who's *really* happy in any *simple* way."

"I've been happy," I said, thinking of Darjeeling, "but it wasn't simple."

"I loathe these proliferating complexities. If I were a god, I'd melt down that whole bloody mob. And you and me, too. The world needs recasting in a simpler mold. Needs it very badly."

We began to stroll across the lawn. Then, abruptly, Martin stopped and looked into my face. "John, if you're going to get married, marry young. Don't wait as long as I did," he continued in a strangely passionate voice. "I love Anila very dearly, you understand, but everything's so very much more difficult than it should be. When one's been used to one's freedom—oh, well, you know. Anyway, my boy, marry young. That's my advice to you. Now, shall we get a drink before we join the others?"

Someone touched my sleeve, and I turned around to see Mirza Ali Khan inclining toward me, one monkey arm stretched out. "I've been sent for you," he said, "by a certain very important lady who wants to make your acquaintance."

"Who?"

"Rosa Maitland." Mirza Ali beamed at me, looking merry and pouting at the same time. Again I was struck by how small his face was in relation to the extraordinary length of his arms and legs.

"I'm busy just now." I started toward the bar again, hating this monkey, this minor devil, whom I saw dancing along the road to Philip's ruin. But Mirza Ali was persistent, hovering at my elbow as I walked. "Really, you must come," he said. "It won't do to disappoint her. Besides, there's another bar there."

We found Lady Maitland and Philip standing at the buffet table, which had been set up at right angles to the bar. Chewing busily, so that the rolls of fat under her chin were in constant motion, Lady Maitland was heaping her plate with galantine of chicken and *foie gras*. Philip swung fiercely toward me. "Are you enjoying my christening party?" he demanded. "Everyone tells me it's a splendid party, but the more often I hear it the better I like it."

"I'm having a fine time," I said, spreading a piece of toast with caviar.

Lady Maitland slowly wheeled around. Cascades of amber beads were looped across the voluminous purple silk of her bosom. "How d'ye do, Mr. Wickham," she said as soon as she had finished swallowing. "I believe Philip tells me you're from Boston?" She spoke with a slow contralto dignity, with much pursing and rounding of her lips. "It must be a delightful city. Quite different from so much of America, I should think."

"No, Lady Maitland, I'm from Baltimore. In the state of Maryland."

"Oh, yes. That's nice, too, isn't it?"

I noticed the sharp, rather pretty English features nearly lost in swathes of encircling flesh. What a sow! A scalded, unhappy sow!

"I've always maintained," she was saying, "that no one has better manners than the nicer sort of American. Except possibly the Spanish. They're so incredibly gallant."

Frédéric de Croye advanced toward us, tall and solemn as a Byzantine saint. A moment later I swallowed the rest of my toast, made my excuses, and moved toward the bar. As I was leaving, I heard Lady Maitland say (in a context that I missed), "You know, I sometimes think I must be rather like Caesar's wife—all things to all men."

Armed with a new highball, I wandered in the direction of the house. As I drew nearer, I began to hear the sound of a piano soaring above the strains of the band. The French doors were open. I glanced in and saw Madame de Croye hunched over Philip's piano, moving with total absorption and tremendous skill through what I soon recognized as the first movement of the *Appassionata*. An unwound coil of black hair had fallen across her forehead. She was alone in the room.

I found Dorothy chatting with Brigadier Leith-Symington. As soon as there was a break in the hilarity, I grabbed her wrist. "Let's dance," I said.

"Hey, not so rough!" But she excused herself from the enchanted soldier and followed me to the dance floor. "You're a little drunk," she said, then added, "I was wondering if you were going to avoid me all evening." We had hardly begun to dance when Kiwi Das Gupta, who was staggering around with the Begum of Chittagong, abandoned his partner in mid-floor and lurched toward Dorothy, his arms outstretched and his soft mouth gaping beneath his mustache. Dorothy squealed out her greeting, they embraced, and then they swirled off unsteadily toward the center of the dancers. I caught Audrey Chittagong's eye and we both shrugged; I noticed that her husband, the Nawab, was dancing with Diane Cummings, who had once been his mistress. A moment later Dorothy dragged Kiwi back, both of them laughing, and gave him a shove in the direction of the Begum. "My God, it's just like the Jungly Wallah," Dorothy gasped as she fell into my arms. "Hasn't anything changed in Calcutta?"

"I have." We settled into the beat of the music.

"Have you?" Then she said, "You look harder, I think. But less mean."

"To tell the truth, I feel meaner tonight than I have in a long time. I'm in a rotten mood."

"You often were. Anyway, it's good to see you again. I mean that."

"I'm glad you do."

I smiled into her glowing face and noticed how young and soft her mouth looked under the flaming poppy-red of her lipstick. Whatever else it was, this was not the face of an ailing orphan. Again I felt the headlong, plunging life that would carry Dorothy until it threw her into her grave. This was not the pallid face of defeat.

"So Phippsie has made you happy," I said after we had danced for a while in silence.

"I hate to disappoint you, but that happens to be the case. I'm happier than I've ever been before. We have a wonderful time in Bombay. Phippsie's a darling, he really is, and he's got more life in him than all the other men I've known put together." She tilted her head slightly, raking me with her laughing blue eyes. "I swear, I have trouble keeping up with him."

"So you've really broken the circuit of your bad luck?" I asked as the music stopped. And I thought, She'll go to bed with me if I play it right.

"You're damn right I have! And what about you? How are things going?"

"So-so."

"Have you and Julia had a fight?"

"Not exactly that."

"Do you think you'll marry her?"

I shook my head. "God only knows. It's not too promising just now."

"You ought to get married. It would do you a lot of good." The glibness of this angered me. "What the hell do you know about it?" I demanded.

"I'm sorry. I didn't mean to pick at a scab."

"That's all right." Then I said, "I'm tired of dancing. Let's get something to drink."

Dorothy agreed, but as we left the floor, she asked what time it was. "Nearly one!" she shrieked. "Good Lord, the McAllisters must be nearly dead. I've got to run."

"Dot," I began, holding fast to her hand, "don't go yet. I'll take you home later. Tell the McAllisters you're going to stay awhile. Our evening's just beginning," I added in almost a whisper.

When she looked down for a second, I was sure that I had won and I began to breathe faster. But in the next moment I heard her say, "If what you've got on your mind is what I think it is, you'd better go home and take a long, cold shower." Her eyes were blazing at me now. "Haven't you believed anything I've said to you this evening? You're the most arrogant, conceited human being I've ever known. Let go of my hand."

I felt like a fool and mumbled something to the effect that she'd misunderstood me. A little later she laughed and said, "My Lord, you don't have to keep on apologizing." We found the McAllisters, said good night, and agreed to meet for lunch at the Great Eastern tomorrow.

Then I returned to the pavilion, still rather crestfallen and angry at myself. I watched Colonel Kelley, of U.S. Graves Registration, trying to jitterbug with Doris Das Gupta; her sari, half-unwound, was flapping like a loose sail, and she waved her arms wildly as he tossed her out and drew her back again. Afterward I danced with Diane Cummings, who was fairly drunk and almost maudlin. She confided in me that the main reason she hadn't gone to the States to become a movie star was because of her little boy. "Did'n know I had a little boy, did you?" she whispered haltingly. "Not many people do. Lives with my mother. Adorable little boy, but his father won't allow him to leave India." Then, with more of the old elegance, "Even if Mummy were willing to keep him forever, one couldn't seriously think of abandoning one's own child. You're nice," she added. "It's so nice of you to sympathize." A moment later Kiwi Das Gupta staggered up to claim possession.

"John, you're a darling," said Anila Fenwick. "I don't know what I'd have done without you." Her sari was askew, half-pulled off her shoulder; she was clinging with both hands to Martin's upper right arm.

"He's a bloody, interfering nuishance. A bloody American bully . . ."

"Shut up, Martin." I was holding him by the left arm. Together we half-carried, half-dragged him along the front walk to where the Porters were waiting in their Hillman.

Suddenly Martin's head dropped forward on his stiff, buckling shirt front and he began to sob—great, racking sobs that threatened to shatter his thin chest with their violence. "I want to die," he gasped. "Want to die. Leave me alone, you bloody fools."

Harold Porter opened the back door, and Anila, Mira Porter, and I managed to shove and pull Martin into the car and to prop him up in the corner of the seat. He was still crying, head down, hopeless, unable to catch his breath.

Before getting into the car herself, Anila turned to me and whispered, "What am I going to do, John? Whatever shall I do?" She touched my hand and a second later I closed the door behind her.

Instead of returning directly to the now-ragged party, I sat down on the concrete door stoop, in the intense shadow of the porte-cochere. My head was swimming. "Oh, God damn, oh, God damn!" I moaned to myself, holding my temples. Poor Martin, poor Anila. Poor Julia. Poor John. . . . I saw Julia push back the sleeve of her blue dressing gown, saw her scratch her poor wrist. How cruel! I got up unsteadily, nearly suffocated with grief, self-pity, and rage. The heaviness of the night was like the pressure of the ocean against a diver's body. An ocean of sadness. I walked down the drive toward Asoka Road and stood looking into the darkness. My foot touched a piece of brick lying in the loose gravel. I picked it up and hurled it clattering down the road. I wanted to break all the windows of my life.

After a while I wandered back to the party, which was now reduced to less than fifty people. The Das Guptas and Diane had disappeared from the dance floor. At the opposite end of the lawn I saw a half-circle of people gathered around Lady Maitland, who sat squeezed into a garden chair. Mirza Ali was on the grass at her feet and Frédéric de Croye and Philip were standing on either side. At some distance from them, Madame de Croye was stretched out in a reclining deck chair, fast asleep.

I got a drink which I didn't want and certainly didn't need. There was no one I felt like talking to, but I couldn't bring myself to go home. Finally, realizing a need to go to the bathroom, I went into the house and upstairs. The door was closed, and behind it I could hear the sound of running water. I was about to move on to the second bathroom, when the door opened and Diane Cummings came out, fumbling with the clasp of her evening bag.

"I thought you'd gone home hours ago," I said.

Standing slackly, her feet wide apart, her bag pressed against her bosom, Diane watched me with a blurred smile. "No, no," she said slowly. "Kiwi passed out. He's sleeping in his car. And I can't find Doris. Think she left with that American officer. Haven't a clue, really. You know?" Diane shrugged, brushed back a lock of hair, which, in the half-light, looked more leaden than gold. She smiled again in her unfocused way. "I've got to get home somehow. One can't be expected to walk."

Slowly I took in the blurred, beautiful, inquiring face; the soft, faintly olive skin of the bare shoulders and arms; the necklace of enormous gold links; the brocaded evening bag held just at the cleft of the breasts; the red fingernails of the hand holding the bag; the loosely held body in its pale-green sheath; the sliding line of the hips and the slight forward thrust of the left leg, bent at the knee.

"I'll take you."

"You think tha's good idea?" The blurred smile was gently questioning.

"Why not? Excuse me a minute." And I walked past her into the bathroom. Why not, I thought, feeling the rising beat of my pulse. It occurred to me that Diane might pass out before I could get her home, which would be awkward. I dashed cold water in my face and rinsed out my mouth, spraying water down my shirt front. God, I hope I'm not too drunk!

Diane was leaning against the stair rail when I came out. "You're all *wet*," she said, moving toward me. "Wet but ved-dy *nice*."

I took her in my arms, drew her close against my body, snuggling my face against the silky cushion of her cheek. *Why not?* Then I moved my hand over her forehead, brushing the gorgeous hair from her face, and at last kissed her mouth. For some time we stood there, our bodies straining against each other. I seemed to be holding Diane up as well as embracing her. She gave a long sigh, followed by a funny half-chuckling sound. At last I pulled back and said, "Come on," but I didn't lead her down the stairs. Instead, with my arm around her shoulders, we crept along the hall toward a room I had seen only once before—an unused bedroom-storeroom at the back of the house. We kept stumbling against each other, like scared but defiant children, and each time I hissed a drawn-out "Shhhh!" against her threatened giggle.

"Not here?" Diane whispered as we leaned against the wall outside the door.

I nodded and then kissed her again before she could protest. To hell with them all, I thought, wild now with this final recklessness. Let it come, let it come! Who cares? I opened the door and we breathed the mustiness of the pitch-dark, airless room. "Come on," I murmured and led her across the bare floor, avoiding boxes and trunks, to the bare mattress of the bed.

Then I went back to close the door, locking it from the inside. The darkness was instant and total, a slap across the eyes. I groped my way to the bed, sniffing the dust and heat, skirting the obstacles in my path. Diane was fumbling with the back of her dress; her face was very hot and her shoulders and arms were slippery with perspiration. I could hear and feel the heaviness of her breathing. My hand rested for a moment on her bare knees and then touched the incredible softness just above. She was murmuring something into my ear. We kissed again, and I felt the dangerous forward leap of sensation. Take it easy, boy! Take it easy, slow down! But it was impossible: I was caught up, hurried along out of all control toward a climax that broke almost the moment our bodies were fully joined.

Something very soft, like the gentlest of feathers, settled over my face, and I woke up in panic. Raising my arm to ward off this softness, I felt my hand become entangled in it. "Jesus Christ!" I cried out, and sat upright with a pounding heart. I was completely enmeshed in this spider's web and for an instant or two experienced pure terror before realizing that what enveloped me was mosquito netting; it must have come loose from the mosquito bar over the bed. Then another kind of terror gripped me. Holding my breath, I brought my wrist watch close to my face and read the luminous dial. It was two fifty-six—I could not have been asleep more than half an hour. Still, I *had* fallen asleep—that really scared me—and there was no time to lose. I was completely sober; I knew exactly where I was and who was with me. Reaching out my hand, pushing aside the netting, I caught Diane's upper arm. "Wake up," I whispered, as loudly as I dared. "We've got to get up. Right now!" My tongue was heavy and foul with hangover. For a long time Diane would not move; finally I had to shake her. I groped in the dark for such clothes as I had taken off, for I was scared to switch on the light and couldn't find my matches. At one point I bumped heavily into a wooden box and stood horrified, my fingers clenched, waiting for the noise to die away in my ears.

I felt my way to the door. It wouldn't open, and there was

another instant of terror before I remembered having locked it from the inside. Then I opened it an inch, letting in a shaft of light. The hall was empty, but I heard the sound of water from the distant bathroom and quickly shut the door.

"Have you found all your clothes?" I whispered, turning in the dark toward the bed.

There was an indeterminate sound.

"All right," I said, making the most favorable interpretation. "As soon as the coast is clear, we'll try to make it to the bathroom. A little cold water will help."

"Mmmm . . ."

Diane turned out to be soberer than I expected, but very glum. Our faces in the bathroom mirror should have made each of us sick on the spot. I remember drinking a great deal of water. Then I told Diane to sneak downstairs ahead of me and try to get out the front door without being seen; I would follow in about five minutes; she was to wait for me at my car, parked at the far end of Asoka Road. After again scouting the hall and the stairway and the hall below, I gave her arm a squeeze and sent her on her way. Diane walked with great carefulness, keeping close to the wall and then to the banister for support. I heard no one speak to her downstairs. Bela Szabo's band was still playing, incredibly, outside.

My turn came, and I met no one. But I did see Mirza Ali stretched full length on the living-room sofa. As far as I could tell, he was sound asleep. There were only a few cars left along Asoka Road. The door of one of them was open, and as I passed, I saw the body of Kiwi Das Gupta slumped across the front seat; I also caught the reek of vomit. When I reached my car, Diane was leaning out of the window. "I took Kiwi's money. And cigarette case," she said. She didn't slur her words, but each one was carefully spaced, as if it might break like a soap bubble. "Those bloody ricksha wallahs might rob him. One can't be too careful."

"Do you think we should leave him there?" At the moment I cared nothing for Kiwi, and I spoke these words from sheer moral habit, forcing them out through a blinding headache.

"Might—as well. Doris will come back for him. Always—does."

I drove in rigid silence to Diane's flat on Park Street, just above her beauty shop. Diane, thank God, had gone back to sleep almost at once, leaving me free to concentrate as fully on the unsteady road as my throbbing forehead would permit. Then, after I had roused her again and we had said good night, she lingered for a moment at the door, her hand on the knob.

Finally, through the din of my headache, I heard myself say, "I don't regret what happened tonight. I hope you don't."

There was just enough light from the street lamp for me to see her shrug. "You Americans are the *funniest* lovers," Diane said, opening the door.

CHAPTER XXIV ❧ **LUNCH** with Dorothy was an ordeal. Ever since awakening that morning—much too early—I had been in a shiver of anxiety, as well as sluggish and muddy-tongued from hangover. Dorothy, on the other hand, was in perfect form. She kept the Great Eastern bearers fluttering around our table, teased me about my lack of appetite and the trembling of my hand, gossiped about people I didn't know in Bombay, rallied me about getting married. Then, when lunch was nearly over, her face lost its glaze for an instant and she said, "Of course Phippsie's no dream to live with. Neither am I. But we've managed pretty well so far. Wish me luck, John."

"I do. But I also think you come closer to making your own luck than any person I've ever known."

"Well, like I always say, it's a great life if you don't weaken."

We parted cordially in the lobby, and I hurried away, remembering with some shame my prediction that Dorothy would be cheating on Phippsie within six months. How long had it taken me to cheat on Julia? Four months? But I don't *feel* guilty, I protested.

I don't feel guilty. That had been almost my first thought when I jolted awake about eight thirty. Next I had caught my breath in a spasm of fright. My God, what a reckless thing to have done! I was practically asking to get caught. But in the stark lucidity of my hangover, I could see only folly, not guilt. The act in itself had meant nothing. I couldn't even recall its physical quality: the smell of the stale mattress and the cobweb touch of the mosquito netting were far more vivid to me than the body I'd embraced. And so were Diane's parting words. Even in my wretchedness I had to smile. The whole episode struck me as basically comic—very dangerous but also very funny. And it had nothing to do with my real feelings for Julia. How could I possibly attach the word *betrayal* to something so ridiculous?

But as the morning wore on and I had been unable to get back to sleep, my anxiety increased. I *had* to see Julia—as if the comforting fact of her mere presence could assure me that what had happened was as trivial as it seemed. Should I try to see her now, or wait until after lunch? Finally, just before leaving for the Great Eastern, I had telephoned to say that I would drop by around three o'clock—only to learn, to my surprise, that Julia had decided to keep her luncheon date with Philip.

And now, as I drove toward Great Russell Street, I was panic-stricken by the thought that she might not have returned or that she might have gone out again. And I didn't think of Julia as she'd been last night but only of the girl who had swung happily on my arm through the bazaars of Darjeeling.

Mary Haakinson, wearing hair-curlers and slacks, met me at the door and said that Julia had gone to her room to take a nap. "She doesn't feel very well," said Mary. "I think you ought to let her sleep."

"I only want to speak to her for a moment. I'll see if she's asleep."

I opened Julia's door just wide enough to stick my head in. The room was very dark: the heavy, slatted blinds had been closed against the brightness of the afternoon and the curtains drawn. Still fully dressed except for her shoes, Julia was lying on top of the bed covers, her hands clasped under her head. But when she heard the door open, she jumped up and sat on the edge of the bed.

"Hi, Julie. Did I wake you?"

"I wasn't asleep."

"Are you feeling better, darling?" I noticed that her dress had long sleeves and a high neck. Coming into the room, I felt, for some reason, the need to tiptoe.

"That's a good question. I really don't know for sure."

"Do you mind if I open one of the blinds?"

"Go ahead."

Now I could see that she was as pale as last night, but the strained, staring look in her eyes had given way to a kind of blankness. When I leaned over to kiss her lips, I found them dry as paper.

"You missed a really spectacular party."

"So I've just heard."

"How was your lunch with Philip?" I asked, drawing up a chair. "I'm glad you felt well enough to go out."

The nails of Julia's right hand touched her left wrist just below the cuff of her sleeve, then drew back quickly. Smiling a little, she caught my eye. "John," she began.

After waiting for a few seconds for her to continue, I said, "What is it, darling?"

"Philip's an awful liar, isn't he? Can you believe *anything* he says?"

I nodded. "He does tell lies sometimes. But I know him well enough so I can usually tell when he's beginning to stretch the truth. At least I think I can. There's something about Philip's eyes when he's posing or lying—they won't let you go, they keep trying to find out what effect he's making on you. What brought this up?" I asked, aware of the intense concentration with which she was following my words.

"He was in a very peculiar mood, different from anything I've seen before. He upset me very much. And I know he wanted to, right from the start."

"Oh? Wh—what did he say?"

"Well, he started out by telling me how bad I looked. You can imagine how cheerful *that* made me feel. But at the same time he was very sympathetic and sweet—you know the way he can be. He took me to Firpo's and made a big fuss about the food, telling me to eat this and not to touch that. He talked on about how much his Catholicism meant to him, how it gave him something firm to hold on to, and how important this was, especially since all human relationships are so disappointing. He went on about how people are always letting each other down and how you can't really trust anyone, especially those you love the most."

"I've heard him on that subject before."

"The funny thing was the way he kept insisting that I agree with him. And when I said I didn't take quite such a dim view of human relations, he gave me a sort of pitying smile and said I was a typical American girl—the kind Henry James wrote

284

about—who could never believe the world was really corrupt and subtle and bad. He said he thought we were basically alike —Philip and me, that is—since we were both too trusting in our natures. And therefore born victims."

"Well, did you agree with him?" I asked as casually as I could.

Julia paused for a moment, but she did not respond to my smile. At last she said, "John, why didn't you tell me Dorothy Eustace is in town?"

"I did tell you!" But in the same instant I realized that I hadn't.

Julia shook her head and primly compressed her lips. "I'm very sorry, John," she began in the voice of an older sister, "but you didn't mention it. Not that it's so important as all that."

"Well, I forgot. I intended to tell you last night, but there was hardly any chance, was there? She's in town for a few days while her husband's on a business trip to Assam. I had lunch with her today."

Julia nodded. Suddenly she looked over her shoulder as though something had moved on the dresser across the room. I followed her glance and saw the dresser and the wardrobe and the dressing table laden with photographs of her family and college friends and a snapshot of myself in a small silver frame. And all the time my heart was beating hard with the terrible realization that Philip had told her something else. Then Julia turned her head and our eyes met.

"How did Dorothy's name come up?" I asked.

"Philip just happened to mention that she'd invited herself to the party."

"I see."

Julia ran her fingers through her hair. Then, after wetting her lips in advance, she said, "Philip thought you were in a strange mood last night. He kept implying I must find you quite a handful at times—that you were so restless and moody and unpredictable. He said he was worried about us."

"Why the hell can't Philip keep his hands off us?" I cried. "I got fairly tight. I suppose that's what he means."

"I think you had every right to be a little moody last night," said Julia, lowering her eyes. "Naturally I didn't go into that with Philip."

"I should hope not!"

Again there was the wetting of the lips. "John," she began, "I—I'm afraid I lost my head. I knew Philip was driving at something but didn't want to speak out. I panicked, and before I knew what I was saying, I asked him point-blank if something had happened between you and Dorothy. . . ."

"Julie!"

She continued without looking at me. "He said no but in such a way that I knew he was holding something back. I got more and more upset, and finally he said you'd behaved in very bad taste and had hurt him very much. . . ."

"I hurt Philip?"

"Yes. By carrying on a big public flirtation with Diane Cummings and then leaving with her at the end of the party. That's a complete lie, isn't it?"

"Of course it is! I did give her a lift home—her date had passed out—but there was not the slightest flirtation or anything like that. I danced with her for maybe fifteen minutes at the most."

Julia blinked as though I'd struck her. "There's no reason at all,"—she faltered—"why you shouldn't give her a lift home. But I—for some reason I was so certain Philip was making it all up." She coughed, nearly strangling. Then, clearing her throat, catching her breath, Julia said, "John, he mentioned something else, something that happened earlier."

"Absolutely nothing happened earlier!"

"John, will you swear to me that you didn't disappear upstairs with Diane Cummings for over an hour?" And at that moment Julia's enormous eyes seemed to absorb all the life in her face.

I knew that my own face had gone as white as hers. For one second I struggled against a terrifying impulse to confess, to throw myself on her mercy. "Of course I didn't," I managed to say. Then more firmly, "It's a God damn lie. I'll kill Philip for this!"

I saw Julia turn away, twisting her body on the edge of the

bed so that she faced the pillow. "I don't believe you," she said. "And it kills me to hear you lie. I saw you hesitate. Now don't say anything. Please don't say another word."

"I'm not lying, Julia."

"Don't!" she screamed. "I can't stand to hear you lie."

I got up and came over to the bed and heard myself say, "Julie, what happened meant absolutely nothing. Darling, it had no meaning, none at all. I'm not lying to you, Julie." I placed my hand on her shoulder. "It hadn't any meaning, darling. Try to understand that. And remember that I love you very much."

"Please leave me," said Julia in a flat voice, shrugging off the touch of my hand. "I can't understand what you're saying. It makes no sense to me. Please go."

"Julia—"

"For God's sake, go! I can't think now, I can't talk to you. John, get out, please!"

"Is Julia feeling better?" asked Mary Haakinson as I came into the living room. I stared at her—hadn't she heard Julia shouting at me? Then I shook my head and hurried out of the room and down the stairs.

The car door slammed behind me like an echo from the night before. And once again I sat stunned behind the wheel, drenched in bitterness, overwhelmed by the senselessness of events. I was like the driver of a car who turns his head to argue with his wife and then learns, on regaining consciousness, that both she and their child had died in the ensuing crash. But I still don't *feel* guilty, I said to myself; and then the irrelevance of what I felt to what had happened made me laugh. I had made my own sacrifice to Kali, and the results lay heaped around me.

I had no right to be surprised by the violence of Julia's reaction. But she didn't have to know! I should have got away with it!

Philip was lying full length on the Bokhara rug in the living room, his head pillowed on a sofa cushion; the Last of the Moguls was sitting on the sofa, his legs drawn up beneath him.

They were drinking tea, eating cakes, and listening to the phonograph. Philip sat up abruptly when I came in. "This is very pleasant!" he said. "I'll tell Ala-uddin to bring you a cup. We've got tons of cakes and sandwiches left over from last night."

"Never mind. I want to speak to you alone for a couple of minutes."

Philip looked at me with raised eyebrows, his head cocked. Then he turned to the Indian. "Mirza Ali," he said lightly, "would you be so kind as to wait for me in the garden? Our guest looks as though he has something frightfully stern to say to me." Mirza Ali put on his slippers and then darted past me, quick and thin as a lizard. Philip got up and switched off the Capehart. "Well," he drawled, "I must say your expression rather becomes you. You look like a very well-dressed and substantial young murderer. I've never seen your face so dark. It makes you look almost Italian."

Ignoring all this, I said, "I've just come from Julia's. If you were counting on her to say nothing about what went on at lunch, you're very badly mistaken."

"I don't know what you're talking about." Philip took a bandanna from the pocket of his blazer and blew his nose as contemptuously as if he were taking snuff.

"You know perfectly well what I'm talking about. Now listen to me, stay where you are!" for Philip had turned his back on me and was walking toward the French doors leading to the veranda. "Just give me one minute and then you can call back Mirza Ali. Now listen, Philip! You've really damaged me this time. You've really hurt me. God damn you, you've been pawing over my life long enough. Now you've really managed to hurt me. I wish I had the courage to kill you. Now you can call back Mirza Ali," I said, turning to leave.

Philip ran forward and caught me by the arm. "I don't know what Julia told you," he said. "I hardly even remember what I said to her. It's not important. She broke her word to me, but that's not important, either. Whatever I said, it was for the sake of our friendship, John. That's what you've got to realize."

"For Christ's sake, Philip!" I broke loose from his grip. His face was white and defenseless, and I knew that I couldn't hit him.

"John," he went on, "you've got to believe me. She's not good enough for you. You know that. For months I've had to stand by and watch you get more and more involved in a situation that could only harm you—you and your career. In some ways I adore Julia, but she's not the right woman for you. You must realize that. She doesn't do you justice. I know she means well, but Julia's fundamentally stupid and childish. . . ."

"Shut up!"

But Philip wouldn't stop. He caught me by the shoulders, his breath beating into my face. "When I found out about you and Diane," he whispered, "I was so hurt and jealous that I nearly died. For *her* to go to bed in *my* house—with *my* friend! But in the next minute I was delighted. Delighted for *your* sake! It meant you were breaking away. It was so much more than I'd dared hope. I knew sooner or later you'd come to your senses. And today, when I saw Julia, I actually felt sorry for her, she looked so ill. I was sure she already knew—by some kind of intuition—and I didn't mean to tell her, I just wanted to draw her out, to hear her admit with her own words that she knew it was all over, that she'd given you up, that—"

"You've gone out of your mind!"

I wrenched myself free, but before I could leave the room, Philip ran ahead of me and stood blocking the doorway, his large body crouched slightly, like a wrestler's. "You can't leave me like this," he said pitifully. But even while he was speaking, his pale eyes narrowed. "Don't think I don't know all about you. You haven't fooled me. And you've dared call yourself my friend!"

"Get out of my way."

"I know all about you," he snarled. "I know the lies you've been spreading about me. And all the while you've pretended to be my friend. I know the filthy lies you've told about me and Mirza Ali. I know what you've said about my reasons for joining the Church. I know—"

I hit him hard on the side of the face, knocking him against the banister rail in the hall. Then I left the house. As I climbed into my car, I heard Philip screaming hoarsely, "John, John! Don't think I haven't seen through you! I saw through you months ago!"

It was after eleven that night when I got out of bed to answer the telephone. It was Diane Cummings. After apologizing for such a late call, she said, "How's your memory?"

"All right, I guess."

"I'm glad mine isn't. I've quite forgotten everything that happened last night. I wonder if I could ask you to do the same? Of course I realize it's asking quite a lot—men *do* like to talk, don't they?—but all the same it would be distinctly awkward for me if a certain person should hear that we left the party together at such a late hour. He might jump to conclusions, you know. I've already managed the Das Guptas. Now I must throw myself on your mercy."

"I won't say anything."

"You're really very nice. It's so reassuring to know one's dealing with a gentleman. Thank you *so* much."

"You're welcome."

"Life's very droll, isn't it?" Diane said before hanging up.

PART V

CHAPTER XXV ❧ E V E R Y day now was brilliant. The sunlight was warm and steady, the air sweetly dry—as if it had blown across wheat fields and prairies instead of the paddy land of Bengal. The third great season of Calcutta had begun—the unblemished months of "cool weather," with their hot sun and chilly nights and the smell of dry gutters and the pleasantly acrid smoke from dung-burning braziers in every poor man's hut. I joined the Calcutta Swimming Club about this time and soon got into the habit of going there during the lunch hour; I would change, have a quick dip, and then eat sandwiches at a sunny table overlooking the pool. In the evenings a tweed jacket or a sweater felt good.

I worked very hard during these weeks, putting in many hours of research on my report on trade unionism. Although I had turned desperately to this project, clutching at it as a life line thrown into the depths of my unhappiness, I soon discovered that there was no magic in work therapy; nor, on the other hand, was loneliness or suffering a guaranteed source of inspiration. Despite all the hours spent, I found it hard to involve myself as deeply in the subject as I needed to. The material, which had once interested me so much, now seemed almost pallid, and I assembled it mechanically. The emotional hemorrhaging had continued, a slow seeping and draining off of my energies which I couldn't yet stanch, though I was no longer so aware of pain. It wasn't until mid-November that the work began to glow fitfully under my touch. An interview with the Secretary of the Postal and Telegraph Workers—a truculent, suspicious, but ultimately friendly man named Arun Bose—opened up a whole new approach to the question of political action. Also, I began to learn more and more about the infighting which had broken out in connection with the Calcutta meeting of the All-India Trade Union Congress, a meeting scheduled for the end of the month.

In spite of his initial irony toward my project, Martin went out of his way to help me, going even to lengths which would have shocked his superiors in the Government of Bengal if they had known about it. He didn't hesitate to talk about those aspects of government policy toward labor which seemed wrong to him. I don't think he betrayed any official secrets, but he was certainly reckless enough otherwise. Once, when I asked if it was proper for me to hear a certain piece of information, Martin merely twitched his little mustache, grinned, and answered simply, "Why not? You won't abuse it." This recklessness was, as I soon learned, a kind of escape valve, all the more necessary because of the pressure of his commitment. Here was one man who really *knew*, who really *felt*, his work. For the first time I could see in practice Martin's efforts "to placate the moral hump" on his back, as he had put it to me months ago in Benares. He hated injustice with the fierceness of a man who knew it could never be avoided. And he fought it with the dedication of a man who knew that his superiors, deeply distrustful, were waiting for the moment when his zeal would betray him. The more hopelessly tangled and fouled an arbitration case became, the more patient and energetic Martin showed himself in his effort to establish the facts. "I spend my life trying to fight hydras," he once said to me. "India is the perfect breeding ground for them." From my conversations with Indian labor leaders, I found out that Martin's decisions didn't favor the underdog quite automatically enough to make him popular with them; but they respected him for what he knew and were scared of his probing, loving, and cynical questioning.

Martin never referred to his breakdown on the night of Philip's party. And although I saw him several times a week, he refused to invite me to his home; his father-in-law was still living with them, he said, and that made it impossible for him and Anila to entertain their friends. Then one day after we had lunched together at the United Services Club, he told me that Anila was pregnant. "It seems rather an odd thing to be congratulated on," he said after I had shaken his hand.

"Martin, that's pure affectation! Of course you're pleased."

He hunched his shoulders. "We hadn't precisely planned things this way. Of course there's a boyish part of me that's very pleased and even rather proud. I shall doubtless spoil the child dreadfully. Still, it's all very odd. I somehow can't quite see myself as the founder of an Anglo-Indian line."

"I wish I were married. I'd like to father a child. I can easily see myself as the founder of a line."

"Can you really?"

"No, not really. I can hardly see beyond the present day, as a matter of fact. Still, I wouldn't mind being a father."

Sweet chance, I thought as I left him. It was still impossible for me to think of marriage and parenthood apart from Julia. I couldn't yet bring myself to let go of the image I'd formed of our life together; I couldn't divorce myself from the days when she had worked with me in the visa office, from our afternoons with the munshi, from our mornings and noons and evenings in Darjeeling. I had already given up hope; it would take much longer for me to give up the image.

I had seen Julia many times at the Consulate, but we hadn't been brought together again socially until less than a week ago, at the Schneiders'. This, of course, was Liz's fine scheme. Like everyone else in the Consulate, Liz knew that we had "broken up," but she was the only one to take the fact to heart; as she had told me, she was crushed, absolutely crushed, and simply couldn't understand it—we were such a good couple and she'd been counting on us to make a go of it. Of course, since nothing could be explained to her, her sympathy seemed almost irrelevant. And on this night the clumsiness of her maneuver annoyed me—and Julia, too, as I could tell by the flash of surprise and protest in her eyes when I arrived. The party was centered around an Indian engineer named Sinha, who was going to the States to study matters of public power, irrigation, and flood control. At dinner, all of the Americans were suggesting things that the Sinhas should do or see during their visit. I took my part in the conversation, but with only half my mind, for the presence of Julia across the table drew my attention like a fire in a darkened room.

I felt hurt that she should look so well. The ailing-orphan expression had disappeared; her lips and skin now seemed well nourished by her blood, and the hazel eyes no longer so dominated her face. I could see no blemish on the skin of her throat or wrists. Wearing a dinner dress of rose-colored silk, Julia looked healthy, poised, and in full command of life. *It's because she doesn't have to deal with me.* The thought filled me with great bitterness.

We talked with each other a little during the evening, and when the party was breaking up, I defied my better judgment and asked if I could give her a lift home. She declined, as I knew she would, saying that she had already promised to go with Mary Buxton and Andy Wanamaker.

"You can change your mind," I said, hating myself for being so abject.

Julia shook her head.

"All right," I said. "I'm not going to fall down on my knees and plead."

"I haven't asked you to. I'm not being coy. I really don't want to go home with you. You can understand that."

It had been the same whenever I had telephoned during those first weeks after the christening party. I *had* to get it into my head that she was really through with me and that nothing was going to change that fact. I had to start making an effort to find a new girl. I did in fact go out a couple of times with an Army nurse, a friend of Marcia Brennaman's, but I felt no wish to see her again. Once, when I was by myself at the apartment, nearly smothered in loneliness and self-pity, I thought of calling Diane Cummings, but my memory of the unaired bedroom, the mildewed mosquito netting, and pointlessness of our embrace proved too strong and too distasteful even for my desire to set the record straight. Let her go to her grave convinced that Americans were the funniest lovers in the world. Perhaps they were. Besides, I kept hearing rumors that Diane was planning to marry Ronny Powell.

Coming back from my lunch with Martin, I arrived at the Consulate just as Herb Schneider was returning from the Bengal Club. When we reached the reception room, he laid his hand on my arm and drew me into his office.

"John, what's been happening to Philip?" he asked.

"I really don't know. I almost never see him."

"I guessed as much. It's too bad."

"Not really."

Herbert's angular and slightly professorial face, which seldom registered any emotion other than a kind of detached (but efficient) good will, suddenly became very bleak. "It looks like there's no one in the office who cares what happens to Philip." He drew a deep breath. "And I'm afraid he's heading for trouble of some sort. Captain Burton stopped me at the club today. Apparently Philip's been seen a good deal in the company of a bad actor the agents are keeping an eye on—some kind of French merchant seaman who may be mixed up in arms-smuggling from Indochina. Of course it's preposterous that Philip should have anything to do with such a person. I told Burton the agents must have made a mistake, but he was quite positive about it. Have you any idea what this is all about?"

"No, I'm completely out of touch with Philip."

"I'd hoped maybe you could talk to him. Even apart from this Frenchman, I'm afraid he's been keeping bad company. Someone should speak to him."

"Herb, I'm the last person in the world for that job."

"I've held off doing it myself, but I guess I'll have to put him on the mat and see what's been going on. There was a report several weeks ago about a fight at the Jungly Wallah—something involving the bartender. My chief worry right now is to keep the C.G. from hearing about any of this." Herbert stood silent for a moment, stroking his chin. "Are you sure you can't throw any light on the situation?" he asked.

"I'm afraid not, Herb. I have nothing to do with him these days. I'm sorry."

There was another pause. "Philip must have hurt you very badly in some way. You were once such good friends. Now you really hate him, don't you?"

"Not really. I just can't be bothered with him any more."

"That's almost worse than hating him, isn't it?"

This was the closest Herbert had ever come to a rebuke, and

I burned under it as I walked back to the visa office. But my indifference to Philip was real. I found it hard to imagine how much that friendship had once meant to me, now that its death was so final. To encounter Philip in the office, as I often did, caused me no pain or embarrassment whatever; even the reports that reached me of his increasingly wild behavior—the unprovoked fight with the bartender at the Jungly Wallah, for example —hardly stirred my interest, though they were told to me with open relish by Ralph, who was looking forward to Philip's quick dismissal from the Foreign Service. I hadn't the slightest desire for revenge. I thought of the house in Alipore, of Philip's collection, of the books I had borrowed, the records I had listened to, the food I had eaten. All of these, like the friendship itself, now seemed permeated with the moldering smell of that upstairs room, and my main concern was to close the door of my consciousness against the whole relationship.

It occurred to me that I might have seen the Frenchman Herbert had spoken about. One night, about two weeks before, as I had stopped for a traffic light at Chowringhee and Lower Circular Road, I heard the roar of a fast car behind me, then the squealing of tires. Philip's Bentley pulled alongside, reflecting the red traffic light in its glossy surfaces. There was much laughter, and I caught the shrill chattering of Mirza Ali Khan. Philip, on the far side, was invisibile, as was Mirza Ali. But on the side nearest me was a third person, half-leaning out the window. His well-muscled right arm was bare to the shoulder, and I could see that his biceps were heavily tatooed; he seemed to be wearing a sleeveless jersey and a scarf knotted around his throat. I couldn't see his face, which was turned toward the interior of the car.

The light switched to green, and after a moment's preliminary racing of the motor, the Bentley had pulled ahead very fast, roaring out of sight down the empty stretches of Chowringhee.

Several days after my conversation with Herbert Schneider, I got an unexpected invitation to have supper at the Friends Service Unit with Walter and Helen Evans, the Quaker couple whom I'd met at Kalighat on the night before the riots. They had interested me and I had thought several times of getting in touch with them but had done nothing about it; hence the invitation was as welcome as it was surprising. We ate communally with about a dozen of the other members of the Unit, both British and American; Ramesh and Sujata were also present. It occurred to me that except for the period of my illness, this was the first evening meal I'd had in India that wasn't preceded by a drink. Afterward I learned that there was some dissension on this subject between the British Friends, who approved of beer, and the strictly teetotaling Americans. We had a lively supper, during which there was a free-for-all argument about the validity of the theory of surplus value. I hadn't been prepared for such good-natured fierceness among Quakers or for such a close knowledge of such a technical subject; later I discovered that the argument grew out of a Marxist study group conducted by a fragile-looking English Friend named Hartley Wordsworth, who was also leading a seminar in Indian sculpture and architecture. I had a very good time.

When supper was over, the Evanses, the Chaudurys, and I gathered at one end of the veranda for our coffee. I talked at some length about my researches into the union movement and found out that the Evanses knew a good deal about that subject, too. Then I asked Walter Evans to explain to me just what the American Friends hoped to accomplish in India.

"That's a pretty big order," he said in his twanging, countrified way. "I guess I better start by saying we can't do a whole lot. That's why we spend a heck of a long time looking around before we act. We try to find some one area where a few workers and a little money will do the most good for the largest number of people."

"That sounds like a kind of spiritual utilitarianism," I said.

"I reckon you could call it that," agreed Walter Evans. "For instance, take our newest project—not the one I'm working on. We hear of a village whose lands have been flooded by a shift in one of those delta channels, so they're now on the verge of starvation—no way to make a living. So we hire a couple of professional fishermen to go down and try to show the village men how to fish. If they take to it, we then try to get 'em fixed up with enough nets and boats and try to figure out a way of getting their fish to market without giving a cut to some middleman. Well, likely as not, there'll be a row with the local zamindar, who claims he owns the flooded lands and wants a big rake-off from the sale of fish. So then we try to get in touch with the right people in the Government of Bengal and see what can be done from that angle. That's where the British Friends make themselves useful—they know how to approach these government wallahs."

"So you don't mind making nuisances of yourselves?" I asked.

"That's right!" Evans grinned in his sheepish way. "Boy, can we be obnoxious! But seriously, we have to be darn practical in these matters. What we're really scared of is biting off more than we can chew. We don't want to waste effort or money. That's why every proposal for a new project gets a real working over. Like this midwife's training outfit Helen's working with. Honey, how long did it take to get that approved by the Committee?"

"Close to a year, I think," said Helen Evans. Perhaps thirty, with large hands and thick legs and a cultivated voice, she was a familiar type to me—the kind of Baltimore or Philadelphia society girl, very plain, who would have been secretly plotting a career in social work or nursing at the very time her parents were insisting that she undergo the agony of being a wallflower at her own coming-out party.

"That's what I mean," said Evans. "We have to fight against our own enthusiasm. There's so much to do and everybody has so many proposals."

"This is such a dreadful country," said Ramesh. "Everything is so appalling no one knows where to begin. But we have magnificent human material," he added quickly.

"That's right," said Evans, nodding with great seriousness. "Another thing we're scared of is getting people too dependent on us. We don't like to start any project that needs American personnel and American money indefinitely to keep it going.

We like to be able to say, 'All right, fellas, it's your baby from now on. Good luck to you.' After all," he went on, turning to face Ramesh, "it's you Indians who live here. You're the ones who've got to run the show."

"I know, I know!" cried Ramesh with a wave of his hands. "It is we—not the British, not even you admirable American Quakers—who must run the show."

"We're great believers in co-operatives," continued Evans. "We think the system has a lot to offer India. Now at Nasirghat —" And he went on, in the calm, twanging monotony of his Midwestern voice, to describe the success with which the produce of this experiment in co-operative farming had been marketed without benefit of middlemen so that the producers themselves were able to plow back their full profits into the experiment. Nasirghat, which was Walter Evans' special project, was not yet self-supporting—an infusion of Quaker money was still needed—but with luck it should one day be able to stand on its own feet. The co-operative system, he thought, was especially well suited to a decentralized agricultural country like India; it suited the temperament of the people.

"I want to go to Nasirghat," I blurted out as soon as he had finished. "Would that be possible?"

Walter Evans looked surprised, almost as surprised as I was at my own sudden fervor. "Well," he said, tugging at one of his big ears, "I'm sure we can manage that. Sure thing!" he added enthusiastically. Then he reddened, cleared his throat, hesitated, and finally said, "But you won't find much in the way of comfort. You'll have to be prepared to rough it a bit. I might as well warn you about that right now."

"I'm prepared," I said, smiling.

"Good! I can promise you a very warm welcome. And I think you'll find it interesting."

We made a tentative date for the weekend before the meeting of the Trade Union Congress.

I left Wood Street that night in a better mood than I'd known for many weeks. I felt the exhilaration of having begun a new, if unlikely, friendship. Once again the world seemed various and alive, holding out more than I could ever see or touch in a lifetime. There's so much! I thought, and I prayed that I could stay in India long enough to make even a fair start on all that it promised. With a thousand images rising and melting before me in the darkness, I again glimpsed that wild excitement and hope which had seized me on the night of the Fourth of July party. But then I had been so confident that Julia would be at my side as I trumpeted my loving challenge to the world. Though my blood was now running freshly again, I felt I'd been diminished to half-size by her loss. Half a man, half-alive—but *alive.*

CHAPTER XXVI ✣ BEFORE I could consolidate this new mood, Philip's situation suddenly exploded in my face.

It happened on a Thursday night, in the middle of the next week. About ten thirty, while I was writing to my mother, the telephone rang. There was no "Hello, John" or "This is Philip" or any other preliminary, just the unmistakable voice, even more drawling than usual, which said, "I'm having a party. A small celebration in fact. It occurred to me that you might come."

"Is this a joke?" I could hear loud music in the background.

"I expect you *are* a bit surprised to hear from me. But it's no joke. I don't seem to see much of you these days, so I thought I'd invite you to this rather special little party. You'll come, won't you?"

"Of course I won't."

"You sound terribly stern and unrelenting. Are you sure you won't come?"

"Yes."

"Yes *what?*"

"I'm *not* going to come. Good night."

"That sounds clear enough. Well, good night. Sleep tight."

I returned to the living room. After puzzling for a few moments over the game Philip was playing, I gave it up with a shrug and returned to my letter.

Half an hour later, the phone rang again. Expecting another encounter with Philip, I was startled to hear a shrill, rapid, Indian voice—so startled that at first I couldn't understand what was being said.

"You must come, please come," the voice repeated, and I at last recognized it as Mirza Ali's.

"Where are you calling from?"

"I'm at Philip's. He is upstairs at his room so I must finish very quickly. Please, you must come."

"I don't understand. What's going on?"

"You may be able to help. He is in such a dreadful state. He broke his records—smashed them! Just now he is upstairs and Pierre is on the veranda, so I can speak to you. But you must come. Everything is so strange. Philip is in a most dreadful state. Please come." Then, almost in a whisper, "I am afraid of Pierre. And Philip is so frightening tonight."

"You're not making any sense. I've no intention of getting mixed up in any of this."

"Oh, please, you must! Oh, please . . ."

I hung up and returned to my desk, disgusted by the image of the drunken, screaming, homosexual cat fight that must be going on. Philip was free to go to hell in his own way. I had no desire to look on.

Nonetheless, in about twenty minutes, I got up and put on my jacket. I hadn't been able to get rid of the note of real terror that shrilled through Mirza Ali's jumbled appeal. And now, in retrospect, I imagined that I could pick out another sound, faint and disguised but also pleading, beneath the insolence of Philip's drawl.

The house on Asoka Road was blazing with light as I drove up. Every room seemed to be illuminated, every curtain pulled back, so that the surrounding grass and trees were nearly as lurid as the windows. But there was no car anywhere in sight. All the windows downstairs were open, but walking across the lawn, I could hear no sound of voices or music. The front door was wide open, too—as if a whole troop of revelers had just passed through.

I hurried into the living room and found Mirza Ali there, huddled on the sofa. In his long black achkan and white pajama trousers, he looked more than ever like some weird gibbon as he peered over his high, bony knees, his face small and frightened.

"You are too late," he said, cringing from me as though I were a keeper advancing to punish him. "They have all gone."

"What the hell's been happening here?"

I glanced quickly around the room. Near the Capehart a great pile of smashed records lay on the Bokhara rug, and there was a glitter of broken glass on the floor near the sofa. The place reeked with the fumes of brandy, which must have been poured from a nearly empty decanter on the coffee table. Every lamp and wall fixture was turned on, making this rich and embellished room stark as a showcase under the glaring lights.

"Oh, there's been such a frightful scene! You can't imagine! Philip called Derek a bitch and threw a glass at him. And he poured brandy all over my sleeve when I held out my glass. You can't imagine! And now he and Pierre have gone to meet a friend of Pierre's—someone from Saigon. It's too frightful!" Mirza Ali hugged his knees even closer, his long-wristed gibbon arms clasped in front. Then, with a sudden brightening of his little face, he said proudly, "*I* was the one who suggested he call you. I told him it would be a fine joke. I hoped you could help."

"Why?" I demanded. "You know there's nothing I can do about Philip. If he wants to throw a tantrum and get hysterical, I'm not going to try to stop him. It's none of my business."

"Don't go!" he pleaded, holding out his hand. And when I stopped, he said, "If you feel this way, then why did you come at all?"

"I thought there might be something serious—or dangerous—going on. Not *this*."

"Then you do care! I was right!"

"No, not really. I don't care about him as a friend. It's just that—" I broke off, unable to decide what I really thought or felt. Then, glancing again at the wreckage on the floor, I sat down and said, "Maybe you'd better tell me exactly what's happened, right from the beginning."

The Indian released his hold on his knees and leaned back. "Well," he said with a more confident look, "I was here when Philip came home from the Consulate. He was so silent. And I thought he was angry at me. You can't imagine how upset I was. He wouldn't say anything, not a word. Then—it must have been about six, I should think—he suddenly ran out to his car and drove away. Just like that! Without a word! He was gone at least an hour and a half and when he came back he looked very wild and excited."

"What did he say? What had happened?"

"I really don't know. I couldn't understand what he was saying—all about lies and plots and things like that. A perfectly frightful jumble. He couldn't sit still. Then he said he wanted to have a party. Pierre—he's that horrid Frenchman—was coming to dinner anyway, and then Philip called Frédéric and he brought Derek. . . ."

"Who's Derek?"

"He's an English boy, a soldier. He's Frédéric's chum. Such a nice boy, and Philip was dreadful to him. It wasn't until after dinner," he continued, picking up his story, "that I realized how frightful everything was. I was simply terrified."

And Mirza Ali told me that when they came into the living room for coffee and brandy, Philip had insisted on having music and had turned up the phonograph so loudly that all the windows rattled. He hadn't been able to sit still but kept pacing around the room, pulling out record albums and books, constantly refilling his glass. "And you know how little he drinks usually," said the Indian, shaking his head. Then, during a lull between records, Philip, after pouring brandy into Derek's glass, had demanded that Derek drink to the joy of being a whore. And when Derek refused, Philip called him a bitch and threw a glass at his head. Then Frédéric de Croye demanded that Philip apologize, which he did. But almost immediately afterward Philip spilled brandy all over Mirza Ali's sleeve, calling him all sorts of terrible names, including bitch and whore and parasite. It was after that that Philip had decided to telephone me. Philip next put on the *St. Matthew Passion,* again turning the volume as loud as it would go.

"It was frightful," said Mirza Ali. "I put my hands over my ears, but then Philip said I had to listen to the 'Protestant noise' and he made me take my hands away. He was sitting next to the machine and conducting the music with his hands and all the time he was laughing at us. Then Frédéric couldn't stand it any longer so he got up to leave, and told Derek to come with him. Philip was furious. But finally he switched off the machine and lifted the stack of records out. I'll never forget the way he looked at us. Then he raised the whole stack over his head and dashed them to the floor—like that! And he said, 'That's enough Protestant noise for one evening, don't you think?' We were all horrified except for that dreadful Pierre and he clapped and kept shouting 'bravo.' "

"Just who is this Pierre?" I asked, looking again at the heap of shards on the rug.

"He's a *horrid* Frenchman Philip met in an *awful* little bar near the Kidderpore docks. Philip thinks he's fascinating. He knows all sorts of criminals and sailors and drug addicts and people like that. I'm sure Pierre has done all kinds of dreadful things. And he's had such a frightful influence on Philip. You can't imagine. Out every night, going to those dreadful places near the docks. Drinking. You know, Philip never used to drink. And he throws his money away on the most dreadful people. Filthy, horrid sailors and Anglo-Indian boys."

Mirza Ali grimaced, and then his face hardened. "I shall never forgive Pierre! He's turned Philip against me. We used to be such friends, and now Philip barely tolerates me. It makes me very sad," he added, lifting his eyes to me, imploring my sympathy.

"What happened after Philip smashed the records?"

"Well, Frédéric and Derek left. Frédéric told Philip he was behaving outrageously. You know how grand and dignified Frédéric can be. Then Philip went upstairs and that's when I phoned you. But when he came down, he and Pierre went off to meet some Polish friend of Pierre's. Pierre had been urging him all evening to meet this friend."

I sat for a long time wondering what to do. Philip was obviously heading for serious trouble—probably a scandal that would rock the Consulate and the American community. Perhaps the police could do something about this Pierre if Herbert or the C.G. requested it, but what then? Would Philip listen to me? What should I say? Should I advise him to resign? My deepest wish was merely to let things take their course. Or else tell Herbert all I knew and shift the burden to him.

Then, for the first time, I felt the threat of Philip's suicide like a freezing wind.

Mirza Ali had been watching me, sipping his brandy, waiting for my reaction. Finally I said, "Do you think there's any chance Philip would listen to me if I talked to him?"

"Oh, yes! You must try! I know Philip still respects you; in spite of everything, he'll listen to you."

"All right," I said, getting up. "I'll try to talk to him tomorrow. Meanwhile, don't tell him I've been here."

"Oh, can't you do something tonight? I'm so worried. Perhaps you could find him, or wait for him here."

"No, I'd better see him tomorrow in the office. When he's less excited." Then, softening a little toward Mirza Ali, I said, "What are you planning to do? Can I give you a lift?"

He shook his head. "No, I shall wait for him here. He may need someone and it would be too awful if he came home and found no one here but the servants."

But I did see Philip that evening. I had just reached my car when headlights flashed down Asoka road. The Bentley pulled up behind me with much skidding and screeching of tires. Philip jumped out.

"Oh, it's you," he said, striding toward me. "So your curiosity got the best of you. Or did Mr. Hubbard send you here to spy on me?"

"I don't know what you're talking about. I thought you invited me to a party."

"Well, the party's over. And I haven't time to talk to you now. Good night." He started across the lawn toward the glaring house.

"Wait," I said, hurrying after him. "I want to speak to you a minute."

I didn't catch him until we had both reached the front hall.

I heard Mirza Ali call from the living room, "Oh, Philip, you've come back!"

"Only to pick up my wallet. I forgot it." Then Philip turned toward me. "Please get out of here. I'm sick of being followed and spied on. I won't have it. I know perfectly well what's been going on. I'm not blind and I'm not without friends."

"I don't understand what you're talking about, Philip."

He stared at me, his face swollen with its own blood, the face of an apoplectic Caesar. "Stop pretending. You saw the letter, didn't you?"

"What letter?"

"The letter Mr. Hubbard was showing everyone today."

"Mr. Hubbard!"

Philip's pale eyes fixed me with infinite scorn. "Stop playing dumb," he said, placing one hand on the newel post. "I can tell from your face you saw the letter. You're actually blushing."

"I haven't seen any letter of Mr. Hubbard's, Philip."

The eyes became cagey. "Well, maybe it was Halpern's. I can't remember." He spoke peevishly, as if the distinction was of no importance at all.

"What in the world?" I began.

"Ha! So you're still playing dumb. I told you I wasn't without friends. Now please leave. I'm in a hurry." And, turning abruptly, he dashed up the stairs.

Mirza Ali came to the living-room door, but I waved him back. Then Philip reappeared at the head of the stairs.

"What, are you still here?" he said, coming down very fast.

I blocked his way. "Look, there's something I've got to talk over with you. Don't go yet. Give me half an hour. . . ."

"You poor fool, do you think I'm going to play your game? Don't you understand, you fool? I've resigned. Ha!" he shouted, laughing in my face. "So you thought I'd let myself be used as a tool. Wait till old Hubbard sees my letter of resignation!"

Oh, Jesus Christ! "Have you turned it in?" I asked.

His flushed scorn turned into a look of wicked cunning. "Do you really expect me to tell you?"

"Philip, for God's sake, don't turn it in! Let Herb handle it all. I can understand why you might want to resign, but talk it over with Herb first. He's your friend, whether you believe it or not. Please don't—"

There was a noise behind me. Philip smiled, and I looked around. A powerfully built man, wearing a striped polo shirt and dungarees, was standing at the front door. Just behind him I could see someone else, a man with yellow hair and a wide, sunburned face.

The first man stepped inside. *"De quoi s'agit-il, Philippe?"* he said, smiling broadly. He was blue-cheeked, with thick brows and well-combed black hair.

"Rien du tout," said Philip. He sauntered past me into the middle of the hall and stood, in the posture of a host, between me and the newcomers. "John," he said arrogantly, "I should like to present Pierre Capus and my new friend of this evening, Vladimir Kosko. And this," he continued with a gesture toward me, "is Vice-Consul John Wickham, who was once my friend and is still my colleague. Or was until this evening." Philip beamed at the Frenchman and the Pole, who both nodded, almost politely, in my direction. I stared back at them. The Pole had now come into the brightness of the hall. He was wearing a blue suit with padded shoulders and wide-bottomed trousers that nearly covered his shoes. "Vladimir," said Philip, again in the explanatory tone of a host, "is on his way to Indo-china to join the Foreign Legion. I rather envy him. I almost wish *I* were a stateless person. Pierre and Vladimir are urging me to go to Saigon, John. Don't you think that might be a good idea?"

He was laughing at me again. The Pole, who obviously spoke no English, whispered a question to Pierre, who answered in rapid French. Then for the first time Pierre caught sight of Mirza Ali, who had come into the hall. *"Comment ça va, p'tit Mogol?"* he said, lifting his tattooed right arm in a kind of salute to the Indian, who glared at him with baby-faced hatred. Then to Philip he said, *"Allons, mon cher Vice-Consul. On nous attends."*

310

I moved toward Philip, half-expecting Pierre Capus and the Pole to leap to his side as bodyguards. "Don't go now," I pleaded, as abject as Mirza Ali had been toward me. "I want to talk to you for just a few minutes." The quills of his madness made me desperate. How could I touch him? There was something mad, too, in the aimless delinquency of the Frenchman's grin. How could I hope to reach Philip while this henchman looked on? "Could we talk alone, Philip? Just for a few minutes?"

Philip laughed at me. "Don't be ridiculous. We are on our way to a party. To which, alas, I am not at liberty to invite you." Then his eyes lost their mockery and became full of suspicion, slyness, and fury. "Why should I stay to listen to your lies? I know all about the plot. I saw the letter. I know what all of you want. Well, haven't I resigned? Doesn't that satisfy you? Why do you keep hounding me?" He curled his lips, narrowing his eyes still further. "I've already called B.O.A.C. I can get a reservation for the States in three days if I need it. Doesn't that satisfy you? Isn't that what you want?"

"Now look, Philip, please. . . ."

I broke off. Philip seemed to be shivering. He closed his eyes for a second, frowning like a man in sudden pain. Then he said in a low, rather irritable voice, "For God's sake, John, stop fretting. If it'll make you happier, I promise not to do anything until I've talked it over with Herb. I'll speak to him first thing in the morning."

My shoulders sagged with relief. *I've won, I've won!* And I said, "That's much the best idea." Then, pressing my luck, I added, "Why don't you take it easy tonight—get a good night's sleep—and then tomorrow I'll—"

"Oh, yes!" cried Mirza Ali, who was now standing behind me. "Please stay, Philip. It will be so much better!"

"Keep quiet," I said, angry at the Indian's bad timing.

"Don't be ridiculous," said Philip, the high color again flooding into his face, which for a moment had become as gray-white and bloodless as cooked veal. Pierre was watching intently, his head cocked to one side, his lips parted; the Pole looked dumb

311

and uncomprehending. "Why shouldn't I go to the party?" continued Philip, smiling at his companions. "I said I'd go and I will." Then he held out his hand. "Good night, John. I intend to keep my promise. You needn't worry about that."

Without a glance at Mirza Ali, Philip turned abruptly and left the house, followed by the shuffling Vladimir and by Pierre, who walked out of the door with the easy-hipped stride of an acrobat.

I stood for a while in the hall, listening to the closing of the car doors and then to the roar of the engine. Aware suddenly of Mirza Ali, I said, "There's nothing else to be done tonight. Are you still planning to stay?"

He nodded, avoiding my eyes.

I was glad to go, immeasurably glad that everything could be put off until morning. I would telephone Herbert before breakfast to warn him.

As I got into my car, I looked back at the brilliant house. Mirza Ali was standing at one of the living-room windows, thin and forlorn as a hanged monkey.

CHAPTER XXVII 🎋 ABOUT ten the next morning, Herbert Schneider telephoned me in the visa office. "Philip hasn't been in yet," he said. "Have you seen him?"

"No, I'll phone his home at once."

Mirza Ali told me that Philip had not come home at all last night. I could tell that he was crying. I consulted again with Herbert, who decided to call Captain Burton. That was how we learned the story.

Early that morning an Indian gardener had come across Philip lying bloody and unconscious in a ditch in the Botanical Gardens, on the other side of the Hooghly River below Howrah. After a long delay the police were notified, and after a still longer delay Philip was taken to the Presidency General Hospital. Since he had been stripped to his underpants, there was no way of identifying him until Herb called Captain Burton. The latter had just received a routine report that a European man had been discovered robbed and beaten and was now undergoing treatment at the hospital. The Bentley had not yet been found.

Herb then called Colonel Merriot, the chief surgeon at the hospital, who knew nothing about the case but who leaped into action as soon as he learned the victim's identity. He called back almost at once to report that Philip was now conscious, though badly confused. He had been beaten or kicked about the head, but there was no skull fracture; his face was badly cut up, and at least two ribs were broken; it was too early to tell whether there were internal injuries. Colonel Merriot considered it most inadvisable for anyone—including the police—to try to talk to Philip just now; perhaps by this afternoon . . . He promised that everything had been—and would be—done.

"Now comes the worst part," said Herb after he had finished telling me what the Colonel said. "We can't keep it from the C.G. any longer."

As expected, Mr. Hubbard went into a complete dither and spent the rest of the morning composing and tearing up telegrams to the Department of State, which would, in turn, have to notify Philip's father, Arnold Sachs, in New York; it was against the Foreign Service regulations for us to notify Mr. Sachs directly. Since I had been closest to the scene of the crime, so to speak, I was called in, along with Herb, for consultations on each new draft. There were new calls to be made to the hospital and to the police every few minutes. Finally a telegram was sent off with the promise that another would follow as soon as someone from the Consulate was permitted to speak to Philip.

Just before lunch I drove to Security Control Headquarters to provide a fuller account of Pierre Capus and Vladimir Kosko than I had already given on the telephone. Captain Burton did not press me about Philip's reasons for associating with such characters as Pierre; he indicated, very urbanely, that these were Philip's own business. The chances were, he said, that the two suspects would try to hide in Calcutta until there was an opportunity for them to get to Indochina. It would be hard to find them in the city, especially since Pierre was known to have a number of Muslim League contacts who might hide him; but it would also be hard for the men to leave now that the French Consulate and the shipping and emigration people had been alerted. "We'll know a lot more," he concluded, "when the car turns up. The only road that leads for more than eighty miles out of Calcutta is the Grand Trunk Road to Delhi, and we'll watch that like a hawk." Before leaving, I gave a list of the probable objects on Philip's person, including the enameled cross, the gold cigarette case, and the gold penknife; Mirza Ali had estimated that Philip carried as much as a thousand rupees in his wallet.

About an hour and a half later Herb and I drove across the Maidan to the Presidency General Hospital. "It's the sickest-looking hospital I've ever seen," said Herb as we looked at the grim old building with its moldy brick pavilions and the rickety, dark-painted balconies that seemed about to collapse under the jungle growth of vines climbing over them. The inside, however, was white and cool, filled with the sinister-clean smell of disinfectant. We were met by Colonel Merriot and Dr. Harlestoun, whom I had called earlier. Philip, they said, was awake, though

314

his mental confusion was still such that they doubted we would learn much from him.

"He seems to be under the illusion," said Colonel Merriot, "that this is all part of some vast conspiracy. The Catholic Church is mixed up in it somehow. I must say he heaped the most frightful abuse upon Harlestoun and me when we saw him a little while ago. Really shocking stuff. I'd have ordered more sedation for him if it weren't for your visit. Wouldn't do to have him too groggy for that. Poor chap, he's in considable pain. Terribly bruised and cut up. I suppose that and the shock can account for any amount of confusion."

"He's not in any serious physical danger now, is he?" asked Herb.

"There's been no evidence of internal hemorrhaging or any other definite sign of that sort. But it's still too early to be sure. Most of the beating seems to have occurred around the upper torso and head. That was brutal enough, to be sure, but hardly so dangerous as if the abdomen or kidneys were involved." The colonel spoke with a professional briskness that implied that there was nothing else we could conceivably wish to know.

"Extraordinary business," said Dr. Harlestoun. "What on earth could he have been doing at the Botanical Gardens at that hour of the night?" The freckled old Scot turned his diagnostician's frown upon me.

"I expect he was forced to drive there at pistol point," I said. "The car still hasn't turned up." This was the line which we had already decided upon at the Consulate; though melodramatic, it sounded plausible enough under the circumstances.

"I suppose the bandits must have forced their way into the car when he stopped at a crossing," continued Harlestoun.

"Probably," I said. So far the existence of Pierre and Vladimir was a secret shared only with the police. We were still hoping to keep it out of the papers.

Philip's lips were so puffed that we couldn't understand him at first. He was looking intently at Herbert through an eye that was nearly closed under the blue-green swelling of its lids; the other eye, like so much of his face and head, was covered with white bandaging.

"What did you say, Philip?" asked Herb. The older man leaned over him, looking curiously more dour and sad than kind. It was only gradually during the course of the morning that I realized what a terrible fight Herb's sympathies were having to wage against an almost overwhelming distaste for the whole incident—and its victim.

Philip's voice now came through loudly, though still distorted. "You're not my father!"

"No, Philip. We're trying to get in touch with your father. We'll let you know as soon as we hear anything. How are you feeling?"

There was no answer to this, but in a moment Philip said, "They didn't kill me." His tone was now vaguely wondering, almost querulous.

"Can you tell us anything about what happened?" asked Herb. I drew closer to the bedside. Thus far Philip had seemed not to recognize my presence.

"You should know all about it," said Philip accusingly.

I now spoke up. "Can you tell us the name of your family doctor in New York? Perhaps you would like us to get in touch with him before you go home."

Again Philip's words were muffled. Finally, in exasperation, he almost shouted, "I told you I don't know! He's some Jew or other. I forget his name." This effort must have been painful, for he gave a low, strangled sound and closed his one eye for a moment.

Herb met my glance and we both moved back from the bed. "I'll come again tomorrow," he said. "Meanwhile I hope you'll get a good rest and feel much better. Have the doctors call me or John if you want anything."

Philip looked up at us both. He seemed to be breathing through his gentian-painted lips. Then there was a mumbling.

"What is it?" I asked, coming to the bed again and resting my hand on his.

"Why isn't Father Bernier here? He's in great danger."

"I'll telephone Father Bernier when we leave and ask him to

come to see you. Good-by, Philip. I'll see you again tomorrow."

We stepped into the hall, and the Anglo-Indian nurse, who had been waiting outside, went at once into the room, carrying a hypodermic syringe. We met the two doctors in the front hall of the hospital.

"What would you say is the earliest possible time Mr. Sachs could be flown back to America?" asked Herbert.

Colonel Merriot stared at him frigidly. "Why do you ask? Have you reason to believe that he will not receive proper treatment at this hospital?"

"Oh, not at all!" said Herbert, embarrassed at the way his question had been taken. He soon mollified the Colonel, who finally replied that if no internal injuries or complications manifested themselves, Mr. Sachs could leave in perhaps a week or ten days. "We'll strap up those ribs of his so he'll be nearly as good as new," said the Colonel, whose professional ease had flowed back with redoubled force. "But I must say I don't quite relish the idea of his traveling such a distance with no one to look after him."

"I wasn't considering *that* for an instant," said Herbert.

As we got into the car, Herbert said to me, "Philip's father is very well off, isn't he?"

"Very."

"In that case, if we put it to him urgently enough, do you think he'd consider paying for a doctor—preferably a psychiatrist—to fly out to India to take Philip home?"

On my way along the corridor leading to the visa section I passed Andy Wanamaker's office. Through the open door I saw Julia sitting there, taking dictation. She looked up as I passed, as though she had been waiting for me to go by; then, leaving the astonished Wanamaker in midsentence, she hurried to the door. "Have you seen him?" she asked. "How is he?"

"Not so good, I'm afraid."

Julia bit her lip. "Poor Philip. I've been nearly frantic ever since I heard—but I can't talk to you now." And she dashed back to Wanamaker's desk.

In the landslide of activity which the outrage in the Botanical

Gardens had begun, I tended to lose sight of the event itself. It was not until now, in the late afternoon, in the relative quiet of the visa office, that I allowed myself to confront the central fact. The image of the dark garden came to me, and the silent, desperate struggle, the soft thud of fists, the heavy breathing, and Philip swaying between the two men until finally he went down. But why did I picture the struggle as silent? I then remembered that Philip's fists, as I had seen them lying on top of the hospital sheet, were unmarked. Had he struggled at all? I now saw Philip standing under the glaring light of the hall in Alipore. "Why shouldn't I go to the party?" he had asked. "I said I'd go and I will." What had he guessed about this meeting with the Pole which Pierre was so anxious to arrange?

My desk telephone was ringing. It was Herbert. Captain Burton had just called, he said, to report that the Bentley had been found deserted near Diamond Harbour, some thirty miles down the Hooghly from Calcutta. It was just possible that the two men had managed, by some sort of prearrangement, to get aboard one of the many merchant ships sailing into the Bay of Bengal early this morning.

I had hardly put the receiver down when the phone began to ring again. This time it was Morris Halpern, who asked if I would come to his office.

"How is he?" he asked when I came in. I told him all I knew. Listening, Morris raised his thick brows; his hooded eyes and wide, down-drooping frog mouth were almost a caricature of the suffering Jew. "What do you think brought on the crisis?" he asked after I had finished.

"Herbert stopped Philip just after work yesterday and said he wanted to have a talk with him sometime. That's all it took."

"So . . ." Morris rubbed a pudgy hand slowly across his face, like a man trying to erase his features. "I'm not really sorry to see him leave," he said, "but I'm very sorry it's worked out this way. I'd hoped that joining the Church might be the answer for him. Even though it disgusted me."

"I'd hoped so, too. But not for long." Then I said, "You know, in a funny way, I feel better about Philip than I have in a long time. What's happened is horrible enough, but at least everything's out in the open. If he can get the kind of help he needs in New York, there's a chance he might pull out of all this."

"I wouldn't count on it," said Morris with a shrug.

"I'm not."

"You look beaten down, John. Why don't you come home for a pot-luck supper with Esther and me? I promise to get you good and drunk and not to mention Philip's name once."

When I got home from the Halperns', I wasn't drunk but I was nearly staggering with exhaustion. Ralph handed me an envelope and said, "Julia left this for you. She came by a couple of hours ago."

"Who?"

"Julia. Julia Cobb. She waited quite a while. I didn't know where you were."

Groggily, I lifted the unsealed flap of the envelope and pulled out a sheet of my own writing paper.

DEAR JOHN,

Our meeting in the office was no good, and I couldn't let the day pass without telling you how distressed I am about Philip. The rumor at the office is that he's had some kind of breakdown as a result of the beating, and I also hear that you've had to bear the brunt of much of it. The recent bad feeling between the two of you can't have made it any easier. I'm *very* sorry.

I wanted to see you but can't wait any longer tonight, so this note will have to suffice. You're very much in my thoughts.

JULIA—10:15.

And at the bottom, in a rapid scrawl suggesting an afterthought, she had written, "Please, John, don't try to read any more into my visit or this note than has been stated above. For your sake as well as mine. J."

Well, that's clear enough, I thought, crumpling the paper in my hand.

CHAPTER XXVIII ❧ THROUGHOUT that next week I looked straight ahead toward the coming trip to Nasirghat. I needed it as I had needed Benares and Darjeeling, and I kept it always in sight as I stumbled along over the rocky waste that intervened.

It was a rough week, for Ralph and I had to take turns in the shipping office in addition to our regular jobs. This left no time for work on my report. I went to the hospital each day, but the visits were pointless, for Philip never once broke out of the endless, mechanical, sterile round of his obsessions. When I last saw him, on Thursday, he was sitting on the edge of his bed, less bandaged but still hideously bruised, closely watched by a male Anglo-Indian attendant who did not leave the room. The doctor from New York was scheduled to arrive on Saturday. I would not see Philip again. My last act before leaving the Consulate on Friday was to validate his passport for return to the United States.

But I would see Julia again. When I sought her out at the office to thank her for her note, she talked about Philip for a while and then informed me that she had applied for a transfer. "These last few weeks have been hell for me," she said, refusing to meet my look. "And I know they've been hard on you, too. If the Department won't authorize a transfer to another post, I'm going to give up my job and go home."

In the dull fog of pain that enclosed me, I could only think to say, "When did you decide on this?"

"After that night at the Schneiders. It's too hard on both of us to keep running into each other."

"So be it," I said, turning away toward the corridor. I would, inevitably, see her many times before she left.

At last Friday came. I had an early supper with the assembled Friends at Wood Street; then, after Walter Evans had kissed his wife, he and I climbed into a jeep and set off on the three-hour trip over bumpy roads to Nasirghat. My sense of liberation was instant and complete. As the headlights of our jeep bored into the dense Bengali night, the cold air rushing past us was like a baptismal flood, sweeping away all the grit and sorrow of my life.

After our walk to the weaving center the next morning, Walter and I decided to take a sun bath during the hour that remained before tiffin. We put on shorts and went into the backyard, where there was a well. I sat on the whitewashed brick wall, which was almost hot to my touch; its crumbling, flaking surface smeared my fingers with a chalky dust and came off on the bottom of my khaki shorts. I subsided at once into a kind of trance, which was, paradoxically, the most wakeful state I had ever known.

The sun poured its twelve o'clock heat over my bare shoulders, thighs, and kneecaps, soaking into my skin, massaging the stiff shoulder muscles and baking the vertebrae of my neck and spine. My leg muscles were also stiff from the plank bed on which I'd slept, but already the morning's walk to the weaving center and now the warm penetration of the sun had begun to loosen the fibers and to dissolve the soreness into a rippling, pliant state of well-being. Looking down at my shins, I watched the dark hairs move under the touch of a light wind that floated across the compound from time to time. The breeze kept me from sweating, and its pleasant tickle made me intensely aware that the surface of my body had a distinct life of its own, an active, breathing, cellular life with trillions of minute antennae and its own medium of air, oil, lymph, and blood. The breeze also brought the dry fragrance of leaves and grass, the smell of sun-baked, crumbling brick, of packed earth, of curry from the kitchen in the rear of the compound, and, from a greater distance, the unexpectedly pleasant muck stench of the shallow river, where a herd of buffaloes was wallowing under the strong sun. This wallowing suddenly struck me as an image of the good life.

I had been in a state of vivid physical consciousness since early morning. It had accompanied the washing of my face and the eating of breakfast and the long hike to the center, where

I had watched old widows and unmarried daughters winding up bobbins and turning out lungis, saris, and tablecloths from the hand looms. Now, as I was sunbathing, this consciousness was so heightened beyond anything I'd ever experienced before that the packed earth and the wiry, yellowish, clipped grass on which my feet rested seemed as momentously real to me, as complex, as rich, as my own reddening shins, my ankles, and my feet with their clumsy spread of toes.

In the grass, just to the side of my right foot, I spotted a whitened snail shell, no larger than the nail of my second toe. Some happy bird must have picked out and gulped down the soft life of the mollusc; I could see the bird's bright eye and the lustful tossing back of its head. Pivoting my foot slightly to the left, I touched the shell with the ball of my big toe, and instantly the delicate spiral collapsed into a pile of tiny white flakes. The next strong breeze would blow them away, but meanwhile those bits of calcium had absorbed, for a few seconds, my most concentrated scrutiny. Caught up in the total physical reality of the moment, I could feel the warmth of a deep pleasure moving steadily outward to meet the sunlight on my skin and the caressing of the air.

"Sun sure feels good, doesn't it?" said Walter Evans, who was sitting on the wall about five feet away.

I nodded. There was no need to answer his comment, which was as freely offered and inoffensive as the chirping of the birds in the bamboo thicket behind the wall; this was the first time either of us had spoken for nearly fifteen minutes. I looked at my feet again but did not attempt to revive my earlier concentration. Then I closed my eyes and tilted back my head, letting the light strike full force against my forehead and the bridge of my nose and glow orange-purple through my eyelids.

"Ah, let me beg you gentlemen not to take too much of this Bengali sun," said an Indian voice. It was Bishnu Das, the young bookkeeper for the Co-operative Experiment in Farming. He stood in front of us, fully clothed in a khaki bush jacket and a dhoti; though well-educated and a socialist, Bishnu, like most Indians of good caste, placed an exorbitant value on the virtue of a fair complexion and looked upon sunbathing as the strangest of Western perversions. "I have come to tell you that tiffin will soon be ready—perhaps in twenty minutes. And I have brought you this for your bath." He handed an unlabeled glass bottle to Walter, who pulled out the cork and sniffed. "It is coconut oil," explained Bishnu with friendly seriousness. "See, it smells very sweet. Rub it carefully into your limbs before you pour on the water and you will find it most healthful for the nerves and the circulation as well as for the skin." Bishnu smiled at us, cocked his head to one side like a watching bird, and then walked back across the compound to the low house.

"Well, what do you say we give it a try?" said Walter, standing up and brushing the whitewash and scraps of leaf from the seat of his green swimming trunks. We strolled over the tickling grass to the well in the center of the compound and seated ourselves on its circular rim, which was also made of whitewashed brick. With his usual awkward deliberateness, Walter removed the cork and poured several drops of oil into the broad palm of his right hand; then he handed me the bottle and I followed the same procedure. We began to rub ourselves vigorously, working the oil into the hot skin of our legs, arms, and chests. A smell of coconut enveloped us, as if drawn up in steam by the sun. Walter was extremely thorough, applying the oil methodically to the back of his neck and even to his big ears. Soon our bodies were gleaming fishlike, seallike, in their suppleness, and I began to laugh aloud from sheer bodily pleasure. Amused and happy, I glanced at the ungainly Quaker, whose countryman's face now shone with a hedonistic glow; even his reddish mustache was now glossily dark with oil.

Walter pulled up the first bucket of water and doused it on me. The water was cold, amazingly cold to have come from a shallow Bengali well, and its shock was painful for an instant before the exhilarated dancing of the blood began. "Ah-h-h!" I cried, slapping my chest and thighs. Covering myself with a lather of cheap Indian soap, I awaited the next shock of water and laughed when it struck. The dust, sweat, oil, and soap all disappeared with the third dousing, and I felt clean all the way down to the bone, clean and glowing, healthier than I'd ever been before. But in the midst of this sharp pleasure, as I was pouring buckets of water over Walter Evans, I suddenly winced with the memory of the bathhouse at Berhampore, where Ronny Powell had emptied a jar of water over Philip. For the first time since coming to Nasirghat, I found myself thinking of Philip.

"Well, this sure ought to give us an appetite," said Walter, and I was instantly brought back to the present—to the cold water, the hot sun, the untainted blue of the sky, and the extraordinary sense of my own health. After perfunctorily drying ourselves with a coarse towel, we went into the house to put on our clothes before tiffin.

Lunch was served on an unpainted plank table in the main room of the house—a white room furnished with spindly wooden chairs and several cushions on the floor. Bishnu Das's wife supervised the other women of the household in the preparing and serving of the food; none of them would sit down with the men. Walter, of course, was right: the bath had given us a really gross appetite. Eating with my fingers, I scooped up mounds of curry and rice with a torn piece of chapatty; the main curry, hot and mustard-yellow, was made from small catfish caught in the nearby river; there was also an egg curry, together with mashed lentils, known as dal, the fried eggplant called brinjal, and three or four other vegetables, all highly spiced. For dessert we had mangoes and bananas and date-palm sugar, which we also used to sweeten the strong, milky tea. All of us ate greedily and belched loudly and comfortably during the intervals. Beside Walter, Bishnu, and me, the company included an elderly Hindu named Shoto Babu, a middle-aged Muslim schoolteacher named Latif Malik, and a boy of eighteen—the son of Shoto Babu—whose name sounded something like Rokul. Bishnu and Latif Malik did most of the talking, while I, besides stuffing myself, asked them questions about the Experiment. Meanwhile, Walter chatted with old Shoto in Hindustani which, I enviously noted, was far more fluent than my own. Thus, with much talking, laughing, noisy slurping of tea, belching, and clattering of tea-cups, the meal took its course—a good meal, eaten in good

324

fellowship, served deftly and gracefully by the shy women who lowered their eyes whenever my gaze met theirs.

After tiffin Walter decided to go over the accounts with Bishnu, leaving me free to take a nap. I went into the white-plastered cell where I had spent the night and stretched out on the thin rice-straw pallet—the only buffer between my body and the crude framework of planks and slats that made up the bed. Bloated with drowsiness from the sun and the heavy meal, I barely had time to draw up the cotton coverlet before subsiding effortlessly into a black pool of sleep. It was a sleep totally without dream or feeling, a real descent into nothingness, and I awoke from it abruptly with a sense of complete disorientation that lasted for several moments; even after I knew where I was, I did not move my eyes from the patch of white wall on which they had opened. Outside the window I could hear the creaking of the well pulley and the voices and laughter of women—the sounds that had awakened me.

These are old sounds, I thought: the creaking of a well pulley and the voices and laughter of women. They were curiously comforting and curiously moving. I had experienced much the same feeling during the morning, when we had visited the weaving center and watched the patient faces of the women—old widows in their white saris, unmarried girls with gentle, dark eyes and braided hair—as they wove the red, green, orange, and purple threads into cloth. That was an old sight, also very moving to me. Afterward we had toured part of the co-operative farm, where an old Muslim, one of the leaders of the project, had led us around, pointing out the gram, tomatoes, string beans, potatoes, and tobacco that were grown in addition to rice and sugar cane. The old man had then led us back to his house—a low building of brick and plaster shaded by two huge pipal trees—where we sat on the porch, surrounded by a good dozen children of all ages, and drank the water of three green coconuts. Here I had again caught the sense of something old and intensely familiar, a sense of patriarchal life, the life of a smiling blue sky and abundant soil. And on our return, just before the hour of the bath, we had passed a single-room school and heard the chanting of students reciting their lessons in unison.

Thinking of these things, staring at the white patch of wall, I was sure that after a year and a half in this country I had at last touched the bedrock of India. I had been led to it by a gawking American Quaker, led to this garden of Nasirghat where Hindu and Muslim sat down at the same table and welcomed the Westerner as their friend. My God, what a homecoming! I marveled at the ease with which I'd slipped into the routine, shedding the rags of Calcutta, bathing myself in the air and sounds and fellowship of this new and familiar place.

A truck changed gears on the road outside the compound; it was one of the two trucks which the American Friends Service Committee had provided for the Experiment—a provision which enabled the Nasirghat farm to market its produce in Calcutta. Then suddenly, and for the first time, I began to question the spell of the place, and a moment later I was struggling against it like a man fighting off the effects of a drug. Summoning my will, digging my fingers into the sand of reality, I forced myself to stare into the *fact* of Julia's fear and Philip's madness and my own suffering and the pitiful strivings of everyone I had ever known well.

What did Nasirghat have to say about Julia huddling in her bedroom, her wrists bared to her cruel nails? How could I bring together the clean sweetness of coconut oil and Philip's battered face and unresting eyes? Or the powerful sense of my own health and the abject failure of my love? Each of these opposites shouted for recognition; each insisted upon its own ultimate truth.

How could I have thought I had touched the bedrock of India in Nasirghat? How ridiculous! The very existence of this garden depended upon two trucks manufactured in Detroit and bought with the money of old ladies and Quaker businessmen living mostly in the suburbs of Philadelphia. At Nasirghat, old Shoto Babu and Latif Malik could sit at the same table in friendship and work together to grow more and better gram, tomatoes, and sugar cane; Bishnu Das and Walter Evans could go over the accounts together without either of them thinking for one moment of the different color of their hands as they turned the pages of the ledger and pointed to the figures; in real friendship they were able to make the garden grow and extend its bounds. In this fretful world, the achievement of Nasirghat was fantastic; I knew that never in my whole life would I lose sight of it. But the thought of its precariousness filled me with sadness. Would the old Hindu and the Muslim schoolteacher still eat their catfish curry and rice together if, as now seemed inevitable, India should be partitioned into two rival communities screeching at one another across the borders? I saw Syed Huq standing like a hunched statue in the tank, his blood trickling like bright new paint. And I thought, too, of the sannyasin (whom I'd not seen) lying face down in a doorway in Hare Street.

Walter Evans puzzled me. He was, after all, a fairly common American type, yet in some ways he was as strange to me as any yogi. Although a Quaker, he had confessed to me, as we talked late into the night, that he wasn't sure he believed in any God that existed apart from, or beyond, man. For all his gawkiness and naïveté, Walter had a hard, sound business head, knew just what the Service Committee should or should not do in connection with the Experiment. Not once, in our talk, did he underestimate the appalling conditions of India, and he was clearly prepared for any amount of discouragement. Poverty, ignorance, and intolerance were his oldest enemies, so to speak. If Nasirghat should be destroyed tomorrow, Walter would sigh and roll up his sleeves and start all over again. Nor did he turn his back on the Industrial Revolution: he was delighted to use any tools which industry or technology might provide. Wherever things could be remedied, bound together, Walter was the man to do it. But there was a kind of simplicity about him that left me uneasy, despite all my admiration.

I had become drowsy again, but I knew that I would not sink back into sleep. A fly was buzzing somewhere in the room. Soon I would have to get up and rejoin Walter and Bishnu. Stretching my arms, filling and emptying my lungs, I again felt

327

a powerful conviction of my own health. A kind of lazy body feeling, a diffused sexuality crept over me. I could again hear the creaking of the well, and I wondered which of the women was drawing water. I thought of the way they held their heads when they walked and the way their shoulders and hips moved under their saris. I wish I could tell Julia about Nasirghat, I thought suddenly. And at that instant I felt an intolerable longing for her. I wanted her *here,* with me now in Nasirghat. I remembered her excitement and pleasure when we had visited the village on the Diamond Harbour road many months ago—the day of the sannyasin. How Julia would have loved Nasirghat! Again sadness broke over me. Could I have handled my love and my rage in such a way that she would be here with me now in this white-plastered room? How was it possible that the health which I had sensed in her, beneath all her sickness and fear, could never be joined to the health which I felt struggling upward through my own sickness and fear? Had I really trampled that possibility into the ground once and for all?

I again thought of her visit to my flat and the note she had left for me. The postscript had seemed explicit enough at the time. Was it conceivable that I had misread it? And that I'd misread our meeting at the Consulate? Probably not.

But I'm better now, I thought, stretching my arms once more and taking a deep breath. The creaking of the well had stopped. The fly was no longer buzzing. The stillness of the afternoon was unflawed. Feeling grateful to Walter for having brought me to Nasirghat, I swung my feet over the side of the bed and stood up.

CHAPTER XXIX ❧ RETURNING from Nasirghat on Sunday night, Walter Evans drove along Great Russell Street on his way to my flat. It was now eleven o'clock, but I noticed that the lights were still on in Julia's bedroom as we passed. When Walter dropped me off at Harrington Mansions and I had thanked him and said good-by, I did not go upstairs. Instead, I left my bag with the lift wallah and hurried back—unshaved, unwashed, dust-smeared, dog-tired—into the street.

Julia gave a little cry when she opened the door and found me there.

"Are you going to let me in?" I asked.

"Of course. You startled me, John. But I'm glad to see you." She was wearing the blue-flannel bathrobe which I had come to hate, and her face was without make-up. But she looked fresh and glowing, just out of a bath. We went into the living room, where she turned on a couple of lamps.

I asked for news about Philip and learned that he and the psychiatrist had left according to schedule during the afternoon. Julia had heard from Liz Schneider that during the last twenty-four hours Philip had withdrawn into total silence; he docilely carried out instructions, Liz had said, but with no sign that he recognized anyone.

"It's so awful," said Julia. "I'd hoped the confusion might clear up once the immediate effects of the beating wore off, but I'm afraid it's not that simple."

"Obviously it isn't."

Then, after she had opened a can of beer for each of us, I told her something about my weekend. "It sounds marvelous," she said, her eyes lighting up. "I'd give anything to be able to go there. I've been feeling awfully trapped in Calcutta. I need to get into the country again."

There was a silence during which we both squirmed a little beneath the unintended emphasis of her words. Finally I said, "Julie, there's so much we could do together. We could have such a fine time. . . ."

She held out her hand with a quick movement. "John, please

don't start on that. Let's leave everything where it is. We're friends now. I'm glad to see you. But let's leave it at that."

"But *why?*" I cried out. "Isn't there any hope for us? I know you've loved me. I think you still do."

Julia shook her head, closing her eyes for a moment. "No, not any more. How can you expect me to love a man who asks me to marry him one week and then the next week makes love to someone he barely knows? And almost in public! What am I supposed to think? Am I supposed to think this little episode hadn't any meaning for you?" she demanded in a voice hovering between grief and scorn. "That I was the one you really loved while you were with her? Is *that* it?"

"Yes! That happens to be exactly true. I don't care how foolish or trite it sounds."

"That point of view's too masculine. It means *nothing* to me, and it never will."

"I was discouraged and hurt—and drunk, too. Not that that excuses anything. There was an opportunity, and—well, I leaped at it, that's all. I felt like smashing a window and I didn't care who got cut. You or me. Or even Diane. I just exploded, I guess. Not that that's really an excuse."

Julia's lip was trembling and she looked away from me. "You succeeded in cutting me all right. I've bled to death from it."

After a long silence, I said, "If you hadn't found out, we'd probably be in each other's arms right now. We might have been married by this time. What happened that night would have made no difference at all, to either of us."

"All I asked from you was a little patience. Do you think I enjoyed being in the state I was in?"

"If you'd never found out—"

"But I *did* find out. That's the fact I have to live with."

"God damn Philip!"

"Don't damn poor Philip. There's no need for that now."

I shrugged. The thought came to me that probably Philip had felt no more conscious remorse for his behavior than I had for that absurd, almost comical act of mine in the unused guest room.

"You're still not sorry for what you did," said Julia. "You're only sorry that *it* happened. And if you hadn't been found out, you probably wouldn't be sorry even for that."

"The act in itself wasn't important enough to feel either glad or sorry about. I'm very sorry about what led to it—and what followed from it."

"There, I told you so!"

I spread my hands helplessly. "All I know is that I love you. If I was wrong and perverse in what I did, then you're being perverse now. You're cutting the throat of your own happiness as well as mine."

"John, I can only deal with myself as I find myself. I know what's possible for me and what isn't. I was afraid of loving you. I don't know why—there's nothing terrifying about you, you're kind and considerate. . . . But I kept losing my nerve, and then each time, with your help, I'd regain my confidence. But now everything's broken down. I'll never be able to regain my footing—not with you, at least."

Standing up, I went to her chair and caught her hands. "Julie, you're unfair to us! You've got to give us another chance!"

She shook her head grimly.

"So you're going ahead with this transfer?"

"There's nothing else for me to do," she said in a stifled voice, her hands limp in mine.

"You want to suffer," I said, letting go. "You want to wallow in suffering and feel righteous about it. You were looking for an excuse to get rid of me. You blamed me for making that eczema come back, and when I handed you the excuse on a silver platter, my God, how you jumped at it! You think you're too good to be happy. God damn you!" I said, slapping her face hard. "God damn you!"

She jerked her head to the side, her profile white against the brown upholstery of the chair. Then, covering her face with her hands, Julia bent over so far that her soft hair fell loosely across her forehead and hung down between her knees.

Perhaps twenty minutes later, Julia turned her tear-streaked and swollen face to me and said, "I'm such a *mess*, John. How can you love such a mess? You must be as neurotic or crazy as Philip to love someone like me. You're a real demon for punishment. I think you're the one who needs a psychiatrist. To say nothing of *me*."

"Maybe," I said, smiling and holding her close to me. Julia was still shivering but no longer racked with sobs.

"God knows I don't want to be unhappy. But when that eczema came back, then everything that was awful and repulsive about me as a girl came back with it. And then when I found out about you and Diane . . ." Her lip began to tremble again.

"The eczema's gone. You're well again."

"But what if it comes back?"

"Well, you can stand that. You're brave enough to see it through. You could have done it this last time if I'd been brave enough and strong enough to—to handle myself. We could have pulled through then. Julie, there's something in both of us that fights like a cornered rat against our happiness. Life's never going to be easy for either of us. We're both going to need an extra portion of love and courage. Don't you think?" I said, kissing her hot cheek. "Let's give ourselves a chance."

And then, after waiting while she looked straight ahead in a kind of trance, I said, "Will you come to the Chaudurys' with me after the Trade Union Congress tomorrow? They'll be so happy to see you again."

"Not tomorrow," Julia said dreamily. She was still staring into the opposite wall. "I can't tomorrow. We're having someone here to dinner."

"Well, we'll get together on Tuesday then. All right?"

She closed her eyes. "Call me on Tuesday. I think so. But I don't want to make any decision when I'm as worn out as I am right now."

CHAPTER XXX ❀ THE November sunlight, as it filtered through the canvas tent, bathed the delegates of the All-India Trade Union Congress in an orange-amber light that seemed dense as water. The smell was dense, too—the smell of hot canvas, unpainted wooden scaffolding, dust, and hair oil, a combination that reminded me of the vacant-lot carnivals I had gone to as a boy. Immediately below the platform (where, to my embarrassment, I had been given a seat of honor) perhaps four hundred Indians were looking up with an expression of fanatic concentration toward the speaker; these were the union leaders, mostly from Calcutta, who had been allowed to sit on wooden benches within the shadow of the tent. Beyond them, thousands and thousands of the rank and file were squatting on the ground, packing Wellesley Square until it resembled an open crate full of tiny heads, arms, shoulders, banners, and placards. For the moment these thousands were very orderly and attentive but ready to leap to their feet and scream their heads off whenever the speaker chose to utter one of the dozen or more well-known slogans demanding worker solidarity or the immediate expulsion of the British. Although distance fused the individual features of the workers, there was a type which I could instantly abstract from the sun-drenched, speckled mass on all sides. This collective worker had straight, parted hair so black that it shone almost blue in the sun; skin the color of burnt sugar; a high-domed forehead; sunken cheeks; a thin, angry mouth scarlet with betel-nut juice; a finely cut, rather aquiline nose; luminous, deep-set eyes, black and glittering. He wore a collarless European shirt, blue or white, plain or striped, fastened with studs in the front, the tails out and reaching almost to the knees; a white dhoti gathered in folds about the bony legs; and cheap black shoes or slippers or sandals without socks. Thinner, darker, more angular than the leaders who sat under the tent, this was the Indian of the organized mob, the sharp-featured militant of the streets and factories, the new Indian of the big cities, and I recognized him as the thin cutting edge of a weapon only recently forged and hardly yet in use.

The men under the tent could mostly have been clerks,

babus with gold-rimmed glasses, paler skins, whiter dhotis, and heavier jowls and paunches; a few even wore European suits. Their eyes were intelligent, and they had the touchy, argumentative look so characteristic of the Bengali who was educated enough to speak and write English but forced to sweat out his living from some job humiliatingly beneath his abilities and dignity. At the same time this group lacked the spiteful obsequiousness of the stereotype babu—they seemed sure of themselves and were, despite their fleshiness, as sharply aggressive as their followers outside—and more controlled, more pointed. Their edgy, nervous mobility contrasted astonishingly with the Mongolian blandness of the delegates from Southeast Asia—the smiling, dish-faced Burmese in their plaid cotton lungis, the Thais, the Malays, and the Indochinese—who were sharing the platform with the speakers. I was the only Westerner present.

Part of this Mongolian blandness (and blankness), I realized, came from the fact that the Oriental visitors could understand no more of what was being said than I. The speaker, a hollow-chested young man who gestured extravagantly with his chicken-bone fingers, had been shouting staccato Bengali into the microphone for the last twenty minutes. Caught up into the loudspeaker system, the sounds blared forth, punctuated by the crackling of the apparatus. I could catch only a word now and then—my study of Hindustani had proved to be of little help in understanding the Bengali dialect. Glancing at my watch, I reflected that the orator, with his Indian passion for rhetoric and prolixity, was good for at least another twenty minutes. This was already the third speech I'd sat through—one in Hindustani, one (by a South Indian) in English, one in Bengali.

Still, I was very glad I had come. Until now, the subject of my report had seemed almost abstract, a little unreal despite all my research. But here, in the orange glow of the tent, nearly deafened by the passionate bellowing into the public-address system, surrounded to the very walls of Wellesley Square by passionate, upturned faces, I sensed the full excitement of human impact—the enfleshed, tangible power of sheer human mass. Ultimately, I distrusted this excitement (for even in this crowd I caught something that reminded me of old newsreels of Hitler's Nürnberg rallies), but for the moment I was glad enough to ride along with it, to feel myself mounted upon its energy. It was now Nasirghat that seemed unreal as a dream—a walled garden where honey-colored women talked and laughed at the well, a pastoral enclave, a green island flowering in a bitter sea. . . .

I glanced at Mr. Arun Bose, the Secretary of the Postal and Telegraph Workers Union, who was sitting not far off, dressed in a dark-brown European suit and wearing horn-rimmed glasses. At the beginning of the meeting he had spotted me standing near the edge of the crowd and had insisted on dragging me along to the platform. Just now Mr. Bose was the only Indian visible whose total attention was not fixed on the speaker; instead, he was thumbing through a stack of yellow papers, presumably telegrams, which he held on his knees. He seemed to have felt my gaze, for suddenly he looked up and gave a flashing smile, a smile brilliant with white teeth and gold fillings. According to Martin Fenwick, Bose, in addition to being an exceptionally clever bargainer, was known to be the leader of the communist faction in the union.

With a scream of *"Jai Hind!"* the speaker finished and raised both emaciated arms to the crowd, which instantly broke into loud cheering. The speaker bowed, pressed his palms together in front of his chest, and finally took his seat, dripping with sweat. Another man, stout and benign as a guinea pig, came forward and raised his arms for silence. This was Professor Devendrenath Tagore, a Brahman of the Brahmans, an economist at the University of Calcutta and, as a staff writer for the *Amrita Bazar Patrika,* a colleague of Ramesh Chaudury's. I leaned forward, much interested, for this was a man of whom I'd heard many things; but a second later I settled back with a sigh, for this aristocrat, who was wearing blue sunglasses and a khaki drill jacket, had also elected to speak in Bengali. Professor Tagore had a high-pitched voice and a monotonous delivery which the microphone translated into a metallic, grating whine. The underwater light and the hot, musty smell of the canvas began to make me drowsy, and at last I closed my eyes. The smell tantalized me, reminding me of something more than carnival tents. It was a monsoon smell of staleness, dampness, mildew. Then it came to me, jolting me wide awake with distaste: this was the smell of Philip's unaired guest room, the odor of the mildewed mosquito netting, of a mattress with dank stuffing. . . .

Someone touched my arm. Mr. Arun Bose, smiling broadly, was holding out a yellow square of paper. "Would you be so kind?" he said in a loud whisper. "Could you kindly tell me what language this is and if possible what it says? Thank you so much."

Pasted in white strips against the yellow paper were these words:

SOFIA 23 NOV 1946 NOUS REGRETTONS TRES SINCEREMENT QUE NOUS NE PUISSIONS PAS ENVOYER UNE DELEGATION AU CONGRES GENERAL DES SYNDICATS DES INDES A NOS CAMARADES INDIENS NOUS ENVOYONS DES SALUTATIONS FRATERNELLES ET DES MEILLEURS SOUHAITS POUR LE SUCCES DE LEURS EFFORTS VAILLANTS DE GAGNER LA LIBERTE LA DEMOCRATIE ET LE SOCIALISME POUR LES MASSES OPPRIMEES INDIENNES NOUS LES ASSURONS DE LAPPUI DES OUVRIERS DU MONDE ENTIER DANS CETTE ENTREPRISE NOBLE ZACHARIA PETKOFF SECRETAIRE DU CONGRES DES OUVRIERS BULGARS

"It's in French," I said. "It's from the Bulgarian Workers' Congress. They're sorry they can't send a delegation, and they wish you all kinds of luck. Do you want me to write out a translation?"

"Would you be so kind?" said Mr. Bose, producing a pocket notebook and a Parker 51 pen. I set to work, rather laboriously because of the lack of punctuation; I had some difficulty in making out LAPPUI. Even so, I found myself unexpectedly stirred, as though I had caught in those sonorous phrases (so much more pompous in English than in French) an authentic echo of the defiant, trumpeting note with which the original

"Workers of the world, unite" must have sounded nearly a hundred years before. And being stirred myself, almost against my will, I could gauge something of the impact which those phrases could have for the glittering-eyed thousands who packed Wellesley Square. What chance did the voice of, say, John Stuart Mill or Jefferson or John Dewey or Mr. Justice Holmes have of penetrating to such an audience—especially when it had to be bellowed out over a loudspeaker system that seemed to heckle the words, to mock their pallid Anglo-Saxon reasonableness, even as they were spoken?

Professor Tagore finished his speech, took off his sunglasses, wiped his face with a handkerchief, and waved both the handkerchief and the glasses in his plump hands. The cheering was respectable but nothing like so extravagant as it had been for his predecessor. Then Arun Bose rushed to the microphone, holding up the yellow telegrams, and as he did so, a compact section of the crowd rose to their feet and began waving their banners and placards. Unable to make out the placards because of the distance, I could not tell whether this group was made up of Postal and Telegraph workers or whether it was a special communist unit drawing on members from a number of unions. Bose now proceeded to read aloud from his stack of papers. The first was from the Trade Union Congress in England, and Bose read it in English and then in Bengali; only on the second reading did it receive any applause, together with a few cries of "Quit India!" After that, he dispensed altogether with English, and I was unable even to catch the name of the senders. Certain messages were greeted with wild shouting by the group who had given Bose his ovation. There was an odd mixture of tumult and order in the cheering, as though high spirits were barely putting up with the rehearsed forms. Once again I felt the pounding of massed energy against the platform, a compound in which violence was lightly but effectively bridled by organization, a mixture of hatred, humor, and rebelliousness with a high potential for explosion.

Then I realized that Arun Bose was pointing in my direction and that every face within the tent was focused on me. I caught the words "Amedicanni vice-consul" and knew that my role in translating the Bulgarian cable was being acknowledged to the crowd. I braced myself for the applause that followed. Bose, of course, was using me—he was deliberately interpreting my presence at the meeting as official American backing for its aims. The British, I knew, would be extremely annoyed when their intelligence agents in the crowd reported the incident, as they were bound to do; eventually some indirect protest would be made—not, of course, to the Consulate but to the O.S.S. for secret transmission to the State Department. Well, so be it, I thought, amused by the prospect. I hadn't been duped; I would have behaved exactly the same way if I'd known Bose's intentions in advance.

The meeting did not break up until nearly sunset, and then did so with a complete throwing away of the lightly resting discipline that had prevailed until that moment. Crowds spilled into the roped-off aisle leading to the tent and into the tent itself, stumbling over the ropes, threatening to bring the whole structure down. I was pushed forward blindly, wedged into a mob of hilarious workers, torn away from Arun Bose, who wanted to talk with me. It was fully half an hour before I was able to reach my car.

Afterward, driving slowly down Dhurrumtolla Street toward Chowringhee Square, I became involved in another sort of crowd. Thousands of office workers were fighting their way into the absurd, broken-down buses and trams; they were like noisy white chickens, all of them flapping madly toward their homes. Again and again I had to stop as yelling Indians dashed nearly under the wheels of my car.

At the Chaudurys' that evening, Ramesh wanted to hear all about Nasirghat. I described the weekend in detail, and when I had finished, I said, "It's a very impressive place. It sounds utopian but it works—at least it seems to. For a little while I thought I'd touched the bedrock of India—the real heart of the country. But that's absurd. What I saw at the Trade Union Congress this afternoon has just as much claim to be the essential India. Just as much and just as little. What I'd like to know is which is going to win out in the long run—the spirit of Nasirghat or the spirit of Wellesley Square. Or neither? Or both? Are militancy and co-operation bound to clash? I really felt today for the first time that India might very well go communist. I didn't see any Quaker—or even Hindu—mildness and patience. I saw men who were determined to force really strong medicine down India's throat. Can all this aggressive class struggle and hatred ever turn itself into the kind of patient lovingness which you need to make a garden grow? Even an industrialized garden?"

"Why not indeed?" cried Ramesh. "I am a socialist, but I'm not afraid of communism. India will cultivate it. We will take our methods from Gandhiji, not from Stalin."

"Oh Lord!" I said, slapping my knees, "if only I could stay here long enough to get some clue as to what's going to happen. I've barely made a start, and it seems such a waste to have to start all over again in another post."

"That's likely to be fairly soon, isn't it?" said Martin in an almost gloating tone. He had come without Anila—whose pregnancy, he said, was causing morning sickness, afternoon sickness, and evening sickness—and had been listening morosely to all that I said about Nasirghat.

"In about a year," I said. "Two at the most. I really don't want to go anywhere else—except to America or Russia. India, America, Russia, maybe China—at the moment everything else seems almost beside the point. Though I suppose there are infinite riches even in Paris, if you know where to dig for them," I added, laughing.

"I suppose I should thank you for that concession—in the name of Western civilization," said Martin. He drained his glass and then turned abruptly toward Ramesh. "Of course India will go communist," he said. "Any fool can see that. And I mean *really* communist. All this talk about India becoming a bastion of social democracy in the East is pure shit."

"My dear Martin!" Ramesh gave an agonized glance toward Sujata and then laughed nervously.

But Martin was not yet through. "Communism is a necessary stage, all right. After the civil wars that are going to tear this bloody country into shreds in the next few years, it's the inevitable next step. Of course it won't be the final step. For all its shiny new appearance, communism is merely the bluntest weapon in behalf of the total dehumanization of mankind. The strong right arm of the faceless future. And Ramesh here talks about the methods of Gandhi! From its vast reservoirs of spirituality, India is going to produce something called Nonviolent Communism!"

Then he swung toward me and said passionately, "Your Quakers make me sick! Has it ever occurred to your new guru, Mr. Evans, that someone who is neither poor nor ignorant nor bigoted might want to lay waste to Nasirghat for the sheer hellish excitement of pulling up the crops and trampling down the flowers?"

"It may have occurred to him, but I think he's incapable, temperamentally, of believing that such a monster could exist."

"He hasn't the honor of knowing me very well," said Martin with a strident laugh. "I'm fully capable of such an act. I expect you are, too. We all are."

"Possibly. Of course, Martin, you're right about Walter. He's no fool, but he's basically what you would call a child of the Enlightenment. He's optimistic about people. Although he wouldn't deny the size of the job, I'm sure he's convinced that a combination of common sense and good will and hard work and faith can overcome most of the problems that beset the world."

"Are you convinced of that?" demanded Martin.

"No. I'm afraid it's not that easy. But still, I'm on his side. I want the garden to grow. And if you insist on blasting it before it has a chance, then by God, Martin, you're my mortal enemy!"

But Martin, to my great dismay, didn't return my smile. He looked down at his empty glass, which Ramesh seemed to be in no hurry to refill, and said nothing.

"I also want it to grow!" cried Ramesh, who had been

fidgeting with excitement. "I'm on the side of Nasirghat! Martin, you may preach your doctrine of doom all you wish, but I will not listen to you. John, you are very fortunate. You have seen India as it will be in twenty-five, maybe thirty years. Why not? It is possible! Listen to me, everyone, listen to me, Sujata, my dearest wife, and you, John and Martin, my dear friends! I hereby swear that I will devote the rest of my life to making this admirable Nasirghat grow until it includes all of India. It is not impossible. And after India, why not the world? England and America are already rich, but they are not yet a garden. Far from it. Perhaps India will show the way! Who knows? We are so poor and helpless now, but we feel strongly and we understand the meaning of love. . . ."

"Are you speaking of your neighbors?" asked Martin. "Those peaceful, loving babus who butchered your friend Huq with such holy glee?"

Ramesh's arms flailed about wildly. "But if we are ever free, there will be no more riots. These are unnatural circumstances. If ever the British leave—"

"Shut up!" yelled Martin, gripping his glass as though he wanted to crush it in his hand. Then, very slowly, he said, "You are my dearest friend, Ramesh, but you are also a tiresome fool."

"My dear Martin!"

There was terrible silence. I couldn't bear to look at Ramesh. Martin continued to scrutinize his glass.

Then Sujata spoke. "That was most unkind, Martin. And quite untrue. You must apologize to Ramesh." And abruptly she looked away, her eyes flashing with tears, and fumbled with the shawl of her sari, as if wishing to veil her face now that she had spoken so bluntly to a man, even though in defense of her husband.

"Oh, no, it is quite unimportant, really quite all right, you know," said Ramesh effusively.

Martin stood up. "I do apologize to you, Ramesh. And to you, Sujata. And to you, John. I apologize to the spiritual nation of India and to the whole bloody world. And you can

341

count on my being properly abject, Ramesh, the next time I see you. And now I think the time has come for me to go."

"Oh, Martin!" cried Ramesh.

"For God's sake, let him go," I said.

"Oh, Martin, please, this is all so silly!" Ramesh jumped to his feet. "Really, you mustn't leave. It's such a silly quarrel." But Martin had already left the room, and after standing at the door for a moment, Ramesh turned to Sujata and me, spreading his palms, his long face collapsed with hurt and embarrassment.

The back of the evening had been broken, and after half an hour of conversational false starts and awkward conclusions, I decided to go. The Chaudurys made only a polite flutter of protest. At the door, Ramesh suddenly cried, "Ah, John, what is happening to everyone we know and love? Why must Martin become drunken and savage? And you also have been unhappy. Forgive me for saying so, but you've looked badly for many weeks—less than half alive. Sujata worries about you, don't you, Sujata?"

"Not too much now," said Sujata, contradicting her husband with a smile.

"And poor Philip," continued Ramesh. "What a dreadful thing! And I know that you quarreled with him. Anila and Martin quarrel and Martin drinks so much. And Martin is unkind to me."

"I hope you won't mind too much about Martin," I said. "He's the one who'll suffer most."

"There seems to be suddenly so much unhappiness. I think the whole world has gone mad."

"It sometimes seems to me that all the world's troubles are only the long shadow of my own. And that I'm the world's sickness engraved on the head of a pin. How's that for egotism?" Then I added, "But you and Sujata stand firm. You are happy together."

"Yes, now we are happy together, but that does not prove very much. You must not sentimentalize us. I am happy, but I am unhappy, too. Nothing will ever restore my friend Syed

342

Huq. Or the baby we lost. Nothing will ever take the sting out of Martin's words to me tonight."

"Still," I insisted, "you and Sujata have found your own island. You have your resting place in each other. That's what I envy. Right now, I feel lucky just to be able to keep my head above water."

"You will find yours, too," said Sujata, blinking at me through her glasses.

"Maybe," I said, hardly daring to let my hope flutter on the ground. "At least the door's open again. And I'm stronger, too. If it's slammed in my face again, I can stand even that. But my God, everything seems so precarious! My own endurance and strength. Nasirghat. India. Your happiness. The whole world. It's so hard to get used to this precariousness."

Ramesh followed me to my car. "It's a bad time," he said. "A very bad time." Then, very cheerfully, he added, "But things will be better when the British leave. You'll see."